Catherine Kidwell talks about Dear Stranger

'Bonnie's a nice girl, an Army pilot's sweetheart in the 40s, a happy housewife, mother of three little girls, and wife of a rising corporate executive ... This woman still hasn't stopped looking for the right man. She no longer needs him to build a nest for her or to rescue her from the real world, but she still wants love, someone to be close to.'

Dear Stranger

Catherine Kidwell

A STAR BOOK

published by

the Paperback Division of
W. H. ALLEN & Co. Ltd

A Star Book

Published in 1983
by the Paperback Division of
W. H. Allen & Co. Ltd
A Howard and Wyndham Company
44 Hill Street, London W1X 8LB

First published in Great Britain by W. H. Allen & Co. Ltd, 1982
Published by arrangement with Warner Books, Inc., New York

Copyright © Catherine Kidwell, 1982

Printed in Great Britain by
Cox & Wyman Ltd, Reading

ISBN 0 352 31309 9

For my mother, Lela,
and my daughter, Jane,
woman to woman.

We're late, darling, we're late.
The curtain descends, everything ends
too soon, too soon.

I wait, darling, I wait.
Will you speak low to me, speak love to me,
and soon.

by Kurt Weill and Ogden Nash
– for the swing bands.

Part One

THE FORTIES

One

She was young in 1943 – when the girls were red-lipped and virginal, and the measure of time was the duration.

That Friday, the February wind hurtled around buildings and scooted across the dirty snow that had packed down and refrozen after dark. Bonnie and her best friend scurried into the protection of the heavy revolving door and pushed it, groaning and resisting, to deliver themselves into the warm confusion of the Wheatland Hotel's Comanche Room.

The wind had polished their skin pink and fringed their high hairdos, but the little felt hats perched on the crowns of their heads still neatly divided pompadour from pageboy. Dribbles of brown water slid from their victory-rubber boots onto the dark tile floor as they surveyed the room. 'See a place?'

Mixed voices rose and fell over the clink of silverware and glass – noise overlaid with smooth, sweet swing flowing from the jukebox, horn notes as neatly clipped and in place as a GI haircut.

The men of the US Army Air Corps coloured the room olive drab; the bright dots were hairbows and skirts and an occasional civilian necktie. Savoury smells of hamburger and onions and fresh-baked apple pie drifted from booths. Up front a veil of smoke hovered over tables weighted with Schlitz and Pabst Blue Ribbon.

The girls spotted a couple leaving a booth, and hurried to claim the space.

The waitress stacked the dishes and pushed them to one side as with her other hand she wiped the dark, varnished tabletop, and with a last quick move, emptied the ashtray onto the saucer that topped the stack. 'Be right with you,' she called back as she walked towards the kitchen. The girls slid into the booth, facing each other.

Bonnie pulled her arms out of the muskrat coat and arranged it behind her, stuffing gloves into the pockets. 'I filed all day. Mr Forbes was out of town.'

Laying back her coat, Maxine regarded her distorted reflection in the chrome napkin holder. 'I noticed you weren't at your desk,' she said as she unpinned her hat and smoothed her curly blonde hair. 'What about Alice Faye settling for Don Ameche? I'd have waited for Tyrone Power any day.'

Bonnie shrugged. 'Maxine, if only we had such a problem!'

As she spoke Bonnie looked around the room, carefully avoiding direct eye contact. Many of the men wore the dark green coats of army officers with one gold bar mounted on each shoulder and new silver wings pinned on their chests. From across the room they looked alike – youthful, lithe bodies, close-cropped hair, uniforms.

Three lieutenants sat together not far from the jukebox, and Bonnie found herself watching the flowing gestures of the dark-haired one in the centre who was doing most of the talking. *Good hands. Maybe a doctor.* She tried to put him in a white coat, but it was hard. He looked so good in the uniform. His right hand suddenly became a fist and landed hard on the table. She jumped, then felt relieved when she saw them all laughing. She was glad he wasn't angry, and sorry to have missed the joke.

'Evening, girls.'

A soldier leaned over their booth and gripped the table edge, swaying slightly until he found his balance. He was a small man, lean and wiry, with weathered, leathery skin like a farmer. He wore the stripes of a buck sergeant, and gunner wings.

'Excuse me,' he continued. 'I saw you ladies come in and I just had to talk to you. May I?' He gestured towards Bonnie's bench and, before she could answer, slid around to a tentative perch close to the end. Bonnie sat up and opened her mouth.

He threw up his hands. 'My intentions are honourable. So help me God, I gotta tell you that what I want most in the world right now is to ask you to marry me.' His face was drawn, his eyes serious.

Bonnie drew back. 'Oh come on, soldier,' she said weakly, 'you've just had too many beers.'

'You're right,' he said. 'Nothing like a few beers to build up a fella's nerve. And that guy's really got his, you're thinking. Fact is, I'm shipping out in a couple of days and in this whole world there ain't one goddamned soul – excuse me, ladies – that's gonna miss me.' The little lines around his eyes tightened. 'Not a goddamned soul, not a goddamned one.'

Bonnie's irritation melted and flowed away.

The sergeant put his elbow on the table and leaned his chin on his hand. 'God, you're pretty,' he said, his gaze gliding across Bonnie's shiny brown hair. 'Goddamn, you're a pretty one.'

She reconnoitered. 'You've probably got a wife and three kids somewhere. You're just lonely tonight.'

'No, ma'am,' came the sober answer. 'I've got nobody. Not a goddamned soul.' He looked down. 'I'm a jockey. Hell of a lot rather be riding the tail of a good horse than the tail of a B-26.'

'Don't you have any folks?'

'Haven't heard from my family in years. Little late to be looking them up now.'

'I'm sorry,' she said.

'Hell, I don't want you being sorry,' he said, drawing himself up. 'It seemed like a good idea at the time.'

Bonnie slowly shook her head.

'Five thousand dollars in insurance, and pretty good odds. I'm not a big guy, but I'm a real terror in the backseat of a car.'

'No.'

The sergeant grinned and rose to his feet. For the first time he looked at Maxine. He gave a lazy wink. 'How about you, sweetheart? Like to come over to my table and let me tell you about the ponies?'

'Sorry.'

The smile lingered about his thin lips as it died in his eyes. 'You're good kids,' he said. 'Don't worry about it.'

Bonnie, watching his retreating back, shook her head. 'I wonder what he would have done if I had said yes.'

'Taken him a wife I guess, if he hadn't sobered up too soon.' Maxine opened her purse and took out a cigarette which she held, unlit. 'He was probably just making a pass.'

'If you're going to die, even a pass is important.'

'They won't all die. Most of them'll come back.'

'They have to kill people. Could you kill someone?'

'I don't think so.'

'Not even Hitler?'

Maxine shuddered. 'Don't ask me. I'm just glad I don't have to. Glad I'm not a man.'

'They're doing it for us. And for our children.'

'Do you think they'll change? After they kill somebody? Or is it easier for men?'

'I don't think it's easy for anyone.'

Maxine took a lighter from her purse and lit the cigarette.

'So you're back to those again.'

'Yeah.' Maxine stared at the smoke. 'No reason not to now.'

'You heard from Jim?'

'Just a note, sending his new address. I've lost him, Bonnie. I'll never see him again.'

'You're not sure.'

'He changed when I told him about Janie. He left so soon, wouldn't talk about it.'

'You shouldn't have sprung it on him at the last minute.'

'How do I handle it, Bonnie? Tell every guy I dance with at the USO that I'm twenty-one, a stenographer, and incidentally have a four-year-old daughter living back on the farm? It just doesn't fit into the conversation.'

'Surely he didn't hold Janie against you?'

'I think it bothered him that I'd been married, that I'd belonged to somebody.'

Bonnie frowned. 'What gives him the right? He's been around.'

'I don't know. Men can't tell you how they feel. I know he likes girls who are feminine – and I liked being feminine for him – even tossing the cigarettes.'

'Well, for Pete's sake,' Bonnie asked, 'what's more feminine than motherhood?'

Maxine shook her head and looked down at her hands. A tear sparkled on her lashes.

Their waitress sidestepped a grope as she came back for their order, and Bonnie and Maxine asked for coffee.

As the waitress turned, a man's hand touched her drooping shoulders, a handsome gold watch showing from beneath a wool sleeve. Looking above wide shoulders, Bonnie contacted blue eyes that looked into hers and held. She recognized the dark-haired lieutenant she had been watching earlier.

'Excuse me.' His voice was pleasant and low, a clipped accent separating the words. 'Before you order, how about considering the case of three lonely soldiers. It's two long hours till curfew.' He turned back to the waitress and smiled as he asked, 'Can you take the order at our table – that is, if these ladies will join us?'

The waitress straightened her apron and fluttered her hand across the crooked hair net. He turned back to Maxine and then to Bonnie. 'I'm John,' he said.

Bonnie heard a distant voice saying, 'I'm Maxine.'

If we had gone straight home tonight this wouldn't be happening. He has been watching me. He saw me reject the sergeant. She said, 'I'm sorry; we really should be going.'

Maxine frowned and squirmed.

Placing both hands on the table edge, John leaned down. She strained to catch his words. 'Please come. Just for a beer. We won't even ask your last names. A month from now you won't remember, but we will.'

I'll remember. I'll remember. 'We really shouldn't, but –'

John straightened up and reached for Bonnie's coat.

'That's not my table,' the waitress said. She looked tired again.

'Thank you, you've been very helpful,' Bonnie said. She felt a ridiculous impulse to embrace the girl.

John folded her coat across his arm. The fur clung to the wool uniform, filling in the spaces between his arm and body. Bonnie slid from the booth into the aisle. Their eyes met and turned away.

Maxine pulled her coat about her shoulders and, chatting comfortably, picked up her hat. Bonnie heard not a word.

Crossing near the jukebox, they sidestepped a dancing couple. 'What did you say you did before you got drafted?' she heard the girl ask as they glided by.

'It's the first table,' John said.

The two men pushed back their chairs and stood up. The blond, stocky one crushed his cigarette in the overflowing tray and smiled. He lifted his hand towards his wings, dropping it suddenly to grab a chair, which he pulled out for Maxine. John introduced him as Joe and the other man as Ed. Ed's movements were as slow and connected as Joe's were spasmodic. He stood quietly, resting the weight of his lean body on one leg. Bonnie felt his eyes sliding over her, touching her, yet the irritation his appraisal aroused in her was laced with pleasure. She slid into the shaky bentwood chair and crossed her legs. John moved in beside her.

'Y'all got a friendly town here,' Joe said, '– for the guys from the base.'

Maxine took a long last look at John and turned to Joe with a flash of even teeth. 'What part of the South are you from?' she asked.

John angled his shoulder away from the other couple, his gaze pulling Bonnie aside, speeding her heartbeat, stealing her breath. 'And what do you do?' he asked.

'Guess.'

He pretended to think. 'Librarian. No – teacher. Nurse. A caring person. There's a softness. . . .'

'I'm a secretary – in our biggest defence plant.'

His head bobbed slowly. 'Efficient, no misspelled words. Files at your fingertips. Brewing hot coffee for the boss, and remembering his wife's birthday.'

'He doesn't have a wife.'

'Well, if he did you'd remember her birthday.'

'Maybe. I have other responsibilities.'

Their eyes, which had been constantly connecting and disengaging, came together again as he said, 'I'm sorry. I would expect you to. You have intelligent eyes.'

No one had ever told her she had intelligent eyes before.

'What do they build at your plant?'

'Airplane parts. Hardware. Bolts and screws.'

Ed caught her reply. 'Hey,' he crowed, 'you work in a screw factory.'

'You could say so,' she answered, forcing a smile.

'It all helps to win the war,' John said.

'Sure, for want of a screw the war could be lost,' Joe joined in, a grin tickling the corner of his mouth.

A funny snorting sound came from Ed, and for a moment, they all teetered on the edge of joining him. Bonnie clasped her hands on the table, one thumb sliding along the other. Then,

14

lean, brown fingers closed over her cold ones. 'Drop it, Jackson,' John said, still looking at Bonnie. 'Would you like to dance?'

He took his hand away and she took it back when they came together in front of the jukebox. The other hand slid around her waist, and her head fit into the space between the hollow of his shoulder and his chin. They were one body as a voice crooned, 'Speak low, when you speak love.' They made the small, smooth movements of the foxtrot on the miniature dance floor.

'All of us are wound up,' he said, close to her ear. 'Don't hold it against him.'

'It's nothing; I've heard it before. Is he a good friend of yours?'

'I just met Joe and Ed. We're crew mates.'

> *We're late, darling, we're late.*
> *The curtain descends, everything ends*
> *too soon, too soon.*
> *I wait, darling, I wait.*
> *Won't you speak low to me, speak love to me*
> *And soon.*

She lifted her head. *Crew mates! That meant he was scheduled to leave soon.* He answered her unspoken question.

He said, 'About a week.'

A whole week. Seven times tonight.

'What are you doing for the next week?' John asked.

'Can't think of a blessed thing.'

The record ended, and she looked down, guarding her pleasure.

The slick, quick beat of the swinging 'American Patrol' intruded. Jitterbug! His hand moved from her back and quickly grasped her other hand. Without missing a step they fell into the split-second synchronization of Lindy footwork. She twisted and spun on the pivot of his wrist, flew away and back again as his strong arm reversed, the push-and-pull intercourse as intimate as a shared heartbeat. Boy, girl, and beat melted together, indivisable as the nation.

When the music stopped they embraced, wetness mingling where her forehead lay against his chin. The world gradually settled down around them. They had an audience. Someone applauded. Bonnie stepped back.

'Man,' she breathed, 'you sure can dance.'

'Found my partner,' he said.

Two girls stood by the jukebox, figures hidden by outsized cashmere sweaters sagging past their hiplines over pleated plaid skirts that stopped just below their knees. Thick, white socks bunched above their dirty saddle shoes. The girls smiled at John and he smiled back, nodding.

'College Girls!' Bonnie said.

John grinned, and looked back over his shoulder after they passed.

'Go ahead, ask them to dance.'

'They're just babies.'

He took her hand and threaded through the tables.

When they were seated, she said, 'I'll bet you're a college man. Ivy League.'

'Why do you say that?'

'Aren't you?'

'Harvard, class of '42. How could you tell?'

'You look like a Harvard man.'

'Known a lot of Harvard men?'

'Nope. You're the first. But you look like one.'

'I've expected to be a Harvard lawyer ever since I can remember.'

'You will be.'

'Maybe. Didn't plan to take to the air, but here I am.'

'The war has improved my life, tripled my salary. Bought me a muskrat.'

'Did you go to the state university here?'

'No, I went to junior college in my home town. Came to Lancaster to work. It's just a little place, my home town.'

Across the table Ed stood up and reached for his coat. 'If you folks can manage without me, I think I'll cruise.'

Bonnie said, 'We didn't mean to leave you out.'

'That's all right, honey. There's bound to be something stirring around here. They can't all be nice girls.'

'Don't you like nice girls?'

'They're okay when you've got the time.' He stood holding the coat like a sad child. 'See you guys at the bus.'

Bonnie and John watched him walk with a little restless

bounce through the congested room. He slowed once as he eyed a girl with curly red hair sitting in the far corner. The girl looked at him, but she was not alone, and Ed put on his coat and went out the door.

John leaned back in his chair. 'Just think, an hour ago I didn't know I'd be sitting here with you.'

'A development not entirely out of your control.'

He grinned and cocked his head. 'Well, maybe I give fate a little push now and then, but I don't give her any trouble when she pushes back.'

'Does it really matter that it's me? Wouldn't any other girl have done just as well?'

'Maybe, we don't know yet, do we? Why are you with me instead of with the sergeant or Ed or the captain over there?'

'Guess I'm swinging with the surprises, too.'

'This has happened to you before.'

She lifted a hand. 'The rules have changed.'

'Of course. We've already established that you're a nice girl.'

'How do you tell? How do guys decide?'

'Interesting question, we'll look into it. I want to see you again.'

'I'm glad.'

'Are you waiting for someone?'

'No. Is there someone waiting?'

'No commitments. There is a girl in Boston I've known all my life.' He leaned forward. 'Know what?'

Her face grew warm. 'What?'

'I don't know your name.'

They shared quick laughter, reliving the intimacy of the dance. She told him her name.

From the end of the table Maxine called 'Bonnie,' and pointed towards the wide door leading to the hotel lobby. Their little sergeant and a tall woman headed for the door. He encircled her waist with his arm, and tried to match his steps to hers as she teetered on three-inch heels. She pulled away from him and bent down to remove the shoes. They seemed to be laughing over the improvement this made in their coupling, and she proceeded towards the lobby in her stocking feet, the sergeant sauntering close behind.

John murmured into Bonnie's ear, 'Lose some, win some.'

Two

Bonnie and John met for steaks and a movie on Saturday night with Joe and Maxine. On Sunday afternoon, bundled against the cold, the two of them explored downtown Lancaster, window-shopping at Murray and Penn's, walking the paths of the university campus, and arriving at the Capitol building in time for a tour. They talked tirelessly, comparing and contrasting their lives and their dreams. Their fathers both had fought in World War I. His mother went to finishing school, hers hadn't finished high school. Her grandparents were farmers, his were sailors and city landlords. They both liked Tchaikovsky, Clark Gable, and rhubarb pie. Also school, October, and Richard Halliburton.

At the bowling alley they stopped in the lounge for a cup of hot chocolate and decided to try a few lines. John was good; she was glad she didn't have to let him win.

Bonnie poised the heavy ball in front of her, swung it back and forward again during three measured steps, then let go out of a graceful swing, knees bent. John watched with approval as her tweed skirt flared and dipped over the old shoes she usually left inside her boots.

Most of the alleys were empty on this gloomy Sunday afternoon. At the end of the lane, the pin boy scrambled to reset the pins and to climb back to his perch above them.

'No matter how well we knock them down, he just keeps putting them back,' John remarked.

'Like recovering from the wars.'

'Suppose we'll find the weapon from which we can't recover?'

'Were you a pacifist in high school?' she asked.

'God yes, weren't we all? I once took the Oxford Pledge.'

She tried to remember what that was.

'A pledge some students took refusing to support the United States in any war.'

'I think I read about it.'

'The radical peace movements were breaking down by the time I got to college. I joined the American Student Union when it was on its last legs. The Communist faction sabotaged the anti-war programme, and the pacifists pulled out.'

He spoke of these things as though they were real – these things you read about, idealized, but didn't do.

He finished, 'We thought we had the simple answers. But life isn't simple.'

'No. Look at you now.'

John adjusted his fingers inside the holes in the ball and lifted it from the rack. 'See the number one pin?' he said. 'That's der Führer.'

His arm swung back. The black ball connected with the alley and spun ahead. The pin setter scurried to safety before the triangle of pins exploded, their perfect order fragmented into chaos.

Back in boots, knitted white stocking cap, and trailing scarf, Bonnie strolled with John towards her apartment at dusk. They walked, eyes lowered, watching the sidewalk for slick spots. They cut through the park, strolling under trees and past bushes heavy with ice. They stopped to rest at a concrete picnic area, sitting on the cold bench and leaning back against the table.

'I'll bet you forgot the watermelon,' John said.

'Thought you were bringing it,' she answered.

'It had to stay in the Frigidaire as long as possible. One hundred in the shade today.' He placed a gloved hand over her mitten on the bench between them. 'I never could stand the heat. Think of me when you share the melon with some other soldier next summer.'

'Can't kid me,' she whispered because he was coming closer. 'There isn't any next summer.'

Their first kiss barely touched, fragile, a small spark in a freezing night. 'Yes there is, Bonnie. That's the way it works.' He kissed her again. 'Hot and cold.'

She stood up, stepped onto the dead grass, the frosted blades

19

crackling under her boots. John sat on the bench watching, then followed. He matched her slow steps. 'What's the matter?'

She shook her head. They stopped and looked back at the cold, white picnic table, silent and empty.

'It looks like a statue,' John said.

She shivered. 'It looks like a tomb.'

'It was alive when we were there.'

'Were we ever there?'

'Yes, Bonnie. We were. Don't forget.'

She turned to face him, and slid both hands up the lapels of his overcoat and under his upturned collar. They leaned together and through layers of heavy clothing she felt him against her. Flesh found flesh as warm mouths and cold noses touched and lingered.

Bonnie strained to control her trembling.

'You're cold, darling,' he whispered.

He kept a protective arm about her shoulders as they turned to walk back to her apartment.

That night, in a room lighted only by the glow of the fireplace grate, his hand sliding down her bare arm, gently touching a cheek before a kiss, resting upon a wool-skirted thigh, cradling an uncovered breast, stirred excitement she hadn't dared dream of. In past experience, touching had set off alarms, produced shields. Tonight touching opened doors through which she dared not – would not – pass.

Three

By Tuesday, they were old friends, sweethearts. After work Bonnie hurried home to change into something loose and soft. She left off her brassiere, but after reapplying lipstick she unzipped and put it back on.

She knew his knock. It was a sound she would always be able to recall. John brought records – Ravel, Prokofiev and Schönberg, a new kind of music.

The new music became a part of the new life. In years to come, its sound would resurrect in memory one special week when the warm walls of a lamplit apartment closed out winter. Shared suppers in the little kitchenette were communion for two. Less than perfect sound from the portable phonograph was a background for the eager flow of words. Words gave way to silent listening as they held each other in the dark, on the mohair sofa, knowing consummation was out of reach.

The night John brought the records they moved to the sofa with cheese and apples after they finished the stew, leaving the scraped, stacked dishes in the sink. Cheese for dessert was new for Bonnie. They did this in Boston.

John readjusted the records on the changer. The stack would play through quickly, another heavy record dropping after each piece ended.

'Are you playing the Ravel waltzes again?' Bonnie asked. 'So beautiful. I only knew "Bolero" before.'

She sat on one foot on the sofa after kicking off her shoes. John dropped into the slip-covered easy chair. He leaned forward, elbows balanced on spread knees. 'No, I saved these for last. This album is Schönberg. Know his music?'

Bonnie shook her head. 'Never heard of him. My school was strictly Bach, Beethoven and Brahms. Oh my, that is strange.'

Rhythm changed without pattern. Melodies leaped and chords were random, chaotic.

'What's the matter, pet?'

'Never heard anything like that before.' She put both feet on the floor.

'A lot of artists were trying to get rid of the rules about the time he was composing. Some of the music can't even be written on a conventional staff.'

They watched the record spinning on the phonograph.

'I had – have – a friend who writes this kind of music,' John said. 'I used to listen with him. He signed the pledge with me in 1938, but right after Pearl Harbor he went out and enlisted. Now he's missing in action.

'He joined the young Communists after the American Student Union. We sometimes talked about it far into the night.'

'I went to some of the meetings, but couldn't ever quite bring myself to join.'

'This girl of yours in Boston, I'll bet she likes this music.'

John looked up. 'Yes, she does.' He shook his head. 'Do you know how often you pick up my thoughts?'

'You were thinking about her?'

'Well, yes. She was with Eric and me sometimes.' He inspected the toe of his shoe. 'I suspected Sara liked him quite a lot, but he didn't care for girls. Just music.'

'He probably figured she was your girl.'

'What?'

'You said she liked Eric but he didn't like her.'

'I didn't say that.'

'Yes you did. You said she liked Eric but he didn't care for –'

She stopped as he moved to the sofa, and took hold of her upper arm. He kissed her lightly. 'We all grew up together.'

The insistent, dissonant chords of the record pounded against her temples as a stranger surrounded her with his body. She placed both hands against his chest and pushed. The strong male wall did not yield. In a flutter of panic she pushed harder. He sat back, surprise stirring across his face.

'Turn it off,' she said, putting her hands over her ears and closing her eyes. When she opened them he was still there, solemnly watching. She dropped her eyes. 'It scares me.'

He stood up, walked over and shut off the music. With care he lifted the stack of heavy records off the machine. He laid them on the table and reached for the old records. She heard the needle scratch. The familiar predictable notes of 'Liebestraum' lay like a calm mantle over the remembered chaos of Schönberg.

Sliding a pack of Camels from the pocket of his uniform jacket draped over a chair back, John sat down out of reach and concentrated on lighting the cigarette before leaning back to look at her. 'This music's nice, too,' he said.

The crook of his finger over the cigarette, and the curve of his hand resting on his knee stirred the pit of her stomach. 'I'll learn to like the Schönberg,' she said. 'It's just so new.'

'Sure you will.'

'I wish I had known Eric.'

'I do, too.'

'Do you think I'm stupid?'

'No, Bonnie. You're not stupid.' He added softly, 'The music reaches you; most people can't even hear it. There's something in you, wrapped up in the sweetness, that I want to uncover – if only there was time. I don't want to leave you, Bonnie. I want to know the woman you will be, as you'll come to know her. I never wanted anything so goddamned bad.'

Could it be that I am superior? Not only not stupid but superior? How good it is, holding our eyes together and not needing to look away. I feel naked before him and I'm not ashamed. He knows me and I know he's supposed to. She lifted her arm and stretched her hand towards him.

John walked over to change the record. 'Clair de Lune' had been repeating for twenty minutes. He switched the machine off and stood with his back to her. The light from the street sliced through the venetian blind, casting diagonal lines across the rug.

'How long does it take to get married here?' he asked.

Sitting in the dark, Bonnie's hand went to her throat.

He spun around and she jumped. 'I mean, is there a waiting period? How long?'

It wasn't the right question, but she followed his lead. 'Three days.'

'Tomorrow's Wednesday. I could get a weekend pass. Can't be sure, but it looks like we'll be here till next week.' He took a

23

step, then faltered. 'God A'mighty, it would be a dumb thing to do!'

He walked over and switched on the lamp. He was restored to her sight, as exciting as the feel of him in the dark. Bonnie straightened and put her hands to her hair.

John's thoughtful gaze moved from her to the muted landscape print hanging above the sofa, to the crushed, petal-dotted pillows at the end, down to the worn leather footstool, over the untouched plate of cheese on the table, and back to her.

'Well, when you make up your mind, let me know.' Bonnie's nervous laugh slid into a hiccup.

'Let's do it,' he said. 'Let's be idiots and do it.'

He sat down and grasped her hands, suddenly reversing himself to stand again and pace. 'Could you get to a doctor tomorrow for the blood test? I can get mine at the base. You'll need to see the doctor for something else, too. Are diaphragms legal in this state? You know they –'

'I *know* what they are!' Her cheeks warmed.

He sat down again and touched one hand. 'Oh, sweetheart,' he asked, 'Is it okay? Do you want to?'

And she said, 'Yes.'

Four

When they came into the apartment the next night, they walked slowly and hung up their coats without speaking. The marriage license they had just applied for made them a different combination. She stood in the doorway, staring at the stove when John came up behind her.

'I like my steak rare, and lots of onion in the meat loaf,' he said, reading her mind again.

'It's a gamble, isn't it, for a man,' she said. 'Taking on a cook

24

for the rest of his life without asking for references. I think I'll just open some cans.'

'It doesn't matter what we eat,' John answered, seating himself on a high stool. 'I'm not hungry, I just wanted to see you in the kitchen tonight – talk to you over our own table. I want to remember you in as many ways as possible. You can't believe all the questions that run through my mind when I'm trying to get to sleep.'

'For instance?'

'Well, let's see. How about high school? Were you a prom queen or a cheerleader?'

Could she tell him she didn't have a steady boyfriend until after high school? She answered truthfully, 'Neither, I'm afraid. I was class valedictorian, and I had the lead in the senior class play.'

'Sweet, untarnished, beautiful, and bright. You'll make those brittle, wiseacre debutantes look like dull brass next to simple, pure gold.

'Maybe we'll go to school together after the war. You could finish up your degree while I'm in law school. It would mean putting off a family for a while.'

She started stirring again. 'I don't think a couple should have children right away. They need to get used to each other.'

'We'll need to, for sure.' He jumped off the stool. 'You're boiling over!'

She switched off the burner, and turned her attention to getting the haphazard supper on the table. Once seated, they could get back to what was important. 'Speaking of children –' she said.

'Another thing we haven't covered. How many? What do you think?'

'Two,' she answered promptly. 'A boy and a girl.'

'Yeah. Okay. Maybe even three or four wouldn't be bad. You were an only child, and my brother didn't come along until I was ten. I think we missed something.'

'Two's enough. About three years apart.'

John put down his fork and reached across and covered her hand. 'It gives me something to think about, plans to make. Something to live for.'

The food she was chewing turned to a soggy lump. She

25

swallowed it, feeling its push all the way down. John slid back his chair and walked around the table. She kept looking at him until he pulled her gently to her feet and began kissing her. She welcomed the kisses, and returned them with love spilling over.

They moved to the sofa, and he unbuttoned her blouse and pushed up her brassiere, touching and kissing her breasts for the first time with the lights on. She was fascinated to watch his long fingers cup the little mounds, and wondered how he knew to brush the nipples so lightly instead of squeezing and hurting as had happened to her before. The sight of his moving hands excited her, made things happen lower, under her skirt. John loosened his tie and top shirt buttons and undid her bra in the back. She was passive at first, but discovered that her enjoyment increased when she felt his ear, or stroked the stubbly hair above it, or slid her hand into his shirt and found hair again – soft and curly on his chest. They continued to kiss and stroke, and occasionally to talk, until it was time for him to leave. They never touched, or disturbed their clothing, below the waist.

She left work early on Thursday, telling Mr Forbes she was having an out-of-town guest. She splurged on a taxi and bought groceries. They planned to stay in the apartment for their weekend honeymoon, but each day had to count for itself. She felt uneasy about sending him away hungry last night.

She considered meat loaf but was afraid it might not be as good as his mother's recipe, and settled for a thick steak to be baked with mushrooms and served with mashed potatoes and gravy. She used a bright blue tablecloth with multicoloured pottery dishes, and bought a new white candle for the clear glass holder, but put it away in favour of a short candle with a blackened wick and dribbled wax streaking its sides and squeezed it into a squatty green wine bottle. She wore the pink housecoat. This time she left off the brassiere. She balanced the Ravel records on the spindle of the record changer so they could be switched on when the knock came.

Rummaging through stacks of notebook paper in the closet, she set aside certain segments, to be taken into the living room and stacked on the table by the sofa.

She expected him around six – shortly after the time she

usually got home. When the knock came she flew to start the record player, then to the door, stopping in front of it to take a deep breath and smooth her hair. It could be fun, getting ready for your man to come home.

When John came inside, he stopped short. 'Hey now,' he exclaimed, 'hey, look at this.'

She smiled and put her arm around his waist. 'Surprise,' she said, 'I got off early.'

Warm, soft arcs of light radiated from the candle, lamp, and fireplace. Thinking of the chasm of time that separated them from a lifetime of such homecomings made her ache inside.

When she went to finish dinner, she pointed to the piles of paper on the table. 'The story I told you about, and some poems. Thought you might like to look at them.'

He hurried to settle himself. She stopped talking while he read, turning the pages quickly; but she glanced at him often, trying to interpret the expression on his face. The gravy became lumpy, and she poured it into the bowl through a large, misshapen tea strainer. Thirty minutes later she called him. Dinner was cooling off.

'Well?' she asked when they were settled.

'It's delicious,' he pronounced, finishing the first taste.

'No, no, I mean the story. What do you think?'

He looked thoughtful while chewing, then swallowed and said, 'It's good, Bonnie, very good.'

She shook her head. 'You didn't like it.'

'Yes I did, I liked it. You have talent, I really mean that. You should keep writing.'

'But – ?'

'Well, it takes a long time, a lot of work. The talent is just the beginning.'

'I've been writing since second grade.'

'I'm sure you have, it shows. You should major in English,' he said as they ate. 'Why'd you set your story in New York?'

'I don't know. It's kind of a fairy-tale place to me. It was fun to imagine –'

'Haven't you ever been there?'

'No. I suppose you have.'

'Sure, often. It's close to home.'

She went back for the coffee. She was always forgetting to pour the coffee.

27

'Why don't you write a story about Lancaster? About things happening to you?'

She poured and sat down. 'I've thought about it,' she said. 'Maybe it's too close.'

'Someday you must. Life in a midwestern Army air base town during the great war.'

'I do write a lot of letters.' It occurred to her that that would soon change. 'But I'll have to stop, won't I? Write and tell them I'm married.'

'Maybe not. Letters are so important to a soldier.'

'You don't mind my writing to other men?'

'Maybe I will mind at that, though it seems selfish.'

'It's not selfish; we'll be forsaking all others.'

'Yes, of course.'

'Is the steak all right?' she asked anxiously.

He had told her he liked his steak rare, and she had served it baked, well-done.

'It's delicious,' he said again.

After the dishes were stacked they sat down together surrounded by the well-thumbed papers accumulated from childhood, through adolescence, into the early bloom of maturity.

'Don't stop writing,' John told her. 'Don't let me or the kids stop you. I may try, you know.'

'I've so much to learn. You're ahead of me, but it's what I want. Help me, John, take me with you.'

'I will, Bonnie, I will. I want to.'

He hugged her and she clung to him. All their plans were fantasies, shining on the other side of a canyon of separation and death.

'You talked about communism,' she spoke from the sanctity of his chest. 'It's very foreign to me. I didn't know Americans ever thought about it.'

They moved apart.

'There's been so much suffering,' John said. 'People who can't find work going hungry and cold or being humiliated by going on relief. I thought about that for a long time. Why *not* divide up the jobs and divide up the money?'

'Simple answers again.'

'Exactly. I wanted simple answers when I was eighteen. But there's a price to pay. The sacrifice of freedom and dreams, the very things America was built on. There has to be another way.'

'Hasn't the war given people jobs?'

'We may have more prosperity than we've ever known when it's over, but first we have to survive.'

'Everybody wants to survive,' she said. 'The war brings us together.'

'And tears us apart,' he remembered, returning to the personal.

Bonnie went to the phonograph and started a record. 'You'd Be So Nice to Come Home To,' a male voice crooned.

'Good choice,' he commented.

'It's the kind of song they're writing these days,' she told him.

A song of separation. Bonnie listened and followed the beat.

Five

He hadn't telephoned her at work before. On Friday morning he said 'Bonnie?' like somebody died. 'Bad news, sweetheart.'

She forced sound from her dry throat. 'What?' The fluorescent light across the aisle flickered. It made her dizzy.

'Our orders came. We're shipping out tomorrow morning.'

Sue, the mail girl, dropped some papers into Bonnie's 'In' box. Sue waited. When Bonnie looked up at her she went on, mumbling something Bonnie didn't hear.

'I'm sorry,' he was saying.

'We can't get married?'

'I'm confined to quarters.'

What's the matter with the maintenance men around here? I asked to have that light fixed two days ago. Or was it Monday? 'This is it? On the phone?'

'Listen, I'll call you tonight. We'll have a long talk.'

'Tonight.'

'I know you can't talk now, but I wanted you to know. You may need to cancel some things.'

'Yes. I will.' *Not much trouble. The arrangements aren't complicated. Not like the wedding I might have had. 'I Love You Truly' and 'Oh Promise Me.'*

'I'm so sorry.'

'Oh, John, so am I.'

'I love you, darling. I always will, remember that.'

'I'll remember.'

She hung up the phone. *The decision wasn't ours. Life will stay the same. No, it won't. I'll wait. Ask me to wait. That other girl is waiting. Without commitment. I'll be committed. Ask me. Come back to me. Just come back. So many good-byes. Even the ones who say 'I love you' stop writing. This time I said it back. This one is different. This one is a two-way street. Come back to me. Come back. Come back. Lord, make him come back. John.*

'Is Mr Forbes in?'

'No, he went to a meeting.'

'When will he be back?'

Not for the duration. Maybe never. 'What?'

'When will he be back? Bonnie, is something wrong?'

'No. What did you say? Oh, he'll be back around noon, I guess.'

'You don't look so good. Too many late hours?' He winked.

'No, it's that light. It makes me dizzy.'

She didn't hear the car pool conversation. Clouds hung low and a damp cold crept into the car. A long talk with Maxine had helped. Maxine, Joe, and Bonnie's pastor were the only ones who knew about the wedding planned for tomorrow. She and John had decided to brave the storm of parental disapproval after the fact. Parents wouldn't understand that you could be sure in a week.

Her feet were heavy on the stairs. She hurried around the landing. He sat on the top step, her lieutenant. Ankles crossed, knees spread, his short topcoat rested over them. His flight cap was pushed to the back of his head, exposing short, dark bristles of hair. He was up in one movement to lift her off her feet and swing her around to the door.

She couldn't stop hugging him. 'Oh, I'm so glad you're here.'

He pushed her gently back. 'The key.'

She dug in the bottom of her purse, mindless rummaging that finally produced a key. They moved inside.

'I had to come. Even AWOL.'

She shut the door. 'You're not!'

'It's okay, the army doesn't know. It's our secret.'

'Are you sure?'

'No problem at the gate, my buddies'll cover in the squad room, but I have to catch the bus before curfew. We take off at eight in the morning.'

Her smile faded. 'Oh. For a minute, I thought –'

'Bonnie,' his voice lowered, 'I can't make the date we had for tomorrow. But we're all ready. It's still six and a half hours to midnight. Do you think your preacher – ?'

'Oh, glory,' she said. She dashed to the phone, flinging her hat and gloves aside as she ran. She struggled with boots with one hand as she held the phone with the other. After a brief conversation she turned a glowing face back to John. 'He'll meet us at the church chapel in an hour.'

'Great.' He grinned as she waltzed about the room in her stocking feet, still wearing her bulky wool coat.

'We can come back here.' She looked about the apartment, in shining readiness for tomorrow's postnuptial celebration for four. 'We'll drink the champagne by ourselves.'

'Bonnie,' he extended a hand and pulled her towards the window. 'Look out there.' They saw a bleak landscape, already sinking into night. The lights in the window of the house across the street framed a fine spray of freezing rain.

'I want in the worst way to come back here, but don't you think we should stay down at the hotel? Close to the church and the terminal?'

She shook her head. 'This is our place; I want you to remember.'

'It'd save a lot of time. As it is, we'll have to depend on the bus. Wouldn't want to try for a cab in this weather.'

'The weather! You can't fly in this weather!'

His face did not reflect her excitement. 'It won't make any difference for us. It could clear tonight. Even if it doesn't I have to go back – to stick around.'

She closed her eyes. 'So stupid of me to keep looking for a reprieve.'

They stood holding hands, looking out at the cold, empty street.

'I wonder if it will be warmer where I am next week?' John squeezed her fingers.

She gasped. 'You know! You have your orders! Where?'

'It's a military secret.'

'Don't tease.' She pulled his hand up and clasped it. 'You know I won't tell.'

He lifted her hands to his lips and kissed her fingertips. 'Let's just say it's good I prefer plum pudding over coconuts.'

She let out a long breath. 'Oh, that's good. Yes, good – it's not the Pacific.'

He nodded. 'It's the assignment we wanted.' He pulled her towards him. She resisted gently and freed her hands.

'I have to dress,' she told him in a low voice. 'I want to wear my wedding dress. It's important, isn't it?'

He didn't answer, and she walked towards the bedroom, adding over her shoulder, 'Turn on some lights and start the fireplace grate if you're cold. I'll hurry.'

Her hand was on the knob when he called her name again. She stopped without turning around.

'Bonnie, could I come in? I won't slow you down, won't touch you.'

She turned slowly. His head was outlined against the window, face in shadow.

'I won't be here tomorrow to watch you dress – Lord knows when we'll be together again.'

'I – I'd rather not.' She forced herself to look at him. He nodded. She went through the door and shut it.

She hurried to bathe and dress. Two walls of guilt pressed in. Had she appeased the right one? She must make it up to him. He wouldn't have long to wait.

When she emerged from the steamy bathroom, she was reassured by the light shining under the door and the sound of the radio. The nasal voice of H V Kaltenborn came through clearly, bringing the evening news. 'RAF and American bombers continue their relentless pounding of military targets in Germany. Allied losses were somewhat lighter this week.'

Reaching for the short, white wool dress, she stopped and grasped the closest doorjamb. She leaned her hand against it, shuddering. She wanted to scream and weep. She wanted to throw open the door. Instead, she dressed faster, and packed a small bag with her high-heeled white satin pumps and her new peignoir and nightdress, tucking the bulky prescription box underneath.

Her work clothes and coat lay heaped on the white counterpane. She took the muskrat from the closet and laid it across her arm, picked up the bag and walked in her stocking feet to the door.

John had switched off the radio when the station reverted to music and was standing before the fireplace, head lowered, hands in pockets. The fire made a yellow glow on the rug, and brass buttons and silver wings glistened in reflected light. *Dear John.*

He turned around. *See me. Remember. I'm part of you, making you whole. Tied to you, pulling you back. The real life. The good part. Your bride.*

'Do you like my dress?'

'You're beautiful.'

She sighed. Spotting the boots, crossing each other on the floor by the sofa, she sat down and pulled out a dusty shoe and put it on.

'Bonnie?'

'Ummmmm?'

'It's hard to talk about.'

'I know.'

'I mean what I've been thinking. I don't know why I didn't think about it before.'

She straightened and put the foot on the floor. 'What?'

'It's what I'm doing to you.'

'Doing to me?'

He walked closer. 'I've been looking out only for myself. Wanting to keep everything the same until I could come back and finish it.'

'So?'

'Have you thought how it's going to be for you in the meantime? I know how you are. You'll wait.'

'Of course I'll wait. That's what I want to do. Wait.'

33

'But can you just put your life on hold? It could be years.'

'Isn't that what *you're* doing?'

She was sorry about the waves in her voice. He was standing over her; she had to look up. 'John, what are you trying to say?'

'Whatever it is, I seem to be saying it badly.' He started to lean over, then straightened. 'Bonnie, are you very sure that you want to be married? Have you really thought what it means?'

'I don't know what *you* mean. I won't be any different from all the other wives. It's what women do.'

He shook his head. 'We've understood each other so well. I don't know why now –'

'All right. Tell me. Do you want out?'

He drew in his breath.

'Because if you do, you can say so. You don't have to make it sound like you're doing it for me.'

He sat down beside her. 'Okay, okay. I'm sorry I mentioned it, please forget that I did.'

She saw him through blurred eyes.

'Forgive me?'

She nodded.

'Of course,' he said, 'I really was thinking of you.'

She gave him a long look before asking quietly. 'What would be the alternative?'

His face drew tight. He stood and raised his voice. 'I don't know. It's not as though I were making plans.' He sat down again. 'I'm trying to be realistic. Maybe it's just everyday pre-wedding jitters.'

'This isn't an everyday wedding. You already said it's a dumb thing to do.'

A freshly starched yellow linen cloth covered the little table where they ate. The square phonograph with its stack of records sat waiting. This room was their whole life together. Outside, the sleet hit the window in uneven gasps.

She forced her eyes to move from her own hands to his face. 'Do you want to marry me without a wedding? Then we wouldn't be committed, we'd still be free.' She watched several answers cross his face.

'That would be an intelligent approach, if we could handle it.'

34

She steadied her chin. 'I'll do it any way you want, John,' she said at last. *It won't make any difference to me. I'm committed.*

This was the moment for him to reach out for her, but a wall stood between them, as solid as it was invisible.

John sighed and stood up. He looked down at her feet, one shoe on and one shoe off. He bent on one knee and pulled the shoe out of the other boot. Grasping her heel, he guided her foot into the shoe. He then lifted the boots one at a time and together they tugged them on over her shoes.

'Please get up off your knees,' she said. 'I feel silly.'

He laid one hand on the sofa arm as he regained his feet, then reached out his arms and pulled her up. Their hands passed on around each other and they held on, fingers spread, his face pressing into her hair. They separated and he picked up her coat.

At the door Bonnie said 'Oh,' and ran back to the refrigerator for the bottle of champagne, placing it in a paper bag and hurrying back. John put it in his pocket, but the bottle bulged and extended out too far.

Bonnie opened her suitcase and laid the tall bottle across the wispy blue peignoir, and snapped the case shut. John paused in the doorway, but without looking back, he pulled the door shut behind them.

Six

A mantle of crystal had settled over the city. Freezing mist veiled the near and obscured the distant. Winter twilight vanquished colour. Diamond trees lined platinum streets. The sidewalk stretched into a flat ribbon of ice.

Noise would shatter the brittle air. She whispered, 'Beautiful. Oh, it's beautiful.'

John dropped the suitcase. He rounded the end of the

sidewalk with a few steps. Bonnie's squeal violated the silence as, arms spread for banking, he slid down the declining walk parallel to the street, skillfully guiding himself onto the grass at the bottom of the incline.

She shrieked again and laughed. 'You're crazy – going the wrong way.'

'Who's crazy?' he shouted. 'You can't slide uphill.'

She took a few cautious steps to the turn in the sidewalk and spread out her arms. 'Catch me. Here I come.'

Her jerky running start turned into a lurching slalom. The boots weren't made for sliding but she managed to keep upright all the way down into John's outstretched arms.

Without consultation, they climbed up the frozen grass and slid down the walk again together.

'Shall we press our luck?' he panted.

'Why not?'

This time they almost didn't make it, Bonnie clutching wildly at his steady, strong arm. Their gasps exploded into laughter, bouncing into a picture postcard world.

'If you think that's good, wait till we put on our skates,' John said.

They climbed back up the incline and she waited for him to retrieve her bag before they threaded their way across the grass in the other direction.

'You'll like our lodge in the Adirondacks. Know how to ski?'

She shook her head. 'But I can learn.'

'You'll be great. I can't wait to teach you.'

She looked around. 'Think there's anybody else out there?'

He looked carefully, pointing through the haze across the street. 'Up in that tree, there's an old man in a pointed cap and cowboy boots. He's the only one.'

She stopped and cupped her hands around her mouth. 'Hey old man,' she called, 'did you know this is my wedding night?'

'I don't think he heard you.'

She raised her hands again, shouting, 'Hey, old man –'

'I'll help. *Hey* –'

Bonnie pulled back on his arm. 'John,' she said, 'we're lunatics.'

'Momma and Poppa Lunatic, talking about a future.'

'Oh, tell me there's a future.'

'I promise. Thirty years from now you'll be a gentle old lady in a shawl with our grandchildren gathered around you saying, "Tell me about your wedding during the big war, Granma."'

She smiled. 'And you'll be an old man in a pointed cap and cowboy boots sitting up in a tree spying on lovers.'

They were the only passengers on the bus. The diminutive driver kept her attention riveted on the icy pavement, skilfully easing the big vehicle up to stop signs and around corners.

Downtown, the few people on the street eased by like ghosts. Out of the mist the grey stone church loomed like a deserted Gothic castle. They rounded the corner, past the steep stone steps, to see a light shining through the small stained-glass windows of the chapel. Like a candle in the window at home, it drew them to the less imposing side entrance. They held each other up one last time on the stone steps, and stood tall again with firm footing in the dry hallway.

The hall was chilly, but when they passed through the heavy chapel doors, warmer air touched their stiff faces and fingers. Mellowed wood panelled the walls here, and the deep red carpet echoed the sombre colours of stained-glass windows with night on the other side. Light was hushed by the amber bulbs in the antique chandelier, and the low-flamed candles in the brass candelabra.

A small man with thinning hair and glasses came towards them, his hand outstretched to grasp Bonnie's.

'Here you are, my dear. Wretched night out there.'

She was grateful for his warm handclasp, and turned to introduce John. Dr Miller examined the bridegroom.

'Glad to meet you. I know Bonnie will have chosen a good man.'

'Thank you, sir,' John replied.

'We're a little late,' Bonnie said. 'You'll be late for your meeting.'

Dr Miller shook his head. 'Doesn't matter, they can start without me. This is more important.'

Two persons stood close to the altar. Bonnie recognized the fuzzy round figure of the church secretary, but she wasn't sure who the man was.

They left their coats and the leather bag at the back of the room, then had to detour around the silent electric organ to join the others up front. With linked hands, they walked down the aisle together. She looked for sadness in the silent organ, the empty benches, the strangers at the altar, the stormy night. Joy kept breaking through instead.

They paced their steps together and reached the end of their a capella processional with grace. Their attendants stood on either side and Dr Miller beamed at them, Bible in hand.

'Bonnie and John,' he said solemnly, 'I would like for you to meet Miss Stapleton and Mr Chap.'

The older people all wore rimless glasses with little nose pieces cutting into the flesh. Miss Stapleton's glasses were smudged. Mr Chap's coat didn't match his trousers. Bonnie wished she could remember where she had seen him before.

Dr Miller cleared his throat. 'Shall we begin?'

The silence of the house of God fell around them, and they straightened their shoulders and fixed their eyes on His minister. Bonnie moved her hand so one finger touched a fingertip that pressed back.

'Dearly beloved, we are gathered together –'

Tears moistened Bonnie's eyes and she looked towards the floor. Dr Miller's black shoes had stayed shiny through the rain. Her own black shoes pointed back towards his – *black*! Her sheer wool dress just cleared the tops of her old black boots. She gasped. John turned. The witnesses peered from the corners of their eyes. Dr Miller finished his sentence and stopped.

'I'm sorry,' she said. 'I'll be right back. Sorry.'

She hurried up an aisle that had no end. *Why didn't somebody tell me? I shouldn't be doing this. I remember, he's the church janitor.*

She changed to the white satin pumps while everybody inspected the floor and the furniture, then she started the long walk again. Mr Chap came to meet her. He was taller than John, too thin for his clothes, with hair that was dark and straight, combed back and oiled, the ends rebellious. His face was a map of little lines, and his eyes behind the glasses were withdrawn, their expression sober. He bent his arm and extended it. Gently Bonnie laid her hand on his forearm, and they covered the remaining distance with dignity. He stepped back with a hint of a bow as he relinquished the bride, and moved to his former place.

'Dearly beloved, we are gathered together today to unite this man and this woman in holy matrimony.'

Dr Miller's voice was as rich and mellow as the panelled walls and warm as the candles. It supplied the missing music. The short ceremony gave her the sanctity and peace she had been seeking. The man she loved slid the narrow gold band onto her finger, and her hand held steady as it received the ring. Looking at the encircled finger, she thought of eternity. She felt relaxed, tired, married.

Mr Chap did not speak or smile, but shook their hands firmly after the ceremony and backed away, quietly watching.

Miss Stapleton embraced Bonnie. She was greying, dowdy, resilient, and she smelled good. Close to Bonnie's ear she whispered, 'How I envy you.' To them both she said, 'Bless you,' several times.

Signatures were affixed to the marriage certificate, and less than half an hour after they had come into the church, they were leaving. They thanked everyone again. Bonnie broke away and went back to put her arms around Mr Chap. When she kissed him on the cheek, she learned a secret. His cheeks were wet.

'My first wedding presents,' she told John when they were alone. 'Envy and tears.'

When they were walking the four blocks to the hotel he asked, 'What's that, envy and tears?'

'Miss Stapleton, she whispered that she envied me. I think that was sweet.' *How can I explain? My friends weren't there.*

'I see. She cried for your mother.'

'No, she didn't cry. Mr Chap cried.'

'He did? Son of a gun.'

Sleet no longer assaulted them, but fog still lay against the buildings, absorbing the couple into its anonymous wetness.

He said, 'You know, it *was* funny.' On the word *funny* his voice broke and he put his hand over his face.

'You're laughing!' she wailed, hating him. 'How could you?'

'I'm sorry.' He walked away into the fog and she was alone.

He was back in an instant. 'Oh, come on, Bonnie,' he began again. 'Can't you see this in the movies with the selected short subjects? You're too close to it; someday you'll look back and see.'

'It was your wedding, too,' she said. 'Why aren't you too close to it?'

He took her hand. 'They're good people who stayed late on a bad night for a couple of strangers. I am grateful, but can't you see? Ichabod Crane and Tugboat Annie, and the bride stopping the ceremony to change her shoes. What a script.'

'It wasn't funny. It was my wedding, and it wasn't funny.'

John sighed.

They walked on.

They passed the frosted windows of the Comanche Room. 'How about a beer?'

She looked up. His eyes were teasing, flirting. Her stomach turned over. She rested her forehead against his shoulder.

They reached the lobby and approached the desk. As John talked to the clerk, Bonnie tugged at her gloves, exposing the left hand now ringed forever. She leaned her elbow on the desk, hand casually close to bell and blotter as he signed the register 'Lieutenant and Mrs John Blake.'

Seven

The telephone bell pierced the dark. John moved after the second ring, breaking the seal of their bodies to throw off the covers. She adjusted the blanket carefully to preserve the warmth in his empty place as he sat on the edge of the bed.

The outline of his bare back projected from unfamiliar background shapes.

'Yes, thank you.' The 11.00 call. He replaced the phone with a quick movement that added a muscular arm to the silhouette.

He dived back into bed after a brief skirmish with the rear-ranged covers that set them both giggling as they embraced again.

'Time to go,' he whispered, while kissing the top of her ear.

'Thirty seconds more?'

'Oh, lady, you've got 'em.'

It was several times thirty before he once again threw back the covers and found his way to the bathroom. The door closed and a ribbon of light appeared below.

Again Bonnie straightened the bed. The air chilled her arms and she pulled them under the blanket. Squirming and stretching, she savoured the warmth and friction of sheets against her bare skin. She had discovered her body. The act of sharing it had brought personal discovery. The annihilation of the artificial wall had freed her womanness. How could she have been whole yesterday when she was more whole today?

Maxine had warned her the first time might be disappointing, even unpleasant. Maxine was wrong.

She had never before been so close to another human. Physically linked, locked together, for the first time in her life she was not alone. They exchanged the warmth of their flesh, mingled their body fluids. In his arms was a place – harbour, nest, cradle. She was in one act his mother and his child. Spiritually joined by their wedding vows, they would never be alone again. Yet she drew up her knees – already she felt severed.

'Where the hell did I leave my pants?' he swore under his breath as he stumbled across the unfamiliar room. The lamp came on. The florid little lamp base showed a colonial maid standing beside a pink and blue well. It sat on a dark desk-dresser next to a stack of hotel picture postcards, a Gideon Bible and an almost full champagne bottle. Two water glasses still holding some of the stale spirits stood together at one side. While frost clouded the one small window.

John found his clothes piled on the luggage rack. He stepped into his officer's pinks and zipped up.

'We'll never be alone again,' Bonnie said solemnly.

'You'd better be alone in about fifteen minutes or I'll be in the guardhouse. I'm not in a position to deal with MPs tonight.'

'Then you wouldn't have to leave tomorrow.'

'I can't miss being on that plane.' He relaxed his firm jaw and added softly, 'I know what you mean, Bonnie. We'll keep remembering that.'

He turned away and picked up his shirt. 'I wish we could have had a nicer room.' They hadn't remembered hotels were busy on weekends.

'It doesn't matter,' she said, as she reached for the pale blue gown on the floor and pulled it over her head. 'Are you sure you don't want me to go to the terminal?'

'We decided. It'd only be a few more minutes, sweet. This is a better place to say good-bye.'

The words hung over them like smoke. She straightened her straps. *We should be saying important things.*

'Remember to see the guy I told you about. I think you can trust him to sell you a good used car. Lots of places take advantage of women.'

'I'll remember.'

'You'll have more money now. Try to loosen up a little.'

'I'll try. John, are we rich?'

He stopped buttoning his shirt and frowned. 'We talked about that. I told you I'm going to make my own way, although the annuity will help.'

'But your parents. You keep mentioning servants and lodges – '

'Well, sure, Dad's pretty well heeled, but he's no Rockefeller.' She didn't like the edge in his voice.

'I didn't mean – of course, I understand – well, it's just that I know so little about you.' *He's wondering if I married him for his money.* 'I mean what will it be like? Will I fit in?'

'You'll be my wife. Of course you'll fit in. In some ways you remind me of my mother.'

'Oh, come on.'

'You do. Short and pretty.'

'All of that?'

He laughed and walked over to switch on the anaemic overhead light. 'Beautiful and well endowed.' He leaned closer to the mirror to knot his tie. 'Of course, I must admit you're going to be a bit of a shock to them tonight.'

'Tonight?'

'Yeah, I'll get in line for the phone at the base. Mom and Dad are expecting the call about shipping out, but they aren't expecting a daughter.'

This isn't happening.

'Will you call Sara?'

He kept working on his tie. At last he said, 'I don't know, a letter would be easier. Yeah, I'll probably just write a letter.'

'You know she'll hear it from your folks. It'll be hard on her.'

'What is this concern? You want me to call her?'

'Not really, but I guess I can afford to be sorry for her.'

'She wouldn't appreciate your sympathy.'

He resents it, too. 'Are you sure you never talked about marriage?'

'Not since we were twelve.'

He isn't going to call her and I'm glad, but I shouldn't be. Poor girl.

She swung her feet out on the floor and hurried into the bathroom. She took care of her needs as quickly as possible, including a quick combing of the long hair, and buttoning into the lace-trimmed peignoir.

When she came out on bare feet, she stopped at the door. John stood at the window not moving, a shoe held in one hand. His shoulders were rounded, his head bent. She took a step towards him and stopped. *What is he thinking? I daren't ask.* She reached back and pulled the door shut with a click.

John straightened and looked hard out the window. He didn't say anything for a long half-minute, then smiled and said, 'I do believe it's clearing. Maybe we won't be grounded after all.' He sat down in the shabby chair and loosened the shoe laces.

She walked to the other chair and stroked the stiff military jacket that was draped around its back. She took it off the chair, holding it until he was ready. As she leaned her cheek against the collar, he accepted the caress with his eyes. He found the sleeves with his hands and she lifted the jacket high and wide over his shoulders. He buttoned the jacket, pulling it straight. After he picked up his cap by the visor, he laid his short coat across his arm. 'Someday it will end and I'll watch you dress every day for the rest of our lives,' he said.

She nodded. *Never. Never. This is the way it will always be.*

He held out his hands. She slid into her place. They tightened their hold and melted together, containing each other. He kissed her on the forehead and then on the lips. They pulled apart and he opened the door.

'Be careful,' she said.

'You too.'

Across the hall the elevator operator held the door. A soldier and a girl got on and turned around and watched. Three pairs of insolent, uncaring eyes blinked at them. He gave her a quick kiss, like a husband going to work, and hurried away. She shut the door before he could turn around, leaning heavily against it. *We never talked about dying.*

Slowly she moved back to the rigid armchair and lowered herself into it. Dry-eyed and wide-awake, she faced the dreary little room.

Eight

May 1943

One Monday morning towards spring Bonnie shared the ladies' room mirror with the president's secretary, Maggie Newcombe. She saw a woman in her mid-thirties, long, dark hair knotted low on her neck. Two permanent creases between her eyebrows gave the impression of a continuing frown, even when she smiled, which was not often. Her dress was dark – fashionable but not new. She had never spoken to Bonnie except about business, but this morning she looked directly into Bonnie's reflected eyes.

'How are things with the new bride?' she asked.

'Fine, thank you.' Bonnie swallowed her surprise and pleasure. 'Not so new. It's three months now.'

A smile touched Maggie's mouth briefly, then disappeared. 'Wait until it's thirteen years. That's "not new."' She carefully adjusted her starched white collar and cuffs. 'Marriage does make a difference in one's way of living; even when you're running the goddamn institution all by yourself.'

Bonnie's throat contracted. 'It's not so bad; we write a lot of letters.'

'V-mail's hardly a substitute for your man around the house,' Maggie answered with a snap of her compact. 'Nor is it much help in dealing with three kids. Harry's been gone a year – overseas for six months – the little one's almost forgotten him. In the thick of it in Africa, Lord knows where he'll land next.'

'Your husband's in the infantry?' Bonnie stretched hair high above her forehead and pulled her comb up through it.

'Right, an infantry sergeant, fighting the real war. Not up there in the wild blue yonder with the fly boys.'

Bonnie tightened her grip on the comb, and its teeth cut into her fingers. She flipped it over, skilfully manoeuvring the rat-tail around her finger, rolling the hair into a smooth, high pompadour, then jabbing hair pins into it.

Maggie washed her hands. 'Some of us from the office get together once a week. Bring our knitting or whatever and visit – gossip – bitch. You're welcome to join us. My house, tonight.'

Bonnie was aware she had received an invitation to court. 'Thank you, but I've already made plans for a movie tonight with Maxine.'

Maggie's expression did not change as she used a paper towel and disposed of it. 'Well, maybe some other time.' Her high heels clicked across the tile floor as she left.

After the movie Maxine and Bonnie headed for the Comanche Room. They had thrown light coats around their shoulders to supplement the warmth of their tailored suits in the chill of dusk. The store windows displayed bright summer clothes and the trees planted in boxes along Main Street were pale green with opening buds.

It was still early evening when they went through the revolving door and found a booth in a far corner.

Maxine watched the ketchup make its way to the end of the bottle and slowly become a gooey, crimson circle on her hamburger. 'Sure you don't want to drop in at the USO? You're still in good standing.'

Bonnie shook her head. 'No, Maxine, I haven't changed my mind. I don't want to go there anymore.'

'I don't want to talk you into anything, but I hate to see you bury yourself. What's wrong with a little socializing? Hostesses aren't supposed to date the soldiers anyway.'

'Ha!'

'Now, you said yourself, the USO makes more friends than lovers.' She put the bun back on the top and took a bite.

Bonnie made an impatient move. 'Who are we kidding? Can't tell me you don't look at each new dance partner with the question, "Are you the one?" Well, I found my "one." Playing the game now would be like playing poker with matches. And I think it's the same for them – there's just one thing they might want from a married woman, and they're not going to get that from me.' Her outburst had interrupted her eating.

Maxine shook her head. 'I don't know; do you really think you would have to defend your honour that often?'

Bonnie relaxed and pulled her milkshake glass closer. 'Well, how would I know? That's behind me now; I know where my place is.' She took a cold swallow, then looked up. 'Is that why you don't tell them about Janie?'

Maxine's colour deepened. 'Of course not – it's just awkward.'

'And you shouldn't have to,' Bonnie hastened to say. 'It's none of their business.' She hesitated. 'We've been close for two years now, but you never talk about your marriage. Don't you miss being married?'

Maxine looked up, then down again to push a french fry across her plate. She raised her eyes. 'Can you imagine a sixteen-year-old girl crawling into bed with a man without the foggiest notion of what was going to happen there?'

Bonnie nodded. 'I can; I would have been in the same boat at sixteen. My mother thought I was clairvoyant or something. I didn't have the faintest idea how it was done. No kidding, it was as mysterious as the Easter Bunny.'

'Did you wonder about those babies in the movies?'

Bonnie smiled. 'Yeah, I sure did. All it took was one quiet little kiss and in the next scene the girl was "in trouble."'

'Remember when Elizabeth Allan just lay down across Clark Gable's bed in *Men in White*?'

'And Clark wasn't even home.' They laughed, and Bonnie added, 'I knew something was going on, but darned if I could figure out what it was. I didn't think you could get it from the furniture.'

'Well, you sure can't find out from the movies.' Maxine

leaned closer. 'Now there's something I'd like to ask you. Has Mr Forbes ever made a pass at you?'

'Frank?' Bonnie exclaimed. 'Are you kidding? He wouldn't know how.'

'Believe me, Bonnie, they're born knowing how.'

Bonnie shook her head. 'He's very nice, we're comfortable together, but he's not the type to chase his secretary around the desk.' She frowned. 'Besides, he's too old. He must be thirty.'

'Too old! The plant's youngest executive? He's quite a catch, Bonnie. I didn't mean chasing you around the desk; I saw him looking at you one day in the strangest way.'

'Like in what strange way? What do you mean?'

'Oh, like you were sugar-coated, you know. He looked down when you turned around. Seems like you would have seen it sometime. Sure you haven't noticed?'

'Oh, you're wrong; I'm sure of it,' Bonnie answered uneasily. 'He never talks about his private life – I wonder if he has any. Sometimes I think he only exists at Scott Manufacturing, like the plant machinery. I don't even know why he isn't in the service. Do you think he has a job deferment?' She considered the question, then answered herself, saying, 'Maybe. Anyway, he isn't interested in me.' She took a bite of hamburger, her chewing growing progressively slower before she swallowed. 'At least, I hope not.'

A burst of laughter began and subsided from the other end of the room.

'I guess I've always been in too big a hurry,' Maxine said. 'I sure picked the hard way to learn the facts of life. We thought we were pretty smooth, lying about our ages and all.'

'Was it really bad?'

'Ghastly,' Maxine answered with renewed gusto. 'For both of us, I mean. Bill was probably just a couple of scores ahead of me, but he thought he was pretty wise. He hadn't had a green kid for a partner before.'

She stared ahead over Bonnie's shoulder. 'We never lived together, but when I found out I was pregnant – Boy, that was the day! We had to put off the divorce.' She shook her head. 'Idiot kids, fooling around with feelings we couldn't understand.'

Bonnie swallowed. 'I'm always feeling sorry for myself

because our time was so short. At least what we did have was perfect.' She sighed. 'Sometimes I almost wish I hadn't found out.'

'I know,' she heard her friend answering. 'That's the way it was with Jim. He was really the first.' She stopped, then quickly added, 'Of course, we didn't go all the way.'

'But he never talked about marriage?'

'No, although I'd gladly be a camp-follower wife. I kept thinking "Next time he'll say it." After all, we saw a lot of each other for two months. That's a long time these days.'

Bonnie felt the shared pain as they stared dumbly at their half-eaten supper. The crooning of the jukebox and the hum of voices in the background seemed far away.

'I could see why Jim might resent your not telling him.'

'But if he really loves me, it shouldn't make any difference. He turned into a different person.'

Bonnie lowered her voice. 'Are you saying he felt cheated because you pretended to be a virgin?'

Maxine's complexion turned a deeper pink, and she moved her hands nervously. 'I don't know what he was thinking. Now I'll never know. Two short letters and then nothing.' She clenched a fist. 'Why couldn't I ask him what was going on? Why didn't I just ask him? Why was I so damned afraid to open my mouth?'

Bonnie shook her head.

'Because he had to bring it up first. It's hell being a woman. All we have is a veto – that's the only power we have.'

Bonnie recoiled from the shock waves of Maxine's explosion. An uneasy guilt over her own better fortune nudged at her. She put her elbows on the table and leaned forward. 'Look,' she said, 'why don't you do something about it? There's a phone booth in the lobby. Go out there now and get Jim on the phone. Talk to him. Ask him all the questions you want to. Tell him what you feel. What have you got to lose?'

'Oh, I couldn't,' Maxine stammered. 'I couldn't do it, just like that.'

'Yes, you could.'

'I'd have to think about it – plan what to say.'

'If you wait, you'll never make it. Do it now.'

Maxine rose slowly and walked towards the lobby door. She

turned once and looked back at Bonnie. Bonnie waved an insistent hand.

Bonnie, my girl, it's none of your business. Guilt refused to attach itself. She took a nickel out of her purse and dropped it into the music machine behind the sugar shaker.

Across the aisle a couple leaned towards each other from opposite sides of the table and kissed. Bonnie turned away and laid her head against the hard wooden back of the bench and heard the songs.

> *I'll walk alone,*
> *Because to tell you the truth, I'll be lonely.*
> *I don't mind being lonely,*
> *When my heart tells me you*
> *Are lonely, too ...*

In the booth ahead she could see part of a man. He wore a dark civilian suit. Stocky build, bulging waistline, his hands gave an impression of middle age. Flesh was only visible in the hand that rested on the tabletop. His hand was large, clean but the knuckles were thick, and purple veins made tracings across the back. There was strength, stability, maleness, in his hand. She held her breath, could not move, as she imagined him touching her. She felt the roughness of his calloused fingers covering her own small fingers, squeezing them. Without asking, using her paralysis, he would go underneath her clothes, release the zippers and hooks. Barely touching, so gentle, his big hand would slide across her breasts. While the other hand ...

A new record had dropped, and the mellow voice of a faceless woman sang out. 'I'll be seeing you,' she was telling her absent lover. 'I'll be seeing you, in every lovely summer's day, in everything that's bright and gay ... '

The half-man slid across the booth, became whole, and stood up. He was too large for his clothes. The broad padded shoulders of his jacket strained from the breadth beneath. He picked up the check and walked away. A woman emerged from the other side, taking quick, small steps to catch up. Bonnie breathed a long, shaky sigh, and pushed the messy dishes aside as she extracted the evening paper from beneath her purse and stared at it.

Maxine reappeared and sat down.

'Well?' Bonnie asked. She sensed no joy in the expressionless face opposite her.

'I did it.'

'Well?'

'No good.'

'Why?'

'He wasn't there.'

'Oh, no.'

'They sent word back he'd gone into town.'

'Did you leave a message?'

'No.'

'Why? Why not, Maxine? He could call you back. At home.'

'It's no use.'

'But how do you know it's no use?'

Anger flared from Maxine's tense lips. 'It's three months already. If he wanted to talk, he would have called me. I'm only making a fool of myself.' She picked up her things. 'I'll see you tomorrow. I'm going to the USO for a while.' She draped her coat around her shoulders. She stopped, then without looking back, said, 'Thanks, anyway,' and hurried out.

Bonnie slowly gathered her belongings. The heaviness of the small supper she had just eaten rested uneasily above the emptiness in the pit of her stomach. *A letter, a letter. I'll hurry home and find a letter.*

Nine

November 1943

The threat of winter lurked in the cloudy November day when Bonnie parked her car in front of Maggie Newcombe's small white bungalow. She sat for a few minutes before she gathered up her purse and knitting bag and got out. In the waning daylight she saw the slight figure of a boy raking wet, brown leaves into a corner of the yard.

As Bonnie approached, he stopped and grinned at her. 'Hi.'

'Hi, yourself.'

'Nice day.' He nodded agreeably and began to work in rapid strokes again. She had an impression of an old man in the body of a child.

She pushed the button, not sure it had worked until the door swung open. Mary Bigelow, the payroll manager, motioned her inside. 'Bonnie, good to see you.'

She stepped directly into the small living room. Three women sat on the matching brown mohair sofa and chair. Mahogany dining chairs lined the wall. Conversation stopped and all eyes turned towards her.

'Guess what, a newcomer,' Mary announced. 'Do you know all these people, Bonnie?'

Bonnie scanned the faces quickly. She didn't see Maggie. 'I think so.' *I can win them over. They only seem hostile.* 'Don't let me interrupt.'

Mary hung her short red coat in the closet and Bonnie eased into one of the straight-backed chairs, aware of being higher than the people on the sofa across from her.

The room was crowded with furniture and people. *Were there really only five?* Unmatched roses, tulips, vines, and fretwork lurked in the rug, draperies, and slipcovers.

Bonnie put her bags on the floor and sat up straight, then reached down to bring out knitting needles and olive drab yarn.

'Well, if you ask me,' Irene Malloy said, 'I'd say she goes around wagging her tail at every man in sight – at the office *and* at every soldier with a weekend pass.'

'Oh, come on, Irene,' Mary objected, settling back on the sofa. 'You don't know how she spends her weekends. Just because she has a cute little behind and brings a tomcat gleam into the eyes of the old guys around the office doesn't mean she's a whore. After all, she's just a baby.'

'Baby, my foot!' Irene exploded. 'I have it on the best authority she's been making it with one of our big shots. That's how she got her last raise.'

'Irene.' Mary straightened up. 'You know as well as any of us

51

that wages are frozen. Do you think the War Labor Board cares who she shacks up with?'

'Well, you should know, Mary Bigelow, that she got a promotion into a different job classification, and she's still doing the same damn thing.'

'Here, here,' Helen Smith's voice interrupted from the end of the sofa. 'Cut it out, you two – I'd just like to know what you're talking about. Come on, Irene, who's the man?'

Irene sniffed and returned to her knitting. 'Never mind,' she said. 'I can keep a secret.'

Mary snorted. Bonnie was confused. She didn't even know who the girl was, much less the man.

'Well, they're down, but I don't know for how long.' Maggie came in from the bedroom hall, carefully closing the door behind her. 'I let them know they'd get their bottoms blistered if they acted up again like last time.'

She moved the ashtrays around; picked up her sewing basket, and pulled up a chair beside Bonnie. 'Hello, Bonnie,' she said. 'Glad you finally made it to join our jolly little group. What do you think of the Merry Wives of Scott Manufacturing?'

She pulled out a strip of daffodil-coloured organdy and pinned it into gathers around the bottom of a tiny bouffant pinafore.

'I just got here,' Bonnie responded. 'Right now my problem is with my knitting. Thought I could learn on a Red Cross sweater – maybe work up to doing something for my own soldier.'

She held up her handiwork and laughed nervously. Mary joined with a controlled titter. The rest of the group looked on with faint smiles.

'It's supposed to be a sleeveless sweater, but it looks like a piece of beef jerky. What a bilious colour.'

'Red, white, and blue uniforms would make dandy targets, dear,' Maggie answered with gentle sarcasm as she laid down the bit of organdy and reached over to take the knitting from Bonnie. 'Your problem is way back here in the beginning – you dropped a stitch. You'll have to ravel it out back to there.'

'British soldiers wore red coats,' Mary said.

'They got shot, too,' Maggie answered.

'Oh, no,' Bonnie wailed. 'Not again. Won't I ever get past the third row?'

'Well, we can't all have the same talents,' Irene interposed. 'I understand you're a very good dancer.'

She would pretend she had never heard Irene's frequent caustic remarks in the lunchroom about girls who consort with soldiers. Bonnie was one of *them* now.

'I guess we'll all be dancing again someday,' she answered.

Their inscrutable eyes all turned and settled upon her.

Maggie picked up a knitting needle and held it with her fist planted on one knee, point standing straight up. 'They'll come back,' she said, 'when all the Krauts and their friends, those little bastard Japs, are wiped off the face of the earth.' Her voice was calm, as soft as the organdy ruffle in her lap. 'This time, we'd better finish the job. Every last German kid should be found and hung up on a hook with a hot rod jammed up his ass. We can't leave a trace of the sons of bitches and their master race.'

Bonnie could see the faces – eyes lowered, red lips straight slashes in pale faces. *Why don't they say something? Why don't I? If I open my mouth I'll throw up.* This suddenly became a possibility. *Where's the bathroom?*

Irene sighed. 'Well, of course you're exaggerating, Americans don't really like to hurt anybody, but basically you're right, they certainly messed up our lives. It would be a better world if we were rid of all of them.'

Stiffly Maggie stood up and tossed the needle into her basket, as though it were not dripping blood. But Bonnie could see the tremor in her fingers as she reached for the back of the chair and gripped it, knuckles turning white.

'I'll go put on the coffeepot,' Maggie said. 'I made a new victory cookie – see if you can tell what replaced the sugar.'

'Irene, is the man Mr Vance?' Helen asked.

Bonnie was exhausted and went to bed as soon as she got home. She had not dozed at all when she reached for the bedside lamp and turned the switch an hour later. Light fanning out from the small shade illuminated a heavy alarm clock, a library copy of *Forever Amber*, and a pillow pounded into wrinkled lumps. She swung her legs over the side of the bed and slid her feet into houseshoes; her pyjama legs were pushed up to her knees, but she felt too tired to push them down.

Every time Bonnie closed her eyes she saw children, faces screwed in pain, streaked with tears, legs outspread and the blunt end of a knitting needle protruding from their panties. It was a dream, a bad dream. *Mother, make it go away.*

On the dresser, Old Bessie and her grinning crew in their flight gear sat in a dime-store frame. Caricatures and names in the spirit of locker room graffiti decorated Bessie's fuselage. The TNT strapped to her belly didn't show.

Children are under the bombs, bombs meant for Hitler, and factories, and camps – Hitler, and workers like me, and soldiers like John; it's only the swastikas that make them different. The children, how do the bombs miss the children? Why John? He doesn't hate the children. I don't hate the children. Why does Maggie hate the children?

It's so dark and I'm so alone. 'I don't smoke – and I don't chew, and I don't go with boys that do.'

She stood up and found the tiny kitchen, fumbling desperately for the switch, for the light. *Don't drink either, I'm a good girl, don't even swear – Jesus Christ – goddamned son of a bitch – bastard – FUCK.* She tried to say the words aloud, moved her lips, nothing came out.

As she dismantled the coffeepot, its basket dropped through her wooden fingers, rolling, spilling its stale grounds on the floor, spreading stains. Nauseated, she turned her back on the mess and replaced the lid, struck a match and held it with trembling fingers over the gas jet. Small yellow flames sprang up, as she set the pot over them.

Pilots don't drop the bombs, they fly the plane while the navigator charts the course and the bombardier says, 'Bombs away!' (good old hot-pants Ed, screwing all the girls in England when he isn't looking into his bombsight), at 'em boys, give 'er the gun, another ammunition dump gone to hell, fighter planes at nine o'clock, praise the Lord and pass the ammunition, comin' in on a wing and a prayer, we live in fame or go down in flame, HEY! nothin' can stop the ARMY AIR CORPS!

She flipped off the burner and walked to the living room, switching on the dim overhead light. Bessie's tail gunner was a nice nineteen-year-old boy from Oklahoma, with a pregnant wife in Okmulgee, but tonight the whining bullets flowing from Old Bessie's tail were being triggered by a little jockey with sad eyes and not a goddamned soul to miss him. Sorry, no mail today for Sergeant What's-his-name.

The tears came at last. Bonnie crumpled to the floor. They were the first tears – the first since she watched him go. Floods of tears, washing out the gates. She threw back her head against the sofa and turned her contorted face to the ceiling. She moaned and cried aloud, and the sound bounced back at her from the walls. In her starkly lighted private world the tempest advanced and retreated again and again, until the crying lost its sound. Little childish quivers replaced heaving sighs, the trembling subsided. Her slick cheeks glistened. Her eyes felt like fire pits.

Stiffly she placed her hand on the cushion and pulled to her feet. In the bathroom she turned on the cold tap full force, cupping both hands to raise the water to cool her ravaged face. She only glanced at the mirror before covering her face with the towel. Her legs barely functioned well enough for her to find the bed. She slid between the white sheets and fell instantly asleep.

Ten

The first letter from Boston arrived airmail a little over a week after the wedding. The stationery was white bond, water-marked, embossed with a delicate monogram. The message was brief:

Dear Bonnie,

John's father joins me in this little letter to welcome you into our family. Needless to say this marriage came as a great surprise, and coinciding as it did with John's leaving for overseas duty in England has left us reeling; but I know that with time we will adjust as John would want us to do.

We thought that John's life was settled into a comfortable pattern we could all foresee; but the war has changed so many things, and of course we must all do our part. There are so many worse off than we are, aren't there? As long as God sees fit to bring him home in one piece, that is the most we can ask.

I'm sure that you must be a wonderful person to cause John to fall in love with you upon so short an acquaintance. It must have been short because he was not in your town very long, and you have never been east, have you?

You must come to see us. In the meantime we will of course keep in touch. God bless you.

Sincerely,
Margaret Blake

Bonnie read and reread the letter. She spent hours composing an answer. She described herself and her life in detail, and prayed that the letter would reach out to touch her in-laws and convince them she was real. She sent it and waited.

The answer arrived. The handwriting, as before, was delicate, the curved lines very round, the straight ones very straight.

Bonnie dear,

It was very sweet of you to write such a long letter. I'm afraid my first letter was not very coherent. It was written under great stress, and I hope it did not sound unkind. We do not wish to be unkind to someone who obviously means so much to our son. Perhaps you will have a son of your own someday and will be better able to understand our concern. What is done is done, and your letter has helped us to accept what must be. We do feel that we know you a little better.

Thank you for the photograph. We have framed it and placed it beside John's latest picture, as part of our family gallery.

*You must come to Boston one of these days so we can
meet you in person. We both love and pray for John, so
this gives us a great common bond, doesn't it?*

Sincerely,
Margaret Blake

There were a few more letters, continuing the tone of the first
two. Bonnie could not escape the feeling that her in-laws hoped
she would prove to be an illusion that would someday fade
away.

Christmas brought from the Blakes a tiny insured package.
A velvet and satin box held a delicate locket with one small
diamond blinking from the pendant. She treasured the gift,
although in her insecurity she felt it accented her isolation. A
coffeepot, a candy dish, even an ashtray would have
acknowledged a marriage.

Shortly after their first anniversary, the definite invitation
was finally extended, the train ticket offered. She wondered
how much pressure from England had brought this about.

March 1944

People in the crowded Boston streets were clutching their hats
and skirts against the cold, hard wind, when Bonnie first saw
them. She rode in the front seat of a 1941 Chevrolet sedan
beside a quiet man. They drove a great distance through the
city from South Station. She was awed by the distinguished
gentleman, even though she knew him to be a member of the
family in the Blakes' service. She wasn't sure whether she was
relieved or disappointed not to be riding in a limousine driven
by a uniformed chauffeur.

Her driver had introduced himself as 'Benton.' He
maintained an attitude of respectful distance, but Bonnie's
excitement over her first exposure to an eastern metropolis
gradually penetrated the chill. His comments and explanations
increased in length and warmth as they drove.

Finally they travelled through rows of large, older homes, all
with extensive grounds, impeccably landscaped. Benton
turned into the circular drive of one of these and stopped
before the porch of the colonial-style brick house. He walked
around the car and opened the door. She waited while he

extricated her large new suitcase from the car's trunk, then she followed him up the steps. Benton rang the bell and pushed the door open without waiting for an answer.

Bonnie stepped into a hall larger than her parents' living room. The gleam of polished mahogany, crystal, and brass blended with the understated elegance of Turkey-red-and-bone-striped wallpaper. Thick, red carpet climbed the dark stairway and muffled the footsteps of the lady descending. Bonnie stopped just inside the door and watched the approach of her mother-in-law.

Platinum grey hair curled coyly into an upswept hairdo. A few wisps escaped at the nape of the neck and in front of the ears. The bluest of eyes, John's eyes, were wide and clear. Her mouth was a moist pink bow against skin flawless as porcelain. She was generously curved, her slight plumpness adding a womanly softness. Ruffles encircled the low neckline of her flowered chiffon dress and the bottom of the long sleeves, partially covering slender, graceful hands. In spike heel shoes she was still shorter than Bonnie. She approached and extended both hands to grasp Bonnie's briefly, then dropped them to her sides.

'Welcome, my dear.' The voice was unexpectedly strong. 'I hope your train ride wasn't too devastating.'

Bonnie shook her head. 'It's wonderful to be here at last. I've thought about it so much.'

'Of course you have, dear. Let Benton take your coat and hat and I'll show you your room; you'll want to rest and freshen up before dinner. How long were you on the train?'

Bonnie relinquished her hat and coat and walked up the stairs with Margaret Blake. 'I left early yesterday morning.'

Mrs Blake shook her head as though she found it unbelievable anyplace could be that far away. 'Trains are so crowded these days. I think it's dreadful you couldn't get a compartment.'

'The pullman was fine,' Bonnie hastened to answer. 'I had lots of company.' She had only travelled by coach before. Her own bed on the train was a luxury. This was one of the things she would not mention.

'I thought you might like to stay in John's room.' Margaret Blake paused before pushing open the door. 'He hasn't spent much time here for several years now, with being away at school and the army, but it's still here for him, whenever he can come – just as he left it.'

Bonnie stepped through the door. This was a boy's room, filled with mementos. Fastened to the walls were pennants with several names she didn't recognize except for the large Harvard one.

She saw a case of ribbons and trophies and a collection of model biplanes. Most of all, snapshots were everywhere – arranged on the wall, pushed into the mirror frame. Formal photographs sat grouped on the dresser.

'I don't know what to say.' *This is a kind, thoughtful thing to do.* She said, 'Thank you.'

Margaret blinked and swallowed. She walked towards the door. In the doorway she turned and with effort said, 'Dinner is at seven. We'll all be down by six. John's father and brother are anxious to meet you.' She took a few steps and came back, her composure still not fully restored. 'Forgive me,' she said, with a motion towards the suitcase Benton had quietly set inside the room. 'I forgot to ask if you would like Mary to help you unpack.'

'Oh no, I can do it,' Bonnie answered quickly. She hoped not too quickly.

'Very well. If you need some things pressed, just push the buzzer by the door and Mary will come for them.'

Bonnie said, 'Thank you,' again, and then she was alone in the room, with the faint lingering scent of Margaret Blake's perfume.

Suddenly her knees felt very weak and she let them give way as she dropped to sit on the bed. *John's bed. He has slept here many times. Nothing happened. Maybe later.*

Her eyes moved once more about the room. She saw now that one entire wall was covered with books. She stood up and walked over to look at the titles. Children's books filled one side of the case. They ranged from Milne and Stevenson to Tom Swift and Tarzan. The rest of the shelves were not so well organized. S.S. Van Dine leaned against Freud, and Richard Halliburton was pushed under Applied Physics. She thought of her textbooks from Centerville Junior College, packed away in the basement at home. The shelves of books through which she had happily browsed over the years were in the local public library. The ones she owned and underlined were carefully chosen and treasured. We can take these with us when we get a home. A house full of books, what a treasure!

She scanned the rest of the room before she disciplined herself to unpack. When she slid back the door, looking for hangers, she found more reminders of John in the closet. John Blake, civilian, was stored here. She tried to picture him in the conservative suits, the blazers, and corduroy trousers. She ran her fingers down the crease of a plaid jacket. It excited her to think of being intimate with the man shelved here. She liked hanging her clothes next to his.

Her dresses were wrinkled, and she looked for the buzzer that would summon the maid. She sat on a chair by the door, a chill of pleasure and guilt tickling her spine as she waited. Once she hurried to the dresser and ran a comb through her hair and touched a powder puff to her nose. She sat on the edge of the bed and casually called 'Come in,' when the knock finally came.

Mary was a girl about her age, probably Benton's daughter. She wore a plain, dark uniform, but without the apron and cap Bonnie had expected to see. She was quiet and unsmiling and took the wrinkled dresses away quickly.

You can't fool me. I know you are interested in what I'm like and are probably making a detailed report to your mother right now.

She wondered if Mary had a crush on John. Of course she did. The family had been with the Blakes for five years. She had a fleeting image of a college boy stealing a kiss from the maid, but instantly rejected it. *Not John.*

After a leisurely soak in her private tub, the bubbles floating away the grime of six states, she pulled a bulky robe around her naked body and stretched out on the bed to rest. Her muscles ached pleasantly. The bed was wide and firm. She closed her eyes and willed herself to sleep, but her eyes kept opening, straining to identify some object in the organized clutter of the room. After turning several times, she surrendered to the siren call of the photographs and silently crossed the room, the imprint of her bare feet lost in the carpet, to stare intently and at close range at the faces watching her.

Here was a younger John, longer black hair pasted straight back except for a cowlick, proudly supporting a bicycle. Next to him was another bicycle held by a girl as tall as he, with windblown hair and a body like a pencil. The next snapshot starred a Model A Ford roadster, no longer new. A couple waved from the rumble seat, their faces indistinct, and another couple peered out of the front window, heads close together.

A chubby child sat on the step of a cabin in another picture between John and his mother. This must be his only brother, ten years his junior. The other photograph of children appeared to be from an earlier era. The adorable little girl and boy with Buster Brown haircuts, standing with their arms around each other, were reminiscent of the boy and girl with the bicycles. This little boy wore a sailor suit with short pants, and the girl had on a dress with the cuffs of matching bloomers peeking out below. Bonnie chuckled with pleasure. Someday, we'll have some like that.

There was a large portrait of boys in swimsuits, lined up stiffly, staring wide-eyed and sober into the camera. The one-piece suits had white tops, cut out under the arms, and dark trunks. She easily picked John out of the group. This would be his prep school swim team, and went with the ribbons and trophies. She imagined slicing through the water with John in some vague summer to come – running on the beach, falling onto the sand. She could smell the damp air and feel the spray of cool water falling across the two of them. She sighed and moved on.

Now she was in front of the mirror. In the centre was her own image, long brown hair pleasantly rumpled by the incomplete nap, escaping strands still coiled by the steam of the bath, the fuzzy bathrobe adding softness and roundness to the reflection. Surrounding the image, more pictures and memorabilia pushed into the mirror frame. The two largest were both carefully posed portraits of a couple in formal dress. John wore the same tuxedo, but the girl beside him was first in pink and then in pale apple green. These had to be successive high school proms – the same photographer in the hall outside the gym at the Boston prep school as at Centerville High. Both photographs were of the same girl. She was even prettier in the green dress, more poised, her fingerwaved hair longer.

For the first time something clicked. It was the same girl, always the same girl, from bloomers to prom. Who else but the inescapable Sara? Her eyes swept back across all the pictures. It seemed that more than half of them – alone, with John, or in group photographs, showed this long-legged, flaxen-haired child, growing girl, young woman.

Bonnie hurried along, peering anxiously at the more recent photos. Here were the campus backgrounds. And yes, Sara with her aviation cadet. At the end of the chronological line came the ultimate turn of the knife. She saw this beautiful blonde creature, still straight as a pencil but gracefully curved where the wind blew against her white dress. Incredible long legs supported by high heels placed her almost eye to eye with Bonnie's lieutenant, as she pinned upon his chest a pair of silver wings.

Bonnie choked. This momentous event, so shortly before she knew him, shared with someone else. *She's the one to pity. He belongs to me.* She was no longer sure. One week against a lifetime.

Furiously she sought the activity of dressing. She opened her suitcase and tenderly lifted up the piece de resistance of her wardrobe – a pair of the sheerest black nylon hose. They were a gift from John, manoeuvred through mysterious channels of the black market, carefully hoarded for the most important occasions.

In a sudden reckless impulse she threw off the fuzzy robe and picked up the brief black girdle that lay by the hose. She stepped into it and see-sawed her bare feet into the carpet. She pulled the lacy garment over her buttocks and gave it a last snap around the waist. Like a surgeon she carefully pulled on and adjusted a pair of black gloves and snapped them at the wrists. She perched on the edge of the bed and began the tedious operation of pulling on the sheer black stockings. She watched the thick ebony seam slowly climb up the back of her leg. She twisted to check the seams in the mirror before securing the tops of the stockings with the long black supporters.

Eyes on the tilted mirror, Bonnie slowly reclined at an angle across the bed, resting her elbow just below the pillow and propping her head upon her hand. She stretched one leg out straight, toe pointed, and pulled the other foot back, knee slightly bent. Striped by black garters, smooth pink flesh glowed between nylons and lace, and continued in uninterrupted bareness above the waistline of the garment.

Confidently she reached for the telephone, a convenient prop on the bedside table, and placed it to her ear, adjusting her arm so that just her nipples were covered in the mirror's reflection. She suppressed a chuckle as the words silently formed. *Hello,* Esquire? *This is your month of March Pretty Girl speaking.* Without moving she rolled her eyes towards the pictures on the wall. 'So save it for the cover of *Vogue*,' she said aloud.

She held the pose until her arm began to waver, a short time, then rolled over on her back and reached out to replace the phone. She pulled a plump pillow from under the spread and put her arms around it, hugging it tightly against her bare skin, burying her chin in the top of it. Her black gloves criss-crossed the front of the stiff white pillow case. She swallowed and closed her eyes and prayed. 'Dear God, help me handle it.'

She threw the pillow aside and sat up and hugged her knees as she looked once more around the room. Something tugged at her mind, somewhere a piece didn't fit. She could imagine a high school boy tucking the picture from the prom into the edge of his mirror. But a whole lifetime of pictures? What teenage boy would arrange his own baby pictures around his bedroom wall? The room was like a stage setting. It had been a long time since someone had lived there. Had the carefully arranged mementos been carefully arranged by someone besides John? It was unthinkable that some of it had been done recently, with her visit in mind.

A light tapping broke into he dark thoughts. When she oriented herself to locate the knock at the hall door, she scooped up the robe and wrapped it tightly about her before calling out, 'Come in.'

Mary entered with the dresses. She walked without a sound and hung the neatly pressed garments in closet, avoiding Bonnie's eyes as she asked, 'Anything else, ma'am?'

'No, that's fine, thank you,' Bonnie answered. Mary quietly and quickly disappeared. Bonnie reached for the simple little black dress.

Eleven

Somewhere the padded baritone chimes of a clock struck six as Bonnie walked along the hall and touched the railing. The house was quiet, and she dragged her feet as she descended the stairs. She had reached the bottom when she jumped back at the sound of shattering glass.

The sound had come from the front of the house. She approached the arched doorway with trepidation. The dark Queen Anne furniture, the heavy tied-back damask draperies, the oriental rug, lay in dignified repose. Then she saw the noise-maker. A thin, perspiring, dark-haired boy stood by the fireplace, in an attitude of frozen motion.

Their disturbed eyes met. Together they looked towards the tile hearth where curved pieces of blue and white china lay, the handles of the elegant Wedgwood vase still intact.

Voices sounded indistinctly in the distance. The boy ran forward and picked up pieces, carefully cradling them in his left arm. Impulsively, Bonnie joined him. He looked frantically about the room before hurrying to the window and pulling back the heavy drapery. Helping each other, they deposited the pieces on the floor and smoothed the weighted curtain in front of them.

With a few quick steps they returned to sit opposite each other on the brocade and mahogany love seats flanking the carved Adam fireplace. As the voices came nearer, the two conspirators regarded each other across the coffee table, and Bonnie found herself returning the grin that twitched around the corners of his mouth.

They were sitting primly, knees together and feet on the floor, when Margaret and Kenneth Blake came into the room. The boy rose clumsily to his feet and Bonnie moved to the edge of the seat.

Margaret smiled when she saw them together. 'Ah,' she said, 'you two have met. Getting acquainted, are you?'

Bonnie felt a sweet stab of remembrance as she looked at Kenneth Blake. Something about the way he moved and stood brought an instant clear picture of John.

'Bonnie, this is John's father,' Margaret said.

Mr Blake sat next to her and touched her hand briefly as he eyed her carefully. 'Bonnie,' he said. 'Well, well, so you're Bonnie.'

'Yes,' she answered. 'I am.'

'Well, well.'

Margaret joined Marc across from them.

'And how was your trip?' Mr Blake asked.

'Long. Tiring.' She added thoughtfully, 'Interesting, too. The train was so crowded, everybody got acquainted. I met some nice people.'

Margaret remarked, 'I should think that could be a mixed blessing.'

'I suppose,' Bonnie said. 'I thought it made the trip easier. I like people.'

Mr Blake had not taken his eyes from her face. 'John was right,' he said. 'You are very pretty.'

Margaret reached for a cigarette from the box on the table. 'Kenneth,' she said, 'perhaps Bonnie would like a drink before dinner.'

Three pairs of eyes rested upon Bonnie.

'Whatever the rest of you are having.'

'Bring us some sherry, would you please, dear?'

Mr Blake moved to the handsome mahogany liquor cabinet.

She heard the voice of John's young brother for the first time. 'John said you don't drink.'

She wondered why John would have told them this. 'I don't go out much.' *Does that make sense?*

'That's too bad.' The timbre of his voice suddenly became lower.

Margaret shot an irritated look at her son. 'Marc, your tie is crooked.'

He fumbled with his tie.

'Use the mirror.'

Marc stood up and walked to the mirror on the wall above

the console table and continued to fumble.

Margaret settled back. 'You're a private secretary. What does your company do?'

'We manufacture a certain type of screw for military planes.'

Margaret paused in lighting her cigarette.

Bonnie shrugged. 'I know it sounds silly. It is a large plant, but that's all we make.' *Why didn't I say hardware? I meant to say hardware.*

Margaret smiled indulgently. 'Well, this is an age of specialization, isn't it?' She finished lighting the cigarette and immediately put it down to accept the wineglass from her husband. 'A good secretary is very important to a business-man, isn't that right, dear?'

Kenneth handed the other glass to Bonnie. 'Indispensable.'

They made a friendly connection with their eyes. *He likes me. I wish she did.* Mr Blake returned to the cabinet to pour his own drink. Marc had returned to his seat, his tie still crooked.

'We have made plans for you to meet some of our friends and John's while you're here. We've reserved a table at the country club Friday evening; just a small dinner for a few friends.'

Bonnie said 'Oh,' and hoped she looked pleased.

'Actually,' Margaret continued, 'there aren't many of the young men left around. Bob Shephard graduated with John and is working in his father's firm, so he and his wife are coming.' She added, 'Bob has a heart murmur. Then there are our close friends, the Andersons, and Bob's parents.'

Andersons. Sara's name. A lump settled in Bonnie's throat that could not be dislodged, even as the evening progressed through dinner. She wondered about the vase, too, and about her involvement with Marc's deception.

When she came into the parlour the next day, the house seemed deserted. She carried a book she had selected from the case upstairs, and eyed an easy chair close to a window, lighted indirectly by the afternoon sun.

Before settling down, she walked to another window and pulled back the lace curtain to peer out into the yard. As she released the curtain, her hand slid down the drapery, pulling it aside to look behind. There was nothing there. She felt a little foolish about her playacting, but somehow in this house she always felt there were eyes upon her.

She curled up in the chair and lost herself in the novel. Some time had passed when she heard the front door open and quick footsteps crossing the hall. Marc shot past the door. In a second he was back, standing in the archway, grinning.

'Hi.'

'Hi, Marc.'

He came into the room. He wore neat grey slacks and a blue sweater, and carried schoolbooks. His walk was more confident, his demeanour different from the night before.

'I've been reading,' she told him. 'There are some interesting books in my room.'

'There are lots more in the library down here.' Marc shuffled his feet. 'I suppose you're wondering about the vase.'

Bonnie nodded. 'Yeah, as a matter of fact I was. What did you do with it?'

'Slipped the pieces to Dad this morning. He knows where to get it fixed. I suppose you think that was a crazy thing I did.'

Bonnie thought about it. 'Well, I think I know how you felt. The timing was wrong.'

Marc brightened. 'Exactly. Hey, how'd you know?'

'Oh, I've experienced some bad timing in my day.'

'I'll have to pick just the right time to give it to Mom. This guy does a fantastic job of putting things back together.'

'Maybe she won't even notice.'

Marc considered, but shook his head. 'I'll tell her. Just so it's the right time. She won't think it's too bad after it's fixed.'

'Your dad didn't care?'

'Well, you know how it is. It was her vase.' He shifted the books to his other arm, then dropped them on a chair. 'I think Dad understands about timing, too. You know what I mean?'

'That's nice.'

'Yeah, it is.' He dropped to a convenient footstool.

This is my chance. How do I say it? I have to know. She tried to keep the tension out of her voice. 'Will Sara be at the dinner tomorrow night?'

Marc looked up quickly, then down again. He seemed to be considering his answer. He said, 'No.'

Bonnie felt muscles relaxing all over the place.

Marc looked up again. 'Hey,' he said, 'don't worry about her.

She's more scared of you than you are of her. Mom was sore because she didn't want to meet you. Sara said, "Nothin' doin'." She's as stubborn as Mom; she won't be there.'

'Your mother likes her, doesn't she?'

'Oh sure, thick as thieves. Mom said it was the only civilized thing to do, but Sara told her, "To hell with the old stiff upper lip."' He laughed loudly. 'That was great. I didn't think Sara had it in her.'

Bonnie reluctantly thought it was great, too. Her opinion of Sara rose a bit.

'Do you like her?' she asked.

'Oh, sure,' Marc answered. 'She's a good guy; she's been around almost as much as a sister.' He looked at Bonnie as shyness changed to bluster. 'You're a good guy, too. That was okay, what you did last night.'

'Anytime,' she replied.

Twelve

Bob Shephard was an ass. Bonnie refused to accept him as representative of John's friends. She couldn't remember John's mentioning him, but they had apparently been college classmates, as well as having grown up in the same crowd. She knew she disliked him from the time they met the couple outside the country club cloakroom.

She liked having Marc as her escort. The older men wore tuxedos, but Marc was boyishly charming in his dark suit and tie, his shoes spit-shine polished, his hair carefully combed back. He reminded her of a boy holding a bicycle. He was always ahead of her, opening the door as they left home and as they entered the Cadillac sedan, where they shared the backseat. He was quick to scurry to the outside of the sidewalk and glowed as he helped her with her coat inside the club. He was as tall as Bonnie. She felt a great affection for him. She wondered if this was a view of young John. Yet in spite of the boys' common background, there was a difference. She sensed a gentleness in Marc, something that left him vulnerable in a way that she had never perceived in John. She couldn't believe that John had ever doubted himself. His strength was one of the things that had drawn her to him – she who was often vulnerable. She couldn't imagine his ever being less sure of himself – even at fourteen.

As the ladies waited for the Blake men to check their wraps, they saw Bob and Marjorie Shephard coming out of the cocktail lounge. The couple joined them and Margaret introduced Bonnie. Bob looked long and hard at her.

'Well now,' he said, 'so this is old John's little Bonnie, the flower of the prairie.' Her evening gown was powder blue crepe with long sleeves and a scooped neckline. She felt Marjorie's quick appraisal, eyes moving from the broad padded shoulders to the skirt, gently flaring from just above the knees. Bonnie had carefully chosen a simple wardrobe for this visit. When Bob looked at her, she felt daisies sprouting from her hem. His wife's dress was strapless, the bodice sparkling with sequins. Bonnie's only sparkle was from the little diamond pendant.

Marjorie smiled, her eyes not cooperating, and said nothing. Bonnie greeted them, glad that the arrival of the rest of their party ended the conversation.

As she turned with the others towards the two couples approaching, the entire setting slipped from reality. She was in a movie theatre, watching characters on the screen. Kay Francis and Lyle Talbot walked across the marble floor of a Boston country club. She was a teenager eating popcorn in the back row of the Majestic on a Sunday afternoon with three of her friends. The awesome responsibility of finding herself up there on the screen with them was overwhelming. Where was the script? She was overpowered by her need for John. How she needed his guiding arm as she moved into each successive element of the plot.

Kay Francis and Lyle Talbot proved to be the Shephards, Sr. They were sleek as a couple of well-fed cats, glossy and well groomed, purring and bowing their heads, sustaining an aura of aloofness, the threat of withdrawal.

She liked the Andersons better. Was it because she had anticipated antagonism? Were they trying extra hard because they resented her for their daughter's sake?

The group gathered at a round table in a secluded corner of the dining room. These people had known each other most of their lives. Bonnie found her own tension relaxing.

They were eating the salad when Mrs Anderson buttered a cracker and remarked to Bonnie, 'Our daughter sent her apologies. She couldn't come because a close friend is getting married soon and they're having a little party tonight.' She toyed with a lettuce leaf as all the conversations at the table ended at the same time. She projected into the silence, 'Sara's her maid of honour, so she really needed to be there.'

Mrs Anderson glanced at her husband, and he stirred. 'Bonnie,' he said, 'tell us what things are like in Lancaster.'

'It's just a nice, clean, midwestern town,' Bonnie answered. 'Things have picked up since the war – a few defence plants. The air base made the biggest change.'

'Yeah,' Bob said, 'Jean finally hooked old Larry. He's just getting a break from sea duty. Lieutenant?'

'J.G.,' Mrs Anderson said.

'John's made first lieutenant now, hasn't he?'

'Captain,' Bonnie and Mrs Blake answered in unison.

'Imagine those guys coming on with all that brass, everybody calling them sir – '

'Joe Peterson's a brigadier general,' Bob's father interrupted.

'Yeah, but he wasn't one of us. Seems like yesterday – matter of fact it was yesterday – we were sneaking off to New York to sow a little wild oats. Man, I'll never forget that one weekend.'

'Forget it.' His wife spoke for the first time.

'We all really tied one on. We hadn't been drinking legal very long, and we made the bars. I remember those chicks.' He gave a low wolf whistle.

'Since when could you and Larry make it with chicks when John was around?'

'That's just the point! John draws chicks like a magnet draws pins!'

He looked around the table into a circle of hostile eyes.

'Well,' he shrugged, 'you know what I mean.' He brightened. 'See what a beautiful chick he finally landed.' He looked sideways at the Andersons. 'So what else is new?' he asked lamely.

'You were telling us about Lancaster, Bonnie,' Mrs Blake said.

After dinner they lingered over hot, black coffee in little china cups. Music from the combo in the next room provided a pleasant live melodic background. They played 'Stardust' a lot, and old Gershwin tunes.

Bonnie relaxed with the wine. She felt increasingly at home with her new friends. They were trying. The wine helped her forget they were trying.

She excused herself and walked back to the foyer. She remembered seeing a LADIES sign at the end of the hall beyond the cloakroom. She followed the hall to where it ended in a stairway marked with a small sign, TO PRIVATE PARTY ROOMS.

Bonnie was alone in the restroom as she washed her hands and inspected her lipstick in the mirror above the lavatory. The door opened. She looked up and in the mirror saw a tall blonde girl move inside and close the door. The girl hesitated, the delicate pink of the panelled door framing her formfitting floor-length black satin dress and brief bolero jacket. When she shifted her weight, movement flowed through her graceful body like the swirls in a liquorice stick.

In the mirror their eyes touched and bounced away. Bonnie panicked. A metal door closed and bolted. She took flight, while forcing herself not to appear hurried. She grasped the gilded doorknob and fell back. The knob was in her hand, the door was still closed.

The rod barely showed in the opening. Slowly and with great care she tried to slip the knob back on, but it would not catch. She breathed faster as she pulled the knob back and groped for the elusive end. Another push with the knob resulted in a dull thud on the other side of the door. A hole remained. She heard the sound of flushing water.

She bit her lip. *You didn't get a good look. It's some other tall, blonde girl. Boston is full of them.*

She inhaled deeply and turned around.

The two women stared at each other. Bonnie saw mirrored panic. Slowly the opposite eyes filled with pain – pain she understood. Even as she recognised echoed emotion, the look

71

changed to hatred, undiluted and terrifying.

Dumbly, she held up the doorknob.

The other girl looked from Bonnie to the doorknob to the hole in the door. Bonnie saw the black-draped Venus wilt and sink into a chair. 'Son of a bitch!' Sara said.

Bonnie walked back and laid the doorknob and her beaded bag upon the washstand counter. *How do you do. I'm Bonnie Blake. You must be Sara Anderson. I've heard so much about you.* She leaned against the counter. She forced herself to see the other girl. Sara was looking – taking in every powder-blue inch, like a long, slow drink of castor oil.

How gorgeous you are, Sara. Not a freckle. But you are skinny, you know, no shape to your arms. Your boobs are no bigger than mine. A spasm of pain. *John knows about that, he watched them grow. Say something. God bless your beautiful, little unfreckled boobs!* 'Will someone find us?'

Sara finally answered. 'Maybe, when someone at this end of the hall decides to go to the john.' She bit her lip.

There has to be a funny answer. This whole thing is hysterically funny. 'I guess the joke's on us. Do you believe in fate?'

'No,' Sara said.

Bonnie sighed. *All I did was fall in love with John. You should understand.* 'They don't keep things repaired like they used to.'

Sara crossed her long legs and took a cigarette out of her purse. 'The main lounge is okay. This one is here for the party rooms.'

Bonnie shifted her weight and continued to lean. Sara had put the cigarettes away when she reopened her purse and took the package out again. 'Have a Lucky?' she asked.

'No, thank you,' and when she thought Sara looked annoyed, 'I don't use them.'

Sara shrugged, and made a lengthy ritual of lighting up and enjoying her cigarette.

Bonnie asked, 'Do you think we should pound on the door or holler or something?'

'You can if you want to.'

Bonnie looked at the floor. The little ceramic squares made designs in two different ways – *optical illusions, it's all in the way you look at it. I have hurt her terribly, she has a right to*

72

hate me. She shook her head and sighed again. *How can I tell her I understand?* She plunged. 'You look like your pictures.'

'So do you.'

Bonnie was relieved. 'I do understand your not wanting to meet me.'

'I don't mind meeting you.'

'We didn't want to hurt anybody.'

Sara straightened in the chair. 'Don't worry,' she said in a firm voice. 'It isn't the first time.'

'I don't know what you mean.'

'I mean I've seen him through other love affairs.'

Bonnie gripped the counter edge. 'Sara, he's my husband.'

'You took advantage of him.'

'You're his sister. He loves you like a sister.'

'Did he tell you that?'

'Not in so many words.'

'He sure as hell didn't treat me like a sister the last time he saw me.' Sara's eyes were fearful again.

'But he told you that, didn't he?' Bonnie took the offensive. 'Didn't he?'

Sara sighed a long shuddering sigh. 'No ... No.'

'He didn't promise you anything. He did promise me. He loves me. I'm sorry. I'm sure he loves you, too. But it's different.'

'Different, hell. Don't tell me you're sorry. And don't think I've given up.'

Sara's words were confident and cold, but her big green eyes were slowly filling until one brimmed over and made a rivulet down the side of her nose. She didn't seem to notice.

Bonnie walked to the door and knocked feebly with the palm of her hand. When she came back, Sara's position had not changed, but the tears were gone.

One more time. 'It would be easier for me if you weren't so beautiful.'

'Thanks a lot.'

'You're not very nice, though.'

Sara grimaced. 'Who says I'm supposed to be nice?'

'You act as though I've committed a sin.'

'You have.'

'How can you say that?'

'I can tell. You are going to say, "All's fair in love and war."'

'John made a free choice. I didn't bewitch him.'

'You took advantage of a time when he wasn't himself. He was under stress.'

'So was I!'

'We loved each other since he proved it by putting frogs in my lunch box and tripping me on the stairs. We undressed each other when we were four. How can you match that in a few days?'

'The important thing is that I did match it. You aren't playing house anymore.'

Sara nodded, speechless. She looked hard at a pink rose in the wallpaper. 'All right, you've won the first round. But I still say, when he gets back I'll be here, too. It will be a different ball game then; we'll see who he wants.'

She's stronger than I am. In her place I would have given up. An icy hand closed around Bonnie's heart. She wanted to beg, but instead of going to her knees she extracted the satin stool from beneath the dressing table and sat, finding her own pink rose. The two women did not speak again, but contained the agonizing words within their own bodies.

Bonnie could not guess how long it was before there was stirring outside the door. She held her breath at the sound of rattling metal, and the sight of the thin rod haltingly pushing through.

In the open doorway, a woman in a green dress smiled. 'Were you locked in?' she asked with amusement.

Bonnie's eyes fixed on the outside wall as she squeezed past the woman and fled down the hall. She saw the other sign, the club's main lounge. She ducked inside and into a toilet stall. Without disturbing her clothes, she sat on the edge of the seat and wept. She knew, as though she could see, that somewhere else Sara was doing the same. Bonnie ground her fingernails into the palms of her hands and her teeth into her lower lip. *Goddamn you, John Blake. Goddamn you.*

Thirteen

They were home before midnight. She had been touched by the controlled concern in the glances she received when she returned to the table. She gave the true reason for her long absence, with an important omission. If Sara wanted to describe their meeting she could, but Bonnie felt it would remain their secret.

Bonnie was halfway up the stairs when Mr Blake's voice reached her, 'Bonnie, you had a call.'

He stood beside the telephone table in the hall, holding a note. Meeting her at the bottom of the stairs, he handed it over. The note gave the number of a Lancaster operator. Disturbed, she turned to go to the phone in her room.

Mr Blake called after her, 'If there's any problem, let us know.'

When the operator completed the call, the answering voice was male. The operator said, 'Go ahead on your call to Boston,' and the voice quickly asked, 'Bonnie – Bonnie?'

'Frank?'

She heard a short laugh. 'I feel a little ridiculous. Actually, I came back to the office this evening to catch up on a few things, and I couldn't find your book of minutes on our meetings with the union, and just on the spur of the moment I decided to call you.'

'It's at the back of the middle left-hand drawer of my desk.' Bonnie relaxed. 'You mean you're still at the office?'

'Well yes, I am; I got started on something and I guess I didn't realize how late it was getting.'

'How are things going?'

'Oh fine. Fine. You were right about Maxine; she's doing a good job. As good as anyone could do, besides you. I'm going to make sure she gets a chance at the next secretarial opening.'

'Oh good, I knew you'd like her. Not just because she's my friend, she's really very clever – nice girl, too.'

'Yes, she is.' Silence. 'How's it going there?'

'Oh – fine.'

'I knew you were nervous when I put you on the train. Have any trouble with the change in Chicago?'

'No, not at all. Some Marines helped me.'

'Having a good time?'

'Yeah,' she said flatly. 'This is a beautiful house.'

'I know it's difficult.' A pause. 'It's just not the same around here. You know, the routine is interrupted; I guess I hadn't realized how much you have to do with keeping the ship on an even keel.'

'Well, it's nice of you to say so.'

'It's true. You might as well let me know when you're getting back; it's no trouble for me to pick you up at the station. Cabs are all doubling up passengers now, and you'll be tired.'

'That would be nice; I'll send a telegram when I find out the time. Be sure to call the station, though; we're bound to be late.'

'Yeah, sure. Well, I'd better let you get to sleep. Nice talking to you, Bonnie.'

She told him good-bye and started to put the phone down, then quickly pulled it back. 'Frank?'

He was still there. 'Yes?'

'The back of the middle left-hand drawer, remember?'

'I guess I didn't. Thanks for reminding me.'

'Good-bye.'

'Good-bye, Bonnie.'

She hung up the phone, her hand lingering before she turned it loose. Then she stood dangling her empty hand at her side, slowly flexing her fingers.

Fourteen

John's new duties were very demanding. The span between letters gradually lengthened; no longer were letters delivered in bunches, to be eagerly sorted for reading in chronological order. More frightening was a subtle change in tone. She searched for intimate meanings. *A wife learns to accept a man's job. He has other things on his mind.*

July 1944

'Seems like wasted gunpowder to me,' Maggie Newcombe said. She evened out the chicken salad on a slice of bread and slapped another slice over it.

'I never did like firecrackers, anyway,' Bonnie agreed, carefully seesawing the broad knife diagonally through a stack of sandwiches.

'I suppose it's good for morale, or patriotism, or something,' Maggie continued. 'They're having the usual blow-out in the park tonight.'

'It's not like it used to be – they've cut back a lot.'

'Well, I should hope so.'

Bonnie arranged the cut sandwiches on a tray.

Maggie asked, 'Are holiday afternoons always this crowded at the U.S.O.?'

Bonnie stopped working. 'Maggie, this is the first time I've been here for a year and a half.'

'Guess you weren't in the kitchen before.'

'No, I wasn't. Not very efficient, is it?' She resumed the stacking.

'I'm not here by choice. "Volunteer," they said, with a gun at our heads.'

'Well, the company donated the food; it doesn't hurt us to take our turn in the kitchen.'

Maggie shook her head quickly. 'Oh, I don't mind; the U.S.O. helps our boys. I've thought of volunteering but I figured there's more in it for single girls.' She looked up. 'Of course, they're not interested in KP, are they?'

Bonnie picked up the tray and approached the swinging door with caution. The sounds of music and blurred voices came through. Her knees weakened as she backed through the door and turned around to face the crowded recreation area. *Here I am, folks. Back again.*

She set the tray on the portable buffet table. The room looked the same. The ping-pong table where she had played a thousand sets; the dance floor where she and Bill What's-his-name had won the contest. Only the faces had changed. Same costumes, different cast. She eased into an empty chair. *They can tell I'm different. Nobody will ask me to dance. Nobody here is like John. But they're laughing.*

Close by, four hostesses sat together, conversing energetically. Occasionally their eyes wandered across the room, returning quickly to their companions. Opposite them, a group of soldiers sat glumly, gazing into space or looking at magazines.

Why are they wasting time? She looked at the faces. *How young the soldiers are now, just children.* Married maturity weighed on her shoulders. She looked towards the club's two pool tables. *Or older. Those men have families.*

She sighed and stood up.

'Hi, Bonnie.'

She turned joyfully. A short, chubby sergeant smiled at her, and she reached back in memory.

'Buzz Arlen. You don't remember.'

'Well, sure, I remember your face,' she said as it gradually became true. 'It's been a long time.'

'Yeah, hell,' he said. 'I guess I've been here longer'n anybody. Where've you been? I looked for you.'

'I got married,' she announced.

'Wouldn't you know it? Congratulations.' He grinned. 'Is your husband here?'

She shook her head. 'He's in England.'

'That's rough.'

She recollected. 'Say, didn't you –?'

'Yeah, I got married. I was getting ready to go on furlough to get married the last time I saw you.'

'That's right. Well, you've stayed here so long, she must be with you.'

He shook his head. 'She has a good job and I keep thinking a WAC will move into my place tomorrow. I'm still in the headquarters office, manning a pencil.'

She pointed a finger. 'You're a mechanic. Saving for your own filling station.'

He nodded. She felt the intelligent blue eyes showed disappointment over her struggle to remember. *Why should it matter, he has someone.*

'Gee, it's nice to see you again, Buzz, but I have to get back to the kitchen.'

'How about me coming along?'

'I'm making sandwiches.'

'I make sandwiches almost as good as I push a pencil.'

'I found a helper,' she announced as they went back through the swinging door.

Maggie looked closely at Buzz. For the first time, Bonnie noticed that his uniform fit too snugly and his ears stuck out.

'That's good,' Maggie said flatly. 'Maybe he could bring in some more cans of chicken salad.'

'Sure.' Buzz straightened to attention. 'Just tell me where to get it.'

'The black car in the alley,' Bonnie said. 'You can't miss it.'

Buzz scooted out the door. Maggie worked over the chicken salad without raising her eyes.

Buzz was a good worker; his enthusiasm speeded things up. They set up an effective assembly line, and Bonnie was soon on her way through the swinging door with another heaped platter.

'LAY THAT PISTOL DOWN, BABE!' Raucous voices assaulted her, ricocheting from a group gathered around the ancient upright piano. A pale private-first-class bounced in the chair as his nimble fingers on the keyboard made the old piano rock. The hostesses and soldiers were alive now, looking each other over while they mumbled the words of the verse they didn't quite know. Each time they reached the chorus the sound swelled as they joined forces in the familiar chant,

Lay that pistol down, Babe. Lay that pistol down.
Pistol-packin' Mama, lay that pistol down!

Bonnie felt isolated. Her vocal cords ached for one good hit at 'Pistol Packin' Mama.' If somebody had a car and enough gas coupons they might all go out to watch the fireworks. On the other hand, she didn't have to play the game today. The flirting, the sizing up that was going on across the room was the gamble that was tantalizing but usually disappointing. Would this be a Fourth of July worth remembering? *The thing I'm sure of is that this one won't be for me.*

She combined the sandwiches from a couple of half-empty trays and covered the new platter with a napkin. Picking up the empty tray, she turned around. At the far end of the room a patch of blue, out of place in a room full of summer khaki, caught her eye. She looked again. A lone civilian had come through the door. Warm recognition flowed her her; she set her tray down and waved.

The man in the light blue shirt recognized her and came quickly across the room, ignoring the glances of the soldiers he brushed against in the crowded desk area.

She smiled as he came closer. 'Frank,' she called to him. 'Hello.' *He looks different. It's the clothes. I've never seen him without a coat and tie.* Frank Forbes's black curly hair was tossed by the humid July wind. His round, pleasant face was flushed. He wasn't the cool, efficient executive she worked with. The sleeves of the blue shirt were rolled back to the elbows, and his high collar stood open.

'I wasn't sure how to get in here,' he said, smiling. 'Should I have used the back door?'

She shook her head. 'It's okay, if you don't mind manoeuvering through the troops.'

He was close enough to speak over the singing without shouting. 'I do feel a little out of place, like I should run out for a haircut. They make me feel so old.'

'Me, too. I was just thinking how young they are these days.'

Frank pulled back and looked at her, without comment. 'I have a car full of doughnuts,' he remembered.

He listened to Bonnie's instructions about the alley entrance, and left to finish the business of delivering the doughnuts.

When he, with Buzz's help, had brought the boxes in, the four of them sat down at the kitchen table for a sandwich and a cup of coffee.

'It was good of your company to furnish all this food,' Buzz said.

'Just good public relations,' Frank answered. 'Where would we be without the army?'

'Do you think the plant will keep going after the war?' Bonnie asked.

'Yes, I do,' Frank answered. 'We're digging in to stay.' He hurried to swallow the bite he had taken. 'Just think of the potential. With all our production turned to defence for years, look at how much catching up we'll have to do. The demand after the war will be incredible.'

'You think, sir, that there'll be jobs for the guys when they come home?' Buzz asked.

'Of course, plenty of work for everybody. The women have done a fantastic job of filling in, but when their men come back they'll be back in the kitchen and nursery, where they were meant to be.'

'That can't be too soon for me,' Maggie said. 'I'm ready as hell to start leaning on a man again.'

'My wife likes her job,' Buzz said thoughtfully. 'She's making more money than I ever did. She has five people working under her – I think I may have a little trouble getting her into the kitchen.'

'She'll be glad to go back,' Maggie said. 'She'll be glad to have someone take care of her.'

Bonnie interrupted. 'What she's doing will help you get started, won't it?'

'Sure, it will; she's putting money in the bank for that filling station. But it's not the way we planned it.'

Frank smiled. 'She'll be too busy having babies one of these days to think about a career. Maybe you can even afford a coloured girl to help out.'

Buzz looked sharply at Frank. 'You married, sir?' he asked.

'No, unfortunately,' Frank answered. 'Guess that's what makes me an expert. How'd I get into this, anyway?' He looked at Bonnie.

She hurried to reassure him. 'You're right; it's natural for a woman to look forward to a home and babies. I know I do.'

Frank's frown deepened. 'You folks through here?'

Bonnie nodded. 'Some of the other girls will be in soon. I think we have plenty of food out until they come.'

'Didn't see your car out back. Need a lift?' he said casually to Bonnie. 'I'm going in your direction.'

'I came with Maggie, but it is out of her way.' She saw the little twitch in Maggie's mouth.

They drove down Bonnie's street. Frank said, 'I bought the house.'

Bonnie had been taking calls from real estate companies. She had been curious, but he hadn't explained.

'You bought a house?'

'It's an investment, you know. A house is the place to put your money.' They saw her apartment ahead. 'I'm going out there now; would you like to see it?'

She thought of the hot apartment – *take off my clothes, two electric fans and a glass of lemonade* – it would still be stifling. 'Sure. I like to look at houses.'

The house was white frame, two and a half stories, with a spacious front porch, and a large terraced lawn. Lilac bushes browning in the July heat climbed the trellis beside the porch. Frank indicated the bushes as they walked up the steps.

'Place needs cleaning up – get rid of those bushes and put on a new coat of paint.'

'Don't destroy the bushes,' Bonnie exclaimed. 'There's nothing like the perfume of lilacs, and those old trees are wonderful.'

'Some of them are all right. Too many trees make it hard to keep up the lawn.'

The empty house seemed even larger inside. The cool foyer was a welcome change, but the space they moved into was warm again. The wide oak woodwork and ornamental wallpaper projected gloom, but the bare oversized windows let in a blast of sun.

'Needs new paper and something on the windows,' Frank said.

'Don't cover them too well; the light is wonderful.' Letting in the light had been increasingly important to her of late.

'Oh, look at the charming window seat.' She walked over and sat down on the low seat. 'Cushions here would make a great spot for reading.'

As Frank watched her, the expression in his eyes brought back an uneasy memory. What were Maxime's words? She uncrossed her legs and tried not to look sugar-coated. 'This is a big house,' she said. 'You don't plan to live here, do you?'

Frank sat on the other end of the seat, towards the front, his legs stretched out. 'Yes, I do; no use paying rent on an apartment.' The look was gone – she had probably imagined it.

'But the heating bill!'

'I suppose it is foolish. But now that I've come this far, I realize that I've always wanted to live in a big house – all my own, that is.'

She had never expected him to be foolish about anything, but how little she knew about him.

He continued, 'I'll close off the upstairs. There are only four rooms down here, and the foyer.'

'It will be lovely,' she said. 'What fun to redo it.'

'I'll be grateful for any suggestions you might have,' he said eagerly. 'I'm sure your ideas would be better than mine.'

She looked at him closely. *He is a human being – but so isolated.* 'Did you grow up in a big house?'

He looked down and shook his head. 'I grew up in many houses,' he answered. 'Some of them very big.' He looked up again. Talking about himself was not easy. 'My parents died together in a flood when I was a baby. I mostly grew up in an assortment of foster homes.'

'Don't you have any relatives?'

He shrugged. 'Some cousins in Iowa. They've never bothered with me, and I have no interest in them. I don't need people; it's a good feeling to know you've done it all on your own.'

She nodded. 'I suppose. I'm not afraid of being alone – there are times I prefer it. But I guess I want the security of knowing there are people out there if I need them.'

'I can't see having people around just in case you might need them. I don't often meet anyone I would put up with for that reason.'

'But some people are special,' Bonnie answered with a sharp intake of breath.

He nodded. 'Yes, some people are special. But you can't always count on having them, can you?'

He stood up. 'Want to see the kitchen?'

The kitchen was large, with a few dark green cupboards on one wall. 'It'll do for a while,' he said. 'I may wait till the war's over to remodel it.'

'You keep saying that like you know it's going to happen.'

'Of course it will end; it has to.'

'I keep saying it, too, but I don't believe it.' *Tell me there's a future.*

'It's hard to buy a winter coat in July, but it's a smart thing to do,' Frank said. 'Where's Maxine now?'

'In Texas.'

'I understand she married a local boy.'

'Yes. He was an old friend, but the romance just developed over a furlough.'

'Too bad she couldn't follow through on the new job.'

'Yes, I was sorry about that,' Bonnie said quickly. 'After you fixed it up for her – I felt responsible.'

'Nonsense, you aren't responsible for other people. We gave her the job because she deserved it. If she wanted marriage more, that's a risk an employer takes.'

When they got into the car, Frank aimed the ignition key at the switch, and then pulled it back and looked at Bonnie.

'Don't suppose you'd be interested in the band concert in the park – before the fireworks.'

'Oh –' she floundered.

'No, I suppose not,' Frank said quickly.

She was surprised, and even disturbed, at how interested she was. It wouldn't mean anything, of course, but it had been so long.

He started the car.

'I would be interested,' she found herself saying. 'It will be cooler in the park.'

He looked up in time for her to see the lights go up in his eyes. 'Yes,' he said quickly. 'It's so damned hot.'

'Muggy,' she said, swallowing the guilt.

He drove away from the kerb.

'We always used to go to the fireworks display – my family, I mean.'

84

'I guess I never did,' Frank replied. 'Just never got around to it. Or band concerts, either.'

'Saturday night band concert was a big deal in Centerville when I was growing up. It was in the middle of Main Street and the stores stayed open as long as people were around. Everybody visited over the music, and we kids ate ice cream. They don't have it anymore – haven't for some time.'

They found a crowd gathered around the bandshell. The green, slatted benches were all filled, and the adults and children dotted their blankets and quilts in an irregular line along the pattern of the shade, which would grow larger as the sun set. Not far away, little boys held firecrackers to the punk and threw them, sizzling and spewing sparks before they exploded in the dirt.

Bonnie shuddered and looked across the crowd. They saw a couple get up and push their way out along the bench. Frank took her and pulled her towards the empty space. She hurried to keep up with his long steps. Her hand rested comfortably inside his bigger one. 'Maybe they're coming back,' she said. Frank did not slow down. 'That's their tough luck,' he said cheerfully.

As they took their seats, the band members filed in. They wore white shirts with rolled-up sleeves, and red trousers with white stripes down the side. A number of women were in the band, and very young boys with no hips or behinds, and men with greying, thinning hair. The first notes that silenced the crowd were on key, if not the sweetest.

As the Strauss polka threw a cover across the voices, Bonnie looked around. One expected to see in Lancaster these days a heavy sprinkling of khaki in every crowd. They were here, the young men who would otherwise fit into the red trousers. They wore summer khaki shirts and trousers, ties tucked in above the third shirt button, and overseas caps over their clipped haircuts. They weren't the same men, of course. *The Lancaster Municipal Band drummer is at Fort Dix, and the trumpet players are in Hondo, Texas, and Guadalcanal. Or in England, maybe, marking off their missions and dreaming of Lancaster on the Fourth of July.* She sent a hostile look towards Frank. *What are you doing here with his wife? It's not fair to blame Frank. He's doing more for the war effort than some private in a foxhole.*

At an explosion close by, she grabbed Frank's arm and ducked her head into his shoulder. She heard boys' laughter, and was shaking as she straightened up. *How can they enjoy playing with gunpowder? How can the soldiers bear it?*

'Are you all right?' Frank asked.

'Yes,' she said.'I'm all right.' But she still shook.

He would steal a look at her occasionally, and she knew he would like to take her hand. A girl could tell.

The featured number was a medley from the new Broadway musical, *Oklahoma!* A skinny boy with pimples belted the back row into corn as high as an elephant's eye before he whisked them away in the surrey with the fringe on top.

After the Stephen Foster medley, the band struck up 'Stars and Stripes Forever' and some of the crowd began to sing. The voices came from a large group of servicemen.

> *Be kind to your web-footed friends,*
> *For a duck may be somebody's mu-ther.*
> *Be kind to your friends in the swamp*
> *Where the weather's cold and domp!*

The abrupt ending of the lyric was less effective when the band kept on playing. Bonnie knew the foolish parody and she was smiling when Frank said with irritation, 'Crazy drunks.'

'No, they're not,' Bonnie said.

Without stopping, the band swung into 'God Bless America.' A few people stood up. Others followed. A strong bass voice joined a wavering soprano. By the time they reached the last stanza the sound had swelled. The second time through everyone was singing, surging to the last home sweet home. The fireworks began and Bonnie felt the stirring in the crowd. *God bless us. God help us.* She knew they were together. This was what their sacrifices were for. It had to matter, or there would be no sense to anything.

Fifteen

September 1944

Margaret Blake's letters were infrequent and polite. Bonnie had no premonition that the one that arrived that autumn day would be any different from the others. When she opened back the familiar monogrammed page, a twice-folded sheet of thin airmail paper fell out. She let it lie at her feet while she read the short message.

Dear Bonnie,

> *I have thought and prayed over the matter, and have at last come to the conclusion that I am doing the right thing in forwarding the enclosed letter to you. Maybe you will hate me for it, but John's happiness is the most important thing in the world to me and I know he will not write this to you himself.*

> *The enclosed letter is one of the kind he writes to me. These are his own words. Make of it what you will. If my doing this destroys something between us, I am deeply sorry, but I think you should know. We both want the best for him.*

> *Sincerely,*
> *Margaret Blake*

Bonnie's heart increased its speed as she dropped Margaret's letter on the table and stopped to pick up the sheet that had fallen to the floor. Her hand shook as she opened it up and spread out the creases on the single sheet. It was John's familiar handwriting. It looked like one of the letters filed away in a box in the corner of her bedroom. She read:

Page 2

> *It has been a long time since I've lived more than one*

day at a time. I think about home and the easy-going, happy times we had. I know I'll never go back to that.

What if the war years were the dream? Sometimes I lie in my bunk and close my eyes and imagine that I might open them in my room at home. You would be dropping in to check out my wardrobe (you never trusted my colour combinations) and Sara would be hollering up the stairs, 'If you're not down in five minutes, I'm going to find a new best friend.'

Has she found one yet? I do hope so, for her sake. I still don't know how I could have hurt her like this. It's all part of the dream. I'm even selfish enough to be damned uncomfortable with that thought, too – her finding someone else, I mean.

Well, here I am, babbling like a child. But what are mothers for?

Some of us are planning to go to Canterbury next weekend. This country is so rich in the past, their –

Bonnie leaped to her feet, the shock of the sharp crack of her shin against the table leg merging with the pain growing inside her. She ripped the page into pieces that fluttered listlessly to the floor in defiance of her angry thrust.

How could she? How could she? No one could be so cruel. His private thoughts, only for her. She betrayed him. His mother. He didn't want me to see. He didn't want it. He didn't want it.

She dropped to her knees and picked up the pieces. She raised them to the table and her trembling fingers pieced them together again, like a simple jigsaw puzzle.

It's all right. It's not so bad. Of course he has such thoughts sometimes. I'll keep reading it to see it's not so bad. It's all right. It's not so bad.

She walked numbly into the bedroom and took the lid off her letter box. It was close to the top, the letter he had written to her about Canterbury. It wasn't necessary to reread it, she still remembered the lengthy description of the cathedral. She already knew it began 'Dear Bonnie' instead of 'Darling.' She had no letter written the same day or even close to his mother's.

Like a slow cancer, the fears ate at her, day by day. The two letters were a presence, inside the desk. Margaret's letter must be answered – some day, some way, but not today. Weeks went by. Each time she wrote to John she was conscious of the rift between his wife and his mother that she could not mention. Her dreams of the future stopped cold. How could she face a life in Boston close to this woman?

Sixteen

'The Fourth of July was lovely, but I hope you understand that we can't do it again.' No.

'It seems innocent, but makes me feel guilty.' No.

'I have so many things to catch up on this evening. I write to John every night, you know.' Better.

She rehearsed the speeches, but never used them. Frank didn't ask her out again. She slipped into the role of office wife. Beyond knowing the correct amount of cream and sugar for his coffee, and the type of reservations he wanted for business luncheons, she was now selecting wallpaper for his house – and once she picked up a pair of socks, size ten. She didn't know John's sock size.

Towards the end of each month, they came back and worked in the evening, Frank dictating the lengthy reports he couldn't get to during the day. In the factory section night was no different from day. The machinery was operated by workers on three eight-hour shifts. But in the offices, occupying the top floor of the building, there was only a day shift. After five, a light burning among the rows of darkened desks indicated a person leaning over papers, putting in solitary overtime. Most often, the lights shone from private offices where non-hourly executives caught up on paperwork in the quiet hours.

Bonnie had sat across the desk many evenings thinking of the previous nights' U.S.O. dance, and later, of a letter, seeing her boss only as part of the furniture. He had been an unlabelled book cover for a long time, gradually becoming someone who needed her. He was a genius with production planning, but he was colour blind; and when it came to coordinating floor coverings – well, he was a man.

While her fingers made Gregg curves and dashes across the pad balanced on her knee, her mind pondered the never-voiced pathos the two people in the room were feeling. The gulf around her island was growing steadily wider, and she knew that the quiet, introverted man across from her also had his island. The evenings at work were a comfort to both of them.

When he dropped her off at her apartment, she always felt a little lonelier as she got out of the car. She had asked him not to walk her to the door every time, but the Buick always stayed at the kerb until she was safely inside. It would be there in case she decided sometime to come running back.

December 1944

December was a grey month, grey with fog and scattered flurries of snow. It was dark by the time Bonnie got home from work, in spite of War Savings Time. She wasn't feeling good. The pain in her heart seemed to spill over, gradually becoming a persistent, low-level pain in her side. She checked once with the plant doctor and he suggested aspirin and a better-regulated diet; she hadn't been eating balanced meals.

She had already mailed John's Christmas package; hopes of seeing him by Christmas were gone.

On this particular grey afternoon nausea added to her problems. She threw up after lunch and later in the afternoon was sick again. She walked unsteadily back to her desk, unable to straighten up because of the pain. Sliding into her desk chair, she wondered how she was going to get home.

The buzzer sounded, and she looked towards Frank's office with new hope. She didn't take her shorthand book, but closed the door behind her with one hand, while the other held her side.

Frank sat behind the mahogany desk, engrossed in a letter he held in his wide sturdy hands. She fixed her eyes on the diamonds in the simple wide ring he wore, willing the nausea to stay under control.

When she didn't sit, he looked up. She saw his expression

change from preoccupation to awareness. They both spoke at once, 'I'm sick.' 'My God, Bonnie.'

Frank stood up with a rattle of his swivel chair and was around the desk in an instant. She could not have stood longer. His arm went around her waist and she leaned against him as she concentrated on the steps to the chair. He eased her into it, his arm slow to move away. The dark-blue serge arm was her focus, she reached up and clung to it. Sliding the arm away he gripped her hands in his, reaching the other arm to the desk to pick up the phone. His voice was strained, but in command as he told the plant operator, 'This is Mr Forbes. Get the doctor up to my office.'

Hastily replacing the phone, he put both hands around hers. 'Bonnie,' he said intensely, 'I think you should put your head down.'

Even as he spoke the room was slipping away.

When it came into focus again, she was lying flat against something hard. The strange object in front of her was a chair leg. The blue serge arm was still there, the strong fingers adjusting her head to a more comfortable angle. His face bent over hers. 'Oh, you're coming to. Thank God.'

Where are we? On the floor? How did I get here? Is my skirt down? It hurts, it hurts.

There was an urgent knock at the door.

Frank pulled his hand away, she tried to hold on. 'It's all right,' he said gently. 'I'll be right back.'

He disappeared and she held her breath.

When the blue legs returned, a pair of white stockings came with them. Things were clearing up now, but she couldn't quite make it to check on the skirt.

'She fainted,' she heard him say. 'I put her on the floor; it's the only place to lie flat.'

'You did the right thing,' a feminine voice answered. 'Has she come out of it?'

'I think so. Where's the doctor?'

'He's gone for the day.'

The cheerful face of Molly Murphy bent over her, her white cap like a halo around her grey hair under the fluorescent light. 'Well, young lady, what's going on here?'

'I don't know,' Bonnie answered, alarmed at her weak voice.

'Oh, I'm sorry,' she gasped. 'I'm sick.'

Molly was already reaching for the mahogany wastebasket and she efficiently assisted Bonnie in using it.

As Molly helped her to lie down she clung to the burning side.

'Hurt you there?' Molly asked.

Bonnie nodded.

'Uh-huh,' Molly said as she stood up. She spoke to Frank in a low voice. 'We should get her to the hospital.'

'I don't want to go in an ambulance!' Bonnie said, louder than she had intened.

'Couldn't I take her in my car?' Frank asked.

'Well . . .'

'Oh, yes, please,' Bonnie said. 'You take me.'

'I'll call for a wheelchair,' Molly agreed. 'You get the car and meet us at the dock; we can use the freight elevator.'

Bonnie struggled to sit up. 'Don't you think I can walk? Do I have to use a wheelchair?'

Frank knelt beside her. 'Look here,' he said. 'Do you want me to carry you down the stairs? It's that or the wheelchair – which?'

She lay down again with a gasp. 'I'm sorry.'

He took her hand and gripped it. 'Don't be afraid,' he said. 'You're going to be taken care of. This'll make you a celebrity at the plant.'

She let out a long breath and closed her eyes, and for a moment the pain was gone.

The hospital was a haven from the time caring hands helped Frank take her from the blue Buick into the white light where men in white jackets nodded and said, 'Aha, we know just what you need,' and they did.

She was drowsy and hurting less when she saw Frank again. He called her name. When she gave a half-smile and opened her eyes, he said quietly, 'Can you give me John's address? I'll call the Red Cross.'

The smile slowly became a frown, and she shook her head. He leaned closer. 'The Red Cross can contact John,' he said. 'They'll let him know right away.'

She shook her head again. 'No,' she said with effort.

'But he must know,' Frank insisted.

'No,' she repeated. 'Wait until it's over; he has enough to worry about.'

When he started an impatient answer she raised her hand. 'I mean it,' she said with effort, the words thickening. 'Please don't do it. Call my mum and dad in Centerville.' She gave him the number. He didn't move. 'Please,' she said. 'Just Mum and Dad for now.'

He nodded and stood up.

'Frank?'

He stopped. She strained to speak. He leaned down.

'Thanks,' she whispered, eyes closed. He stood by the bed until her breathing was heavier, but she knew when his lips brushed her forehead. She floated away on a gentle cloud.

Daddy was there. Sometimes the lights came on, and sometimes fireworks exploded, and sometimes she retched until the bed was wet. She heard Daddy's voice. and saw him sometimes, maybe. Once Mother was washing her face with a cool cloth. Or was it Mother? Some of the time Daddy had black curly hair. A girl in a blue striped pinafore kept disturbing Bonnie's sleep to make conversation while she wrapped a black cloth around her arm.

There were red and yellow streaks in the sky. Sunrise or sunset? A high-backed chair was silhouetted by the window. She moved and grimaced with pain. Just a little to relieve the cramp.

The door opened quietly and she looked for someone to appear in the reflected light from the inverted fixture above the bed. He tiptoed to the bed. She watched the tired, drawn lines in his face change when he saw her open eyes.

'Hi,' Frank said. 'Feeling better?'

'Depends upon what it's better than.'

'So, you *are* better. Making jokes now.'

She squinted at him. 'You look terrible.' A dark shadow of beard circled his face and his tie hung loose. The top button of the white shirt was unfastened, and the shirt was wrinkled and awry under the dark coat. *Actually, you look rather handsome – that curl down on the forehead.*

'Look who's talking,' he chided while his eyes said things

they shouldn't. 'I don't know who has a better right. We've been through something, you and I.'

She discovered her left arm was fastened to a board. Tubes carried strange liquids into the back of her hand.

'Did I dream that my folks were here?'

He shook his head. 'No, you didn't dream it; they were here all night. I got them to go to your place for a nap about an hour ago.'

'Were you here all night?'

'I can sleep sitting up in a chair. I know I shouldn't have.' He looked embarrassed.

'Don't apologize; you've been wonderful.'

A curtain came over his eyes. 'I didn't have anything better to do.'

She looked at the red liquid going into her arm. 'It was only a simple appendectomy. Wasn't it?'

He looked weary. She wanted to push the wayward curl back.

'You had some problems; we were pretty worried. But it's all right now. Doctor says we can relax.'

'I think I'll sleep.'

'Sure, you go to sleep. I can go home now and clean up and get to work.'

She pulled her eyes open and tried to answer, but didn't make it.

By the third day she could be cranked up in bed enough to write a letter. The tubes were gone and she no longer needed pain shots. She wrote a long letter to John. Now there was something to write about. She worked at the letter several times during the day, and breathing a sigh when it was finished and addressed, she settled back for a nap.

The pretty student nurse in the blue pinafore bounced into the room. Close behind her was an orderly pushing a wheelchair

'Guess what?' she bubbled. 'We're supposed to get you up. There's a big surprise!'

Bonnie moaned. 'You and your surprises. What are you going to do to me?'

'No, honest,' the girl said. 'This is a genuine, super happy surprise. Have you dangled yet?'

94

'Yes,' Bonnie answered, suspicious of the subject change. 'I dangled this morning, but I haven't been out of bed.'

'We'll help you,' the girl promised, and she and the orderly proceeded to do so.

The difficult transition to the wheelchair accomplished, the nurse stood back and grinned. 'Now I will tell you,' she announced.

'Yes, why don't you do that?'

'It's a phone call. They're holding a person-to-person call for you on the switchboard.' She hesitated, for full impact, 'It's an *overseas* long-distance phone call.'

Bonnie leaned her forehead against her hand.

'Are you all right?'

She nodded.

They sailed down the hall to the nurses' station. The chair was braked by the low telephone table, reserved for patients' use. Her escorts retired to a discrete distance, saying, 'Wave when you need us.'

The phone was heavy. She propped her elbow on the arm of the chair and spoke timidly to the operator. The call went through quickly.

'Bonnie, is that you?' It was John's voice. He sounded different – older, strained.

The phone crackled and sputtered. She hesitated, then talked into the noise. 'Oh, John.'

'Bonnie, can you hear me?'

She raised her voice. 'Yes, I hear you. How did you know I was here?'

'Bonnie, I can't hear you.'

She pulled the crackling phone back and looked at it helplessly. She tried again. 'I can hear you; why can't you hear me?'

'Now,' he said, 'that's better. Are you all right? How sick are you?'

'I'm fine.'

'I can't hear what you're saying, darling. I just got back to the base and there were a bunch of messages from the Red Cross. Scared hell out of me. They said you'd had surgery, but were doing fine. Is that right? You're doing fine?'

'Yes, I'm fine. Are you all right?'

'Oh, sure, I'm fine.'

95

She jerked the receiver away as a loud screech came through. She cautiously brought it back to her ear as the sound subsided.

The robot voice of the operator interrupted. 'Are you through with your call?'

'No,' Bonnie answered. 'We haven't even started.'

'Will you hold a moment?'

She waited. There was silence, then the static started again. 'Go ahead.'

'Hello, Bonnie?'

'Yes. Can you hear me?'

'Not very well.'

'I just wrote you a long letter,' she shouted. The entire corridor was sharing the conversation now. 'I told you all about it. I don't know who told the Red Cross. I don't think you should have to pay for this call; we have a terrible connection. Are you paying for it?'

'What?'

'This call. Do you have to pay for it?'

'No, no, it's on the Red Cross.'

'Oh, that's nice of them.'

'What? Oh, Jesus Christ, I wish I could hear you.'

The tears spilled over. She let them flow, too weak to turn them off.

'Listen, Bonnie, I could ask for emergency leave. But I am involved in something big here. Not that Hitler would win if I left, we're all expendable – but it is important. Do you understand?'

She realized she was nodding. *He can't see me. Can't hear me either.*

'Are you sure you're okay?'

'I'm fine.'

'Your time is up,' a voice cut in, clear as a bell.

'Oh, hell!' he said.

'I love you,' she whispered.

She managed to hang up the phone. She laid her hands in her lap and allowed the tears to roll unchecked, dripping onto her new robe, making dark streaks on the shiny material. The little student nurse looked around occasionally, but made no move to come over. At last, when the need for a handkerchief could no longer be ignored, Bonnie made a feeble motion and her two escorts moved at once to take her back to the room.

When Frank stopped in after work that evening, she was ready for him. He laid a little volume of poems on the bedside table. 'I don't know anything about these things, but the girl at the bookstore thought you'd like it.' He never came empty-handed.

'Thanks,' she said. 'I've got a bone to pick with you.'

He smiled. 'Oh, yeah? What have I done now?'

She had put on the new robe and makeup in anticipation of his stopping by, but she was determined to be stern with him. 'I had a phone call this afternoon. A call from England!'

'Really.' He straightened up. 'What brought that on?'

'That's a good question.'

Frank shook his head. 'Well,' he said, 'I would guess that it had something to do with my call to the Red Cross.'

'You did it. And I asked you not to. And you didn't tell me.'

'Yes, all those things. Actually, your parents and I decided John should know what was happening. We called while you were still in the operating room.'

'But I asked you not to.'

'I guess I – we – just put ourselves in his place. He had a right to know. I'm sorry if it makes you mad. I think it was the right thing to do.'

'Why didn't you tell me?'

'I didn't want you to worry. They couldn't reach him; he wasn't at the base. Nobody seemed to know where he was; said he'd left on a pass.'

'You didn't believe that?'

'Well, you'd talked about a top-secret assignment. That was what came to mind; I thought he might be missing or something. Or that you might think so.'

'Yes, I suppose I would have.'

'What did you hear today?'

'I talked to John.'

'Then everything's all right.'

'Yes. We had a bad connection; it was very unsatisfactory. It was awful, in fact.' Her voice broke.

'I'm sorry.'

She shook her head, unable to speak. In her distress, she looked at Frank. He looked as stricken as she was. She felt a surge of pity and affection.

'It's all right,' she said. 'You probably did the right thing;

I've involved you far too much in my problems.'

Frank looked sicker and turned around and walked to the window. His broad pin-striped back made a solid block against the December grey of the world outside.

He didn't mean me when he wished it was a dream. It's not so bad.

Seventeen

Major John Blake, USAAF
APO210
c/o Postmaster
New York, New York
February 20, 1945

Dear John,

I finished eating Sunday's stew and tried to sew, but quit after putting the right sleeve in the left armhole again. This has been my week for doing things backward.

Happy Anniversary, darling. I was hoping for a letter, but even you, clever as you are, couldn't time it that well. It has been two weeks and the last letter was very short. Things can't be duller in England than they are here. But then, of course I understand there is so much you can't write about. It doesn't seem fair that you have to stay so long overseas without a leave. But I know someday you can tell me why.

Anyway, I've been Mrs Blake for two years now. I'm quite comfortable with the name. I'm lucky to be able to look forward to being a real wife. The war must end someday and we will have the house and kids – but we've said this so many times.

Last night I woke up and I couldn't remember what you look like. I kept getting wider awake. You know how it is when you can't go back to sleep. It was so dark – cloudy I guess. Finally turned on the light but the picture by my bed wouldn't do it. I got up and dug out all the snapshots you've sent. Have you changed? You seem a little different. Are you different in England? Of course you've changed. God, what a question!

You know, I always pretend you're sleeping beside me. Last night you weren't there. I couldn't make you be there. Couldn't find you. We never even spent a whole night together. How am I supposed to know what it's like when I've never slept all night with a man? I mean how much imagination am I supposed to have? Do we do it again when we wake up? Do we do it in the middle of the night? Will I ever know? How can ...

Major John Blake, USAAF
APO 210
c/o Postmaster
New York, New York
February 20, 1945

Dear John,

I finished eating Sunday's stew – it was still very good. I sewed awhile but I found I wasn't in the mood.

Happy Anniversary, darling. I was hoping for a letter, but even you, clever as you are, couldn't time it that well. I know there is such a large part of your life now that you can't write about. We just have to visit about the past and the future. We shared so little of the past, but the future will be all ours. We know that we belong to each other, and someday we will look back at these times and know it was worth waiting for.

How many times have I said this in the last two years? How many ways are there to say it? No wonder you don't write so often. How long can we exist on reliving that night in the Comanche Room? I can still see you across the room when I go there. But it isn't you, it's a lot of other soldiers. They're not ...

Major John Blake, USAAF
APO 210
c/o Postmaster
New York, New York
February 20, 1945

Dear John,

I finished eating Sunday's stew and sewed awhile. Happy Anniversary, darling. I was hoping for a letter, but even you, clever as you are, couldn't time it that well.

I really miss Maxine. We weren't together as much after I got married, but still she was there when I needed her. I could always talk to her. I needed her today.

My married friends at the office aren't like me. I wonder if there's something wrong with me. Why does their talk bother me so much? They make me feel guilty about being happy.

Yet tonight, I feel like they're right. You'll never be back. We thought there was a tie between us that could span the ocean. Our spirits had become one – two halves of one spirit, or was it just me said it? Tonight I want to touch you. I need to feel your flesh with my hands. I need your body, not your spirit. I need, I need, I need ...

Major John Blake, USAAF
APO 210
c/o Postmaster
New York, New York
February 20, 1945

Dear John,

I finished the stew and tried to sew. It has been cold and dry. The sun keeps shining. I wish it would snow. Winter will be over soon.

It's almost a year since I went to Boston. Your folks were good to me, but they don't write often.

I am terrified of how it will be when you discover what I found out there. It was like accidentally wandering into a play with the cast of characters already complete. You

*needed me for a little while. What does that have to do with
your past and future? How will you ...*

Major John Blake, USAAF
APO 210
c/o Postmaster
New York, New York
February 20, 1945

Dear John,

It's cold and we need rain ...

Major John Blake, USAAF
APO 210
c/o Postmaster
New York, New York
February 20, 1945

Dear John,

Harry Newcombe is dead. Maggie's father brought the
telegram to the plant today. I knew as soon as I saw him. So
did Maggie.

Maggie has memories. If I got the next telegram, I would
have nothing left but a stack of V-mail and a lot of fantasies
and dead hopes.

There is someone here who loves me and needs me. He
hasn't said it, but it's real to me without words. I honestly am
not sure how I feel about him, but I want to be free to find
out. I've been frozen so long.

Nobody else will ever touch me the way you did. But that's
gone. We'll never go back to that place again. I want to let
you go. I want you to cut me loose, if you haven't already.
Something died for me today, too. Dear John, please don't
blame me. I tried. God help us both.

Bonnie

Part Two

THE SEVENTIES

One

This soldier was ten feet tall. His sleeves were rolled above his elbows, wrinkled and saturated with the sweat of honest labour. The muscles in his arm bulged from the grip on his heavy musket. The other hand lay on the handle of a resting plough. First things first.

COMING NEXT YEAR – 1776–1976 AMERICAN BICENTENNIAL, the sign said.

He was the only soldier in sight as he kept his watch from the side of a Manhattan building. On the street below his countrymen jostled, ran over, mugged, cheated, annoyed, chased, helped, supported, loved, and lusted after each other in their daily quest to find themselves, do their own thing, get a piece of the action, get it all together, find the good life, and form a meaningful relationship.

May 1975

The colonial soldier could be seen from the window of Anne Forbes's walk-up apartment. He fit into a slot just above the shorter town house across the street and to one side of the tall building on the corner. When Bonnie let herself into the apartment with the two keys her daughter had mailed to her, his image wavered through the windowpane, as she stopped inside the door to put down her suitcase and rest her arm.

The studio-living room was larger than she had expected. Next to the windows a drafting board caught the best light. Pencils, charcoal, and clean brushes lay neatly beside it. Half-filled paint jars were dabs of strong colour on the shelves against the wall beside stacks of poster board.

On the other side of the room a deep sofa smothered in pillows caught the brilliance of the paintings and pottery in the pale room. An inside-out tweed sweater lay across one end of the sofa, and Sunday's *Times* was folded on the floor beside it. Warmth seeped through her tired body at the sight of the sweater.

She stopped to lift the suitcase again and turned to find the bedroom on the right. Anne had written it could be hers for her stay in New York. She laid the suitcase flat on the black-and tan-striped bed and set her bulging canvas tote bag beside it. The bedside clock said 5 p.m. It had been a long day. She sat on the side of the bed and kicked off her shoes.

The plane ride had been quick and comfortable. It was the treadmill she walked before and after that had exhausted her. Was it just this morning that she had had the last confrontation with Frank? A conversation that left her boarding the plane with extra carry-on baggage called guilt?

She went into the bathroom for aspirin. In the old-fashioned medicine chest, next to the Lectra-Shave, she found some. She swallowed three tablets and automatically examined her reflection in the mirror after the door clicked shut. Her makeup was wearing thin. A good night's sleep would lighten the dark circles. She picked up the comb on the counter and ran it through her short, tightly curled brown hair. Tossing the comb onto the counter, she turned back to the bedroom.

Tempting reading protruded from the tote bag. She had stopped at the hotel and registered for the convention on her way in, and picked up the literature. *Rest a little. Get my breath before Anne gets home. So much to talk about.*

She pushed the suitcase aside and pulled a pillow from under the spread. She punched it, found it to be unyielding polyester, and tossed it against the headboard. Her skirt slid above her knees as she settled herself on the bed, leaning back against the pillow. *Good-looking legs.* She let the skirt creep higher as she reached into the bag. EARTH SAVERS, THIRD ANNUAL CONVENTION, WELCOME DELEGATES, she read.

'*What the hell do you know about factory wastes?*' Frank's voice intruded. '*Why can't you play bridge or baby-sit for your grandchildren or take up china painting? Why are you always wanting to change the world?*' She shook her head to get rid of the sound. That was a year ago. They had long ago moved into a policy of not talking about it.

Yet, it was only this morning in Lancaster that she had been folding the last pants suit for packing when she heard the door close and footsteps on the stairs. She recognized Frank's walk. They had said a chilly good-bye a few hours earlier. Why was he back? *Don't be defensive. Maybe it bothers him, too, that the good-bye kiss was so empty.*

She felt him come into the room. Silence finally forced her to turn. He stood by the window, staring out. As she watched, he turned back. *He looks terrible. Does he really mind that much?* She braced herself.

'Why are you taking that suitcase?'

She didn't answer, but pulled the lid down and tugged at the fastener.

'You know the blue luggage is lighter weight. Why must you always do things the hard way?'

The fastener almost caught before it slipped out of her fingers.

Frank took heavy steps to the bed. 'Put it on a chair. The bed's too soft.' With a few quick movements he placed it on a chair and latched both fasteners.

She tried to speak casually. 'Why are you home? I mean, did you decide to take me to the airport after all?'

'Isn't Linda taking you?'

'She offered, but there was no use taking the baby out. He still runs a temperature at night. I was going to call a cab.' She clasped her hands nervously. 'You don't need to, but it would be nice.'

Frank nodded. 'Sure. Okay. Are you ready?'

'Almost. There's plenty of time.'

He paced slowly in front of the window, his back as always very straight. His thick, white hair had broken loose here and there from its sculptured styling with an undisciplined ringlet, as it had a tendency to do when he was warm.

'What's the matter with the baby?' he asked.

'Babies just run temperatures sometimes. I hope it isn't the ear infection coming back.'

'Well, you can't worry about not being here if they have another siege with him.'

'They can manage,' she said, raising her voice. 'Mike will just have to help out more.'

'Mike's got too much going at the plant right now to take care of babies.'

She swallowed the lump in her throat and picked the suitcase up off the chair and set it on the floor. 'Linda plans to have you over for dinner. Karen should, too, though she hasn't mentioned it.'

'I don't know if I'm up to Karen's vegetarian cooking.'

'She knows you're meat-and-potatoes man.'

'Don't worry about it. I can eat out.'

She sat down in the chair. 'Mrs Myers will cook for you on Monday and Thursday when she comes to clean.'

'I said, don't worry about it.'

She knew she should drop the matter. 'There was a day when you could cook for yourself.' She attempted to smile. 'You haven't been in the kitchen for almost thirty years. Do you think you could still do it?'

Frank was looking out the window. He pulled himself back after she had decided he wasn't going to answer.

'Oh, of course I could,' he said shortly. 'I just have more important things to do.'

Sudden rage gripped her throat. Disgust at violent feelings in herself increased the violence. She jumped to her feet and snatched her trench coat out of the closet.

In the car Frank clutched the steering wheel, staring glumly ahead. Once they remained stopped before a green light. When she reminded him, he lashed out, 'I can see the light,' and the car shot forward as the amber light came on.

They had turned onto the highway when he said in a flat voice, 'Clem called me in this morning.'

She jerked her head to look at him. *A call from the president's office.* 'Was it important?'

'You might say it was important.' His tone was casual, but she knew him well enough to see the little quivering muscles around his jaw, and the way his fingers moved while his hand remained fixed on the steering wheel.

She quietly released a long breath. *It isn't me. Something happened at the office. It's not my fault.*

'He's quitting. Now, by God, at last he's decided to quit.'

She knew what was coming. 'What else did he say? Did he say who – ?'

Frank nodded. She sighed. His foot let up on the accelerator in the slow lane of the divided highway.

'Well, we knew all along.' His voice was louder. 'It had to be George Ames. He's a born executive. He's done miracles.' He swallowed. 'He's young – forty-two, what the hell!'

'Frank,' she said softly, 'why didn't you tell me before? That's why you're upset. I thought all your anger was for me.'

'I'm not upset. I gave up the idea of the presidency years ago, when the old man didn't retire.'

'Frank,' she said, 'you know very well you've been the crown prince at Scott Manufacturing ever since Clem took over. You should have had it then. You *weren't* too young. Who would have thought he'd hang on so long?'

'You can't blame them for not wanting to take on another old man now.'

She looked sharply at him and away again. 'I won't even answer that. You're above such remarks.'

'Bonnie, it's a fact of life that sixty-five is just around the corner for me. Why duck it? They didn't.'

He's right. It's hard for me to face. She looked down at her hands. 'I'm sorry.'

I could comfort him tonight. In my arms, in bed, I could comfort him. It's the only place he recognizes tenderness. We give and take for our needs without words there. But I'm leaving him alone.

They both watched the highway. He speeded up and passed a long truck. When the car was settled back in the right-hand lane, Frank sighed.

'I suppose there'll be a goddamned cocktail party this weekend after the announcement. There won't be any way I can duck it.'

'Why don't you call Dorothy Vance to go with you? She's been out of things since Fred died. I'll bet she'd like to go.'

'Now why would I want to do that?'

'It would be a nice thing to do for her – and you wouldn't have to go alone.'

'Bonnie, I don't need anyone to hold my hand.'

What's so bad about needing someone? You just can't say it, can you? Go ahead and say it. I need you, Bonnie. I hurt and hurt and I need you. Why can't you say it?

She looked out the window at a brilliant sky behind marsh-mallow clouds. *I don't want him to say it. I'm glad he can't say it. I'd sell my soul to the devil for this two weeks. Friendly Skies of United, I want you, I lust for you. New York, New York – freedom, choice, change. Streets packed with strangers, people climbing over people, all strangers who want nothing from me. Scott Manufacturing has been Frank's mistress. Now she has spurned him and he's crying for me.*

'Don't worry about leaving.' The words gradually registered through her thoughts. His voice was quieter. 'I know this trip means a lot to you. I want you to have a good time.'

Tears came close.

'Frank – I do still love you.'

He took his hand from the wheel and, without looking from the road, covered her hand lying on the seat. 'I know that,' he said quietly. 'You know how important you are to me. You put up with a hell of a lot.' He put both hands back on the wheel and manoeuvred the cloverleaf turn onto the airport road.

The sands of guilt sifted out of the plane all the way to New York – a substantial dump into the Great Lakes, a final shake over Ohio. Now as she looked over the itinerary of celebrity speakers her spirits grew increasingly higher. The separation would be good for their marriage. Frank's last-minute show of affection was a good sign. He had been so proud of his model wife and three beautiful little girls. It was hard for him to accept change – and their life was changing.

She stuffed the half-read itinerary back into the bag and swung her feet onto the floor.

Sliding open the closet door, she noted that Anne had provided hanger space at one end of the closet. Pushed tightly together were man-tailored jackets and blazers. She slid back the other door to find a row of trousers. There were twelve pairs when she counted, neatly creased and hung.

She took a step back and looked around the room. The hair brush on the chest didn't have a handle. Lectra-Shave? She walked back to the medicine cabinet and took another look. It was.

She remembered Anne's letter. 'You'll love the new apartment, Mom. Sharing expenses with a roommate makes it practical. My roommate travels a good deal so I have the whole place to myself much of the time.' Part-time roommate – male.

This would never have happened to Linda or Karen. Anne was the child who asked 'Why?' as soon as she could talk. And never stopped asking. The one who never turned down a dare. The only member of the family who had spent a night in jail. Yet she was the one who seemed the most solidly anchored. Bonnie kept holding out her arms to catch a toppling child, only to find the child racing along ahead of her, looking for new worlds to conquer.

She stepped back to the closet for a closer look. As she pulled back the sleeve of a corduroy jacket, she had a disturbing sense of having been there before. The styles were casual but conservative. Size forty, tall, with a good athletic breadth in the shoulders. They didn't belong to the actor Anne was dating during her last visit. That was a relief. She dropped the sleeve and turned to her unpacking.

Two

Dinner that night was soup and salad on trays. The stylish young woman who had embraced Bonnie so enthusiastically an hour ago had changed into a sexpot in factory-faded blue jeans and a tight T-shirt with a small, sans serif 'Anne' printed discreetly on the left side, just above the nipple bump. Her bare feet curled under her on the sofa. Her black curls were shoulder length, styled to frame big brown eyes, like her mother's.

'I'm impressed with the apartment,' Bonnie told her. 'If one can survive the stairs, it's very nice.'

'Can you believe it – four rooms in the city? Even if three of them *are* closets. And my career is really happening.'

'We're so proud of you, darling.'

Anne stirred her coffee. 'Of course, I couldn't have swung the apartment without a roommate.'

Bonnie looked at Anne, waiting until the other pair of brown eyes slowly raised. She could feel Anne anxiously appraising her own expression. A smile broke through.

'Do you mind? I wasn't sure if you would.'

Bonnie shook her head. A lump of love for this girl lodged in her throat. 'Oh, Anne, you're a woman now. I'm completely convinced of your ability to run your life. A few years back, with the other girls, yes, I would have minded.'

'No way,' Anne said. 'Linda and Karen got stuck in the housewife mud early.'

'They have what they want. You just hear another drummer.' She put her crumpled napkin on the tray. 'As a matter of fact, I envy you. To be in love and not sure what's coming next. The sweet torment.'

'Would you be as understanding if I lived in Lancaster?'

Bonnie looked at her thoughtfully. 'I'm not sure. Perhaps things do look different here. Anyway, thank you for caring what I think. And, by the way –'

They spoke in unison, 'Just don't tell your father.'

They laughed and Bonnie felt guilty again. 'I don't think it would surprise him much,' she explained, 'but he's more comfortable not knowing.'

Anne nodded. 'Yes. We've played this game before.'

'Tell me about your roommate.'

Anne straightened out her legs and burrowed her bare, brown toes into the carpet. A glow settled across her face like dust settling silently in the sunlight.

'His name is Bill Evans. He's twenty-nine, a native New Yorker. B.A. in art from N.Y.U. He represents a gallery and travels a lot on buying trips. He's in Europe now. He's handsome in a rugged sort of way, sensitive, personable.'

'Well, at least he has a steady job. Your father would like that. This part-time arrangement, are you sure he's not married?'

'As sure as I can be. I think we're being honest with each other. I know that he sees other girls sometimes, when he's away. But for now he says I'm the best.'

These words coming from my rebel?

'Are you seeing others?'

'Well, no. But I could, if I wanted to.'

'And what will you do if he decides you're not the best anymore?'

Anne shrugged. 'When that happens, I'll decide.'

Bonnie stared at the signed graphic on the wall and with her eyes traced the course of a purple line that began lush and thick and wound around into oblivion.

'Hey, Mom,' she heard Anne say, 'are you still with me?'

'Sorry,' she answered soberly.

Anne pushed her tray aside and leaned forward. 'I won't get hurt. You don't need to worry.'

'I'm not worried,' Bonnie said flatly.

She stood up and carried her tray to the tiny kitchen. Anne stacked her dishes, and followed.

'Dad will have a hard time getting along without you.'

'Anne, your father is first vice-president of a billion-dollar corporation. He should be able to find his socks for a couple of weeks.'

'Is he still angry with you?'

'The pure-water thing is pretty sticky. If the environmentalists win out, it'll cost the company a lot of money.'

'Are you sure it's worth it?'

Bonnie squeezed the tray onto the small counter. 'We're right. The company's wrong.' A cup tilted onto its side, and a small stream of coffee rolled across the cabinet top and dripped onto the floor.

Anne said, 'There isn't room for both of us in here. I'll straighten this up in a jiffy.'

Bonnie stepped over the puddle and returned to her chair. She reached for the canvas bag and pulled out the stack of material. She rummaged through the pamphlets, looking for the five-page printed itinerary. She had worked enough on convention committees at home to be impressed with the magnitude of this one. Seminars and lectures filled every day and night. 'Senator Callahan, yet,' she exclaimed.

The last evening scheduled the usual banquet, formal dress optional. There was a small picture and writeup about the speaker. She dropped the paper in her lap and pulled off her glasses.

'Did you get the Philharmonic tickets?'

'Ummmm, great seats. They're sold out.'

'Your father takes me to symphony now. He doesn't enjoy the music any more than he ever did, but he decided it's good for business.'

'We'll do some plays, too. We'll have a great time next week.'

Bonnie picked up the convention itinerary again. The banquet writeup – the picture – the name – blurred. She put on her glasses. 'John Blake, distinguished Boston trial lawyer of the internationally known firm of Anderson, Blake, Jones and McCloskey.' Her eyes slid back to the photograph. This man had long, wavy hair and the colour was too light. But something about the mouth, and the eyes – oh, yes, the eyes. Ice-laden tree branches and the scratch of a metal insignia against her cheek. The smell of smoke and beer and a jukebox playing 'Sentimental Journey.' The chatter from the kitchen became distant static.

Only when it stopped did she become aware that Anne was standing in front of her. 'What is it?'

Bonnie handed the printed sheet to her. Anne stared at it and shook her head.

'The banquet speaker,' Bonnie said. 'I hadn't realized.'

'John Blake. John Blake.' Anne's lips slowly formed a circle. 'Ohhhh, do you think it's really him?'

Bonnie found her voice. 'I'm sure of it. The picture. Sometimes I can't remember what he looked like, and sometimes it's clear as yesterday.' The dreams. The face was always clear in her dreams.

Anne threw up her hands. 'Fantastic! How exciting, Mom. You haven't seen or heard from him for – how many years?'

'Thirty.' It was hard to say. 'He didn't answer my letter.'

'Your "Dear John" letter. You broke his heart!'

'Stop it!' Her anger was like a jet of cold water.

Anne's smile faded. 'Hey! You are upset, aren't you? Call him up. Call him up and we'll have him to dinner.'

'We'll do no such thing.'

'Why not? Aren't you dying to see how he turned out?' She picked up the picture again. 'He looks dreamy here. Of course, this might not be a recent picture. He still has his hair. He could have a potbelly. Hey, I'm sorry.' Her voice followed Bonnie into the bedroom and continued through the closed door. 'Mom, I'm sorry. I don't know why you're so upset.'

Bonnie didn't know either. She did know that she didn't want the reunion taking place with her daughter as chaperon.

I am going to see John again. In bed that night she stared at the ceiling. Although he was less in her conscious thoughts, John had continued to appear in dreams – always in uniform – forever twenty-three. Gradually the dreams had become less frequent, almost disappearing during the last ten years.

She had never been back to Boston. Once she had looked up his name in a Boston telephone book. She never considered calling the number, but seeing the name in print stirred a strange excitement. There were three 'J. Blake's,' but only one of them was associated with the firm of Anderson, Hornby, and Blake. Blake was last then. The Anderson would surely be the Mr Anderson she once met at the country club dinner party in Boston. He would be an old man now. Did Sara have a brother? She didn't think so, but couldn't be sure. Lord, it was so long ago!

By the time she went to the Philharmonic she would know. The banquet would be over. Concerts had become a part of life in the last twenty years.

A day in 1955 focused in clearly. She had come back in the station wagon from delivering the three girls to the school door. Anne enrolled in kindergarten yesterday, and Bonnie faced the prospect of two whole hours to herself every morning, in a quiet house, for the first time in nine years.

She felt the bind of the tight Capri pants as she bent down to pull out the drawer of the oiled Danish modern entertainment centre. She was reaching for a record – Mantovani on the hi-fi this morning instead of 'Ding-Dong School' on the tube. She said 'Damn,' when a gold earring fell into the record drawer, and she dropped to her knees. Digging back she found no earring but uncovered the old 78s stored in the back of the drawer. She manoeuvred a record through a small passage. It was 'Concerto for Violin and Orchestra' by Arnold Schönberg. Slowly she sat back on the heels of her ballet slippers. *Schönberg*.

She adjusted the speed on the record player, and when the turntable started spinning, put the record and needle in place.

balanced unsteadily on her knees, she breathed shallowly as the music began.

The ever-widening repetition of ripples in a stream – she remembered the impact of the strange music upon her that day in the protected world of young motherhood.

The untamed music stirred yearnings for unattained happiness, in sight but out of reach. In her chlorophyll-clean living room it had spread an uneasiness over an unearned peace. Her little dinners for eight were a triumph. Her PTA minutes were always approved as read. Her daughters' dance costumes were sensational, and the girls all learned to play 'The Happy Farmer' in piano recital at an early age. But Schönberg still waited in the shadows. She had forgotten he was there.

She had tried then to pull him into the light of day. A small ache still nibbled with the memory of playing the record again. Her guests at the next morning coffee klatch were just the women on the block, but she had waxed and polished and buffed with extra vigour. That was pre-Mrs Myers, when Bonnie didn't feel justified in paying anyone to do the work that was her portion of the marriage contract.

The big old house had bloomed under her hands. Those were the days when Ozzie and Harriet basked in the cozy comfort of early American, and Bonnie was the first on the block to blossom into provincial print, hard rock maple, fluted lamp shades, and Hitchcock stencils on her deacon's bench. Now three of their neighbours had gone early American, and Bonnie was giving pep talks every morning about the warmth generated to the family psyche by the room-sized braided rug, while she secretly lingered over the pages of sleek Danish modern in *House Beautiful*. The teak entertainment centre was a stroke of rebellion, a wedge directed towards change – a redecorated house could lend spice and variety, challenge and excitement to living.

She was mildly fond of the young mothers who gathered that morning. They had come to know each other quickly as their little ones wandered off to find new playmates, and turned up in the kitchen next door. 'I'm Linda's mother,' or 'Karen's,' or 'Anne's,' became a standard form of introduction, depending upon which child she was tracking that day. This was a separate world from her other social life centred around the plant. There it was 'I'm Frank Forbes's wife. Your husband is in Production, isn't he?'

The conversation that morning was broccoli-oriented. One husband rather liked it; two tolerated it (one because he never commented on anything he was eating); and three got very unpleasant about it (unless it was only served about every six months – four at the very least). Two unusual children just loved broccoli. The rest refused it completely, or pushed it around their plates until they got yelled at by their fathers (not necessarily the same fathers who liked it).

After thirty minutes of broccoli, Bonnie set down her milk-glass snack tray – she didn't eat as many gooey cinnamon rolls when she was the hostess – and walked over to the hi-fi, pulled out the drawer below the television screen, and set the needle in place. The turntable whirled at 78 rpm. The talk had lagged, but was already picking up, splintering off in many small conversations. She waited for the surprise, the contemptuous laughter, the rejection. She waited for the quiet, when she could say with a big smile, 'Listen to this, what do you think of it?'

Nearby, Julia and Marge raised their voices to be heard over the record. They were arguing over which of their husbands had acted like the biggest baby when he had the flu. Betty was staring into space with a pucker between her eyes. Probably replaying the remark she didn't get in about broccoli.

Bonnie sat flat on the floor next to the spinning record. She wore the new hot-pink Capris this morning with her smart Italian-style stand-up collar blouse.

'Most people don't hear this music at all, Bonnie. It reaches you. Moves even as it disturbs.' Longing for John rolled over her. It was one of the moments when his face and voice were crystal clear. She surrendered to the reclaimed pain. She needed the ugly music. Its ugliness was more real than her pretty lamp shades. It was out of reach, calling her to stretch. She shuddered and pressed her face against her bent kness, allowing all the sounds in the room to merge into one kind of gibberish. *I'm past thirty. Locked in. Nothing is going to change. This is all there is.* From a far distance, a voice separated itself from the general buzz.

'Cream. Bonnie, do you have cream?'

She raised her head and stared at Betty standing over her.

Betty's eyes were questioning, concerned. 'Are you okay?' she asked hesitantly.

'Sure. I'm okay. Cream. Yes, sure. Coming up.'

She found the cream pitcher in the refrigerator and carried it to the dining table. Then she lifted off the record, put it into its jacket, and squeezed it into the back of the drawer where it had been hidden for the past ten years.

That afternoon she fixed Frank's favourite pot roast, and laboured over a fresh apple pie. She put a coloured tablecloth over the Formica table in the breakfast room, and fussed over which glasses to use. When he came through the kitchen door after work, she pulled him back, not content with the light brush of his lips across her forehead as he passed by. The second kiss was as absentminded as the first. At the table that night, she watched his hands. They were wide, short-fingered, they were a man's hands – her man's.

He said he wasn't hungry, and waved her away, saying 'None for me,' when she brought out the pie. After her little cry of disappointment, he explained, 'I had a huge lunch – took out the government inspector who's been here this week. The University Club on my expense account.' She set the plate back on the cabinet. 'Maybe I'll have a piece before bed,' he said in a conciliatory tone.

She was glad to see him settle down with the paper in the living room after dinner and hurried to get the girls started on the dishes. Five-year-old Anne helped clear the table, and Bonnie scraped and stacked to get everything in order for the two older girls to wash and dry. Their part was relatively small (the part that would be taken over by the dishwasher someday), but they always had to be dragged back to the sink against their will – the same ritual every night. She never was totally in control. Once in a while she gave in – maybe the child really did have a headache – and she supposed that was the reason they continued to test her every time. They never understood that she was in command. She was there too much. Perhaps there *were* good reasons for non-fraternization between ranks in the army. The commanding officers didn't have their control weakened by the obstacle of loving their men. Or even of just tolerating them twenty-four hours a day. They were more like fathers.

By the time she was able to join Frank, he was watching *Gunsmoke*, and she watched Chester and Doc and Kitty with half a mind while the other half thought about this morning, longing to share it with someone. Preposterous thought that it could be Frank. *You should try. You don't try enough.*

The final scene between Matt and Kitty faded out. She wondered what Matt and Kitty did when they were alone. They never kissed on camera. The old tradition of the cowboy petting only his horse. The little boys in the audience at the Hoot Gibson movies groaned and slid down in their seats when Hoot held hands with a girl. Now they were grown up and watching *Gunsmoke*, and they still liked their cowboys tough. Frank smiled when Matt gunned down the villain.

She hurried to find the record again and get it ready before switching off the TV at the next commercial. She started the record and reached up and turned off the set.

'What are you doing?'

'I found this record. It brought back a lot of things – old feelings.'

'Do you have to play it now? You know I don't like this Beethoven stuff.'

'It's not even close to Beethoven. You're lumping things together again.'

Frank put his hand on his forehead. 'Bonnie, I've had a hard day. I just want to relax. And I don't choose to do it by listening to Beethoven. Is there anything wrong with that?'

She came back and sat in the chair opposite him, forcing her voice to be quiet and friendly. 'I found this old record this morning. It made me feel funny. I guess it reminded me of things I felt when I first heard it. Ten – no twelve years ago.'

'That inspector was hard to deal with today. I don't feel like arguing about our different tastes in music.'

'I don't want to argue. I just thought maybe I could tell you how I felt.'

'All right. Tell me. How did you feel?'

She didn't answer.

'Well, I'm listening.'

'I'm just trying to think of how to say it. This music, it's

119

different. So much of my life is always the same.'

He smiled. 'Is that it? What's wrong with the same if it's good? Haven't I given you a good life? I'm not an alcoholic or a chaser. You don't have to worry about paying the bills or having enough groceries. Are you saying it would be better if you had to struggle more?'

'No. Well, maybe you should share the decisions more. You don't even let me help pick out our new car. You just drive it home.'

'You did the house by yourself.'

'You can help next time –'

'Hell, what do I care what colour you paint the bedroom?'

Like an echo, young voices crescendoed in the kitchen.

'Why don't you care?'

'You mean you're unhappy because you have to decide what colour to paint the bedroom?'

'Mo-therrrr!'

'What are we talking about? The bedroom doesn't need painting.'

The discordant record jabbed at them, unsynchronized.

'Hellllp! She threw hot water on me. Owwww!'

Bonnie jumped up and lunged across the room.

'Honey, turn on the TV. Please. And tell them to cut out that noise, for God's sake. You complain because I don't stay home!'

Three

Bonnie turned over in Bill Evans's bed and saw strange shapes, not immediately identifiable in the darkness in the strange room, and remembered that the Schönberg episodes had not been totally unproductive. She had called Betty the next day and they made plans to buy tickets together for the symphony season. She had dug through boxes in the basement until she found the stack of stories and poems that had been packed away since she moved into this house with Frank and spent a day reading them. They sounded a little silly. She put them away again.

Ten years later, in 1965, Bonnie had become very old.

The toothbrush is in the holder with a little catch on the side. If I can get it out of the drawer and walk into the bathroom. I'll have it made. Flip up the little catch. If up won't work, try down. Squeeze out the toothpaste. Brush. Where's the toothpaste? In the drawer by the toothbrush. Back up. Pick up the toothbrush holder and the toothpaste. Walk to the bathroom. No, shut the drawer, then walk to the bathroom. Turn on the light? Light in the daytime? Can't remember. Check when I get there. Right. Open the drawer, the rest will come. But might forget the toothpaste and have to come back. I'm tired. God in heaven, I'm tired. Why can't I sleep?

Getting back up on the hospital bed wasn't all that easy, either. Brushing would mean going through that again. *Doctor says 'Keep walking.'* Bonnie was stretched across the bed, on top of the covers, robe and slippers still on from the last walk. *That much done.*

Someone came through the door. She could wait a few seconds to see who it was, and then she wouldn't have to turn her head. *Quick turns can make the old head swim. Have to watch that.*

Sure enough, the authoritarian male figure materialized at the foot of the bed. He was handsome and young, his suit expensive and freshly pressed. This was Dr Bradley (Brady?), the internist her family doctor had called in to supervise a complete physical examination. Dr Adams couldn't pinpoint the problem in his office. 'We'll bring in another opinion,' he told her. She was sure Frank had requested it, but nobody told her that.

'Mrs Forbes,' Dr Bradley said, as if he were proud of his achievement in remembering her name. 'How are you today?'

She said 'Fine,' and clutched the edge of the blanket. *Maybe it will be operable.*

Dr Bradley had papers in his hand. He waved them at her

and smiled. 'Good news,' he said. 'All the tests are negative. You're in perfect health.'

'What?' She felt the panic again, about not being sure she could move her arm. She moved it, as she always did, to prove she could. 'But Dr Bradley, you just didn't find it. I *am* sick.'

'Brady. Yes, Mrs Forbes, I know you're sick, but it's my opinion – and Dr Adams concurs – that your trouble is emotional, not physical.'

The statement sat on the wall before it crashed into view. 'Emotional?' she repeated. 'I don't have emotional problems. A little trouble with my nerves when I had a houseful of babies, but it wasn't like this. I'm dizzy. Sometimes I can't walk.'

Dr Brady looked at the sheets in his hands. 'Well, that's possible, you know. Genuine physical distress from emotional causes.' He looked up. 'You mentioned some change in your periods.'

'Oh, just that they've been straggling out. It's no problem really. Last month was perfectly . . .' She stopped.

The man's expression was smug, knowledgeable. He looked at the papers again. 'What's your age? Forty-three? It's very possible that we have some menopausal problem here. It's not an illness you know, but it lowers the threshold. Makes women more vulnerable to emotional upsets.'

She was braced for multiple sclerosis, muscular dystrophy, even cancer. Not menopause. Not even after Mary had said hesitantly, 'Do you think it could be your age?' Not even that, because Bonnie had said, 'Of course not.' She wouldn't be fifty for years. She wasn't old yet.

Dr Brady smiled. 'There are things we can do. Hormones – Vitamin B. We'll get you straightened out. Don't worry.'

Don't worry, he says. I can't walk or think and it's only menopause.

'I didn't think I was old enough,' she said weakly.

'Oh, yes. It could be. How old was your mother?'

'I don't know; she never mentioned it. I never knew she had it. I don't think it made her sick.'

'That's good. Have you noticed periods of feeling very warm?'

'No. I don't know. I've felt so bad lately.' *Hot flashes. He means hot flashes.*

'Well. Don't worry. It's a natural part of life. You'll cope, I'm sure.' She felt patted on the head. Like his mother. *There, there, Mom.*

'Dr Adams will be in tomorrow. He'll talk to you about treatment.'

She had had time to think about it before Frank came that evening. She was, after all, relieved that she wasn't going to die. Life runs in chapters. Slowing down might not be so bad. She could resign from committees, say no to the cancer drive. She considered the twilight pleasures of long, quiet hours listening to music. An elaborate new stereo system would be of more value now than the faraway-places vacation she had been trying to get Frank to take for years. *Too late for that now. All that running around, looking for the hotel.* Frank was right.

Early the first night they had given her a sleeping pill, and she had assumed the fetal position on the hard bed, waiting for the knock-out. The TV across the hall was still going. *When you aren't watching, TV is noise, NOISE.* The male voice boomed from beyond the door, 'But Laura, going to Miami can't be as important as what's happening to your children.' Laura's voice was a soft mumble. Then the man said, 'Jimmy is ... and besides ... love you (them? me?)' 'Did you get 32?' 'Yes, 34 still needs a backrub.' Giggles overshadowing the low hum of wheels under the staccato rattle of metal. '... Jimmy. And besides ...'

Bonnie threw her body to one side and put her arms over her head. The room rolled on, revolving like a carousel, slowly, gradually, coming to a halt as she held her head very, very still. The sleeping pill – bringing back the dizzies.

Finally the TV was turned off, and only the occasional full-voiced comments of the nurses in the hall broke the silence. She had to go to the bathroom. It was hard enough when she wasn't dizzy, how could she make it after the sleeping pill? Her bladder strained to bursting before she remembered the button for summoning a nurse. It had been so long since she had called upon anyone to lean on in the night that she hadn't thought of it. So many years it had been the other way around.

She managed only a couple of hours' sleep that night, which

was no better than nights without the sleeping pill, so she refused to take one again.

The third day, after the report from Dr Brady, she asked the nurse to call her husband's office and leave a message for him to come tonight. She didn't want to call home. She didn't feel up to talking to the girls. She knew she should, they would be worried, but she couldn't.

A young woman with problems in her pregnancy had moved into the other bed that afternoon. Her company during evening visiting hours filled all the chairs. Their loud talking among themselves gave a sort of privacy to Bonnie's side of the room.

Frank had sent flowers, and he was empty-handed tonight when he pushed through the crowd around the other bed. He looked miserable, a little frightened. Different from that other male figure at the foot of the bed. Her heart went out to him, but she held up a barrier, like a silver shield, against guilt. Frank always blamed her for her small illnesses, but he seemed to know this one was different.

'How you doin', honey?'

She shrugged. 'How are you and the girls doing?'

'Oh, we're all right.' He sat tentatively on the edge of the bed. It wasn't allowed, but Bonnie rejected the responsibility. 'They're finding out they can cook. It's good for them.'

Linda was living at the sorority house by then, but the other two girls were still at home.

Bonnie said, 'Dr Bradley ... Brady ... whatever ... gave me the report this afternoon ... on the tests.'

Frank leaned forward. 'What did he say?'

She laughed. It came out as a dainty snort. 'He says I'm in perfect health.'

Frank's eyes opened wider. 'But that can't be,' he said. 'There's got to be something ...'

'He says it's emotional.'

Frank stared, looking uncomfortable. 'Do you think that's possible?'

'I don't know. I didn't think so. He says I may be going into menopause. He says it lowers the threshold.'

Frank stood up and began to pace. 'I've worked hard to see that you and the kids had things. You seemed happy.'

She laughed the funny laugh again. 'I thought I was. I haven't been nervous. Just dead.'

'Dead? How dead?'

'Oh, just like I couldn't make another decision. Remembering whether I'm out of cinnamon while I'm at the grocery store, and whether your suit is still at the cleaners or if I've already picked it up, and deciding if the dog needs to go out again before I leave the house, and whether the girls' headaches are bad enough to miss school or not dry the dishes, and putting away the phone book, and folding up the papers, and hanging up the bath mat –'

'We all have to deal with details,' Frank interrupted, his voice a notch higher. 'I get tired of it too.'

'But yours are important.'

'Are you saying important decisions are easier to make than unimportant ones?'

She shook her head.

He came back to the bed and sat down and took her hand under his. 'We're not making any sense as usual, but I do know that you had trouble walking into this hospital, so something is wrong. Can women's complaints really make that happen?'

She shook her head again, and said in a tiny voice, 'I don't know.'

'Shall we call another doctor?'

'Frank, don't make me decide.'

He leaned over and kissed her. It was a small kiss, but he did it with other people in the room, and she was grateful.

'You don't have to make any more decisions until you're ready. I'll talk to Dr Adams. Just rest.'

She nodded. A few hot tears trickled out. She hadn't cried hard in years. She was all dried up.

She left the hospital two days later, still tired. She hadn't slept. The tranquillizers didn't do it, nor the shots. Some of the shots were male hormones. A little manliness in her system to balance out the inconvenience of being a woman.

She hadn't been anxious to return home. It didn't matter where she was until she walked through the door Frank held open for her. Linda was at the door, quick to embrace her. Her hair long and shiny, she was dressed in coordinated corduroy. Linda was a fashion merchandising major, long since dedicated to a career in the life a la mode. Close behind her, in jeans and gingham shirts, her other two daughters waited their turns to touch and squeeze. They looked more grown-up than she remembered. Karen, now a high school senior, was engaged and looking forward to being the first bride in the family. Fifteen-year-old Anne was always deeply immersed in her latest cause. Whether it was the plight of local black children, saving sinners, or the necessity of mapping out her life's career, everything was important. Her enthusiasm was refreshing to others, if a little taxing to her family.

The house was neat and shining. They brought her tea and cookies as if she were a guest. She knew it was only today, but it was sweet to be cared for. Like the last time she came home with a new baby.

The bed was turned down, with clean, green leaf-patterned sheets, and when she slid aching legs between the smooth, cool sheets early that evening, she already knew that things were going to get better. Anne came in and sat on the bed on top of the covers and talked awhile. She was too lovely for her fifteen years. She talked about school. Then she told her mother, 'Dr Adams called us all in, one at a time, and told us it was up to us to help you get well.' She looked at her hands twisting in her lap. 'He made me feel like it was my fault.'

'No, oh, no,' Bonnie said. 'It's nobody's fault. The time comes when you have to stop and refuel. Maybe I need to think about where my energies should go. You children won't be around much longer.'

Anne's big brown eyes glistened, and her chin quivered. 'Mom, I thought when the doctor wanted to talk to me that he was going to tell me you were dying.'

'Oh, Anne, darling.'

Anne buried her face in the pillow, her cheek pushing into the hollow next to her mother's neck. Bonnie turned over and put her arms tight around Anne and they lightly rocked, releasing the warm women's tears. The spring was not dry. When they straightened up and smiled and kissed good night, Anne left and Bonnie resumed the bliss of weeping. Her limbs no longer felt paralyzed, only heavy.

She fell asleep and did not come fully awake for twelve hours. But in the midst of her weariness and dreams, she roused to the gentle touch, the asking, that for twenty years had been the bond with the man in her bed. Again and again in the daylight hours, in their clothes, surrounded by possessions and the other people in their lives, they reached out in different directions and slipped past each other, coming out in opposite corners of the room. But once in a while, as on this half-conscious, dreamy night, they found each other, happy that it could happen sometimes. Bonnie was to learn that during the menopausal years she would have the extra bonus of sharpened sensuality. Orgasm came sweet and easy, as it had during pregnancy ... a compensation from nature for womanly endurance.

After the nightmare struggle with Jell-O knees and floating vision, she surrendered to immobility, accepting assistance and love from her family. In a few weeks she was able to gradually reassume the small tasks that had overcome her ... still tedious and dull, but taken on again with renewed strength. When she started going out again, she reevaluated her priorities, and discovered that guilt did not necessarily follow every *no*.

It was not long before the girls were again dropping their clothes on the floor in their rooms, amid the Coke bottles and wayward hair rollers, and being honked for by friends before the dishes were done. Bonnie pulled shut their doors, and loaded the dishwasher herself. Frank had again begun returning to the office in the evening or closing himself off in the den.

She found that in a house no longer filled with little people, she could read the books that had waited so long, write poetry again, and contemplate who she was, as distinct from family and friends. But it was to be a long time still before she would find out how separate she really was.

Four

The movement into the midst of a mass of people fired with enthusiasm for a common cause intoxicated Bonnie. She passed through the New York convention week a few feet off the ground. She listened intently, occasionally took her turn at the microphone, and filled a notebook with scribblings to be deciphered and incorporated into speeches at home. She was already booked for the Rotarians and the Women's Club.

Close friendships formed quickly, born of the temporary total involvement. She hadn't been close to her fellow Earth Savers in Lancaster. They had other interests needing their time, and she was shy about pushing herself onto people. She had wondered, sometimes, what people would think if they knew that underneath she was somebody else. Bonnie now found a common bond with Sir Grahme, balding banker from Ohio, and his beautiful white-haired wife, Madge. Madge was a highly successful organizer and their money was important to the cause. Bonnie did not contribute as much as she would have liked because it seemed unfair to Frank – giving his money to a cause to which he was not sympathetic. Special, too, were Cal and Mary Briggs from Pittsburgh. They ran a health food store. Mary was noticeably pregnant; Cal had a beard; and they both wore blue jeans most of the time. Frank would call them hippies.

Bonnie didn't miss a meeting, and Anne greeted her weary mother at the apartment each night with a hot drink, a little small talk, and early quiet to crawl into bed by, with a book.

The book was a prop. Bonnie never turned the page. Bedtime was the time to think about Friday. During the day she pushed away conscious thoughts of John, but stole anxious second looks at every man over thirty-five she saw at the hotel.

Bonnie had one bad moment when a striking blonde girl with

128

long, graceful legs, stopped to talk to a group of people ahead of her. Beads of perspiration formed in hidden places before logic came through. This girl was no more than twenty-five. She couldn't be Sara – Sara'd be older looking.

Anne lingered one night to talk. She came to the door as Bonnie finished rereading her letter from Frank. He had dictated it to his secretary. At the bottom, after signing 'Love, Frank,' he had scrawled in his almost illegible hand, 'Miss you, every night.' She supposed he had handed it back to Miss Nolan for dispatch with the rest of the mail.

'I had one, too,' Anne said. 'From Bill. He's in Rome.'

'Did you? When's he coming back?'

'Didn't say.'

Bonnie pulled off her glasses and held the tip of an ear piece against her lip.

'How long have you known Bill, Anne?'

'Over a year. He was one of the first people I met here. I knew right away that I wanted him.' She leaned her head and shoulders against the door frame. 'Of course, we really got acquainted after he moved in – between trips.'

'Do you think this might lead to marriage?'

Anne's wide eyes looked into Bonnie's. They held sadness, cupped tentatively behind large pupils before she blinked it away. She straightened and walked over to adjust a crooked window shade. 'No.'

'You sound sure.'

'Just being realistic.'

Bonnie dropped the glasses on the bed beside her. 'I see.'

Anne sat on the foot of the bed and smoothed the spread where it dipped from Bonnie's knees.

Bonnie said, 'You didn't sound this way Monday. Something in the letter?'

'Not really.' She looked at her sandals. 'He's got someone over there. I can tell.'

'Maybe that's not it. Don't assume too much from one letter. People have moods.'

'No, I know. He'd tell me if I asked.'

Bonnie sighed. 'Well, wait until he comes back. You'll get to talk to him face to face. You can clear it up then.'

'I intend to.'

Should I talk about it to her? 'I'm nervous about tomorrow.'

Anne stared without comment before catching her breath. 'Oh, you mean seeing him tomorrow night? Why are you nervous?'

Bonnie leaned forward. 'Why am I nervous? For heaven's sake, what a question!'

Anne laughed uneasily. 'You're still very attractive, Mom. I'll bet he'll be surprised.'

Bonnie shrugged. 'I've changed a lot.'

'Well, of course, you have.'

Like a revelation she heard the sound of John's voice, *'Thirty years from now you'll be a gentle old lady in a shawl with our grandchildren gathered around you . . .'*

I can't see him now, I can't destroy his memory of me. I've been deceiving myself. How disgusting.

Anne stood up. 'Well, you'd better get your beauty sleep. Don't lose your nerve. Just walk right up to him. See how he acts.'

She doesn't understand. Bonnie said, 'Good night, I hope things work out right for you.'

Anne nodded and walked to the doorway where she stopped and looked back. 'You too,' she said unsmiling.

Bonnie switched off the lamp, turned over and pulled the sheet over her shoulders.

Complex girl, this youngest child. An honour student in college, she spurned her sister's sorority to throw herself into serious campus business. Life was earnest, life was real for students in the sixties.

Bonnie was working on a mailing for the Playhouse Guild when Anne's dormitory roommate, Susan, had interrupted with a phone call one Sunday evening in the spring of 1969.

'Annie asked me to call.' She stopped talking and Bonnie impatiently tapped on the desk with the pen she had carried to the phone.

'Yes, Susan?'

'She won't be home tonight.'

'Oh? And she asked you to call?' Anne was always good about calling.

'Yeah. She's – well, she's spending the night in the ROTC building.'

She's decided to join the ROTC – the first woman.

'What did you say, Susan? She's spending the night where?'

'In the ROTC Building. It's a peace protest. They're occupying the building.'

'They're *what*? Good Lord, Susan, who's they? Did you say occupying?'

'We're protesting the military presence on the campus, Mrs Forbes. It's a nonviolent occupation.'

'We? Are you in it, too?'

'Well, I was. But my uncle from Indiana is coming this weekend and I haven't seen him for years.' Her voice choked up and stopped, then continued. 'My dad said I should come home. But they're right, Mrs Forbes. Somebody has to stand up and be counted.'

'So, wouldn't you know it would be Anne. Oh, Susan, what are you kids thinking of? Do they have guns?'

'Of course not.' Susan's voice was suddenly cold. 'We don't need guns. Not even if they use force against us. We're peace protesters.'

Bonnie had been tolerant of the peace marches, but she had toned down protest talk at home. Perhaps Frank was right. They should have taken a stronger stand.

'What's the university doing? What will happen to them?'

'The police are just standing around outside. A lot of people are milling around. I'm surprised you didn't hear it on the news.'

Bonnie had a vague recollection of seeing police cars around a building on television while she was stirring the gravy. She hadn't realized it was local.

'The police. You say the police are there?'

'They weren't doing anything. If they do arrest us, we'll just go to jail, peacefully.'

'What do you mean "we," Susan? You're home with your uncle.'

After a brief silence she heard a click followed by a dial tone. Bonnie's numb fingers fumbled with the phone book. *Susan – Susan – Johnson, that's it*. She finally found the number and dialled it. Susan answered immediately.

'I'm sorry, Susan,' she said. 'Forgive me. I appreciate your calling. Where is this ROTC Building?'

Susan placed the location in Bonnie's mind. *So that's what that building is.*

After Susan hung up, Bonnie sat by the phone and lifted the receiver twice, each time replacing it slowly. Frank had gone back to the office. The need for his decisive presence pushed her towards calling him, but at the same time a warning voice pulled her back. She sat for several minutes by the telephone. What, exactly, could he do? *He'll know what to do. He's good in emergencies.* But what help could he be? Ask his friend, the chief of police, to go easy on the one with the long, black hair and big mouth? Anne was good at making speeches. Call her out of the building and order her home? Bonnie shuddered. Sit with Bonnie and hold her hand and wait it out? *That's the one. That's what he could do.* She reached for the phone again – dialled one number, hung up, then stood up and hurried to the bedroom to change her clothes.

What to wear to a sit-in? She dug in the drawer and pulled out an old pair of Anne's jeans, a tight fit over her slender hips. A loose sweater pulled over her head, an old suede jacket, and she was ready to go.

She drove the small car, leaving it some distance from the campus, and walked towards the Student Union. Things appeared normal there, but she could see people walking towards a gathered crowd a few blocks ahead. The students along the way were calm. They could have been strolling to the movies or a rock concert. Across the street from the building, they stood in groups – watching and talking.

She counted three police cars. *Blue and white campus police. The national guard arrival must not be imminent, if the city police aren't here yet.* She wondered about the men talking earnestly with the men in uniform. *Plainclothes detectives? University officials?*

She continued around the building. There was no audience in back, but an officer sat in his car, leaning back, observing the door. Her shaking knees carried her up the walk. A car door slammed and she heard footsteps behind her. She turned around.

The officer smiled. 'Looking for someone?' he asked.

'Yes,' she answered. 'I think my daughter's in there. I'd like to talk to her.'

He nodded sympathetically. 'I don't know,' he said slowly. 'I'll see what I can do. Want to wait a minute?'

She stayed where she was while he went to the door and knocked. He talked to someone who summoned someone else. She could see a person with lots of hair and an unkempt beard. The officer still wore his winter uniform – dark trousers neatly creased, shoes shined, necktie in place. He stood on the outside stoop, conferring with the kid on the inside. Uncombed, unpressed – unwashed? Authority deferring to anarchy. The officer motioned for her and she hurried to join him.

The hair and beard surrounded eyes that were blue and sharp – eyes that looked at her with a certain amount of hostility.

'What's your daughter's name?' the officer asked.

She told him and saw a light appear in the man's eyes. He looked at Bonnie closely, then stepped back and motioned her inside. 'Come on in,' he said.

Bonnie looked back at the officer, then slowly went in. The door closed behind her. Her guide led her through a dark hall and down to the other end where, in dim light, two sentries sat by a door. They sat in desk chairs, probably pulled from a classroom. One was reading a book, the other stared out the glass door at the crowd across the street.

She had to run a little to keep up with her guide's long-legged pace. As they descended the stairs, she realized this was where everybody was – in the basement. The hall was full of people, and at the end of it a door opened into a large room where there were more people. They lay on the floor, or sat in small groups talking quietly. Some leaned against the wall with their eyes closed.

A boy in military surplus dungarees sat with his arm around a girl. Her head rested on his shoulder. She was a plain girl, her features unaccented by makeup, hair skinned back tightly into a little bun. She wore round gold-rimmed glasses like the ones that had belonged to Bonnie's grandmother. A strange little Granny with smooth, fresh skin in an oversized blue workshirt and tight, worn Levis.

Bonnie looked back to see the bearded one coming towards her with Anne following him. She was a colourless sparrow like the rest of them – deliberately blending into the grey mass –

133

personifying their joyless state. The thick brown hair was pulled back and clamped low on her neck so that it lay flat against the faded Levi's jacket. Bonnie braced herself.

'Mother!' Anne spoke in a frightened whisper. 'What are you doing here?'

Bonnie's throat was dry. She straightened to her full height; her daughter still stood above her. 'I wanted to see what was happening. I didn't know they'd let me in.'

'I'm not leaving.'

'I'm not asking you to.' *Why are you here? Convince me you're right.*

Anne's set jaw softened. 'Don't worry, Mom. We just want to make a point. We have to be heard.'

Why this way? What will people say? 'All right. I'm not interfering. I'd just like to understand.'

The beard wiggled a little, and the blue eyes challenged. 'You can join us. It's an open cause.'

She looked at him sharply. 'What are you trying to prove? Tell me.'

'We're protesting the American military presence in Viet Nam in an unnecessary, immoral war. The ROTC represents the military on campus.'

'But what do you expect to gain?'

'Attention.' His voice was quiet but his eyes were fiery. 'They're asking for our lives, lady, and those people out there,' he made a wide gesture with his arm, 'they don't know there's a war on. The fuckin' military doesn't give a shit about human beings. Us or them.'

'You're exempt while you're in school – '

'What the hell does that mean? Some other hungry bastard, my fellow American, has to back up the system in my place.'

Anne laid her hand on his arm. 'Easy, Joe.'

He put his hand over Anne's and held it. 'I'm sorry, Mrs Forbes,' he said, 'I'm just telling it like it is.'

Bonnie nodded. 'I'm sympathetic. Anne knows that. But I'm not sure about the method.'

'We're sure,' he said, closing the matter. 'Excuse me, hon,' he said to Anne. 'They want me over there.' He spoke to Bonnie as he left. 'Stick around. See what you can learn.'

Arrogant S.O.B.

'I don't think you should stay, Mom,' Anne said uneasily. 'We think things will go okay, but we can't be sure.'

'I know I embarrass you by being here. I won't stay.'

'I'm not embarrassed. I'm not a kid.'

She's nineteen. Older than I was at nineteen. What about her and Joe? All that hair.

She left Anne and headed for the stairs where Joe was talking to a sandy-haired, slender man. Bonnie pulled back quickly. She recognized the man. He was a reporter from the *News* who had done some articles involving Frank. *'Frank Forbes's lovely wife, active in community volunteer work.'* Shivering at the thought of how Frank and his company would react to publicity that gave her a part in *this* story, she moved back into the gymnasium.

The strum of a guitar and the recorded blue denim and straw voice of Bob Dylan floated a layer above the dull hum in the room. Dylan twanged of refugees, the luckless, the outcasts, of the gentle and the kind, equating the conditions of these characters at a time when the flower children were going to jail. A torn placard was propped against the wall. 'Give a Damn,' it said. In a corner a group passed around a roughly formed hand-rolled cigarette. She wondered at the shortage of cigarettes. It was grass, of course. She had been naive about such things then.

She was still there, sitting alone in the back of the room when President Walker came in and the group drew slowly around him. Some stayed seated on the edges, listening. She saw young backs straightened, shoulders steadied to support the chips on them, eyes brightening with anticipation and excitement.

He stood out in the room in his conservative dark suit, a tall man with iron-grey hair. His voice was calm, his manner uncondescending but firm.

'We appreciate the sincerity of your convictions. Some members of the faculty have supported your efforts in the past. We have voted not to prosecute anyone involved in this matter, provided,' he paused significantly, 'provided there is no damage to school property. We will not interfere with your sit-in tonight. However, anyone still on the premises after 7.00 tomorrow morning will be arrested and jailed. You can talk this over. I hope that you will feel we have handled the matter fairly. The administration has a duty to the community. We also feel we have a duty to our student body of which you are a significant part, although by no means a majority.'

After he left, the debate began. Slowly at first, gradually growing more bitter. Many voices were heard, including Anne's, but from the first the prime voices were those of Joe and Carla. An English department graduate student and instructor, Carla rallied behind her a small but very vocal group of radicals.

The blunt ends of her shiny straight blonde hair reached the middle of her back and her flared miniskirt and neat blouse were strangely at odds with her militant manner.

'Fuck him!' had been her response to the university president's proposals. 'He's gonna *let us* have our little demonstration. Pat us on the head and send us home. Jesus!'

'We've nothing to gain by shovin' it,' was Joe's fiery response. 'We're antiviolence. Use your heads for Chrissake. What are we here for?'

'There's a roomful of rifles locked up in there,' Carla said with a toss of her Rapunzel hair. Her green eyes sparked fire.

'And that's where they stay,' Joe said.

'We could dump them all in the creek.'

This suggestion found strong favour with a few. Others looked uneasy.

'All right,' Joe said. 'I guess it's time to stop bullshittin' and take a vote. Everybody who wants to tear down the door and carry off the rifles raise their hand.'

The response was negligible.

Berkeley, it was not; but coming out of the heart of Nixon country and the Bible Belt, the occupation made its mark. It was good small talk for the next company cocktail party where everyone agreed it was fortunate the protesters had straggled home the next morning before the 'Rotsy' boys came to class.

'The Rotsy boys would have shown these long-hairs where to go,' Fred Vance said, rattling his ice cubes. Bonnie watched Frank nod in firm agreement.

Anne gave a farewell party for Joe, quietly and away from home of course, when he went to jail for burning his draft card.

They tried to do it. What we couldn't do. The young, trying to vomit out war. They had no Hitler or Tojo, no Pearl Harbor or Bataan. Yet they were just as scared, just as separated, just as crippled, just as dead.

Five

It was very warm for May. Bonnie's pyjamas clung damply to her skin. She needed a good night's sleep in order to stay alert at the convention tomorrow. She squeezed her eyelids shut and slid back to another convention, another room, at the solitary hour of 3.00 AM.

July 1972

The flickering light from the television set and the lamp above it balanced the lamplight next to her chair. The last cold cup of coffee sat on the table along with remnants of salty snacks that had filled out a long, solitary evening. She had switched off the air conditioning and opened a window in the room. The open window picked up the draught coming down the hall from the bedroom, where Frank had long ago retired.

The hullabaloo ended, the speech she had waited for was about to begin. Delegates milled around the screen, signs still bobbing and dipping, despite their holders' weariness from a long day and night of choosing a candidate. A lot of people were still awake at the convention, and she wondered if she were the only one watching in Lancaster. She had been nodding at midnight, but was wide awake now.

She had shaken hands with George McGovern at the University Student Union early in the campaign. He was a tall, handsome man with long, dark hair thinning on top. Bonnie had been strangely drawn to the quiet strength of the man whom the press later suggested had no charisma. The feel of his firm hand clasping hers so briefly was with her again this evening, as she heard him implore a sleeping America to 'come home.'

> *I have no secret plan for peace. I have a public plan. As one whose heart has ached for ten years over the agony of Viet Nam, I will halt the senseless bombing of Indochina on Inauguration Day ...*
>
> *Within ninety days of my inauguration, every American soldier and every American prisoner will be out of the jungle and out of their cells and back home in America where they belong. And then let us resolve that never again will we shed the precious young blood of this nation to prop up a cruel and corrupt dictatorship ten thousand miles from our shores ...*
>
> *Come home, America ...*
> *This is the time.*

Now they'll see. It's not just the long-haired kids.

Her body jerked as the telephone bell shattered the silence. She grabbed it up to interrupt the second ring.

'Mom, were you watching?'

She could hear mixed loud voices behind Anne's words. Somebody was awake in Lancaster. 'I heard,' she answered.

'They didn't think we could do it! We're going out for a victory breakfast.'

'Celebrate for me.'

She put down the phone and looked about the family room, richly furnished in dark walnut and leather – sombre when one stood alone in the early morning hours, inside solid panelled walls.

She set Frank's plate of bacon and eggs on the table at the same moment he came into the bright breakfast room and joined him, pouring the coffee after they were seated.

Frank was freshly shaven, faintly fragrant, his curly white hair still damp from the shower. He looked complete in his dark suit and maroon striped tie. Her long nightgown showed beneath the clean striped brunch coat, and she hadn't used lipstick this morning.

'You were late coming to bed,' he said.

She nodded. 'I wanted to hear the acceptance speech.'

'Beats me how you can sit and watch all that political hoopla. Grown-up people making fools of themselves.'

'It was better this year. The rule changes made it better.'

'Like scheduling their major speech after everyone was in bed? That was really smart.'

Bonnie slowly pushed the jelly over her toast. 'It was a good speech,' she said.

'Well, if you've heard one political speech, you've heard them all. I'm sure the world won't miss it.' He smiled and reached for the butter.

'He's sincere.'

'He's an idealistic fool. The American people have more sense.'

'Don't you want to hear what he said?'

'Not really, but I have a feeling I'm going to.'

Bonnie laid the toast on her plate. She compressed her lips and sat in injured silence.

Frank consumed his breakfast, appetite unaffected by the conversation, or the end of it. As he pushed back his chair he said, 'Don't forget to take my suit to the cleaners. And be sure to show them the grease spot; they don't always get it out.' He hesitated in the doorway. 'Cheer up,' he said. 'Nixon can handle it.'

She didn't look up. She stayed at the table until she heard the front door close. The sound of the car leaving the driveway was filtered through it. The last cry of the Buick tyres going around the corner towards Seventieth Street was overtaken by silence. She looked at the egg stains on the plates.

'As one whose heart has ached for ten years over the agony of Viet Nam, I will halt the senseless bombing of Indochina on Inauguration Day.'

Bracing her hands against the table edge she stood up and hurried down the hall to shower and dress in a slim blue cotton shift and flat-heeled sandals.

She was on her way through the service entrance towards the garage when she remembered the bed and went back to pull the king-sized spread over it. A quick stop in the kitchen to clear the table and load the dishwasher, and she was off.

The storefront was small, the large letters MCGOVERN FOR PRESIDENT stretched across the upper third of the plate glass

139

window. The doors stood open, and Bonnie felt the outside heat barely modified when she stepped through. Papers on the tables around the room rustled slightly in the breeze stirred up by the two big electric fans.

A man lay stretched out on an army cot, breathing deeply and regularly. His butterscotch-coloured hair was awry, straggling across the arm tucked under his cheek. A red shadow darkened his chin where whiskers sprouted, darker than his hair. Flesh above the shadow looked smooth and brown.

As she hesitated, her quiet staring communicated. The eyelids half opened, and the man jerked himself upright to stare blankly at her with red-rimmed blue eyes.

'I'm sorry,' she said.

He stared, raised his hand stiffly to his head. His eyes slowly focussed.

'You didn't get any sleep last night.'

'Right. Thought I could last till noon.' He struggled to his feet, overcompensating with quick movements. 'What can I do for you?'

'I came to volunteer. Sorry if I'm too early.'

'Don't be sorry.' He squinted at her and her cheeks grew warm.

'I can type ... '

He held out a wide hand. 'Rick Baker.'

'Bonnie Forbes.'

'Sit down. I'll get coffee.'

She pulled a folding chair away from the cluttered table and sat in it.

'Guess we didn't make it yet this morning,' she heard Rick say.

Bonnie was on her feet. 'Can I do it? You're tired.'

Rick waved her away and carried the large coffeemaker to the sink on the back wall. 'Don't get off to a bad start.'

She slowly sank back into the chair, liking it here already.

'I know all about the hazards of volunteering,' he said in a loud voice from across the room, 'from the Army.'

'Are you a Viet Nam veteran?'

'Yeah, I was in Nam.'

When they were settled, he talked to her about plans. 'We

need wisdom and experience to harness all this youthful energy. How are you at organization?'

'I've been president of everything.'

'Terrific. You're going to be important here.'

People drifted in. By early afternoon bodies and noise filled the room. Rick introduced her to Jan something-or-other before he left. She wore tight jeans and a wrinkled T-shirt. Her smile was quick and warm, and Bonnie asked her, 'Who is he, anyway? Is he in charge here?'

Jan nodded. 'He's the organizer sent in before the primary. He'll stick around to get us going in our new quarters.'

'Did you work on the primary?'

'Worked my butt off. Nice to win.' Bonnie liked Jan's short black hair and sparse makeup. She had flair, but was natural.

Jan's husband, a botany professor at the university, joined them occasionally. He was a big man, towering over his wife, but gentle, like an oversized dog.

Bonnie learned to make decisions without agonizing over them, to walk faster, to speak positively. Rushing home from headquarters, she managed each day to grab an apron and put dinner together on time. As she sat quietly at the table listening to Frank, she was careful not to mention sore feet or problems in her day. If there was telephoning to do at night, she waited until Frank vanished back into his own busy world at the office or in the den. He knew she was doing volunteer work for the Democratic Party, but he did not realize the extent of her involvement. He never faced an unmade bed or an unwashed shirt because of it. The subject of politics was mutually understood to be off limits.

Since social afternoons had been left behind, she found herself looking forward to dressing up for a dinner party at Clem and Eva's. It was a night to have her hair done and wear diamond earrings and a low-cut neckline. The company president was entertaining his two top executives and their wives. The little group had been friends for a long time.

Bonnie and Frank were the last to arrive, and as she handed over her little velvet coat, Bonnie was surprised to see Jenny Ames posed on the brocade sofa. How beautiful Jenny looked in her short, revealing dress. Frank moved on into the other room with the men. Only later did Bonnie think about the significance of the new younger couple in the group. Even then she had not realized the fear that must have been planted in Frank's mind. George Ames was moving in.

Eva sat down on the edge of a chair, looking for attention after Bonnie's arrival. 'Well,' she said with an expectant look around the circle. 'I have news this evening I can't wait to tell you.'

They all watched and waited.

'I'll bet some of your husbands have already told you what happened at yesterday's board meeting.'

No response.

'Well,' she started again, 'anyway – we're going to get it. The Playhouse. The grant from the company.'

A murmur passed around, like a sigh.

'The Board voted to underwrite Playhouse expenses for the next five years.'

The sigh expanded.

'We can start tomorrow morning to make specific plans. Full-time paid director, a new building. We should be rolling by the first of the year.'

Eva's eyes returned to Bonnie. Through some peculiar protocol, she was second in command to Eva here, just as Frank was next to Clem.

Bonnie tried to sound enthusiastic. 'Maybe we can improve upon the quality of the plays, too.'

Eva's head jerked slightly. *Mistake. Eva is chairman of the play-reading committee.* 'I think there's a danger in going too intellectual. Let the university theatre do that.'

'That's right, Eva,' Bonnie heard. 'Let's face it, the average playgoer in Lancaster can't handle much beyond Neil Simon.' Bonnie shot a quick look at Dorothy Vance.

Eva continued. 'I want you, dear friends, to be the steering committee. Plan to give some full days next week, working together and at home on the phone.

'Bonnie, we've missed you this year. I'd like to see you take charge of finding and hiring the new director.'

'I'm flattered, Eva, I am.' *Careful, careful.* 'But I couldn't get started on it,' she said, 'until after the election.'

A faint smile touched Eva's mouth. 'The election? What does that have to do with it?'

'I'm working – working on the campaign.'

'I didn't know that,' Eva said, as though she should have been informed. Her smile broadened. 'Now, Bonnie, don't we all know that Mr Nixon will get elected with our without your help? Isn't there more challenge in the job I'm offering?'

Bonnie squirmed and shifted her feet. 'He won't if I can help it – I'm working for McGovern.'

In the corner of her eye, as she and Eva spoke, she had seen Clem come into the room. Frank was with him. They were all caught in a block of silence until Clem said, 'Brenda says she can serve dinner any time we're ready.'

'Well,' Eva said, moving out of her chair, 'perhaps it's time. We'll get back to this later.'

Bonnie managed to avoid eye contact with her husband as they moved towards the dining room. After twenty-seven years of living with Frank, she could sense his mood without seeing him. He was upset.

Clem didn't look seventy – he was a big man and handsome. Bonnie sat on his right at dinner. He had always seemed awesome and mature to her. He had already been a vice-president at Scott when Bonnie had gone to work there during the war, as Frank Forbes's secretary.

Fred Vance was at her other side, and Jenny Ames across, next to Frank. It was at this point she wondered why the Ameses were there. And was Jenny seated close to Clem because she was the only lady at the table under forty? *Unfair. Those were only rumours.*

They had finished the shrimp cocktail and consommé when Clem sat back and turned his magnetic gaze upon Bonnie.

'So, Bonnie, you've gone over to the Democrats.'

'I've always been a Democrat, Clem.'

'Well, they can use all the help they can get. You ladies need your little projects.'

The room was oppressively warm. She said, 'I think it's important.'

Clem nodded slightly. 'I'm sorry. I didn't mean to put you down. I think many of the ladies' projects are important. I'm as enthused as Eva over the company grant to the community theatre.'

Bonnie nodded. 'Yes, it's exciting.'

She looked at Frank. His face was a thundercloud.

Fred Vance said, 'McGovern doesn't have a prayer in this state. People here are leery of radicals.'

'I admire your sincerity,' Clem continued to Bonnie. 'I hate to see it misplaced.' He laughed politely.

Jenny leaned forward and breathed into her first statement. 'I will be thrilled to help with the theatre. I can't believe I'm going to be on the steering committee.'

Clem turned to her. 'Have you done any acting?'

'Mercy, no.'

'I thought maybe you had. You have the presence for it.'

The shape, Clem. It's her shape.

Brenda began serving plates from a cart.

Bonnie said to Fred, 'Aren't the people in this state bothered by the Watergate burglary?'

Jenny blinked. 'The what?'

'Watergate.' Bonnie looked hard at Jenny, who looked confused until Clem came to her rescue.

'It seems the Republicans got in a little campaign monkey business,' he explained. 'This sort of thing goes on all the time; these guys happened to get caught.' He glanced at Bonnie. 'You can be sure the Democrats will make the most of it.'

'It's just politics,' Fred said.

'George says McGovern is for pot and abortion,' Jenny said. 'That he isn't nice and steady like Nixon.'

'And what do you think?' Bonnie asked.

Jenny levelled her violet eyes at Bonnie. 'I think McGovern talks like Liberace.'

A titter passed around their end of the table. Jenny looked pleased.

Bonnie set her jaw. 'Nice, steady Nixon isn't stopping the war.'

'You can't just *stop* a war,' Fred said with a polite little smile.

'We have to prevent a bloodbath,' Jenny added with growing confidence.

'*Why* can't we stop it?' Bonnie's voice quivered as it crescendoed towards shrillness. 'They're all dying, for nothing, and you don't want to be bothered.'

All conversation had stopped and everyone was looking at her. Bonnie squeezed her eyes shut. She covered her contorted face with one hand.

'Well, as for me, I'll take some of that chicken,' Clem's voice boomed out. 'Brenda has outdone herself tonight.' Everyone started talking about the chicken.

Bonnie steeled herself to remain at the table. She fiercely wiped her eyes and straightened up. She was so lonely. When Frank joined her after dinner, she thought how good it would be if he would squeeze her hand. He looked at everyone but her, and didn't get close enough for her dress to brush his leg. She dreaded the ride home.

She hardly spoke during the rest of the evening. Goodbyes were pleasant. She told herself that she had been far more upset by the outburst than anyone else.

In the blue Buick, she leaned her head back. Her closed eyes suddenly came open when she heard Frank's voice, soft, but razor-sharp. 'That was a hell of a show. You sure as hell did it tonight.'

She sighed.

Frank's voice grew louder. 'Why do you do that, Bonnie? Why do you always rock the boat?'

She answered in a monotone. 'I'm sorry, I didn't mean to.'

'What do you mean, you didn't mean to? How do you do it every time when you don't mean to? What the hell does that mean?'

Her voice grew more animated. 'It means I don't plan ahead to embarrass you.' She forced herself to look at him. 'Once in a while I have to be myself. Do you have any idea what it's like to always be wrong when I'm myself?'

Frank's face looked lined and old. Grim. 'I don't ask much of you, Bonnie. I haven't complained about this campaigning, have I?' He waited. Said again, louder, 'Have I?' She was frightened by the remoteness of his eyes.

She said 'No,' hating being forced to say it.

He jammed on the brakes at a red light. Then quickly slid the car around the corner in a right turn.

'Well, it's your own fault. Now, you're going to have to stop the campaigning.'

Her nerves suddenly came alive. 'Oh, no,' burst out of her. 'Frank, please don't ask me to do that. Please.'

His voice was settling. 'Eva's counting on you to help with the theatre thing. She even talked to me yesterday, asked me to let her break the news tonight. She expected you to be thrilled.'

Bonnie racked her brain for the right words. 'I'll help. After the election. I'll do a good job for her.'

'That's six weeks. She needs you now.'

Bonnie bit her lip. 'You're the one on the company payroll, not me.'

'You know that's bullshit!'

She did know it was bullshit.

They rode the next mile without speaking. She formed the words carefully. 'I think Clem admires my having convictions.'

'He also believes wives should put their husbands' careers first. I'm sixty. Ames is thirty-nine. Five years ago I was the coming president. Tonight I'm not so sure.'

I won't do it. He can't do this to me. She went to sleep holding to this conviction. She woke up knowing that she would do it.

Monday mornings were quiet at headquarters. Bonnie went in early to talk to Rick. She joined him as he finished visiting with some new young volunteers. When they left, he leaned back and grinned. 'More house-to-house canvassers for you. We'll get some mileage out of those two.'

Bonnie nodded feebly, and looked out the plate glass window where a woman was passing with a white poodle on a leash.

'We're sending in reservatins for the dinner,' he said. 'Put you down for two?'

She shook her head. 'Frank wouldn't be caught dead at a Democratic fund-1aising dinner.'

'I don't have a date,' she heard him say. 'How about going with me?'

How sweet. What a sweet gesture. 'I'm going to quit, Rick.'

He stood up. 'Hey, come on.'

'It's true. I'm on my way to another meeting; I'm not going to have time.'

He looked like she had struck him, she couldn't understand. 'Did somebody step on your toes?'

'You know better than that.'

'Well, what then?'

She sighed. 'It's a conflict at home. Frank asked me to.'

Rick said softly, 'Christ, what a fuckin' pile of shit!'

She steadied herself against the desk, stammering. 'No, you don't understand. It's important. Thirty years with the company, I can't jeopardize Frank's promotion for six more weeks of my little job.'

'Little job! Jobs like this can change the country – the world.'

She tried to swallow the lump. 'Not really,' she said. 'Somebody else can do it.'

'Bonnie Forbes can do it, you know that? What'll it mean to you to let somebody else do it?'

She took a deep breath. 'I really don't think you need to get belligerent.'

Rick threw up his hands. 'Okay. Okay.'

Stinging from the attack, Bonnie looked around the desk. *Is that my stapler?* 'A lot of the ground work is done,' she said, fumbling with papers. 'Maybe Jan can handle some of my people along with hers now. And Anne can come in more –' Bonnie had been trying to throw her daughter and Rick together for weeks. 'Well, thanks, I guess,' she said finally. 'I didn't know I was this important.'

'You really don't know, do you?' he said slowly. 'How important you could be?'

The front door closed. Others were coming in.

'I can still do some mailing at home. Have someone call me.'

He nodded and turned away.

She put her things in a little box, erasing herself too quickly from the room. When she reached for her coat she saw Rick had come back. 'I'm sorry, Bonnie,' he said. 'I don't know why I did that.'

'It's what I have to do,' she replied anxiously. 'I don't want to.'

Rick nodded, but his eyes were dark again, and she felt he was tasting bitter unsaid words. 'Appreciate the help you gave us. You did a good job,' he said before he walked away.

After the ties were cut, she didn't see much of the campaign crowd until election night. She found it painful to go back – the familiar room was like a reminder of an old love affair. But she did go back on election night to mingle her tears with theirs. Quiet, unashamed tears were shared in a room silent as death during the concession speech.

They had come in braced for defeat, but as they saw one state after another reaffirming Nixon – the count rolling towards the worst defeat in United States history – the bitter taste galled. One of the student volunteers wept noisily, not bothering to wipe her glistening face. Bonnie put her arms around the girl's shoulders and hugged her.

'How can they do that?' the girl sobbed. 'Nobody cares.'

'McGovern cares too much,' Bonnie answered. 'They don't trust a caring man.'

She looked around her, loving them, grateful for their tears.

This was a Valium night. Bonnie rolled out of bed to find the bottle.

Six

Bonnie walked in the dark across the end of Anne's living room, striding towards the switch inside the bathroom door. The streetlight outside filtered through the sheer curtains, giving her a clear view of the window side of the room. She gasped as one of the shapes framed by the window became human. She recognized Anne's still profile. Anne sat in the overstuffed chair, more stationary than the curtain that moved gently with an occasional breeze. Through the window, sounds of distant traffic were dotted with a roar when a car sped through this quiet block.

Bonnie contemplated her daughter. Their crusader, settled back into her putty-coloured sitting room. Without benefit of clergy, committing herself to her absent man. Her mother's way rejected, but ultimately imitated.

'Anne?' she said, as she walked towards the windows.

Anne turned quickly. 'Mom?'

Bonnie walked over and sat on the sofa. 'I couldn't sleep either.'

Anne's bare legs curled beneath her. She wore a long T-shirt over her flowered bikini panties. Bonnie felt outdated in her man-tailored pink nylon pyjamas.

'What's it like, Mom, to have your life all settled? To not have to worry about the future?'

'If that were true, I would find it grim. It's called growing old.'

'Is it terribly hard, having your children grown and on their own?'

'Of course not.'

'But you were depressed ten years ago. We all worried. I felt like it was my fault.'

Bonnie shook her head. 'I don't know what caused it. I've always had a good life. Sometimes when women are forty they just run out of gas. One day I couldn't make all the silly little motions one more time. Deciding what to cook – on everybody's different schedule; and deciding whether to shorten my dress again; and asking you to clean your room again; and cleaning the spots off the bathroom mirror again; and remembering whether I shut off the iron.' Even the words made her weary. 'But you all helped me. I was able to get back on the track.'

'Yuck!' Anne put her feet on the floor. 'I make Bill clean up his own spots.'

Bonnie stood up. She churned with anger. And guilt about the anger.

'You're always telling me not to talk to Daddy about it,' Anne said. 'You and he don't talk much either, do you?'

Bonnie walked to the other end of the sofa. She would love a cigarette, but Anne wouldn't like it. 'We talk, but if we go very deep, we disagree. We've learned to stay on the surface.'

Anne's tone became less confident. 'Do you still love him?'

Bonnie lifted her chin. 'Of course I do. We've been through so much together. And our sex life is good.' She sat down. 'He's a very virile man, you know. He's never had a problem – even though he is past sixty.'

No answer from the other chair. 'Anne, what's the matter? Lord, I do believe you're embarrassed.'

'You never talked like this.' Anne's voice was small. 'I mean sex was always theoretical, not specific.'

149

'But parents do do it, you know. And not just three times for you and your sisters.' Bonnie was suddenly embarrassed, also. Grateful for the dark.

'It's him. Ever since you saw his picture, you've been different.'

'I've been thinking all week about when I was young. When I was all in one piece – before I sectioned myself out. I didn't know then how good it could be. If I could just – '

' – have known then what you know now. It's already been said, Mother.'

'Do you remember when I worked on the McGovern campaign?'

'Yes. What made you think of that?'

Bonnie's mind returned to those months when she had made a magnificent gesture (in her life of gentle moves) directed against a war that had become horrendous enough that its end was the simple answer.

'I guess I thought of it because I feel the way I did then.'

'How?'

'Alive. Yes – just – alive.'

'You quit, just because Dad asked you to. I guess you felt your first loyalty was to your family. When it comes down to it, the few people close to us matter more than the masses out there.'

Why did she feel choked? 'It was more than Frank's personal prejudice, I think I would have fought that. It was because of the situation at the plant. I was an embarrassment to him. He thought I wasn't acting like a company president's wife. He wanted to be president very much, you know.'

'Yes.'

They were both thinking that this battle, too, was over.

'Dad is doing his suffering alone.'

'He's always alone. I can't reach him, Anne. So many years I've tried. We keep reaching, and not touching.'

She knew that her confidante was distressed. *I shouldn't say it to her.* But Bonnie was tired of guilt. It felt so good to say it.

Anne could handle it, after all. Her voice sounded okay when she said a minute later, 'I'm still young. What should I do?'

'Don't be afraid to take the good things that show up.'

Through the dark, she saw her child, and added in a less sturdy voice, 'But be careful.'

Seven

Bonnie sat quietly through the morning seminar. At lunch break, she picked up her overloaded bag and scooted quickly for the door. Her decision to skip the afternoon meeting grew firmer when she emerged into the beautiful, mellow day. The noontime sun shone in the slits between the buildings here and there with exceptional brightness for the city. Its warmth seeped into her limps, and she stood on a street corner, feeling it.

The nearness of a corner telephone booth dared her to put a random thought into action. She stepped inside, closed the door snugly behind her, looked up the number of the hotel she had just left, and dialled.

'I'd like to speak to Mrs John Blake, please.' She waited, ready to hang up the phone before the call was completed.

The operator returned. 'I'm sorry. Mrs Blake is not registered. We have a Mr John Blake. Would you like me to connect you?' Her heart gave a little leap.

'No. No, thank you.' *Not yet.* She fumbled with the receiver as she hung it up.

Mrs Blake is not registered. How strange to say the name again. It used to be mine.

She folded back the door and took a deep breath of fresh air. *So, you didn't come along, Sara. Too bad.*

Stacks of green, blue, and gold luggage with large black price tags, five foolish puppies, lingerie in black and white next to a fan of panty hose – the succession of shopwindows registered in her eyes, but not in her thoughts. She walked without direction.

SEX! The sign was taller than she was. It stood next to a box office the size of the phone booth. 'Confessions of a Cheer Leader' and 'The Waitresses' said a smaller sign above some still photographs. Bonnie resisted the impulse to look around before she moved closer. The pictures showed naked couples in interesting but unrevealing positions. X-RATED. POSITIVELY NO ADMITTANCE TO ANYONE UNDER 18. *I'm over eighteen.* She bought a ticket and went in.

There was no ticket taker or popcorn. An accommodating darkness immediately closed around her, and she stood uncertainly, uncomfortable with the awareness of being seen when she couldn't yet see.

On the large screen the cheerleaders were doing their thing at a game. They waved their pom-poms and jumped around to reveal cute thighs under their little pleated skirts.

She squeezed past a man in the back row, pressing hard against the seat in front, barely brushing his knees with the backs of hers. He moved his legs and she stumbled in her haste to slide into the seat. She held her arms tightly to her sides and kept her eyes on the screen.

As the darkness receded she looked around the theatre, moving eyes more than head. The place was very small, and it was crowded. *What kind of people come to a place like this?* Silhouettes did not reveal gender with any certainty, but she decided there were a few other women there. They probably had escorts. Frank had never taken her to one of these. She had tried to persuade him once, during a rare vacation without the children. Of course, he was tired from a long drive. She turned her attention to the screen.

The cheerleaders and the waitresses all had the same thing on their minds. They took their clothes off sooner and oftener than the ladies in the R-rated movies, and did a great deal of sighing and moaning. Bonnie was sorry they overdid it. The plots were slim and the acting bad. Little literary foreplay for romantic mood building. They just had at it.

She found pleasure in watching a coarse-featured man handle the waitress's breasts. His hands looked so strong and brown and his fingers moved around the girl's nipples like a musician's or surgeon's. Truck drivers would have strong hands, but this man seemed gentle.

The man sitting next to her wore dark shoes and dress trousers without cuffs. She stayed in her seat when she needed to go to the bathroom, because she didn't want to crowd in front of him again. He left in the middle of the second feature and the seat next to her remained empty.

When *The Waitresses* was over, the lights came up. Now she could see the other patrons. They looked like a cross section of people anywhere. There were, indeed, very few women in the place. Two couples came in and found seats, laughing and talking at once in high-pitched voices as though they asked to be seen as unsophisticated visitors.

As the lights dimmed she thought, *I forgot to eat lunch. I need time to wash my hair and soak in the tub and do my nails.* She decided to do without the opening reels of 'Confessions,' and returned to the street, moving quickly onto the sidewalk and into the crowd.

Those were not my fantasies. The couples weren't close. They didn't touch.

The man was half a block away when she saw him. Between them people hurried along.

He leaned against a tall iron fence that set apart a dirty stone church. His arms hooked over the top of the fence, the heel of one black Italian boot rested on the lower rail. His head was turned towards her. His languorous pose did not change as she drew closer.

From his wide shoulders, his Qiana nylon shirt sank into valleys where the arrested ripple of muscle dipped and curved. The plunging unbuttoned front of the contoured shirt revealed shadowed darkness – a black glimpse of moist, curling hair. Its V-line complemented the tapering waistline which vanished into hip-hugging bell-bottom trousers. The perfect little high-riding curves behind accented the solidity of stomach and thighs, and the gentle roll in front.

Bonnie's shoulders were back, her spine straight. Her heels struck the sidewalk squarely and rhythmically. Only the two of them could see the seductive twist of her hips.

She was in the shade – he in the sun. Now she could see his blond hair – long, tapered flat to his neck, meeting the high

153

collar. Shaped sideburns framed a smooth-shaven face – unsmiling, watching.

She was close enough to see his face. Their eyes connected. She did not slow her pace. Lazily he unwound himself from the fence and stepped forward. She emerged into the sun.

'Pardon me, miss,' he said, his voice unexpectedly animated. 'Could you tell me how to get to the Museum of Modern –?'

They were both too close now. She could see the little lines around his eyes. He extended an arm as he spoke, but the arm stopped with the voice. The arm dropped. She could barely hear the word that slipped from tight lips.

'Shit.'

He turned on one boot heel and walked quickly away.

Bonnie stood in stunned silence, then slowly drifted back down to a dirty sidewalk. Drivers honked horns and a taxi driver shouted an obscenity at another driver on the avenue. A sudden breeze engulfed her in exhaust fumes from a passing bus. A seedy little man brushed against her and she gripped her handbag. She was cold and the apartment was five blocks away. She walked again.

The apartment door clicked shut. Her fingers flew to fasten the extra locks on the door, and she walked slowly to the bedroom, closing another door behind her. She sat on the bed, reluctant to let go of the protective numbness she had wrapped around her. Slowly, and painfully the feeling came through.

Have I missed something that others can see? Did I turn a corner somewhere, passing another decade, and leave myself behind?

She put two hands on the bed on either side of her hips and pushed painfully to her feet. At the bathroom mirror she gripped the counter and leaned forward to examine her face – each line and sag a wound. She raised an arm and looked critically at the looseness of the flesh.

Who am I?

She switched off the strong light over the mirror and fluffed up her hair with the comb. Back in the bedroom, she looked down into the street at people going about their business. Some have passed down the street more times than others. Others have more walking left to do.

Carefully, soundlessly, she opened the closet door and

pulled out the long copper-coloured gown, its soft, silken folds drooping like the willow, without a body to cling to.

I am not somebody else. I am the girl who loved a soldier. I am more woman now. Not less.

She dropped the dress across the bed, kicked off her shoes, and reached for the zipper on her skirt.

Eight

Masses of lilacs in plain white bowls decorated the white tablecloths lined up in the hotel ballroom. At the head table, elevated at one end of the room, spring flowers were the centrepiece.

'Hey, lady, you're gorgeous.' God bless Cal for his sweeping appraisal, and Sid Grahme for the look in his eye when she joined the two couples.

Madge wanted to sit close to the action, and Bonnie was relieved that the first rows of tables were already filled. *He won't recognize me.* Still, she held back.

Before she sat down, she carefully placed beside her plate the half-finished highball. It was her second. *What happened to the first?*

'I love your dress,' Madge told her.

'Yours is lover, too.' Bonnie frowned, and pondered her mistake.

Words fled as she saw a line of people moving towards the head table.

She knew him at once. He was very like his father as she had seen him in 1944. But mostly he was John. Not vanished into the mist, but real, of solid matter, smiling at Convention Chairwoman Martha Boyd as he pulled out her chair. He sat down and looked about the room.

He was a larger man than she remembered. Body thickened,

155

hair a pleasant mix – greyer at the sideburns and above the forehead. She couldn't see his eyes, but she remembered the little half-smile he wore when his mind was somewhere else. He pulled back suddenly and the smile broadened as a waitress served his meal. The girl smiled, too, and backed into a waiter, bringing another serving.

Serving, eating, closing business – things to be endured until the speaker of the evening was introduced. It occurred to Bonnie that it would be natural to tell her friends that she was acquainted with the speaker, but she could not. *The last time I saw him we kissed goodbye at midnight in a hotel room doorway.* She could not speak of it casually.

Martha Boyd's introduction was enthusiastic. There was an uncharacteristic flutter about her tonight. Bonnie had learned this week that the well-publicized case of Jerome vs. Custer Manufacturing had been carried through the courts by Anderson, Blake, Jones and McCloskey. The important Supreme Court decision had followed the eloquent arguments of John Blake. His picture had appeared with the writeup in *Time* magazine. *Must look it up in the basement.*

John stood up and moved to the microphone. He carried no notes. Gripping the top edge of the lectern, he leaned forward slightly and looked out over them with a promise, wooing his audience without words. Gradually the coughing and movement subsided. A deadly quiet filled the room. Bonnie's back moved away from her chair. The first word would be an exquisite penetration of the silence.

'Madam Chairman, fellow Earth Savers,' *beautiful, beautiful sound.* She sat back and took a handkerchief from her bag, to dab at her lip and forehead. She tuned her mind to listen to the words.

The audience was in his hands. Their silent attention carried through to the last sentence. How appropriate that this man had found his niche in the courtroom. He always knew where he was going. No agonizing indecision about direction. Only a brief detour to fight a war. Forgotten now. Something apart. Not real life. He doesn't know that a survivor of that detour is watching.

As the applause died down and people began to stir, Sid commented, 'Fascinating speech.'

156

'Fascinating man,' his wife added with a lift of her eyebrows.

'Wow, you can say that again!' Little Mary hoisted her pregnant body around to face them. 'They're bringing in a group. Want to dance with me, Cal?'

Cal grinned. 'Sure, honey.'

Bonnie didn't think they would, but they did.

Bonnie sat behind a bouquet of lilacs, wondering what to do next. People swarmed around John as soon as the meeting adjourned. She didn't want to approach him in a crowd. *The band will play 'Speak Low' and he will suddenly appear at my side. He has spotted me in the crowd and recognized me immediately. 'Dance?'*

The tune was not 'Speak Low.' It was 'Rhinestone Cowboy.' A few couples moved onto the floor. They did not find each other's arms. They wiggled and squirmed and shuffled their feet. She watched a couple nearby. The young man's body writhed bonelessly, his feet barely moved. An air of lazy boredom hung about him. A few feet away, his partner wiggled and jerked, her miniskirt a half beat behind her grinding buttocks, her braless breasts vibrating to the beat of the electric guitars. *Do they know each other? They're sharing nothing.* She remembered all the times she had concentrated on missing the beat in order to follow her partner's lead. *Where he leads me I will follow. Amen.*

Her eyes scanned the room again. She found John near the door. He was backing away from people who were shaking his hand. *He's leaving.* She gripped the table edge. *You blew it. He's leaving.* With a final nod of his head he was gone. She looked down at her hands, swallowing the disappointment. She pushed back the sudden thrust of panic. *Be sensible about this. What to do.* She rummaged in her bag and found a stale cigarette. The lighter still worked and she leaned back and inhaled. *He's registered at the hotel. He's staying over. I'll call him in the morning. Calling may be the thing.*

She danced with Sid. He still did the box step. Made a good try at dancing loose with Cal. Both couples eventually returned to the floor, leaving her alone at the table.

The perfume of the lilacs had been riding the edge of her consciousness all evening. For the first time she looked squarely at the purple blossoms. She could see them in masses

157

of colour and aroma at the end of the porch of the old white house on Maple Street. She had watched them through so many springs.

They were in full bloom the last time she sat in the slatted swing on the wide porch. The packing was done, ready for the van in the morning. They were leaving the big white house.

Bonnie had dropped, exhausted, into the swing. Linda and Karen, long-legged teenagers, came one at a time through the wide screen door and sat silently in the swing on either side of her. She reached out both hands to squeeze the responsive fingers of her sombre daughters. They silently shared their separate memories of the old house, the only home the girls had known.

The door opened again and Frank came through, carrying a bulging briefcase.

'I can't work here,' he said, stopping in front of the door. 'I'm going back to the office.'

Bonnie nodded, not sure he could see. He stood with his hand on the door, then turned and walked towards the steps. There was a noise in the hall and the door flew open. Eleven-year-old Anne ran after her father.

'Wait, Daddy,' she called.

He stopped on the top step and turned as Anne clutched his arm. She buried her face in the curve of his arm and said shakily, 'How can you leave? It's our last night.'

Frank rumpled Anne's short hair, saying briskly, 'What about that new room you've been so excited about? You're not fooling me with those tears.'

Anne pulled away and dropped down on the steps, turning her back to him.

Frank walked on and they heard the sound of the garage door opening. The follow-up sound of the car motor did not come. No one had moved or spoken when Frank reappeared around the corner of the house. He walked slowly up the steps, propped his case against the railing, sat down beside Anne, and reached for her. With a rush she moved into his arms, and Bonnie knew she was crying on his shoulder.

Hot tears welled up in Bonnie's eyes then. *Frank has not touched his children in years, except when they come to him for a quick good night or thank you*. The pair sitting on the step were holding together with a crisis-like urgency. The curve of Frank's grey flannel back decried the rigidity to which Bonnie had become so accustomed.

She had stored away the memory of that moment and pulled it out to be handled over and over again.

Frank left the briefcase behind that night and they all went out for ice cream. They laughed a lot and touched one another. Frank put his arm around Bonnie in the drive-in and the girls forgot to be embarrassed. They had drawn together in familial strength against the threat of severed roots.

She hadn't meant to remember this now. The memory was out of place tonight. Frank wasn't good at speeches, either public or private. Frank was a worker. Clem could never have carried the presidential burden as long as he did without Frank's long hours of patient manipulation behind the scenes. He was the rod around which Bonnie's family was built. But he wasn't good with words. And sometimes a woman needed words. Or even a look. Something more than a deed. More than the charge accounts and the new house.

Bonnie leaned her forehead on her hand and looked down into her lap. She slipped past the drive-in, all the way back to an icy street where two people clung together, holding each other up in a world with no tomorrow. They had come together to merge their seeds, only to be pulled apart before the blossoming.

With trembling fingers she opened up a paper napkin and wrote on it,

I have a splitting headache. It's been great, will keep in touch.

Love,
Bonnie

She left the ballroom, retrieved her mink jacket, and turned with halting steps to the lobby.

Nine

When, in a small voice, she asked the desk clerk for Mr Blake's room number, he smiled. 'Yes, ma'am. I'll see if he's in.' He picked up the house phone. 'Whom shall I say –?'

'Mrs Forbes.' She fumbled in her purse, then snapped it shut. 'I'm from the convention committee,' she said in a raised voice to cover the lie. 'I'm sorry to bother him so late, but there are some details we missed. It won't take long.' Her voice trailed off. She was sure she was blushing.

The clerk didn't care. He talked to someone who answered, then told her, 'Room 618. Go right up, Mrs Forbes.'

The self-service elevator stopped at six without a sound and the door slid open. The hall was modern and plush. The carpet red, the wallpaper silver-striped, the woodwork dark, the ashtrays streaks of unadorned chrome.

She thought of the halls at the Wheatland. In memory, probably wrong, they were narrow and badly lighted. Her mink became muskrat, her hair touched her shoulders. She tapped on the door marked 618.

They had exchanged places. The gently lamplit room was behind him when he pulled back the door, fastening the buttons on his jacket.

It wasn't the same. He looked older up close. She sensed a controlled annoyance behind the courteous smile.

'Hello. Mrs Forbes? Come in.'

He stepped back. Bonnie stayed.

Her rehearsed speech fled down the hall. 'John,' she said in a very weak voice. Then louder, 'John, don't you know me?'

Slowly she watched the cool charm change to a puzzled, penetrating appraisal. The lines between his eyes deepened. Like surfacing bubbles a joy emerged inside her. She felt beautiful. *This is the way I always feel with John*. She laughed.

In slow motion he raised a hand and barely touched her arm.
'Bonnie? Is it Bonnie?'

She nodded. They were awkward, dumb. She laughed again.
His hand closed on her arm and he pulled her inside and shut
the door.

'I can't believe it.'

They were standing very close, very still. It only felt like each
started and drew back at different instants. They were familiar
persons in different bodies.

'Well,' he said, taking hold of both her hands. 'Let me look
at you.'

'You didn't recognize me.'

'Well, of course you've changed. Who'd want to stay twenty-
one forever?'

'Yes, twenty-one. I was, wasn't I?'

He inspected her carefully and nodded. His eyes had turned
warm and happy. 'Yes. Yes, it's good. You look just like you
should. I couldn't have planned it better.'

She believed him. 'I was very proud of *you* tonight.'

'You were there? At the banquet?'

'Yes.'

He moved behind her and took her jacket. She stood still
while he hung it in the closet.

'Are you really on the committee?'

They were in the parlour of a suite, a room of black leather,
chrome and glass.

'No. That was a lie.'

There was a spring in his step as he came back and touched
her elbow. 'Sit down. I was going to order a sandwich. I can't
eat when I'm speaking. What can I get you?'

'Maybe some coffee.' She hadn't eaten much either, but the
thought of food made her sick.

'Some wine?' He smiled. 'I remember you didn't like to drink
much.'

She nodded, remembering the two highballs. 'All right. I
have learned to live with cocktail parties.'

He waved towards the black chairs. She sat and placed her
elbows on the glistening chair arms, turning her head to watch
him at the phone. His fingers rested along the smooth, white
plastic – long, large-knuckled, fingernails immaculate. A plain

gold band encircled the third finger. *He has already touched me three – five – times, more than I can count.*

He came over and sat across from her. He spoke carefully, in a low confidential tone. 'Well, girl, it's been a long time.'

She shook her head. 'Oh, yes.'

His eyes sparkled. 'Jet planes and astronauts.'

'Automatic washers and television.'

'Beatles and –' he groped for a word.

'Beatniks,' came out in a rush of laughter. She kept wanting to laugh.

'That's not what we want to talk about. What about you? What's happened to you?'

She breathed out. 'Did you marry Sara?'

'Yes. We've a silver anniversary coming up soon.'

'Really? I – I thought it would have been longer.'

'No. 1950.'

I had my third baby that year.

'She had a brief modelling career. I knocked about a bit after I got my law degree. Worked a couple of places.'

'I'm sure she's still beautiful.'

Was there a slight hesitation before he said, 'Yes, of course. Put on a little weight.'

Bonnie tried to picture a fat Sara and failed.

'Forbes,' he said. 'Wasn't that the man you worked for?'

'Yes – Frank.'

They weren't looking at each other now. His hand slid inside his coat and pulled out a thin cigarette case. After extracting a cigarette he started to close it, then remembered to extend the case to Bonnie. She reached across and took one. He lighted her cigarette and his before speaking again.

'Sorry, I don't think of you as a smoker.'

'I started when the children were small. Now I'm trying to quit.'

'Nasty habit.'

She examined the toe of her satin pump.

'You have a family?' he asked.

'Yes,' she responded quickly. 'I – we have three daughters and two grandchildren. Linda and Karen are married, still in Lancaster. My youngest, Anne, is launching a career as a graphic designer here in New York. I'm staying with her now.'

162

'Nice for you. They must be lovely young women, like their mother.'

'Do you have children?'

'We had a son. He's dead.'

'Oh, I'm sorry.' She was. His pain showed.

'You accept it,' he said slowly, 'because you have to.'

She waited for more, but he did not continue.

'Your parents – and Marc?' she asked at last.

'Dad died in 1954. Mother took over the business. She's still chairman of the board, going strong at seventy-five. Marc's president, but he's not really in charge. You probably didn't see it in mother, but there's a steel spine beneath that flowered chiffon.'

I saw it! Poor Marc.

'Marc was such a sweet boy. I hope he's happy.'

John hesitated. 'I don't honestly think he is – very happy. He's one of those people who keeps missing the boat.'

'Oh, John, why?'

'I suppose I shouldn't say that. Just because he hasn't followed the conventional pattern of marriage and working his way to the top.'

'He's not married?'

'No. Know what he told me one time?'

'What?'

'That he hadn't been able to find a girl like Bonnie. That's what he said. You were his ideal.'

Bonnie blushed. 'Oh, my goodness. He hardly knew me.'

John grinned. 'You won people over rather quickly, remember?'

Her face grew warmer still. *How sweet it is.*

She looked down at her hands and said quickly, 'My parents are both still in good health.' *I'm acting twenty-one.*

John didn't respond and she looked up. 'But that's right, you never met them.'

'Your mother wrote to me several times,' John said. 'Nice, warm letters. I appreciated it. What about your friend – Laverne?'

'You mean Maxine.'

'Yeah, I knew it was one of the Andrews Sisters.'

They laughed suddenly and Bonnie had trouble answering.

163

'Maxine just got her third divorce.' The laughter didn't fit. She tried to stop.

He was laughing too. 'That's too bad. Third one, you say.'

They looked away from each other to gain control. She slowly stole a look at him, and they were off again.

A tapping intruded. John crushed his cigarette and went to the door. The waiter wheeled in a cart-table. As the waiter removed the two silver covers, Bonnie and John snickered. The waiter looked up, startled, then finished his task. With an injured air he accepted the tip and departed.

John shook his head. 'Guy thinks we're off our rockers.'

The funny business ended as quickly as it had started and they settled down on either side of the cart.

The covers had protected a dark sandwich and a plate of potato salad. The cart also held a chrome coffee carafe, a bottle of red wine, two white cups and two slender wine goblets.

'I can't eat alone.'

'Well, maybe a little potato salad.'

They looked at the single setting. John handed Bonnie the fork and picked up the spoon. 'You start on that side,' he said.

They looked at each other, not at the food. The cold silver handles balanced loosely. Slowly they lowered their eyes and slid tines and bowl under the tender, moist morsels. In ritualistic unison they raised the food from a common plate to their parted lips. Bonnie chewed and swallowed with difficulty. The fork awkwardly extended in midair, eyes focused on mayonnaise and pickle, she said, 'John, why didn't you answer my letter?'

Carefully she placed the fork on the table and raised her eyes to his. The indentations over the bridge of his nose had deepened again. He spoke carefully.

'That's all done. We can't go back.'

'I wish you'd try. I've carried questions in my heart for so long.'

He said, 'We had a trim, silver ship, propellers turning, engines roaring – and ceiling zero. They didn't let us get her off the ground.'

Bonnie worked on the lump in her throat. 'You must have been relieved when I ended it.'

'I'm not a very humble person. "Dear John" letters were bitter medicine.'

'But you *were* relieved.'

He sat back in the chair, his shoulders straightening in the trimly tailored tuxedo jacket. 'I don't like post mortems. I think we should stick to the recent history of our relatives and friends.'

'Maybe you'd like to discuss the current political scene.'

'Ecology. We really took the big boys down in that court case, didn't we? It cost us money to defend the little guy, but we got a million dollars worth of publicity.'

'Now you sound like Frank.'

'Is that bad?'

'In this context it is. Relating everything to money.'

'I don't do that. I'm sorry if it sounded that way.'

'Would you have taken the case, just on principle?'

'I did. My partners hollered like hell, but I'm the senior partner. The old man backed me up.'

'Sara's father?'

'Yes. He's in his eighties now, and his memory slips sometimes. We keep his name on the door, even though he doesn't do much. He was a brilliant man. I owe him a lot. I think I'll have a try at that sandwich. I'm starved. Sure you won't share?'

She shook her head. *How can he eat?*

'Finished with the potatoes?'

She nodded.

He poured two cups of coffee, set one on her side, and pulled the potato salad and sandwich plate closer. 'So Maxine didn't hit it lucky in the marriage game?'

'No. She's still looking for Mr Right.'

'Well, I hope she finds him.'

Bonnie silently watched John bite into the sandwich. She felt as though her wrists had been slapped.

'I suppose I should be going.'

He put down the sandwich. 'Oh, Bonnie, please don't. I've upset you. We're a couple of friends talking about old times. I don't look back much. What's done is done. A lot of things didn't turn out the way I wanted them to, but there's always something new around the corner. Or just the possibility of something new around the corner. Know what I mean?'

'You're saying there's still a future.'

'Of course there is. Probably when I'm eighty, I can help some young guy of fifty-three change the world a bit.'

165

'By then you'll have the answers.'

'Oh, no. It's the young who know all the answers. The more alternatives you discover through the years, the harder it is to be certain of anything. The sweet ambivalence of choices! This can be the excitement that makes a day worth facing, or it can be scary as hell. Depends upon whether you decide to live excited or scared.'

'Most of the people I know just live bored. They don't see alternatives.'

'There's something to be said for that, too. There's security in black and white. Those of us wandering in the greys have our own kinds of problems.'

'You'll always be my brave soldier.'

'Oh, Bonnie, if you only knew. That's one thing about not getting airborne. We've kept our illusions.'

'When weren't you brave?'

'How about this brave guy sitting on a bench in a railroad station for four hours, waiting for a train to get away from a town full of ghosts?'

'You? What town?'

'Lancaster. Christmas week 19—? 1946 it was. My first semester in law school.'

'You did? You were there?'

'I spent Christmas break with a friend in Chicago. Decided on the spur of the moment to take the train to Lancaster. I didn't even know it was an eight-hour ride.'

'Did you look for me?'

'Bonnie darling, why else would I go to Lancaster? I didn't know what had become of you. I didn't know anyone else there.'

'You couldn't find me?'

'I found you. That's where the cowardice comes in. I went to your old address and your landlady told me. I couldn't face visiting you in a cottage. Chatting with your husband and bouncing your baby on my knee. She said you had a baby.'

Bonnie remembered her world of diapers and dishpans. *That was the year we had the scrawny tree. Frank fixed the lights.* Tried to imagine John dropping into it. Wondered if it would have made any difference.

'You knew I married Frank.'

166

'Yes, I did, but I'll have to confess I didn't recognize the name tonight.'

She excused him, at the same time realizing that she could never hear the name 'Sara' without remembering.

'Why didn't you answer my letter?'

'You don't give up, do you? What would any brave soldier do? Throw out your pictures. Throw a party. Throw up.'

'I can't believe how you're evading me. You can't answer.' She swallowed the lump and felt it slowly rise again. 'I can take it. I just want to know.'

'All right.' He set down the coffee cup. 'Because it damned near killed me.'

Her defences were set the wrong way. The blow came from behind. It wasn't fair.

She stammered, 'I thought you wanted it. I thought I'd pushed you. That when you'd just needed a woman, I'd made you take a wife.'

'You didn't say that. You said I was hurting you. You said there was another man.'

'I thought you'd fight if you cared.'

'I thought you'd write again and take it all back.'

She stood up and walked to the window, turning her back. ANGELO'S the red neon sign said, ITALIAN CUISINE. She heard the muffled, unbalanced roar of traffic from below.

His soft voice reached her. 'I wrote. Every day for a week.'

She knew about tight crumpled wads of words scattered over the floor.

'Then I got legal papers. I signed them. "Thanks for the memories" and "Good luck" – I just couldn't say it.'

She jumped when he touched her arm. The thick white carpet swallowed footsteps, and her nerves were surfaced and open. He slid both arms around her waist and put his face in her hair. She slid around, touching all the way, and reached her arms up around his shoulders. Drowning, drowning in the merging of mouths and tongues, clutching at the tuxedo jacket. She had never kissed like this before. The movement slowed and sweetened. She could feel his body changing. His hand moved across the front of her dress. Finding the little amber buttons. Releasing them, one by one.

A bell rang.

At the next shrill shout they stopped.

Reality grabbed her throat. The telephone was close by.

It rang again. She put her hand back on his arm and the sound struck again.

She jerked away and in a few steps picked up the phone. She held it out uncertainly. A loud voice came clearly from the receiver. 'John? John, darling, are you there?'

John took two long strides to the back of the table and yanked at the cord. The plug flew out of the phone jack. Bonnie laid the dead thing on the table.

'I'm sorry,' she said, looking at the floor. 'I never could stand to let it ring.' She added in a monotone. 'That was your wife.'

John moved slowly into the circle of light by the chairs and pulled the cart back. 'No,' he said flatly. 'That was not my wife.'

The leather chair back was soft and yielding, but she tried to steady herself against it. She was breathless and dizzy.

'You'd better sit down,' John said. He uncorked the wine bottle and poured the red liquid into the stemmed glasses.

She edged around the chair and slid into it. She took the glass and lowered it to her knee as John sank into the chair opposite. Looking at the glass, the open bodice of her dress came into peripheral view, exposing cleavage and flesh-coloured lace. The wine sloshed to the rim as she set the glass on the table. Her fingers rewound button loops around buttons, fingers lingering briefly across her bosom before locking together on her lap.

He watched without comment.

The wine soothed her tongue and warmed her throat. She watched the circles of light from the table lamps make overlapping shadows on the thick, white carpet into varied shades of grey.

Odd to sit, willing the pulse to return to normal, the blood pressure to go down. Odd to find the old feeling still there, like yesterday. Immaterial when yesterday was. The hungers, the primeval urge, not hidden as it had been before. This time I know the beast. Friend or foe, it no longer lurks in the shadows.

They sometimes looked at each other, sometimes not. They could still share an empathetic silence. Sorting out.

You're not as cool as you look. Your pulse and blood

pressure need calming too. You want me again, but today the beast has a new set of chains.

He sat effortlessly straight, the very cut and cloth of his clothes calling to something sweet and wild in her. She looked at the hand resting on the chair arm and burned with the feel of it slipping across the front of her dress. *How would our child have been? A child from such sweetness. A boy like his father, to cherish, to nurse at my breast, to love.*

'You'd have liked my boy.' Her heart jumped. 'Sara and I had him. It's one great thing we did together. He was blown to pieces by a land mine. We never saw him dead.'

The grief from all the wars, all the dying boys she hadn't mourned, came at once. 'Viet Nam.'

'Yes.'

She waited for the next words, then groped for a question, sensing his need to talk about it. 'What –?'

'Different from our war. Did you think so?'

'Oh yes, I did. We had a protester, but she was a girl. She didn't have to –'

'Brad was a protester. I helped him go to Canada. Gave him money.'

'Then –?'

'That's why it was such a waste. He was the type that could understand dying for a cause, but it wasn't his cause.'

Bonnie waited. He didn't need her questions.

'He was a bright boy – very bright. Graduated from Harvard at twenty. Such a day. Do you remember certain days when you were really happy? It never came to us again, never will. Just before we left, he let us have it. He wasn't staying in school like we'd planned. Was leaving for Canada with his friends. Sara had hysterics. She still showed her feelings then.'

Bonnie nodded. She could see.

'We knew how he was about the war. Still, it was a shock. Your son, you know, you want him to be strong and brave. He had a low number. Once out of school it was the Army, Canada or jail. He thought staying in school would be the real cop-out. What do you think? What would you have done?'

'I guess it was his decision. You could only –'

'That's what I kept saying. And I had this growing feeling that he was right. Not like our war.' He picked up the cham-

169

pagne goblet and twirled the stem between his fingers.

'He came back?'

'Yes. His mother got sick. He came back for her.'

'Sara's sick?'

'It was emotional. She was hospitalized for a while. Withdrawn. She had a rough time. She couldn't help it. Her life was built around Brad and me. When we let her down she fell apart. She thought I was helping Brad to shame her.'

'But you were doing it for yourselves, not against her.'

He set the glass down hard. 'I didn't even do that right. I didn't speak out after I knew the war was evil, that my country was wrong. It was more convenient to let my son take the rap. My clients, my associates, they wouldn't have liked my marching in parades or writing a book. I sent Brad money, but I'm not sure he knew I believed in what he was doing. I think maybe I told him, but I should have said it louder. I should have told him to stay.'

'He was a man. You couldn't have told him what to do, any more than anyone could have told you.'

He looked at her sharply. 'Do you really think so?'

'He had to know about his mother. He had to decide for himself.'

He leaned his head on his hand, touching his forehead and looking at the floor. 'He came back in time for his draft call. They got him. He was only overseas a month.'

The ambiguous 'they.' The Army? The Viet Cong? His mother? His father?

'How is she?'

'She was okay after he went to the Army. Put on a bright face as though those months had never happened. When he was killed, she went through the expected motions of a grieving mother. If there's some terrible rage bottled up inside her, nobody saw it. Nobody got that close. Certainly not me. Yet, I could feel her holding on. I had this egotistical conviction that if I weren't there she'd break in two.'

Tears were on her cheeks without her having cried them.

'And what about you? We all let you down.'

Slowly his eyes focused on her. 'Oh, Bonnie, no.'

'I've never stopped blaming myself. I did it all wrong.'

'No, you mustn't. I didn't want to make you feel bad.'

170

'Why not? When you were alone, in a strange place and offering your life, I was the one who quit.'

'Bonnie, listen to me. I wasn't always alone.'

'What?'

'It was an unreal world – like a series of separate lives stretching from one mission to the next. Sometimes I took what comfort was offered. Do you understand?'

She shook her head slowly. The past couldn't change after it had been moulded and fired and glazed and worshipped on an altar for half a lifetime.

'What do you mean?'

'How else can I say it?'

'You mean there were other women?'

He nodded. 'Sometimes.'

She felt detached, like a spectator at a play. 'It never even occurred to me that you might be unfaithful. I never thought of it ever. Not once.'

He shifted in the chair. Lifted his hands. 'I'm an ass to bring it up. I just can't see you taking all the guilt.'

Her eyes felt tight and hot. She laboured with the words. 'What were they like? A different one every night? One that was special – ?'

'No, no. Nothing like that.' He leaned forward. 'God, Bonnie, don't do this to yourself. It wasn't important. I can hardly remember. Something of the moment, "a celebration – tonight I'm still here." It had nothing to do with you.'

'Was that what I was? Something of the moment?'

'You were the centre of all my dreams of a sane, normal life.'

'Why didn't you tell me?'

'I did, you know I did.'

'Not at the end.'

'You always represented all the things I wanted to come back to.'

'Not Sara?'

'Not Sara. Everybody else decided that for me. Even you.'

'I wanted life to be good for you.'

'Bonnie,' he leaned towards her. 'Don't you see that it was your sacrifices that did us in? Not my transgressions.'

She pulled back. A different kind of heat spread over her. 'We were programmed to sacrifice, Sara and I. Living for our

171

men and our children. They told us that to look for happiness in anything else, the way they could, was to be less than a real woman.'

'I know that.' They were the 'differents,' reaching across the divide.

'And you,' she said slowly, 'you *man*, with all your choices, you get to pick up the check.' She could see it now, the bitter justice of it. 'It doesn't come free.'

He said, 'That's man and woman. Now where does it leave you and me?'

She looked at him soberly. 'Frank and I live black and white. We don't cheat.'

'Just don't forget, lady,' John said in a voice as quiet as hers. 'Good old Frank is the son of a bitch who stole my wife.'

She stood up. 'I want to leave,' she said. 'I don't know how I'll feel tomorrow, but now I need to get out of here.'

Rustily John rose and brought her jacket from the closet. Bonnie had never been so tired.

He put the jacket around her shoulders.

'I'll go down and get you a cab.'

'You don't need to.'

'I'm going out too.'

'Oh.'

She sounded young. Of course she's young. They don't say 'Shit' to him.

He switched off the lamps, leaving a small one faintly illuminating the abandoned setting. They went out and he checked the lock. They walked down the hall and waited for the elevator without looking at each other.

The walls of the elevator were close. She stole a sideways glance at the silent figure sharing her isolation. They had been a pair once more – for a few hours. The door slid noiselessly open and the other people were there again.

At the far end of the lobby a revolving door stayed in motion. They wound through chattering groups, together but not touching. They each stepped into a moving compartment of the door without contributing to its momentum.

The doorman gave them the first cab and she hurried into it before John could help her. She scooted back. He leaned in and took her hand. 'Will I see you again?'

172

'I doubt it. We could keep in touch. Maybe at Christmas.'

He nodded. 'Sure. Shouldn't wait another thirty years.'

He hesitated, his hand still loosely covering hers. 'Sometime, dearest,' he said, 'try doing it for Bonnie. The world will keep on turning.'

A dull ache passed down her shoulder and into the passive hand. His fingers went away and he shut the door.

Her cab squeezed into the line of traffic, waiting for the light. In front of them, another taxi waited for a noisy group threading through the cars. Her driver swore under his breath as the delay caused him to miss the light. Bonnie saw John walk back to where the doorman watched for another cab.

She lifted her chin and pushed against the seat with her back. She was returning to the security of her cushioned box – static, stable. Only steps away, a New York sidewalk stretched towards an unknown horizon. The revolving door turned faster. Red lights flashed and faded on the backs of cars, on street corners, on moving neon signs.

Another cab pulled up and she watched John step towards it. He stopped, waited, waved it away with one quick motion. His head was bowed, his shoulders curved. She saw a young man in uniform before a frosted window, with a shoe in his hand and the same curve to his back. A private moment of resignation, fear, defeat, all things strong men deny themselves. *He's not Superman. He's a person like me. It's a celebration. Tonight we're still here.*

Her cab rolled forward. She frantically dug in her purse and pulled out a bill without looking at it. 'Wait!' she called. 'I changed my mind.' She pushed the bill into the fare box and got out of the cab.

A noisy crowd was coming out of the hotel, moving against the people going in. The two groups collided and mingled and she was caught in the crosscurrent.

She raised her bent arms and with all the power she could muster plunged elbows into flesh and bone blocking her way. She heard gasps and unfriendly words – but the way opened.

She reached around the last human obstacle to close fingers around John's arm, feeling the muscle beneath the hard cloth. He straightened and turned his head. She held on, moving closer, their eyes pressing intimacies that had never been said.

Silently she moved her hand down to lace her fingers into hi
and, against the crowd, they walked together back to th
revolving door.

Ten

The room was dusky. The morning sunlight, captured and held
in the heavy cloth of the drawn drapery, telescoped into one
bright sliver on the middle of the sill. She was suspended in a
timeless, feathery cocoon. Naked, a slight turn touched coo
sheets to her warm thighs. The covers were turned back, she
was alone.

Suddenly she was awake, wide eyes moving around the
room. The huge ebony dresser – a deep shadow on the white
carpet – held a crystal lamp with a darkened silk shade; and a
Bible behind scattered studs, a man's black bow tie, and he
own diamond earrings.

Then she saw him in the high-backed chair, still as the New
York hotel furniture. The only movement was the silen
spiralling of grey-blue smoke from the cigarette held between
his fingers. The smoke clouded the grey streaks in his hair, and
she thought how handsome he was – as handsome, in anothe
way, as the boy he had been when she had loved and lost him
thirty years ago.

He had put on a pair of dark trousers, and a tight short-
sleeved undershirt, dressing without waking her. She hadn'
slept much. For hours she had lain looking at his profile in the
dark, listening to the heavy breathing that sometimes ended
with a slight, gentle whistle. She had moved carefully, sometimes barely touching her hand against his skin. When he did
wake, she would move close against him and his hands would
stroke her, as though gently acknowledging the fragility o
their union. They had made love again as the drapery was
taking on the rosy glow of morning.

His eyes turned towards the bed. He sat forward.

'Good morning.' Bonnie signalled him that she was awake.

'Good morning,' John answered.

'I didn't hear you get up. What time is it?'

'After eight.' He stood up and walked over to take a laundry-folded shirt from a small leather bag.

Strange little ripples of energy sparked and radiated through Bonnie's body when she watched John move. His hands, unfolding and smoothing the shirt, captured her eyes and held them. Her body was a wind chime, played upon by his slightest movement. The room was beautiful; life was a gift.

The hands found their way into sleeves, and fastened buttons. He unzipped his trousers and smoothed down the shirt-tail, quickly readjusting all to a smooth fit. She tried to recall how her husband fastened his trousers. She couldn't remember.

John looked at her again and broke into a slow smile as he reached for the sitting room door. 'I'll order breakfast.'

'John –'

He stopped.

'When you're through, come back. Sit and talk.' She was suffocating with excitement. 'Watch me dress.'

An elusive softening, a fraction of delay, then he nodded. He remembered.

She had not been so alive in years. The tartness of the orange juice painfully set against the sweetness of the roll – at once delicious and sickening. They slipped through multiple emotions like auditioning actors. John grew increasingly sober.

She stopped in the middle of a sentence as she felt him staring, memorizing her face.

'Bonnie,' he said, 'we still don't have our dream.'

She reached over and touched his arm and said, 'It's all right, darling. Did you think I thought we did?'

He gave her a Boston box number, scribbled on hotel stationery, and she gave him her home address. He said, 'If you need me,' and neither of them knew what that meant.

They held hands to the door. Their good-bye kiss was controlled, but the feel of it took root inside her, to grow alongside last night's memories.

She never expected to see him again. She knew that life would never be the same.

Eleven

Bright sunshine burst over her as she came out of the revolving door. Her copper-coloured formal gown just cleared the sidewalk below her high-collared mink jacket. The people crowding the Manhattan sidewalk didn't turn to stare. She made a sharp turn, her high-heeled sandals clicking on the pavement.

They think I'm an actress. Or a model. Or a lady who was having too good a time to go home. A fat man pushing back the squealing metal grate to open his store grinned openly at her. She grinned back and nodded. She was headed in the right direction for Anne's apartment, but it would be too far to walk. She could hail a cab when she was tired, or climb on a bus. Cabs and buses awaited a snap of her fingers. She wasn't tired. She could walk forever.

The world looked different. Fresher, as though it had rained. Had it rained? She felt giddy, like she was soaring up above the traffic. She could fly across the street instead of walking if she wished. *Is this what it feels like to sin?* She stopped, dead still. *I sinned. When will the lightning strike? It feels so good.* She resumed walking at a slower pace. Anne's voice on the phone last night, 'Mo—therrrrrrr!' *Oh, Hallelujah, I sinned and it was beautiful.* Her stomach flipped and breathing quickened as she remembered John moving over her. Her first time out of wedlock.

Bouquets of butter-coloured daisies and jonquils winked at her from fruit jars stacked on crude shelves close to the curb.

'Yes, ma'am,' the young man smiled. He towered over her, skinny and tall and black, like the stems on the flowers,

176

bursting at the top into a massive hairdo – black fuzz in a neat, round blossom. He grinned with a brilliant display of even, white teeth.

'I'd like that one.' She pointed to a large bunch of daisies. He took them, dripping, out of the fruit jar and wrapped them in a newspaper. 'One bunch of daisies for a very classy lady,' he said as he handed them to her. 'That's a buck fifty.'

She gave him the money and walked on.

'Yes, sir, very classy,' she heard from behind. She looked back over her shoulder and smiled. She would have kept her eyes straight ahead if it hadn't been for the long, slinky dress, and the kind of fresh, warm day it was. He raised his hand in what she took to be a friendly salute. He seemed like a nice young man.

She waited on a corner for a large truck to go around.

'Lord, that's a pretty dress,' she heard someone say. The voice came from a bundle of soiled rags, fluttering in constant, slow movement beside her. The smiling face was a mass of wrinkles, the eyes bare slits beneath the folded, baggy lids. 'What's the material, honey?' the crone asked.

'I – I'm not sure,' Bonnie stammered. 'Yes, it's silk. I –'

'I used to have dresses like that,' the voice droned on. 'I used to be a star, you know. Now I don't even have enough to eat. That's life –' the voice trailed off.

Bonnie opened her purse and took out a bill which she pushed into the clawlike hand.

'Oh, bless you, honey,' the old lady said, bringing the bill closer to her eyes. She scrutinized it with one eye squeezed shut. Agilely she pivoted on one foot and trotted away.

A taxi rounded the corner, available. Bonnie waved.

She had two phone calls that evening. Late afternoon, Madge Grahme called to arrange lunch before she and Sid left for Cincinnati. Bonnie struggled to bring her scattered thoughts into focus when Madge said, 'Hope you're feeling better.' Was it only last night she had made up the headache after the Earth Savers banquet?

Madge and Sid had become close to her in the convention week she had known them. When she hung up, she felt the pressure of unshed tears. There were no friends like Madge and

177

Sid waiting for her in Lancaster. Why, she might even be able to tell Madge about last night.

The buzzer sounded. Bonnie flipped on the intercom and heard, 'Rosencranz Florist. I have a delivery.' When she looked through the opening past the chain lock minutes later, she saw a messenger with a large florist's box. She carried the box to the kitchen counter before finding the card. The name on the outside of the small envelope was 'Bonnie Forbes,' not Mrs Frank. With shaking fingers she pulled out the enclosure.

One word on the card – 'Remembering.'

She started to cry, softly, without anguish. She walked back to the big chair and sat down and cried and blew her nose and cried some more. This was the climax of a week of sentimental journeys – journeys into the past set in motion when she had seen John's name on the convention itinerary.

There was this girl with soft brown hair resting on her shoulders – a tall mass of it rolled back from her sweet face and tucked under and pinned securely to a cotton-filled hair rat. She touched the hearts of young soldiers – exchanged kisses on the sofa, sometimes allowed small liberties – always slightly clouded with guilt, never worried about going too far for it was already written that she wouldn't. She had been sure then that there was a map for her life, and she had only to be careful to find the right way. Each night she prayed for guidance, and each day she followed the master plan. She was a good girl. She was fifty-three years old, and last night for the first time in her life she had taken an unscheduled flight.

Now she had a memory – a shining new one to replace the old dreams. And there was so much more to this couple now, Bonnie and John. They had expanded and mellowed from the good times; smoothed off the rough edges; rebounded and reconnoitred from the bad times. What children they had been. What tender, trusting children back when youth was supposed to be that way. Bonnie had struggled with Anne and her cohorts who always questioned everything – and had found that sometimes they were right, even though it's harder when you have decide. 'There's security in black and white. Those of us wandering in the greys have our own kinds of problems.' John again. He was so incredibly wise, so wonderful. His wonderfulness made her ache and cry.

She was still sitting in the chair, legs tucked under, clutching he soaked handkerchief, when she heard Anne's keys in the door. Anne walked slowly across the room to stand before her. Bonnie saw the question in Anne's eyes change to alarm. What's that goddamned son of a bitch done to you?' she exploded.

Bonnie put her feet on the floor. 'Oh, no, no,' she protested. I'm fine. These are happy tears.'

Anne stood unyielding, feet planted apart.

'Such language, Anne. I never heard you talk that way before.'

'I never saw my mother being seduced before.'

Bonnie stood up and put her arms around her daughter. She clung to the unresponsive shoulders and laughed. 'It's all right, baby. Put away your shotgun, I'm fine. Better than fine. It's 1975, we're liberated, remember?'

'You're my mother!'

Bonnie pulled Anne to the couch and sat beside her. 'Baby, I'm sorry you had to be in on this. I don't want to cause you problems.'

Anne breathed deeply, then asked, 'What happened? And stop calling me "Baby." '

Bonnie drew back.

'That shouldn't be so hard to answer.' Anne's voice was cold. What happened?'

Bonnie stood and looked down at the arrogant young body. You have no right to interrogate me like this. I don't owe you an explanation.'

She slid her feet into the houseshoes in front of the chair, and went to her room, closing the door with a bang. She stood in the middle of her bedroom. When she realized she was not being followed, she walked to the bed and sat on the edge. How tired she was, how sleepy.

She heard the telephone bell, Anne's muffled voice, and a tap at the door. 'It's Dad on the phone' came through. *Oh, no. I can't.*

She painfully pulled herself off the edge of the bed and went back into the studio to pick up the phone.

'Hello, Frank.' Her voice was husky.

'Hey, Bonnie.' Frank sounded unusually boisterous. 'How are you, hon? I've missed you.'

'That's good,' she finally said.

'What's the matter? You sound funny.'

She raised her voice. 'Nothing's the matter.'

'I can't find the light blue shirt the kids gave me for Christmas. I wanted to wear it to the board meeting.'

'I'm sure it's in the closet. You never wear it.'

'There's something else.' He hesitated. 'I hate to ask you, but it's important. Clem is leaving next weekend. It seems our president's retirement was ordered by his doctor. They're moving to Florida. You know it's up to us to give them a party before they go.'

I can't do it. I can't.

'I know it's a lot to ask, but do you think we could have the party at our place Saturday night?'

'I can't come back Saturday and entertain one hundred people Saturday night.'

'It wouldn't be one hundred. Maybe only fifty. You're so good at this. It's been a hell of a time for you to be gone.'

'All right.' Her voice was dead. 'I'll come Friday.'

'That's my good girl. You're a good wife, Bonnie. I probably can't get away to go to the airport, but I'll see you at dinner Friday night. Your cooking is going to taste great.'

Good girl. Sit. Roll over.

'Did the convention go well? Did you enjoy it?'

'Yes. Very well.'

'You sound tired. Maybe you can rest now, hum?'

'Yes. I am tired.'

'You get a good rest before Friday. You'll be ready to go again. Good-bye, hon.'

'Frank – wait.' She bit her lip. 'Why don't you call Barton's Catering Service and ask them to take care of things?'

'Barton's! Since when do you need them? They charge a hell of a lot and you can do it better. You got those coloured girls to come in last time. You have a reputation –'

'Never mind my reputation. I don't want to do it. We can afford Barton's.'

'Bonnie, what else do you have to do that's more important?'

'Don't say that.' She knew her voice was getting too loud. 'Don't say that to me again.'

'Look. It's no good arguing over the phone. I'll see you Friday.'

180

'Tell Mrs Myers to get the house ready. And call the caterer.'

She hung up the phone and stood motionless beside it. She waited for it to ring again, but made no move when it did. Anne's voice came to her. 'Aren't you going to answer?' Bonnie shook her head. Finally, it stopped.

Bonnie's numbness was physical, dead fingers and toes actualizing the guilt held at bay. Her husband was at a crisis time in his career, although he spoke only of parties and shirts.

The refrigerator went off and left a surplus of silence in the room. Anne spoke from the sofa. 'Mom, I'm sorry. I was way out of line. I'm sorry.'

Bonnie turned slowly, then hurried to Anne and they hugged each other.

'Anne,' she burst out. 'I don't know what's happening to me. I'm not ready to be old.'

'You aren't supposed to change.'

'We've always been friends,' Bonnie said. 'You told me things.'

'Not everything.' Anne caught her breath. 'I'm not sure I want you to tell me everything, either.'

'Anne, I want to talk about John. I never told you children about the war. You just barely know his name.'

Anne looked back in mute misery. Bonnie reached over and took her hand. 'Please, dearest. Please.'

Anne settled slowly back against the sofa pillows. 'All right,' she said in a small voice. 'Tell me.'

'Well, we met one night in the Comanche Room. That's what it used to be called – in the Wheatland Hotel.'

They talked until the sharp edges of things in the room softened and ran together, and the streetlight outside came on. The pictures were sharp again, rehearsed during the past week of remembering. The years between were blurred ones now. Anne listened quietly. Bonnie wasn't sure how Anne was reacting, but it didn't matter. Bonnie was filled with love and wonder. They could have made it. Anything should have been possible. If only she had known.

It was dark when Anne left the sofa. She switched the lamps on, and went into the kitchen. Bonnie looked up when she heard Anne's exclamation. She found her daughter folding back the tissue paper in the long box to expose a mass of lush

181

crimson blooms and long, deep, green stems and leaves.

'Lordy,' Bonnie exclaimed. 'I forgot to open the box.'

They found a tall vase and searched for an appropriate setting for long-stemmed roses.

'I didn't need the daisies,' Bonnie said.

'Poor Daddy,' Anne murmured, so low that Bonnie didn't have to answer.

Twelve

Bonnie met Madge the next day at the little health food restaurant their young friends Cal and Mary had found during the convention. The two women made their way downstairs from the sidewalk to sit in a dark varnished booth next to an uncovered mortar-spattered brick wall. They ordered herbal tea and a vegetable casserole topped with sunflower seeds and almonds.

Madge had news. 'I saw Martha Boyd this afternoon and she was beside herself. Seems her right arm here in New York office, Joyce Carr – you remember Joyce – resigned last night.'

'I don't remember Joyce.'

'Yes you do. She was the little blonde girl who was scooting around at the convention with all the answers. She's one of the paid people at Earth Savers headquarters who keeps things going. Well, anyway, she got proposed to during the convention. Marriage, I mean. She's marrying a man from Idaho, or Utah, or one of those God-forsaken places, and she's going to move. Gave a month's notice.'

Bonnie was sympathetic. 'Oh, my. She'll be hard to replace.'

'You bet. Do you think Anne might know someone who'd be willing to take an interesting part-time job that doesn't pay enough? Does she have any rich, bored, intelligent friends?'

'I haven't heard her mention anyone of that description. I'll ask, though.'

'It's a real pain, isn't it? When are you leaving?'

'Friday.' Bonnie bit her lower lip. 'I just changed the reservation.'

Madge reversed the direction of her teacup, returned it to the saucer as her eyes lit up. 'Hey,' she said, 'do you want to hear a piece of gossip? About our good-looking banquet speaker?'

The flavour changed in her food; Bonnie swallowed quickly.

'Martha says John Blake has something going with Barbara Aiken.'

A blank stare from Bonnie brought further quick information. 'You know. She's the little blues singer over at the Leopard Room. Don't you remember? Some of the delegates were talking about her at coffee break. Of course, he's married but –'

Bonnie held up a hand. Madge stopped. 'What's the matter?'

Bonnie caught her breath and talked rapidly. 'There's something I didn't tell you, Madge. I want to tell you.'

'Yes?' Madge looked frustrated, her momentum interrupted.

Bonnie plunged. 'I know John Blake. I knew him a long time ago.' She took a deep breath. 'I was once married to him.' The effect was all she could have hoped for. 'Watch your chin, Madge,' she said. 'You're going to lose it.'

Madge leaned slowly back. 'Bonnie, Bonnie Forbes! How could you do this? Not a word, not a hint. You let us rave on –'

Bonnie put her hand to her head. 'I'm sorry, Madge. I couldn't talk about it. I was too upset. I didn't know what to say.'

'I don't understand. Martha said he's been married for years to a Boston socialite. I don't think she knew he'd been married before. And she thinks she's so smart! Are you sure –?' She stopped and laughed. 'Well,' she said blushing, 'I mean, it's just such a surprise.'

Bonnie knew Madge was waiting. Bonnie took a sip of tea before looking at Madge again across the expectant silence.

'It was a very long time ago. During the war.'

'Which war?'

'Our war, Madge. World War Two.'

'Great God,' Madge gasped, 'way back then.'

'Yes. We were married for two years, but we were only together for one week.'

183

Madge's eyes were going soft. 'Oh, yes. One of those. It happened. I wonder if any of them survived.' She sat back and fumbled for a handkerchief in her purse. 'The marriages I mean. Everything was so different when they came back.'

'We didn't get that far. We got an annullment after two years.'

'Was he as attractive then?'

'Oh, yes. He was a pilot.'

'Well, of course, wouldn't you know it? I mean what else? Silver wings and pink pants and the stiffening out of his cap. Sid was in the infantry. A ninety-day wonder. We married when he got his commission. A miserable hot day in Georgia. I was sick from the train ride. We decided on the spur of the moment, but of course we'd been dating for years.' She gazed at the far wall. Bonnie identified a piece of cauliflower on her plate and wondered why there was a rock in her stomach. *Barbara Aiken, you said?*

Madge came back. 'How could you let him go, Bonnie?'

She shook her head. 'Many reasons, I suppose. The biggest was that I thought he wanted it. I felt guilty. There was a girl he had dated for years – and a life in Boston. Those days while he was at the base in Lancaster were separate. Seemed like everything at the time.'

'And you haven't seen him since?'

'Well – not until last night.'

'What you must have been feeling during his speech.'

'I mean after the speech. I saw him after the speech.'

Madge gasped. 'Well, weren't you the sly one? A headache. Oh, it's so exciting. They do say it's disappointing. Going back.'

Bonnie shook her head. 'Not with John. Nothing's disappointing the way they say.'

'Oh, shit!' Madge's expression matched her tone of voice. 'Here comes Martha Boyd and Joyce. Talk about timing.'

Bonnie only had time to frown and barely move her head, to signal a change of subject.

Martha Boyd, convention chairperson, descended upon them. 'What luck! But of course, you're friends of Cal's, too. Isn't this place cute?'

Martha had a way of assuming control of an encounter. The twosome became a foursome, and Madge's plane time grew nearer. They all left together to look for cabs.

'We aren't going in the same direction,' Bonnie said.

'You can share a cab with me, Bonnie,' Martha said decisively. 'It will be my treat.' She moved off the curb and waved.

Bonnie leaned towards her friend and sent a hoarse whisper into Madge's ear. 'I stayed all night.'

Madge seized Bonnie's arm and hollered to Martha. 'Bonnie's going with me.' She beat Martha to the door of the cab, dragging Bonnie behind her. 'Thank you, Martha, you're a jewel.'

They scrambled into the cab and disappeared into the traffic, leaving Martha in her navy blue polyester pants suit, one arm frozen in the air, balancing on the street side of the kerb.

Thirteen

Bonnie sat in a window seat, looking out at the undiluted blue, and at the curdled carpet of clouds sliding slowly under the plane. She was weightless, detached, eternal. She was Diana and Venus and Aphrodite. She had wept quietly at the last sight of New York City. It occurred to her that she had laughed and cried a great deal in the past week – her emotions were just under her thumb, popping out all the time like a slippery spring. She was a freed canary, returning to her cage, and this thought made her cry again.

The lady sitting next to her put down her book and leaned over. 'Good-byes are sad, aren't they? I'm pretty good at sizing people up. I'll bet you just left your grandchildren.'

Bonnie blinked. 'No,' she said. 'No, you see I'm in love with this married man.'

The lady blinked back. 'Oh,' she said.

'And even if he wanted me, I could never take his wife's place

– with all the friends they share. And his clients, and all.' She appealed, 'Could I?'

'Well, no,' the lady stammered. She closed her book, found her place and opened it again, and then carefully closed it. 'You know, dear, you can't break up a marriage. It isn't the Christian thing to do. You'll just have to give him up.'

'I know,' Bonnie said thoughtfully. 'Unless we could have an affair. I think maybe we could have an affair. If only I didn't have this husband.'

'Oh, my dear.'

'Do you live in Lancaster?'

'No. I live just outside Chicago.'

'Good. Neither do I,' Bonnie said quickly. *The first lie. Another commandment busted.* She turned back to the blue sky.

Fourteen

She made the change in Chicago, and in midafternoon saw the Lancaster terminal below. She had always seen coming down on an airstrip as an act of great faith. The setting down of the giant plane on that little ribbon rendered other miracles more comprehensible.

She stayed in her seat until the rest of the passengers had pushed past her through the narrow aisle. When the white-haired man leaning on his cane brought up the rear, she sighed and fell in behind him, bulging tote bag bumping against her side.

Her steps were slow as she came out of the ramp into the waiting room. She looked out the glass walls at the runways. This building had been constructed on the site of the abandoned air base. Those runways had once been squadrons of B-17's and B-26's taking off one after another on their way to

England or the South Pacific. She stood still, hearing the motors, seeing the glisten of their wings in the cold dawn mist. She clung to the vision, fighting the reality of the big jet that slowly revolved into position, lights blinking.

'Nana!'

She turned quickly and the people in the room fell into focus. A small body flew across the floor, short round legs blurring in motion. She let go of the bag and bent her knees to receive the little arms that locked around her neck. She swooped the two-year-old boy off the floor as she stood and squeezed his solid, wiggling, warm body against her own.

The tears and laughter, both so close to the surface, emerged together and she held him close with all her strength. The body grew rigid, clinging softness suddenly turning to rebellion.

'Oh, sweet,' she said, 'did Nana squeeze too tight?'

He was squirming to get down, and she reluctantly put him back on his feet. Through the mist in her eyes she saw Linda smiling at the reunion. Linda was in her usual disarray. Her trench coat with its crooked hem had been hastily fastened with a twisted belt. The baby was getting to be a load. He leaned his head against Linda's shoulder, wide eyes looking with distrust at unfamiliar surroundings. The distrust extended to Bonnie, as he examined her long and hard.

'Oh,' she said tearfully, 'you can't have forgotten me.'

Slowly the round, blue eyes melted and a wisp of smile played with his lips. Bonnie kissed him three times, brushed a kiss across her oldest daughter's cheek, and turned to retrieve her bag.

'I wasn't expecting anyone to meet me.'

'Of course we wanted to meet you,' Linda said. 'Besides, it was an excuse to get out of the house.'

Bonnie extended a free finger to little Luke, and they moved together to the baggage conveyer.

In the car she learned that nothing of importance had happened except that the children had survived a bout of vomiting and diarrhoea. Linda felt that Frank had missed his wife very much.

'I don't see why,' Bonnie answered defensively. 'He doesn't spend that much time with me.'

'He kept the television blaring when he was home, even when

he wasn't in the room. And he showed up at the party in a blue tie with a green shirt.'

Bonnie shifted the baby to her other knee.

'It almost seemed like he did it on purpose. He was so sorry for himself. Going alone. He hates those parties anyway.'

'Why couldn't he just enjoy it?' Bonnie burst out. 'Flirt with somebody, get drunk?'

Linda stole a side glance. 'Of course, you're kidding.' She pulled around a truck. Linda was a fast driver. It was one of the few daring things she did. 'Actually, this party was an especially bad one for him. It was George Ames's night and people were looking out of the corner of their eyes for Dad's tears.'

'All the more reason to get drunk.'

Linda gave her a quick, puzzled look. From the backseat Luke called, 'Nana, I threw up on the rug.'

'Did he ever,' Linda muttered.

Bonnie clucked the expected sympathetic acknowledgement of this bit of news.

At last Linda asked, 'How was your trip? Was it worth all the trouble?'

'It was –' Bonnie was startled at a choking in her throat that made her start over. 'It was wonderful.'

'That good, huh? The people at the convention weren't too kooky?'

'Oh, no! All kinds of people are interested in the environment, Linda. Everybody should be. We had some impressive speakers. Senator Callahan for one.'

For the first time the problem of mentioning John appeared. She didn't want to. The prospect of anyone in her family being interested enough to read the itinerary seemed remote. Yet if they did find out, her not mentioning it would raise questions. She quickly decided to keep quiet.

'Dad doesn't like Senator Callahan.'

'He doesn't like anyone more liberal than Calvin Coolidge.'

'Was Coolidge terribly conservative?'

'I think so. I wasn't much into politics in kindergarten.'

'I was. I wore an "I like Ike" buttone to school every day.'

'I know. You and your button. Your dad put you up to that.'

'I didn't think Dad could be wrong.'

'Neither did I. But looking back on it, I wish I had voted for Stevenson.'

Linda and the children came in with her. Linda wanted to hear about the Broadway plays Bonnie had seen and the shopping she had done. Bonnie's enthusiastic description of Anne's apartment and career was received by her sister with silence, finally broken by a halfhearted, 'Well, if that's what she wants. Anne knows how to look out for Anne.' Bonnie knew she had made the right decision in omitting mention of Anne's part-time male roommate.

As Linda watched Bonnie unpack, she suggested, 'Shall I call Mike to come here after work? He'd like to hear about your trip.'

Mike couldn't care less about my trip. 'Of course. Call him.'

Linda picked up the phone from the night stand. 'Dad ate with us several times.'

'I'm sure he appreciated that.'

'He enjoyed the kids. In small doses, of course. Thirty minutes is about his limit.'

Bonnie fixed her eyes on the window and tried to think about dinner. She couldn't remember a menu. *Start with the meat. Take it from the freezer and thaw it in the microwave oven.* Painfully the details were drawn out. *Like riding a bicycle. How many people in a pound of ground beef?*

Somehow, in her sunny, daisy-papered kitchen, she put together a dinner. Linda's chatter laced through Luke's clattering the pans pulled from his special drawer, and the baby's persistent demands for the rubber chicken thrown to the floor. Bonnie often stood immobilized in the middle of the kitchen, waiting to remember where to find a utensil that had been stored in the same place for fourteen years. *Too many daisies. Roses would be enough.*

She heard men's voices in the hall. A cramp twisted her stomach. Frank and Mike appeared in the kitchen doorway. Frank stood tall, his curly, white hair in place, shoes shined, dark suit and sombre striped tie straight as always. He looked handsomer and younger than he had been in her recent thoughts. He smiled broadly and crossed the room to give her a quick, dry stab of a kiss. He reached around where the children couldn't see and pinched her bottom. Irritation flashed. Resolutely she laid down the spoon she was carrying, and pulled him back for a longer hug and kiss. The exchange was self-conscious. Frank had trouble with public display of affection. Or private either, for that matter, except in bed.

They were sitting down to eat when Bonnie remembered she had forgotten to make the coffee. Even when they found she had salted the mashed potatoes twice, Frank was patient. 'We'll let it pass this time,' he said magnanimously.

Linda, Mike and the children left early, and Bonnie dutifully called her third daughter, Karen, and checked in. Karen, after almost ten years of marriage, had enrolled as a freshman in the university and they weren't seeing much of her these days.

'I would have come over,' she apologized, 'but I have a paper due Monday and a French quiz. I just don't have time to breathe.'

She sounded happy. Frank thought she was being absurd, but Bonnie thought she sounded happy.

'Karen sounds happy,' she said thoughtfully as she hung up the phone.

'What's she going to school for?' Frank lowered the evening paper.

'She'll find a direction. She didn't like any of the jobs she's had.'

'It isn't too late. She might still have babies.'

Bonnie tapped a pencil against the telephone pad. Neither Karen nor her mother had ever been able to say to Frank, 'Karen doesn't want babies.' Bonnie put down the pencil. 'Karen doesn't want babies,' she told him.

Frank stared at her, then covered his face with the paper again. 'Of course she does. Every woman wants babies.' A full page ad on Murray and Penn's anniversary clearance sale covered the back of the paper. 'She just hasn't realized it yet.'

Bonnie sighed and walked away.

Fifteen

She took a long, hot bath, smoothing her pink body with pink lotion afterwards, fluffing her short hair with the brush – hair curly and thick from the steam. She slid the long satin gown over her head and walked barefooted back into the bedroom.

She heard water running in the other bathroom, and realized Frank was shaving. She scooted between the sheets on her side of the king-sized bed and closed her eyes, leaving the small lamp burning. Frank would switch off the lamp and reach across to pull her over to his side. They always wriggled out of their nightclothes under the covers in the dark. This was the way it was done in the 1940s, and the way they still did it. In fact, the whole procedure hadn't changed much. Well, there were worse things than predictability.

Worse things like wanting another man, Bonnie? She pulled the sheet over her head. She allowed herself one short moment of wanting John, wanting him from the smallest emerging cell, wanting him from the most protected inner cave. Then she pulled the sheet down and opened her eyes. This was home. The sight of the flimsy gauze curtains moved gently by an evening breeze, the hand-printed full-blown roses scattered sparingly across the white paper, the celadon velvet chaise, usually confirmed her sense of security and peace – prelude to the whole procedure.

When Frank turned out the light and reached for her in the dark, she closed the door on reason and dropped into a mindless drift of feeling. She was open, abandoned, aroused. She could feel Frank responding. It was good for him tonight.

When it was finished and they lay back, tired, their lingering perspiration turning cool, Bonnie told herself she was home. Her kitchen would look more familiar tomorrow.

'I should send you away more often,' Frank told her. 'You were really hot tonight.'

True. I might even be able to go round again. Knowing this was not possible, she stayed on her side of the bed. She didn't respond to his comment and he leaned across and kissed her quickly, before settling down under the covers. She thought he might be asleep when she asked, 'Are we set for tomorrow night?'

'Yes.' Frank stirred. 'I had Miss Nolan call Barton's. Christ, they want a hundred dollars plus liquor and food.'

'It's tax deductible,' she answered defensively. 'You don't realize how much work it is to entertain on this scale.'

'I just know that your parties work. You make it look easy.'

'It isn't,' Bonnie answered. 'It's not easy at all.'

'You told me you enjoyed it.'

'That was a rash statement made years ago. I used to.' *When did it change? How long has it been work?* 'I don't like it any more. I'm tired.'

'I thought this trip would give you a break. Hell, I'm always raring to get back to work after a vacation.'

'Maybe the nature of our work has something to do wth it.'

'Woman's work is important.'

'You constantly belittle everything I do.'

'God, Bonnie, I don't know what's happening to you. Ever since you got in with that bunch of do-gooders trying to save the planet. No, before that. The Viet Nam War. Those people are just troublemakers. They like to stir things up – anything for a cause.'

'And you're opposed to change just because it's change. You never give a thought to the nature of the cause.'

Frank sat up in bed, his bulk in the dark high above her frozen in tension. 'All right, Bonnie, you want a fight? We're doing it your way. What do you want from me?'

Bonnie laid the back of her wrist across her forehead. 'No, Frank, no, I don't want to fight. I'm sorry. I'm really sorry. You have other problems. I don't know how we got into this.'

Frank slowly lay back on his pillow. 'I knew I shouldn't have let you go on this trip. I thought it might help us. Jesus Christ, you can't even remember to make the coffee.'

Her anger swelled like a helium balloon. She swallowed it and felt it pressing against the walls of her chest, and pushing up into her throat. *I know it's my fault. My fault. We can talk when things are settled at the plant.*

She hated Frank at this moment. She hated him because it was her fault. She hated him for falling asleep so quickly. *I've hated him before. It happens when you live with someone. You get over it.* The fight used to precede the lovemaking. *Why can't we talk? I didn't even ask him how he's making it at work. My fault.*

Frank's predicament at the plant loomed over her in the dark as a monster that had not been given its proper dread. After fifteen years of waiting to become president of Scott Manufacturing another man had been promoted over him. When Clem hung onto the presidency long past the usual retirement age, he brought his first vice-president to the age of sixty-three and the board was afraid of another old man. They had just given the position to George Ames, age forty-two, only ten years with the company compared to Frank's thirty-four. Frank said it was no surprise, but she knew he had hoped until the end. His impending presidency had ruled their lives for years. She sat up and shook her feather pillow, threw it down and lay on it again.

Sixteen

It rained on Saturday. A soggy, grey drizzle clouded the horizon and made them turn the lights on. Frank dressed for the office, but he seemed reluctant to leave. After breakfast he stood at the bay window off the breakfast room, looking out at the yard through the hanging plants. 'It's greening up. Going to need mowing before we know it.'

Bonnie answered from the table, 'We'll have a houseful tonight if we can't use the patio.'

She pushed back her chair and walked over to stand beside him. 'I'll bet the tulips broke through while I was gone. The rain'll bring them along.'

'We'll never get rid of the cigarette smoke!' Frank said.

'The furnace fan circulates pretty well. I wonder if we'll need heat or air conditioning.'

Frank walked slowly down the two steps into the family room. There was much she needed to do, but Bonnie felt he wanted her to follow.

He dropped heavily into his chair. She stooped to sit on the other side of the coffee table, changed her mind and moved to the oversized ottoman closer to Frank. He looked haggard, and she wanted to reach over and take his hand.

'Frank, what are you going to do?' she asked instead, willing her voice to speak handclasps.

He shook his head slowly. It was a big question. 'I change my mind every day,' he said dully. 'It's for damned sure Ames would like to be rid of me. On the other hand, he knows he needs me.'

'He'd never make it without you.'

'Nonsense, of course he would. George isn't short on brains, but he has new ideas. With Fred dead and Clem retired, I'm the last of the old guard. I had some ideas, too, but they'll never be carried out now.'

She groped for the right words. 'Frank. Have you ever considered that this might be a good thing that happened? That you could be free. Take an early retirement.'

His expression was unchanged. 'I thought about it. Bob Miller was telling me about a retirement community in Arizona. Nice apartments – golf course – no snow.'

A cold hand closed around Bonnie's heart. 'Retirement community?'

'He think's there's opportunity there for business know-how. The place is just getting started. I could get paid for consulting – get away from the long hours. God knows you've done enough complaining about that.'

'But a retirement community? I'm not old enough.'

'You wouldn't have to be. I am. Anyway, the limit's fifty-five. You'll soon be there. We'd be all set for old age. They have great facilities.'

Bonnie stood up and walked to the window, so she could turn her back.

Frank gave a short, quick laugh. 'You're really sensitive about this, aren't you? Well, don't worry. I'll probably stick with Scott at least two more years. I don't think Ames'll put on any pressure knowing how close I am to retirement age.'

Bonnie spoke with her back turned. 'I didn't mean that kind of retirement. I thought we could travel – do things there wasn't time for before.'

'Well, I thought about that, too.'

Bonnie turned slowly.

'How'd you like to move into one of those motor homes – just wander around the country?'

Bonnie's eyes widened in horror.

'No,' Frank responded wearily, 'I suppose not.'

She seemed to be slipping into the canyon that divided them across the family room. She stepped carefully and slowly, speaking as she walked. 'A trip around the world, Frank. All the places we've only read about.'

Frank's weary expression did not change. 'Living out of a suitcase in hotels and cruise ships?'

'We could take study tours. Learn about places and see them at the same time. Frank, I've never seen Paris!' She had to control a sudden impulse to break into sobs. The injustice of it.

Frank put his elbows on his knees and lowered his face into his hands.

She pushed her feelings into the canyon and laid a cover over it to walk across. 'Well, we have time to think about it,' she said with forced lightness. 'I have to call the catering service and find out how they're handling this tonight. We haven't had anything catered since Linda's wedding.'

She stopped by Frank's chair and reached over and laid her hand on his shoulder. 'One thing at a time, hey?'

He stood up and left the room, and she felt that she had failed him again.

It was a good party, in spite of the rain. Bonnie stayed at Frank's side as much as she could. She was the beautiful and charming hostess, at the right hand of the company's elder statesman. Frank was already assuming the role, even as George Ames had taken on a quiet self-assurance with the race over and a new yoke of responsibility settling around his shoulders.

Bonnie was disturbed by how old and tired Clem looked. The indestructible man seemed shorter than he had a few weeks ago. She watched him speak with uncharacteristic sharpness to

Eva when Eva suggested they sit down during the course of a conversation with the chief accountant and his wife.

Jenny Ames, on the contrary, talked more than usual, her movements quick and constant. As the new president's wife, her colour was high and there were little half-moons under her carefully outlined eyes. Bonnie wanted to take her by the hand and lead her to a quiet corner and say 'Shut up.'

Bonnie was surprised to find Jenny standing quietly at the bedroom window watching the rain. Bonnie had hurried back to the master bedroom in search of a pin for a wayward strap.

They saw each other at the same time, both startled. Bonnie smiled, Jenny did not. The bubbles had vanished. *Has she been crying?*

Jenny's pomegranate-coloured chiffon dress just covered her knees. Her long pearl necklace outlined its décolletage. Although cleavage and legs were at their best advantage, her face was drawn.

'Bonnie,' she said, nodding slightly.

'Jenny?' Bonnie smiled. 'It is getting stuffy in there.' She walked to the dresser and took a safety pin from the cushion, reaching inside the shoulder of her dress to find the strap. 'Strap popped in the middle of the latest evaluation of President Ford.'

'Your evaluation?'

'Don't be silly. They didn't even see me leave.'

The two lamps in the room showed the wraps hiding the spread on the big bed. Bonnie's pale beige dress blended with her skin and the highlights in her brown hair. 'Could you lend me a hand?'

Jenny helped locate and hold the strap while Bonnie pinned.

'There we go. Thanks,' Bonnie said, looking Jenny full in the eyes.

Jenny crumpled. Putting her hand to her mouth, she cried.

'Oh, now,' Bonnie exclaimed. New warmth towards Jenny came in a rush.

Soon Jenny wiped her eyes and straightened, the half-moons darkened. 'I'm sorry,' she said. 'I'm better now.' She moved back towards the window.

'I can't take Eva's place,' Jenny said, quietly desperate. 'Bonnie, will you do it? You're prepared. You know how.

Everything works out for you. It's a beautiful party tonight. I'd die!'

'This is a catered party. You could do it. Besides you don't have to be Eva. Be yourself. Do what you feel like.' Even as she said it, Bonnie wondered. *Just cool it. Turn down your volume.*

'You're always so calm. So in control.'

Bonnie looked at her sharply. 'Really, Jenny?'

Jenny plunged ahead. 'Well, now, that's what I mean. You know that these people don't want you to be different. You've handled it.'

'I handled it by giving in.'

'Women don't like me.'

Ageing sex kitten. The red dress a terrible mistake. 'I'll help you.'

'Eva asked me to chair the playhouse committee after she leaves.'

'She was just being courteous. Dorothy Vance will be the one.'

'Really? How am I supposed to know that?'

'Scott is the big benefactor – its president's wife gets to run the show. You could accept the honour and let others do the work.' Jenny looked dubious as she listened. 'On the other hand, I think you would be respected for asking for a little more time.'

Jenny sighed and walked over to the mirror. 'Gawd, I look awful!'

'Adjusting our faces is the easy part. Meanwhile, don't worry. It'll come along.'

'I didn't realize. I didn't pick this job. I don't know what to do with it.'

'Just grit your teeth and buy another fur coat,' Bonnie answered, knowing her cynicism was out of character. *Who is this person saying these things?*

They returned to the party where Jenny continued her low-key flirting.

Bonnie was emptying ashtrays in the family room when Eva approached her, their converstaion made private by the level of noise in the room.

'Thank you, Bonnie. It's been nice.' Eva looked weary.

'We're going to miss you.'

'We've been around a long time – you and I. Well, Florida isn't all that far away. We'll be back from time to time. And of course you'll come see us.'

'Of course.'

'Clem isn't well, you know.' She lowered her voice and Bonnie had to listen carefully. 'He doesn't like me to talk about it. But honestly, I'm terrified at the thought of being without him.'

'You have a good marriage, Eva. You've stayed close.'

Eva shook her head, her mouth working. Bonnie was bothered by the sight of the little puckers around Eva's lips. 'I'm truly not whole without him,' she got out at last.

'Nonsense,' Bonnie chided. 'Don't diminish yourself because you've had a good marriage.'

Eva reassumed control. 'We have a lead on a beautiful house in Florida. Clem talked about a condominium, but we have all those lovely antiques. I'm not ready to parcel them out to the children yet. I've been working like crazy getting things sorted out so we can send for them when we're ready.'

Bonnie found herself saying, 'Let me know when I can help you.'

'You're a good friend, Bonnie,' Eva responded eagerly. 'I may need you.'

Bonnie had never been close to Eva. Their friendship was more like a friendship between men – all tied up with common responsibilities and goals. She wondered if she would find it hard to be generous now that those ties were broken. She watched Eva walk away and realized that she was old. *When did she get old?*

Everyone was gone by midnight. When the last group of cars left the driveway, Bonnie and Frank switched off the lights and went to bed. Frank was soon breathing heavily and regularly. Bonnie lay a long time in the dark, reviewing conversations of the day and thinking about wives and friends and jobs.

Seventeen

They slept late. After breakfast, Frank read the Sunday paper and Bonnie put the house back in order. She threw herself into the straightening and cleaning – a physical catharsis. Frank lifted his feet over the sweeper without lowering the financial page.

Linda and the children dropped in during the afternoon. With the baby sleeping in the crib in the guest room, and Luke crawling around the kitchen floor pushing a tiny automobile and vibrating his lips in automobile noises. Linda joined her mother. Bonnie was starting the dinner roast. Mike had to stop by the office for a minute.

'He'll be there all afternoon,' Linda said. 'I know Mike cares for me, and he loves his kids, too, but he really likes it at the office better than at home.'

'If that's true, Linda, it's sad. Men need a home. Even when the office is important.'

'He's getting just like Daddy. What did you do about it?' Bonnie shook her head. 'I don't know. I'm no model.'

'I've been working on him to take a vacation. If we could get away by ourselves for a week – maybe he could see me, without the kids. I don't exist without the kids. Luke even follows me to the bathroom. Howls if I shut him out.'

'You need a vacation. I could keep the kids.' A tight band fastened around Bonnie's middle and pushed the pressure up into her chest. Linda dived at Luke as he strained to reach a glass near the edge of the counter. Only a second ago he had been pushing the car on the other side of the room.

'I was counting on that,' Linda answered quickly, lifting a writhing child. 'The big problem is getting Mike to go. He think's he's indispensable.'

'Nobody's indispensable,' Bonnie said slowly. 'They could always get along somehow.'

'That's what I keep telling him.' She gave Luke a drink of water and returned his attention to the little car.

'Mom, do you know I'll be thirty next year?'

'Don't remind me.'

'Remember when I was headed for a big career in fashion? All down the drain.'

'Thirty isn't old. You can still try your wings when the children are a little older.'

'Rubbish! All those pretty young things just out of college to compete with. It's not as though I've been growing. Just a couple of years part-time clerking during school.'

'In a good store. They were interested in you.'

The words came out in a rush. 'Mr Barnes is still there. He said I could make buyer. I've been thinking about it a lot. If you – if you would keep the kids.'

Bonnie laid down the onion and knife. 'Oh, no.' The band grew tighter. 'No, Linda.'

'Why don't you think about it?' Linda's fists were drawn tight, her arms suspended. 'Please think about it. I know it's sudden. I didn't lead up to it very well. You don't have a family anymore. You've had your chance. I've still got time.'

Bonnie managed to get out something about a baby sitter.

'Mike wouldn't let me get a sitter,' Linda moaned. 'He says I shouldn't leave them while they're little, but he'd let you – just until they're old enough for nursery school. I need you, Mom.' Bonnie knew that she did.

Bonnie steadied herself against the cabinet. 'I'll think about it.' Linda threw her arms around her mother's neck. 'Don't get your hopes up,' Bonnie protested. 'In fact, no. I'm pretty sure the answer's no.'

Linda withdrew suddenly. 'I haven't even talked to Mike or to Mr Barnes. I hadn't really decided on it before, but now I'm so excited. You think about it. I know it's probably no, but you think about it. How wonderful it would be.'

Bonnie slowly picked up the knife and the onion. She was sliding backwards. Those teenage years when the girls were always testing. Bonnie's legs grew weak. Linda moved quickly to pull Luke out of the wastebasket, his hands covered with

200

coffee grounds. Better straighten this out right now. As Bonnie stood erect and opened her mouth, Frank's voice came down from the doorway.

'It's a beautiful day. Why don't we walk to the park?'

Bonnie swallowed her cries, feeling them stuck in her throat. 'Go ahead,' she said. 'I'll stay with the baby. I'm not through in the kitchen yet.'

She could reach back in her head and draw on the memory bank. As vague as remembered pain was the recollection of ecstasy when each tiny mite first closed its eager mouth over her nipple and sucked its life from her breast. Their first wobbly steps, and the curves in the fair smooth flesh where you pushed the oil and powder, the big, round eyes changing from anxiety to peace when they settled on Mommy. She had to reach deliberately for such memories. The blanket impression of those years was of an endless treadmill world, ruled by persons under three feet tall. She had forgotten about the bathroom thing until Linda brought it up. She could see the three of them, all eyes, lined up watching. And the way they would materialize out of nowhere when she wanted to take a nap. 'What can I do?' She read stories in *Good Housekeeping* about the mothers who wept when the last child started school, and she wondered what was wrong with her. Those two blissful hours. For a while she made a point of sitting down with a book, but that didn't last long. The book should wait, like dessert, until the errands were run. Sew a tutu, march for polio, recruit teachers for vacation Bible school. During the two weeks that she had read a book every morning she had always returned it to the shelf, not leaving it around for Frank to see. *Why did I do that? WHY DID I DO THAT?* The sacrificial lamb – self-appointed. *My fault.*

Mike arrived at the same time that Frank, Linda, and Luke returned from the park. Luke had enjoyed the mud puddles, and after he was bathed and redressed they were ready to eat. Bonnie had opened a novel, but didn't know what she had read. She left it on the chair when she went back to the kitchen.

How could it happen again? Frank had almost finished carving the roast when she remembered she had forgotten to make the coffee. She stammered something and pushed her chair back. She felt Frank's eyes burning through her. Out of the corner of her eye, she saw him lay down the knife. All he said was 'Bonnie.'

Peace settled over her. Her legs were strong when she stood up. She looked only at Frank, and said in a calm, modulated voice, 'I quit.' She laid her napkin on her plate and walked out of the room.

It was a long walk to the bedroom. She stood in the middle of the quiet room. She had spoiled everyone's dinner – it was an expensive roast. A smile tickled the corners of her mouth and she didn't know what to do with it.

Frank appeared in the doorway. She was still standing. 'Tell them to go home,' she said. He looked more worried than angry. He left. Ten minutes later he came back and closed the bedroom door behind him, standing in front of it.

'I'm sorry, Frank.' She was, and not so happy now. 'You're going to have to let me go.'

'You can see Dr Adams in the morning. You're not well.'

'I'm all right,' she said. 'I'm not crazy. I've lived thirty years as your extra arm, or the children's extra legs. I want to be the whole thing.'

She could see him holding on, manoeuvring. 'What is it you want?'

'There's a job in New York,' she said. She had just thought of this. 'In the Earth Savers' office. I'm going to take it.'

He looked frightened now. 'Just promise me you'll see Dr Adams.'

'No, I won't promise. That old chauvinist wouldn't understand me any better than you can. Oh Frank ...' They were still standing – far apart. 'I'm sorry, so sorry, but I can't stop it. There's more than this to life. I've got to find out.'

'You're acting like a goddamned teenager.'

'It's not too late. I've paid my dues. I've earned it.'

'Paid your dues? God, Bonnie, is that the way you see it? I've worked my butt off to make it good for you.' He checked himself and lowered his voice, desperation creeping in. 'Please, Bonnie, give us time.'

'I've been a long time coming to this place. I'm sure.'

It hurt to see him frightened. He never had been before.

'I'll leave,' she said .'We won't have to get a divorce right away.'

'Divorce?' he whispered.

The essence of bad dreams hung on the word.

'A legal separation,' she mumbled. 'We can start there.'

Frank whirled and left the room.

Eighteen

The man in the aisle seat opened a novel with a beautiful blonde bleeding on the cover. Bonnie closed her eyes.

Less than three weeks ago, she had been on this same flight. She had said, 'It's a little windy,' to the man next to her on that flight, and they had pursued the matter of air currents for some time. All the while, her memory had registered him as a blank face and body. Her mind behind the empty words had churned over Frank's loss of promotion to company president, and their grandchild's infected ear.

A tornado had rolled across her life since then, dipping and churning and altering the landscape. Now she had left the shocked and injured behind, to find their own rejuvenation.

She realized the man had spoken. She inclined her head towards him and said, 'What?'

'I said, that must be Des Moines down there.'

'Oh. Yes. It could very well be.' She didn't lean forward to check on Des Moines. The man returned to his book.

Marriage was forever, and the thought of leaving Frank had not entered her conscious mind until she told him. The surprise came to them both. 'I quit,' she had said, reversing a thirty-year thrust with two simple words. They were all still back there, and she was here. They would lean against her and find her gone, and tumble and be bruised. But their bruises would heal, just as her own bruises would heal. The leaning post was not exposed, no longer protected by the leaners. Let them handle their own bruises, as she strained to handle hers.

'Something to drink?' a smiling voice intruded and Bonnie ordered diet soda. She lowered the tray in front of her to support the cold can and ice-filled glass. Her neighbour ordered Scotch, and offered Bonnie his package of peanuts.

Oh, thank you, no. We'll be having lunch.' She smiled though, and for the first time looked at him. He had straight hair, cut short, and a thin moustache. He was neither young nor old, and she did not find him attractive. He wasn't wearing a ring. She wondered if he had someone to sleep with, or how he managed if he didn't.

'Matter of fact,' she said. 'I get two lunches. Another one when I change for New York.'

'How about that?' he answered enthusiastically.

She wondered if he could tell she was different now – free to wonder if he wondered. Not that he would be interested, but if she wondered, maybe he wondered.

She looked at the hand holding the plastic cup and saw the rings still on her finger – reached for the discarded magazine on the seat between them and opened it on the tray, turning away.

She had reservations at the Rialto Hotel in New York. The woman at the travel agency had chosen it – moderately priced and centrally located. Still too expensive for an extended stay, it would do for starters. Her first thought had been of Anne's extra bedroom. She had dialled her New York daughter's number. The 'Hello' came in a bass voice. Bonnie repeated the number.

'Yes,' the voice said. 'That's the number.'

Bonnie said with a flash of memory, 'Is this Bill?'

'Yes, it is,' he answered. 'May I ask who this is?'

'It's Anne's mother. Is she there?'

'No, she isn't. Shall I have her call?'

'Yes. It's nice to meet you. You're back from Rome.'

'I got back last night. Anne said you'd been here.'

'On second thought, she needn't call. I'll try again. Thank you, Bill.' Anne's extra room was no longer empty.

'You're welcome. I'll tell her.'

Staying alone might be better. She would call Anne after she arrived.

'Staying in New York long?' her companion asked.

'Yes.' Her tone was pleasant, but she didn't look up from the magazine. The man beside her returned to his book and did not speak to her again.

Nineteen

The Rialto Hotel was relatively clean, respectably shabby. As the bellman closed the door after unloading her two suitcases and small trunk, Bonnie stood in the small walkway left in the middle of the room. Against the forest green walls, the blond oak dresser loomed large. Its mirror reflected a slender, middle-aged woman, rooted into the tweed carpet, clutching a purse and shopping bag.

She walked over to deposit her bags on the dresser top, and took out her comb. Neatly fluffed hair would make her a little less middle-aged. She shuddered, dropped her eyes to the floor, and allowed herself a long minute of panic, a drop to the bottom of the pool before pushing off for the top again.

She looked at her watch and found it was almost five o'clock. She went to the bathroom, came back and sat on the edge of the bed. She wasn't tired. She stood up, retrieved her purse and the key, and went out.

The gloomy, quiet hotel opened onto a groaning, singing, whistling, sighing street. She stepped into the melee and speeded up to pace herself with the rush-hour crowd, like entering an auto onto a freeway. She glided along with them, absorbing the vitality. They certainly were going somewhere.

The orange juice and hot dog stand on the corner was blantly offensive. A few doors down, the Moulin Blue restaurant with its faded awning was threadbare-elegant, deliberately inaccessible.

A poster on a light post announced a Tchaikovsky concert at Avery Fisher Hall. On the spur of the moment she joined the

205

end of a line getting onto a bus, stopping on the bottom step to raise her voice to the driver. 'How would I get to Lincoln Center?'

The driver ran a perspiring hand back and forth on the steering wheel and shouted a string of instructions. Occasionally a number emerged that she could understand. She was trying to sort out the sounds when he said clearly, 'Lady, will you get on or off?'

Bonnie stepped back to the street, mumbling, 'I'm sorry.' She blinked at an unexpected tear.

'Aaaaaaa, bus drivers!' She heard the voice and turned to look into a tired, round face. It belonged to a plump lady with one fat roller in her bangs, who was carrying a sack of greengroceries. 'Take any uptown bus to Sixty-seventh Street and change to crosstown.'

Bonnie smiled and said, 'Thanks,' and the lady's voice softened as she trotted off after the next bus.

Bonnie turned against the current and regained the sidewalk. She stopped for a 'Don't Walk' sign and felt the crowd surge around her. She plunged ahead.

As she watched for restaurant signs on the storefronts she passed she noted a bookstore and made a stop. She emerged a few minutes later, feeling good about her purchase – a small paperback, *Welcome to New York*, full of maps and information for the newcomer. Something to study over dinner.

In the soup and salad place, the tables looked new and clean, but the floor was not until a dark young man with enormous black eyes pushed a wide broom down the aisle, clearing a path. Bonnie saw him pinch a waitress as he sailed past. The girl jumped and hissed an unintelligible word, its tone four-lettered.

The faces around Bonnie kept changing. Bowls were emptied and scooped up by busboys, then instantly replaced by more bowls. She studied the maps in her new book, looking up to new faces that never looked back. She wondered how many people she had looked at today that she would never see again. The pretty black girl who sat ramrod straight, haughty as an African princess; the man with a short, thick scar on his cheek who hunched over his soup as though he were guarding it. She

206

wanted to know them, to find out their secrets. She went back for soggy cheesecake and ate it very slowly, so she could stay at the table.

When it was time, she rode the bus to Avery Fisher Hall. Inside the hall the floors were clean. People strolled to their seats. Concertgoers conversed in voices melting together in muted harmony appropriate to thirty-dollar seats. Jeans sat next to diamonds.

The Tchaikovsky was as good as a long, hot bath. Nerves and muscles let go as she surrendered to the passion of the Fifth Symphony. She cried. She hadn't cried over Tchaikovsky since she was fourteen. As she wiped away the first tears she stole a sideways glance at the gentleman next to her. His face was stern. Bored as Frank. She opened up her handkerchief with a flourish, ready to wipe and eyes and blow her nose with gusto.

At Fifth Avenue she got off the bus and walked back to the hotel. The crowd had thinned, and the pace slowed. She hesitated at window displays of real silk gowns and floor-length furs and a single jewel worthy of its own Fifth Avenue window. The evening was warm with a slight, cool breeze. The moisture in the air softened it, creeping under her loose jacket, and curling her hair. She still had some distance to go when random drops of rain appeared on the sidewalk. She looked down the street for a cab, saw none, returned her attention to the walking.

The drops accelerated into a gentle spring shower as she walked on, head high. By the time she reached the hotel lobby, her hair and clothes were wet, her forehead shiny. She winked at a mirrored reflection and shook her head like a puppy. The desk clerk grinned as she passed, and an old man dozing in the lobby woke up and watched her go by.

In the ugly little room she quickly unpacked the smallest suitcase and prepared for bed. In the gathered pocket inside the lid she had packed her jewellery case, and she pulled it out carefully now. She set it on the dresser, opened the lid, pushed aside the pearls and raised the false bottom. Tenderly she pulled out a sheet of paper with a torn edge in familiar handwriting – a box number and zip code. She held it, remembering another hand that had held it, summoning up an image of the hand, feeling it against her cheek. The paper

207

presence was with her tonight, instead of a real man. A shadow extending into a future of uncertain substance. She smiled covertly and extended a timid hand to the stranger under her skin, wanting to love and guide her into a path sprouting unnamed buds.

She returned the paper and the jewellery to the box, stopping short of closing the lid. She held her left hand out in front of her and slowly spread her fingers. With right thumb and forefinger she grasped the rings and pulled. The knuckle resisted, but she pulled harder. The rings were off, leaving a white circle – exposing flesh that had long been protected. She put the solitaire and the narrow gold band into the jewellery box. Rummaging in the box, she found a ring set with two garnets. It slid backwards, too large for the ring finger. She considered whether the naked finger was too much to bear in the cold, little room. Decided it was not.

She set the alarm clock, then turned it off decisively. The sheets were clean and crisp, the pillow and covers soft and amiable. She could hear street sounds and the room was brightened by city lights. She remembered waiting for Santa Claus, her first dance, being pregnant. She caressed the blanket with her fingers and fell asleep.

Twenty

Martha Boyd was on the telephone when Bonnie came in. Martha's strong, deep voice carried into the outer office.

Earth Savers, Inc, headquarters consisted of a large room with two small offices partitioned off by free-standing panels. Martha was in one of these. The place was a mess. The two desks and the row of plain wooden tables against the wall were covered with disorganized stacks of papers and pamphlets.

'Next month's issue for sure. Dirty shame you didn't call a

few days sooner. Yeah. Gotcha. Bye-bye now.' The telephone slammed down and the place quieted except for faraway outside noise. Bonnie walked to the door opening and looking in.

Martha leaned back in her swivel chair, staring out the window. Her forehead puckered. She needed a rinse, the grey showed at her temples.

Bonnie cleared her throat. Recognition cleared Martha's eyes and she sat up straight.

'Bonnie! Am I glad to see you.' She stood up and came over and grasped Bonnie's hand in both her large ones. 'How are you, honey? When did you get in? Come and have some coffee. Oh, shit, I haven't made it yet. See if you can find the filters.' She waved an arm in an ambiguous circle, taking in half the room as they emerged from the little office. 'I don't think I've seen them since Joyce left, and I can't seem to remember to buy any.'

'When did Joyce leave?' Bonnie's eyes circled the dishevelled room.

'She left a few days after the convention. What a mess!'

'Are there only two of us?'

'Just volunteers. Volunteer help. You and I are the paid staff. I didn't try to find anybody, after you called. I know you'll be great. You type.'

'I used to be a good secretary. A long time ago.'

'And you're neat. I can tell you're tidy as hell.'

Martha triumphantly waved a tea bag in the air and laid it down. She picked up the glass pot and disappeared through an unmarked door. Bonnie heard water running and saw Martha emerge to set the pot on the coffee maker.

'I'm dying to hear why you're here,' Martha continued. 'What in God's name caused you to abandon fresh air and wide open spaces to come back to the Big Apple?' She turned to face Bonnie. 'Sit down, honey, I didn't mean to keep you on your feet. You're looking good, you know that? You're older than I am, did you know that? God, I could be your mother.'

Bonnie pulled out the desk chair and sat down while Martha walked slowly back and took the chair on the other side.

'I've left my husband,' Bonnie said.

'What'd the bum do?'

'Oh, he didn't do anything,' Bonnie said quickly.

'Really?' Martha looked doubtful. 'I'll bet. How long you been married?'

'Thirty years.'

'How about that, so was I. I would have been if he hadn't left me for a showgirl last year. How about that? A couple of war brides.'

'Frank wasn't in the service. He was an executive in a defence plant.'

Martha nodded. 'Well, we might as well face it. We're being phased out.'

'Not me. I'm going to start living.'

Martha stared, her lips apart. She stood up and walked back to the boiling water. 'Okay,' she said. She poured water into two cups and carried one back to the desk. She stood still, holding the cup carefully. 'Okay.' She set the cup down and went back for the other one.'

Bonnie shifted in the chair and sighed. 'You think I'm crazy.'

'Well, no,' Martha said. 'It's perfectly normal to walk out on a good husband when you're fifty, and start to live.'

'What's normal? May-maybe I'd like being subnormal,' Bonnie stammered. Martha's second chin was beginning to show. 'Abnormal?'

'You came to the right place. Lots of kinky people here. Just pick your brand of kinky, we've got it.'

'I don't want to be kinky,' Bonnie said positively. 'Kooky might be nice. Not kinky.'

'I don't believe we're having this conversation. A nice lady like you.'

Bonnie winced.

'Well, I only met you three weeks ago when you came to our convention. I sized you up right away as president of the Kansas, or Ohio – one of those western states – Women's Clubs. Trying on the liberal label, token conservationist.' She raised her hand as Bonnie leaned forward. 'Maybe I was all wrong.'

Bonnie swallowed.

'Was I wrong?'

If not, the minutes stand approved as read. 'I came back to be by myself and think.'

Martha sighed. 'You probably won't last. We can't keep anyone in this job.'

'Martha,' Bonnie said, 'you've been independent for some time now. Isn't it good?'

Martha considered. 'Well, I can stand it now. Is that good?'

'You have a responsible job. You ran the convention single-handed.'

'Well, not quite single-handed, dear, but I was running the show.' She reflected. 'Yeah, that felt good.'

'Well, you see.'

Martha stared at the opposite wall. 'I haven't been laid for a year and a half.'

Bonnie pondered. 'Well,' she said. 'You've got a point there. But sometimes something happens that changes everything. Your whole life looks different.'

'Like your husband finding a showgirl. Everything you've built your life on is gone.'

'You thought it was over, and it isn't. The world is full of new things.'

'You're too old to start over. Tired.'

'And you need to be free. You want to start growing again.'

'He went crazy. He forgot what he owed me.'

'It's all right to think of myself. It's my turn.'

'I'll never forgive the son of a bee.'

Bonnie reached for her bag and stood up. 'Could I start work Tuesday? I need to find an apartment.'

'We can pay you for only twenty hours a week. Maybe you could start half-days Monday.'

'All right. Monday.'

Twenty-one

Bonnie sat on top of the stepladder and carefully lifted her masterpiece off the table. The cherry on top was the crowning touch to the rich vanilla mould, just starting to melt its little outside edge of thick creamy thick goo onto the chocolate and cool white marshmallow. This was dinner at the beginning of the fourth week in her new home in New York. Almost a month had passed since that trembling night in the Rialto Hotel – a night of new beginnings orchestrated to Tchaikovsky's Fifth. She pulled her knees together, resting the dish on paint-splattered jeans. Jazz drifted pleasantly from the small radio on the floor nearby.

She tasted the sundae on her tongue and her spirits lifted as she surveyed the bright new room that was emerging under her paint roller. The rose-beige walls looked dirtier beside the delicate ivory that was transforming their neighbours. The large room was brightened by an oversized window at the end that for thirty minutes every morning caught the sun in its bevelled glass transom and made rainbows on the walls.

A letter from Frank lay on the folding metal table, filed there temporarily on top of the papers she had brought from the lawyer's office. He had sent a cheque – an amount that had sounded large in Lancaster, but seemed smaller every day in New York. His letter was cold and to the point. Frank never wrote warm letters, even when she was expecting them.

Gordon, their long-time lawyer and friend in Lancaster had advised Bonnie to consult a lawyer when she reached New York. 'I can't represent both of you,' he had told her. 'It just isn't done that way.'

She had Martha's assurance that Matt Fineberg would take good care of her. His youthful appearance bothered Bonnie, but his confident manner reassured her. He would contact

Gordon. He immediately told her, 'Get it in writing. A legal separation providing definite financial arrangements.'

Bonnie wasn't sure. 'Frank will be generous,' she had said. 'I don't want to be greedy.'

Matt leaned across the desk, frowning. 'What do you mean, generous, greedy? It's *his* money? What were you doing for thirty years? Eating chocolates and reading romances?'

Bonnie drew back under fire. 'Well – I didn't have a – I worked – it is my fault – I can take care of myself.'

'We'll talk about alimony when and if you start divorce proceedings. Maybe you won't want it. But from what you tell me it sounds like you have a considerable estate acquired during a long marriage. You've earned your share. Hell, it's yours.'

With her spoon, she slowly dug a whole pecan out of the chocolate syrup. She didn't need the money as much as Frank did. She could have chocolate-marshmallow sundaes for dinner whenever she pleased, and rainbows every day on a wall she had painted herself.

She slid off the stool when she heard a tap at the door. It was her young neighbour, Hannah, fresh from the shower in a short terry-cloth robe, her hair still wet.

'Couldn't wait to see. Hey – really tough!'

Bonnie readjusted the locks on the door, and turned, smiling. 'Do you like it? Better than white?'

'It's almost white – higher butterfat content.'

'I'll have to stay now – investing all this work. But what's the risk? A more beautiful world.'

'Of course you'll stay.' Hannah circled the room in barefoot grace.

'Want some ice cream?'

'Bad for my figure. Lord, are you eating that?'

Bonnie resisted the impulse to hide it in the refrigerator and went back to the stool to finish. 'I had a salad for lunch.'

'Well, they're your thighs.' Hannah gazed at the French moulding that squared off the walls. 'What do you suppose this room was like when this was a house?'

'I think it was very elegant. Ladies came calling here on Tuesdays "at home."'

'That would have been lovely. Lifting my bustle into the

213

carriage.' Hannah pantomimed the operation, manoeuvring into one of the folding chairs.

'Where did you learn about bustles?'

'I've done some summer opera, in the chorus.' She crossed her legs and pointed a red polished toe. 'I had an offer today.'

'Opera?'

'No. Another bar date. Best money yet.'

'Terrific.'

'No, not terrific. Topless.'

'Oh.'

'Think I should take it?'

'Is this just conversation or do you really want to know?'

'I want to know.'

'No.'

'That's what I think.'

Hannah stood up and walked about the room. 'What are you going to put in here?'

'I plan to rent a few more pieces, but it's a temptation to buy furniture.'

'You aren't going back, are you Bonnie?'

The spoon stopped over the last sweet, dark bite. 'Not yet,' she answered softly, and stood up to put the dish in the sink.

'I've got the right size boobs for topless,' she heard Hannah say.

'You've got the right size everything.'

'I mean, they're not too big. They don't like big ones. Did you know that?'

'No, I didn't know that.'

'It's not that I'm ashamed of my body.'

'Of course not.'

'If there was a good reason for it, I wouldn't mind. Things will start slipping soon. I'm twenty-five already.'

'What is the reason?'

'A gimmick for customers. They wouldn't notice my voice.'

'That's right.'

'That would be disgusting.'

'You want to do it, don't you?'

'Like crazy!'

Bonnie shook her head.

'It's a high-class place, expensive. All the women who work

there go topless. I'd be on a stage, not close to the audience.'

'It's very sexist, you know. Those men don't have the right – just because they pay.'

'It's a mixed crowd, not just men. Once when I was in high school, I went skinny dipping with some girl friends. I thought I heard somebody in the trees, but I didn't say anything. I screamed loud as everybody else when we saw them move, but actually, I liked it.'

'Not the same. You weren't getting paid.'

'I guess not. One night would pay a month's rent.'

'Does this pay better than where – where you wear all your clothes?'

'Well, yes. Well, it depends you know. For somebody who isn't well-known yet.'

Bonnie turned the hot water on and prepared to wash the day's dirty dishes. Her kitchen was a short row of built-ins across the back wall of the high-ceilinged room.

'Do you know Barbara Aiken?' she asked without turning.

'Sure. I mean, of course I don't know her but I know who she is.'

'Is she pretty good?' Bonnie asked, not wanting to talk about it.

'She's great. Why?'

Bonnie shrugged. 'No reason.'

Madge's words had stayed alive, needing to be constantly pushed away. 'Martha says John Blake has something going with Barbara Aiken.' The voice on the telephone in John's hotel room. Bonnie could not cope with these things, so she blocked them out. *Don't mess up my memories.*

Hannah walked over to the full-length mirror propped against the wall. The reflection was somewhat elongated by the angle, but served the purpose as she slipped her arms out of the robe and let it hang from the belt, looking hard into the mirror.

Barbara raised sudsy hands from the water and glanced at the bare windows and back to Hannah.

'What do you think?' Hannah asked.

'I think I'm green with envy,' Bonnie answered.

'No, I mean, really.'

'I think you've already decided to do it, and are trying to get my approval to salve your conscience. No dice. You're old enough to make your own decision.'

Hannah raised the robe back over her shoulders. 'Very clever of you,' she said.

Bonnie slid the saucers into the water.

'I'm so glad you came to borrow a cup of sugar,' Hannah said. 'I'd lived here two years and that was the first time a neighbour knocked on my door.'

Bonnie smiled, remembering the enthusiasm with which Hannah had invited her in, only to remember she didn't have any. She used brown sugar and honey.

'Didn't it occur to you to knock on theirs?'

'You know, it never did.'

Knock on doors, Hannah. You're twenty-five already.

Twenty-two

Summer came to New York, bringing longer daylight evenings, Shakespeare in the Park, sweating crowds on the subway platforms.

Bonnie enrolled for an early morning class in summer school – A Survey of Twentieth-Century Music. She slipped into a seat in the back of the room, hiding from real college students wearing their wisdom, knowledge, and youth with a nonchalance that made her feel awkward and misplaced. She watched anxiously for someone over twenty-five to come through the door. The young man in jeans with a gold chain showing under his open-collared denim shirt and wearing a neatly trimmed beard barely qualified. He proved to be the teacher.

She forgot the others when the instructor handed out the course syllabus. Records, John's offering, spinning at 78 RPM in her wartime apartment had introduced her to Ravel, Prokofiev and Schönberg. Here they were alive and listed in the intellectual climate of a college classroom. The list took on the titillating qualities of a gourmet menu. *All for me. No one to say 'You shouldn't like this thing.'*

At break-time she stayed in her chair. A woman in one of the front seats turned around. Bonnie smiled. The woman stood up and came back, her eyes seeking out Bonnie's. She said, 'I'm Jeanne Hoffman.'

They spoke briefly, and after class walked together to take the uptown subway to their respective jobs. By the time they changed to different trains they knew that they were women on the same journey, even though Jeanne had only left the other side of the river.

Their first chance to talk came soon with homework under the stars in Central Park. Jeanne brought a blanket that they spread out on the grass beyond the benches. At first they sat with their arms around their knees, then, stretching cramped muscles, lay semi-reclining as they listened to the New York Philharmonic play Stravinsky in the Sheep Meadow.

Her blue denim jump-suit accentuated Jeanne's small, firm body.

'I thought you were one of the undergraduates,' Bonnie had told her at school.

'I am,' she had answered. 'Just took a twenty-year break between my junior and senior years.'

Before the concert they looked at pictures of their children. Bonnie showed her dimpled grandchildren.

Jeanne extracted from her billfold a plastic container which she opened to facing pictures of two grinning teenagers. The girl had long shining blonde hair and blue eyes. The boy had long shining blond hair and blue eyes.

'Chuck is thirteen,' Jeanne said. 'He stayed with his father. Charlotte is eighteen. She's starting Juilliard. Moved into a dormitory last month.'

'Beautiful children,' Bonnie said. 'Is your divorce final?'

'Yes. Doug got in a hurry when he learned his assets were going up next year.'

Bonnie's throat tightened as she asked. 'How do you feel? Cut off? Alone?'

'Sometimes. But mostly I feel bigger.'

Bonnie said, 'You're a musician.'

'No,' Jeanne responded quickly. 'I'm a poet. My daughter's the musician. She's beautiful at the piano. You're a musician?'

'No. I don't know what I am.'

The small breeze caused the microphones to crackle occasionally, and the volume to vary, but the breeze was refreshing. Bonnie lay back to close her eyes, opening them again to massed green leaves against real sky. The leaves moved lazily, just as they did at home, constantly changing shape. The earth beside her was cool and moist. Above the trees in the near distance rose skyscraper spires, shooting straight into the sky, dotted with light – spangled and sparkling. Jack-and-the-beanstalk castles in the air. The stuff of fairy tales. Dwarfing the humans who swarmed through them by day. Yet, they were built by humans and were no larger than the minds and hands that had conceived and built them. Like the music that soared through the park, only as powerful as the humans who composed it, who played it, who received it. *This power is in me.*

After the concert they scrambled to roll up the blanket and walk quickly along the cinder paths with the crowd. Reaching the bright avenue, they slowed to a small-town stroll. There was so much to say. They found a booth in a secluded corner of a small bar, and continued to talk.

Jeanne. 'I have two years alimony, then I'm on my own. One is already gone. I'll have my degree in December.'

'Then what?'

'I'm thinking of graduate school. I wouldn't mind being a student on the poverty level.'

'No backlog?'

'Doug and I spent every cent he made. We lived well. Money isn't important.'

'What is important?'

'Finding myself. Like a goddamned teenager.'

Bonnie flinched over the exact words Frank had thrown at her a few months ago. The growing bond made her reckless. 'Women stay married because they figure that's the only way to have a man when they're older. You snare them when you're young and then they still love you when you get old. It's because they remember how you used to be.'

'Nonsense. Men aren't so stupid. Not all of them anyway.

218

I'm not through with men.' There was fear in Jeanne's eyes.

The room around them was a smoky blur. The shapes focussed into people. The room was full of men. There were women there, too, but they were background. The people wore pants – and coats and tight collars and neckties. Different.

For the first time, Bonnie sipped her drink self-consciously, aware that they were two women alone in a bar.

'I'm not good at this,' Jeanne said in a low voice.

Bonnie wanted to giggle. 'Neither am I.'

'If someone comes over, it's okay. But you don't let him pay for your drink.'

'I don't think they can see us over here.'

'Do you think anybody noticed we brought our blanket?' They giggled.

Bonnie tasted the Vodka Collins through a thin plastic straw. 'They're not coming,' she said in a low voice.

'Remember the school dances?' Jeanne said. 'They all stood around, and you waited?'

'I didn't understand then how hard it was for them.'

'For them?'

'Well, it was. Facing rejection.'

'I always got stuck with a creep because I was too nice to get rid of him.'

'How about that, Jeanne. We're back on that scene again.'

'Hope springs eternal. Prince Charming once more around the corner – or the next.'

Bonnie sobered. 'I don't think I like it here.'

Jeanne nodded and they gathered up their things. They walked close to the bar, down the full length to gain the front door. Most of the stools were occupied by men. As the two women passed, heads turned, eyes lifted and followed, assessing, not turning away when the look was challenged by a meeting of eyes, waiting for a rearview inspection. Bonnie gasped when they reached the sidewalk. Jeanne said, 'They're pigs. Big fat chauvinist pigs!'

Bonnie walked watching the sidewalk. What were the odds of finding Prince Charming twice?

Twenty-three

Bonnie uncovered her typewriter to address the envelope for the paste-up of the monthly newsletter she and Martha had just completed. This was the third one she had sent off to the printer.

'Bonnie, love, where's the letter from the mayor of Birmingham, what's-his-name?' The voice came from Martha's office.

Bonnie finished typing the information on the manila envelope, hesitated after taking it out of the typewriter, put it down and opened the file drawer. She carried the letter in and laid it in front of Martha.

'Oh, thank you, dear. I guess we'd better wait until Friday to tackle this.'

Bonnie hurried back to finish gathering the material into the large envelope. Martha's desk was in the same kind of disorder it had been when Bonnie arrived, but the outside office was in order. The clutter once scattered over the office was now organized, labelled, and tucked away inside file cabinets. The volunteers who reported for duty found their work set up for them, to be handled in a fraction of the time it had once taken. Bonnie had put in considerable overtime the first weeks, but now found she could handle everything in the three days a week she was paid to work.

She walked to Martha's doorway. 'All done,' she said. She laid the envelope on the corner of Martha's desk, ready for the delivery service pick-up in the morning.

'Wil you be coming in earlier next week, with summer school over?' Martha asked.

'I thought I would just sleep later. You don't come before ten, do you?'

Martha straightened. 'I'm practically always here by nine. Someone needs to answer the phone.'

'I'm trying to hold it to twenty hours,' Bonnie said.

Martha sighed. 'Ah, well, like a wife, I'm not privileged to count my hours. Did you remember to pick up stamps and coffee this morning?'

Bonnie nodded. She returned to her desk and took her purse out of the bottom drawer.

'Bonnie,' Martha called again. Bonnie returned to the door. 'Are you busy this evening?' Martha asked, her brisk manner suddenly reversing to a timid one.

Bonnie set her purse on the desk. 'Not exactly,' she answered hesitantly.

Martha picked up her handkerchief. 'I just wondered – thought maybe you might like to go home with me. I made homemade lasagna. If you're not busy – '

Bonnie relaxed. 'I think that would be nice. No, I'm not busy.' She still experienced a glow of illicit pleasure when she could make a sudden change of plans.

Martha brightened. 'We keep intending to get together, but you're so busy.'

They had seen a couple of Broadway plays, with dinner before, but had never visited each other's homes. The brownstone that housed Martha's apartment was a variation of Bonnie's. When she stepped inside, Bonnie knew that this was Martha's place. The tiny living room was jammed with furniture. Open doors suggested an equally crowded bedroom and kitchen. The furniture was dark, traditional, and of large proportions. Every available flat surface was covered with knickknacks.

Martha scooped up a pile of knitting from one chair and a stack of unopened mail from another. 'I didn't know you were coming,' she explained.

While Martha chattered from the nearby kitchen, Bonnie moved around the narrow path in the living room to look at the mementos on the tables and shelves.

A large selection of photographs was grouped in a corner. Bonnie saw a younger, thinner Martha with a stocky, pleasant-looking man and three stocky, pleasant-looking children. Other photographs appeared to be the same children at various ages.

She examined an exquisite bone china madonna and

realized that individually, the knickknacks were of fine quality and good taste, yet their crowded arrangement made them seem vulgar. She commented on the figurine.

'I bought it in Rome in, let's see, Jody was ten, that would have been 1960.'

'I know the place is crowded,' Martha said when she brought the heaped plates and iced tea into the living room on a tray. 'I don't need more room for myself, but I could use it for my things.' She said 'things' with affection, looking around the room at them as though they were her pets. 'It took me a long time to accumulate the furniture for my big house, and I was so proud of it. I kept as much as I could.' She stood in one place, holding the tray. 'It seemed sensible to sell the house and move close to work. Silly to commute every day for hours to a big, empty house.

Bonnie knew that Martha's children were married and scattered, though not as far away as Bonnie's.

'Of course, after I sold the house, I didn't need the job – except for something to do.' She looked at the pictures. 'I wish the children were young again. That was the only time in my life when somebody thought I was perfect.'

She transferred the food to a small table and motioned for Bonnie to pull up a chair. Martha filled the small chair, her large lap extending over the sides. She looked strong, as if she could pick up the little table by one leg and balance it above her head. This was the woman in the office who controlled a nation-wide organization, who directed Bonnie to wait on her while she worked. Martha had not talked this way to her before, although Bonnie had seen such feelings poking through. She knew this was what she had been invited here for so she listened patiently.

'I used to be pretty,' Martha continued. 'Soldiers wanted to dance with me.'

'Me, too. Until I cut them off by getting married.'

'What times those were. I wrote to a lot of boys. My letters were important to them.'

'Martha, have you always measured yourself by other people's ratings?'

Martha stopped her tea glass in midair. 'Is there another way?'

222

'I think so.'

Martha said sadly, 'The tree that falls alone in the forest doesn't make a sound. How can it matter what you are when you aren't attached to anyone?'

'We don't exist in a vacuum. We touch more people when we aren't attached; there are good things to do besides serve.'

Martha's face was drawn and serious. 'What good thing are you doing now?'

Bonnie thought carefully before answering. 'I'm developing an interesting, happy human being. The only human being I have total control over, and the one I've neglected the most.' Bonnie had never put this into words before, and the two women sat and thought about what she had said. Bonnie felt good because she had said it well, and wished she had written it down.

'*You're* still pretty.'

'You could be more attractive, Martha. Anyway, looks don't matter.' Even as she spoke, Bonnie knew she was still addicted to her comb.

'I'd give it all up, Bonnie.' There were tears now, brimming over and coursing down Martha's cheeks. 'They could take the job and stick it if I could just be somebody's woman again.'

They sat, motionless and silent, aware of Martha's exposed and bleeding heart. Bonnie stood up. In one quick movement she walked around the table and put her arms around the other woman. Martha sobbed into Bonnie's chest as Bonnie held firmly the heaving shoulders. Bonnie was using her mother arms again, and her mother voice, saying, 'I know, I know, it hurts.'

When the storm passed, they were able to talk in a way they hadn't talked before. It was even possible for Martha to say, 'You're so goddamned cheerful all the time. It makes me sick.'

'I know it does. And sometimes you act like a husband. I mean you treat me like a wife. At the office.'

'I didn't know I did that.'

'Well, you do. Like you're getting even.'

'I'm sorry, but you're so goddamned cheerful.'

Before the evening had ended, they were exchanging confidences about old love affairs. Remembering when they were young and virginal and full of dreams.

It was dark when Bonnie came up the steps from the subway station. She walked past her street, feeling the need for movement to augment the movement in her head. She was restless and hesitant to seek confinement.

She was still replaying the bittersweet nostalgia. The fifties and sixties had become a colourless blur and the forties were alive again. Sleeping Beauty had picked up the thread. What stories she could tell! She turned back towards home.

Bonnie had preregistered for a poetry class with Jeanne in the fall semester. She had brought a folder of original poems from home. And a box of old letters from the war days. Tucked into the trunk at the last minute like the things one rescues from a fire. She hadn't read them yet. She walked faster, half running up the stairs. Inside her door, she switched on the air conditioner, kicked off her shoes, pulled a chair to the closet and climbed up, reaching for the top shelf, carefully balancing the box as she pulled it down.

She curled up on the bed and dumped the letters out. They were arranged in chronological order. First came the letters with varying handwriting and return addresses – Fort Dix, Eglin Field, APO numbers from Postmaster, New York or San Francisco. She had to reach back hard, and sometimes in vain, to remember who they were from.

Then the handwriting became the same, the APO the same. The only progression was from Lieutenant John Blake to Major John Blake.

The time was approaching 2.00 AM when Bonnie slowly straightened her stiff legs and got off the bed. She went to the table she used as a desk and took paper and pencil from the drawer. She pulled out the chair, sat down, and started to write. She dated the page March 24, 1943. She made it all up, but she wrote from the pit of her stomach. The letter began, 'Dear Joe' and was signed 'Julie.'

Twenty-four

Sprays of big yellow flowers splashed over the new sofa. The day it came she shoved it from spot to another, not willing to settle for the place marking off the kitchen she had chosen before the delivery men came. After pushing and tugging it to four different spots she put it back where it started and thought, *That's right. This is the place.*

She had bought a jonquil-yellow linen tablecloth for the white aluminium table, and plain white dishes. Two thick, white area rugs broke the expanse of old polished wood floors.

She borrowed some multicoloured pillows from Hannah to try out. Bonnie realized she had knocked too early. There was a long pause after she had given her name through the door before it opened. Hannah admitted her cheerfully, left Bonnie standing just inside the door while she trotted into the bedroom for the pillows. Bonnie heard subdued voices, one in a low register. When Hannah came back with the pillows, Bonnie apologized. 'I didn't know you had company.'

'S'okay,' Hannah assured her. 'I have a lesson at ten-thirty. Good you interrupted.' Hannah had quit her day job and was seriously studying voice, now that she had a good-paying nighttime spot.

'Well, tell Earl hi.'

Hannah screwed up her nose. 'It's not Earl.'

'Oh. Well. Whoever.' Bonnie let herself out and hurried back to her own place.

Her renewed apartment was like the inside of a buttercup, beckoning her to come in and warm herself. Sometimes Bonnie sat in Hannah's apartment and restrained herself from going after the little curls of dust. Bonnie belonged to a generation of dust fighters. Her apartment was not only clean, the articles on the tables were arranged – arranged carefully to look not arranged. Tastefully unmatched.

225

After her lesson, Hannah stopped by. She admired the sofa, and sat on it, kicking off her shoes and tucking her feet under.

'Who's the new man?' Bonnie asked. 'Something exciting?'

Hannah tipped her head. 'Oh, yes and no. I'm not sure.'

'I haven't talked to you lately. I didn't realize there was anyone.'

'I only met him last week. He subbed on guitar one night.'

'Oh. Must be a mover.'

'Not really. It was the third date. I let him stay over because he lives way out in Queens, and he had a noon appointment. At least he said he did.'

'The third date. Hannah, do you know how I worried about the timing for the first kiss?'

'Well, there are always decisions about something.'

Bonnie switched the pillows around. 'Do you like blue and green, or pink and orange?'

'No matter. Get some prints, or tie dye your own. There's a neat little Indian shop near Union Square. They have tons of pillows.'

'Good idea. Let's go some afternoon.'

'You're on. Right now, I need a nap.' She closed her eyes, but made no move to leave.

'Well, don't take it here,' Bonnie said after some consideration. 'I've work to do.'

Hannah opened her eyes. 'How's the writing coming?'

'With great difficulty. I'm getting schizophrenic, turning myself into Julie, reliving the war.'

'I can't imagine all the men being gone to war.'

'There was no man shortage in Lancaster – just a big turnover. We had an air base.'

'Wow. And you're telling me you only worried about kisses?'

'We were very moral,' Bonnie reassured her. 'I was married and faithful. I married a man I had known for a week.'

'Wow,' Hannah said again. 'And you stayed married thirty years.'

'No. Only two years. I married Frank later.'

'What happened to your soldier?'

'I saw him recently. A brief reunion that was quite wonderful.'

Hannah blinked and straightened up. 'Oho, I'm beginning to get the picture. Does he live here?'

'Close,' Bonnie answered hesitantly.

'Well. What's happening? You've been holding out on me.'

'Nothing's happening.'

'Nothing?'

'Nothing.'

'Why?'

Bonnie shook her head impatiently. 'He's had a long marriage, too. He's inaccessible.'

'Is that what he told you? Surely you aren't going to buy that if it was so wonderful.'

'Oh, Hannah,' Bonnie said impatiently. 'You don't understand. The parts of my life I shared with him are the beautiful times. I couldn't risk spoiling the memories.'

'Memories, shmemories! I thought you were making new memories.'

'I'm not sure he wanted to see me again.'

'So – he probably wasn't sure either. Why can't you decide for him – or change his mind?'

Bonnie had enjoyed watching Hannah's uninhibited reaching out for whatever she wanted at the moment she wanted it. *That's for Hannah, not for me. Six months ago the only decisions I had to make were seating arrangements in my formal dining room.*

Bonnie stood up and walked to the chest of drawers to open her jewellery box. She laid aside the pearls, opened the false bottom, and took out the paper, waving it at Hannah.

'It's here,' she said, 'a box number. He said, "If you need me ... " You think I should write?'

Hannah grinned. 'I think you just want my permission. You're old enough to make up your own mind.'

The edge of the small chest top cut into Bonnie's ribs as she leaned into it to support her weak knees.

That afternoon Bonnie again became 'Julie,' turning herself inside out, reliving the vulnerability of young love. The emotion that had been surfacing over the summer now overflowed to be channelled day by day into her new typewriter. What she was writing was never good enough. It was too sentimental. Bonnie would leave the typewriter aroused, restless, to pace the floor, before returning to it again and again.

Now she pushed back her chair with a strong movement,

switched off the music, combed her hair, and went outside to find a stationer. She spent half an hour selecting a simple linen-textured paper, with envelopes lined in a sky-blue flowered print. Back at her desk, she practised on the back of discarded pages,

> I need you.
> > Bonnie.

Stood up and went to the kitchen to put on the teakettle. Dragged her feet coming back. Sat down quickly and copied the message with care onto the new stationery. At the bottom of the page she wrote her address and phone number. She addressed the envelope and went down the stairs once more to drop it in the box on the corner, touching the edge of the envelope to her cheek before letting it go.

Twenty-five

The following week Martha and Bonnie plunged into an end-of-summer Save the Whales convention. Bonnie built up overtime again, and her feet were hurting when she and Martha left the convention hotel early Friday evening. Everything was wound up and the delegates had been released on the town.

The push of the rush-hour crowd was no longer as stimulating as the anticipation of the quiet in her apartment. By habit, she looked at the faces. She wondered how many of them had a quiet nest waiting – how many were going someplace they especially wanted to be. What were the odds for peace? She was one of the lucky ones.

Bonnie looked down and saw wrinkled brown bags and popsicle sticks blown against a caved-in Pepsi can. 'The streets would be cleaned in one day if everybody would handle his own litter.' She looked at the faces again and tried to decide which one might put his empty gum wrapper in his pocket.

'That's right, Bonnie. But maybe when you've never had a clean place –' Martha replied.

'Or always had some woman to tidy up for you. I have this conditioned reflex that makes me want to pick up the junk.'

'I rather get a kick out of letting it lie there.'

Bonnie's bus came first. She stood for four blocks, then agilely scooted into a seat close behind the fat man who vacated it. She ignored the hostile stare of the well-dressed lady she had squeezed out, and relaxed to enjoy the rest of the ride.

Her feet felt better by the time she alighted at her stop, and she hurried, thinking of the piece of cold chicken breast in her refrigerator. She wondered how the leaves would look on the cement-surrounded trees on her block when fall came. The mailbox yielded a stack of impersonal mail, and she tucked it under her arm as she went up the stairs.

When she rounded the last landing, she stopped short, reaching out to clutch the rail. Someone waited, sitting on the top step. In the low-level light from the ceiling fixture she saw a man, leaning against the wall, long legs bent in front of him. He unwound and stood up, extending his hands. His grey flannel arms had opened for her. She could anticipate the roughness of the wool, needing it past all reason.

Sliding her hand along the rail, she started to run, flying against him, dropping the mail, hugging him, being hugged by him, pulling back to see his face, raising her arms to encircle his neck while he kissed her, pulling him closer, kissing back.

Then John's chin was in her hair, while he gently spread his fingers around it, surrounding her with his maleness. He was holding her up. She found her balance and pulled back. They both laughed, and kissed again quickly.

She said, 'Come in,' and pulled him by the hand to her door. When she let go to use the key, he went back and picked up his attaché case and Bonnie's mail. She held the door open and watched him walk through, closing and bolting it behind him. Everything was in its place. World order was achieved for the present moment.

She turned around. She had never seen him in his daily lawyer costume. The faintly striped coat and vest lay smoothly across wide, erect shoulders. The maroon tie was silk against an unwrinkled pale blue shirt and weathered brown neck. The skin around his eyes broke into soft sunbursts when he smiled, and his greying dark hair lay in soft, thick waves, now barely disarranged. He held out her mail. She took it from him, disappointed when their fingers didn't touch.

He set his case on the floor, against the chair, and walked about the room.

'Your place?'

'Yes.'

She watched him without stopping, their eyes connecting off and on in spurts of current.

'Nice. Looks like you.'

'I've left Frank.'

'You had a yellow tablecloth, and a flowered thinkamajig before.' He stopped walking and turned to her. 'When did you do this?'

'Months ago.'

He was a beautiful stranger, distressingly aware of her most intimate secrets. She hurried over to the coat closet and took off her jacket.

'Sit down,' she told him. 'May I get you a glass of tea?'

'All right.'

'Are you in town on business?'

'No. I'm in Philadelphia. I tried to call last night – until midnight.'

'Oh. We had a convention party last night.' She put the glasses on a small tray. Her voice softened. 'And you came anyway.'

She set the tray down on the table beside his chair, took a glass, and sat on the sofa across from him. They started to speak at the same time, both stopped and laughed.

'I checked in at the hotel and chanced coming on over.'

'It was a nice surprise.'

'How are you Bonnie?'

The smile that had become part of her that summer played across her lips.

'I don't need to ask,' John said. 'You're blooming.'

'Really? You can tell?'

He nodded, face tender. 'What was he doing to you, Bonnie?'

230

Her eyes widened. 'He loved me. He gave me everything.'

'Then why did you leave?'

'I don't know.' She spoke softly. 'I found this open door.'

'That was all you needed. An open door.'

'Is it so easy?'

'Yes.'

'I'm a very neat lady, John.'

'Yes. You are.'

'It took me so long to find you out.'

'I knew a long time ago. I told you.'

'Tell me again.'

'You're a very neat lady.'

Her fingers were cold. The condensation on the glass of tea threatened to drip on her skirt. She set the glass on the table.

'I have a part-time job at Earth-Savers headquarters.'

'And what else do you do?'

'Go to school. I took a college music class for fun this summer. Start poetry writing next week.'

'Finishing your degree?'

She put one knee across the other slowly. 'I hadn't thought of it. I could, couldn't I?' There was a faint black smudge on the toe of her shoe. 'I have no plans. I love living for today. I never did that.'

He nodded. 'It's all there is. Today.'

The room was crowded with the mature, self-aware persons they had become, the kids who shared their love on an icy night shadowed by war, the couple who joined in adultery in a New York hotel last spring. These persons looked at each other with curiosity and some embarrassment, and wondered what to say.

He said, 'You've travelled with me a great deal since last spring. I keep finding you in every revolving door.'

She answered. 'I've never been without you.'

She extended her arms, palms up, curling beckoning fingers selfward. He moved in beside her and they sat together on the sofa. Their scenario developed in separate acts with intermissions of kissing. Talk awhile, touch awhile. She kicked off her shoes and curled her feet beneath her. She helped him get rid of his coat. The vest and tie were loosened and her blouse became disarranged as they first tested the magic in their fingers through cloth.

231

He told her he had taken up flying again – being involved at first by unanticipated nightmares about flak and bombs – soon moving on to a new sense of freedom, of escape for him. He was trying to cut back on his case load, he said, wanting to live before he was old, but it was difficult.

His hands were warm against personal flesh by the time she spoke of her smothering. How the anonymity of city crowds had given her solitude to find herself.

The objects of the room were disintegrating into outlines to their night-adjusting eyes when they opened up the sofa bed and took off their clothes to meet again at last, skin to skin.

The months of sleeping alone had stored up a hunger in Bonnie that exploded like skyrockets, bursting again and again, sending showers of sparks into all the extremities, leaving toes and lips alive with all the little needles, fading slowly to weakness and overpowering love for the man who had brought it all to finale.

They lay quietly for a long time afterwards, on their backs close together, her head on his arm.

'I'm not the girl who gave you her virginity.'

'I loved her too.' He brushed his lips across her forehead.

'Do you think it would be this good – on this night – if we had stayed married to each other?'

She waited for an answer. Finally turned on her side and laid her hand on his chest.

He answered, 'I think the question is totally irrelevant. Since we didn't.'

'Yes, I suppose you're right.'

'There's something I have to tell you –'

'What?'

'I'm starved. I haven't eaten since eleven this morning.'

Relief washed over her face as she rolled away, laughing, and sat up.

They had supper on the yellow tablecloth. Things salvaged from the refrigerator, cheese and crackers, sardines, one piece of chicken, yoghurt, dill pickles and wine. She put Ravel on the record player, reminding John of how he had introduced her to Schönberg, and he promised to bring the next time some old custom recordings made by his dead friend, Eric.

'He didn't come back?' Bonnie asked softly.

'He did come back. He died a suicide in 1954. His health was bad after the years in a Japanese prison camp, but he made a career for himself in Hollywood – composing and conducting for the movies.'

'He did? The movies?'

'Very successful for a short time. He was fired during the Un-American Activities purge.'

Bonnie gasped. 'You said he joined the Communist Party in college.'

'A "card-carrying member." '

'You almost joined.'

'– but for the grace of God.'

'And he killed himself?'

'Yes. I only saw him once after the war, lost track, I'm not sure what happened. He was a man of great talent. And sensitive for a guy.'

'You have some of his recordings?'

'Early ones, experimental stuff.'

'Please bring them.'

Long past midnight they straightened the covers and lay down again. This time to lie close together, and to sleep.

Twenty-six

He left before noon the next day. The door closed and she adjusted the chain lock, and turned around to the pale ivory room. The sofa was a sofa again. She turned on the stereo, choosing chamber music over jazz to avoid the talk on the jazz station.

She walked uneasily back and forth from the FM component to the sofa, straightening pillows, adjusting the music volume down and back up again. She brightened when she noticed used breakfast dishes still on the table, needing stacking and washing. Fortunately, there were other weekend chores needing her attention. Her hand churned the water in the sink, stirring up a froth of suds. Even while the dishes were being submerged, her mind was moving on.

Drying her hands she hurried to the telephone on the desk. The number she dialled rang many times before she slowly hung up the receiver. No answer from Jeanne. Disappointed, she edged down into the desk chair. Words formed in her mind, telling it to Jeanne. This would be the next good thing. She tried to imagine how John would confide the same story to someone, 'There's this beautiful, extra thing being added to me.' She couldn't imagine it, and then realized that he would not confide in anyone. He's a man.

It was all right to imagine his going back to the hotel to pick up his bag. And on the train. She wouldn't think of him going home. Sara had not been with them last night. Her name had not been mentioned. He had not even talked about home. A certain house with a yard and staircase and furnace.

She turned around quickly. No beautiful blonde ex-model, ex-Radcliffe coed ducked behind the sofa. Bonnie was still alone. She was the most alone she had been in this room. She returned to the dishes.

Sara was tall. In high heels, almost as tall as John. Bonnie and Sara had met only once. They faced each other for – how long? – fifteen minutes? thirty? Bonnie's insides twisted in the grip of the same pain she had felt then – and knew Sara had shared. Two women mutually feeling their unwanted connection because of their attachment to the same man. The link between them, a man whom they both were sure they needed to be whole.

I was his wife then! She bent over with the pain in her stomach, and turned away from the sink. *I was his wife. I was his wife.*

'Don't think I've given up.' She could hear Sara's voice, the exact timbre of it.

'You're his sister. He loves you like a sister,' Bonnie had told her.

'He sure as hell didn't treat me like a sister the last time he saw me.'

'He loves me. I'm sure he loves you, too. But it's different.'

'Different, hell. Don't tell me you're sorry. And don't think I've given up.'

The scene was alive, although it had been stored in her memory for over thirty years.

'We loved each other since he proved it by putting frogs in my lunch box and tripping me on the stairs,' Sara's voice went on. 'We undressed each other when we were four.'

And I told her I was sorry. I worried about what I had done to them. I felt like a thief and I was his wife!

Bonnie began to pace the wood floor. She was breathing short shallow gasps of air. *I gave him back to her. Handed him back. I didn't even give him a chance to choose. He had chosen me, and I handed him back.*

'*Dear John,*' *I wrote:*

Nobody else will ever touch me the way you did. But that's gone. We'll never go back to that place again. I want to let you go. I want you to cut me loose, if you haven't already.

I told him there was another man.

There is someone here who loves me and needs me. He hasn't said it, but it's real to me without words ... I've been frozen so long.

I was safe with Frank. I knew he needed me more than John did. What a fool I was. What a fool. Cool, cool Sara. Fool, fool Bonnie.

Feeling light-headed, Bonnie sat in the overstuffed chair. She saw herself with John as it could have been. Saw them standing together with the son who didn't want to go to war. Not the same boy, of course. But yes, standing together with him. Not calling him to duty – to country and to mother as Sara had done, and killing him. Killing him. John's boy.

She picked up a coffee cup off the table by the chair and pulled her arm back, wanting to throw it against the wall, to smash it. She could not. Her arm was frozen. She could not smash it.

Slowly she lowered her arm, and put the cup back. She looked at the puddle of coffee on the table and wanted to wipe it up but couldn't do that either.

Sara's last words to Bonnie: 'You've won the first round. But

I still say, when he gets back, I'll be here, too. It will be a different ball game then. We'll see who he wants.'

The bitter smile was inside Bonnie, not surfacing. *'We'll see, Sara.'*

The knots in her stomach loosened. She leaned back in the chair and felt herself relaxing, almost into unconsciousness. She saw John waiting on the stairs on nights to come. Needing her and seeking her out. Both of them giving what they wanted to give, and accepting what they needed. Both existing separately, supporting each other only on special occasions. Always special.

She stood up, took a light jacket from the closet and went out to walk. She didn't walk towards the park, but chose the crowded sidewalks, walking fast. Not pushing, but not allowing herself to be pushed. She stopped at a fruit stand, haggled over the price of some bruised peaches, and won.

As she slowed her steps going home, enjoying the premature autumn bite in the air, she thought of the young lovers who had been finding themselves through her typewriter. She anticipated losing herself in a new rewrite of their love scenes. Regretting that their youth must wait to know the felicity she and John had shared in last night's deep, quiet coupling.

Twenty-seven

Debby dropped a string shopping bag on the floor beside her desk-chair on the day they were asked to bring to class some poems they had written in the past. Peeking through the holes were green and yellow spiral notebooks, loose sheets of paper large and small – pounds of paper in the same disarray as Debby herself. Debby's stringy, sun-streaked hair reached the middle of her back. Her sandals showed bare feet with the big toe separated from the rest by a sturdy thong. She wore jeans, or gathered, wrinkled shirts to class, and tight cotton T-shirts, frankly revealing a boyishly flat bosom. She said the poems had been accumulating forever. Dating all the way back to 1960, when she was only five. Debby's poems had a lingering lyrical sound, their lack of logic hinting at vague hidden messages.

Bonnie quailed in the presence of genius, and blushed for the three carefully chosen poems tucked into the back pocket of her new notebook. She had realized the first day of the fall college poetry-writing class that she was the oldest member, and the least experienced in poetry writing.

After class that day she hung behind, watching the professor gather up his papers as he listened to a young man who needed a shave. That person out of the way, the teacher moved towards the door, looking back at Bonnie with a smile.

'My high school poetry,' she said from across the room. 'I couldn't bring it. It's sweet. And it rhymes.' A confession so disgusting, she blushed at mentioning it.

He waited for her to catch up and they walked slowly through the door together.

'Don't worry,' he said. 'You have more to write about than they do.'

He was right. Bonnie threw off the bonds of rhyme and structure and aimed for feelings. She bought a wrinkled cotton skirt and sandals without the thong and after she came home from work and class she would sit with a yellow pad on her knee, chewing on a No. 2 yellow pencil, searching the thesaurus for gems. Julie and Joe and 1943 were temporarily laid aside.

One Saturday afternoon her wandering mind settled upon a new thought and she reached for the phone, not waiting for the thought to prove itself as she once would have done. The number she dialled was Karen's, back in Lancaster. Her middle child answered promptly and Bonnie wondered what to say.

'Mom?' The disbelief in Karen's voice stirred guilt in Bonnie.

'How are you, honey? I just wondered how you are.'

'I'm okay.' A pause. 'Are you?'

'Oh, yes, I'm very okay.' Silence. 'I'm happy, Karen. I really am.'

'That's good.' Her voice flat. 'I'm glad.'

'I'm taking another college course. Poetry writing. I just wanted to tell you. I wanted to tell you I understand, about your going to school.'

'You are? Poetry writing?'

'Yes. Well, you remember I always liked to write poems.'

'Mom. You're not using that stuff about babies?'

'It wasn't so bad. It came from where I was then.'

'In a college class? In New York?'

'New York's not so different.'

Silence.

'The local Earth Savers are into it again with Dad's company. Water pollution.'

'I know. I heard about it.'

'Do you like your job? Do you feel like you're doing good?'

'Yes.' She pushed up the pitch of her voice. 'We're helping people to work together, to feel they can do something.'

'But can they?'

'Of course. Can't you see it there?'

'I'm not sure. I believe in it, but can't get excited about it.'

'Sometimes the job is dull,' Bonnie admitted. 'I'm not always excited.'

'I think I'll go for a Ph.D.,' Karen said suddenly. 'I want to be a professor.'

'Wonderful. That's what I called about – '

'Nobody else thinks so. There aren't any jobs.'

'So the competition is great. It's where you want to be.'

'Bob says I'm escaping from reality. He says academia is a phoney world.'

'It's not his world.'

'Exactly! Mom, we just exist in the same house. Why did I get married so young?'

Bonnie didn't want to hear this. 'You've both grown up.'

'I don't think we can salvage it. What's the use?'

'Can't you talk to him?'

'We've been married ten years. I don't think we even like each other anymore.'

Bonnie sighed. 'Then perhaps you should end it. Your best years are still ahead of you.'

Shocked silence. 'You really mean that?'

'I can't decide for you. But I can tell you. A woman can make

238

it on her own. There's no security like knowing you can handle your own life.'

'I wish I could see you.'

'I have to come back soon. I haven't moved my things. Probably Christmas.'

'You're not coming back to stay?'

'I don't think so. I'm pretty sure.'

The conversation ended with both of them on the edge of tears.

Twenty-eight

'Tell me when Santa Claus comes by.' Anne Forbes opened the oven door a crack, just to enjoy the sight of the big Thanksgiving bird. A peek helped its aroma escape to creep into every corner of the efficiency kitchen, and to wander on beyond.

She barely heard the 'Hummmm?' that came from Bill, relaxed on the sofa with the *Times* obstructing his view. The television set in front of him was chronicling Macy's Christmas parade, taking place at that moment not far away. Bill in his old jeans and a T-shirt reading 'I love New York' half-reclined, with his bare feet on the sofa.

'Santa,' she said again. 'I want to see what the old boy looks like this year.'

'Why? He's not going to bring you anything. You're too old.'

Anne took a wooden spoon from the rack and sent it spinning. It reached its target with a splat, pulling the *Times* from Bill's fingers and into his face. He swung his feet to the floor and hollered, 'Hey!'

Anne stood grinning, hand on hip. 'You're supposed to be running the sweeper, Smarty.'

Bill settled back on the sofa. 'Soon.'

'Come on, Bill. Mother'll be here any time now.'

'Why do we always have to run the sweeper before your mother comes?' Bill mumbled from behind the paper.

'It's Thanksgiving. The house is supposed to be clean on Thanksgiving.'

Bill slowly lowered the paper. 'Why?'

'It just is. Didn't you grow up with a clean house for Thanksgiving?'

Bill grimaced and cocked his head. He started to raise the paper, then lowered it again. 'But my father didn't run the sweeper.'

'Well, things have changed. You do.'

Bill grinned and said 'Okay.' He raised the paper. 'Soon.'

Anne shook her head and took the sweet potatoes out of the refrigerator. At the sink, she peeled them.

She heard Bill say, 'Does your mom know we're going skiing over Christmas?'

'No. She'll probably go home.'

Linda's tearful voice on the phone came back to Anne. 'Whatever will we do about Christmas?' Last May that was. When the sisters first faced together the black news that their parents were parting. 'Oh, Linda,' Anne had said. 'There are more important things to worry about.'

'But what will we do? Who do we spend it with? Who gets left out of dinner?'

'Well, if Mom is still in New York, she can eat with us.'

'Still in New York?' Linda had quavered. 'She won't stay there. She'll never do that.'

'Well, wait and see,' Anne had said, impatient with her oldest sister, who was the least self-reliant one. Yet, the time was getting close and Anne wondered what they were going to do about Mother.

'She should be here by now,' Anne said to Bill. 'Oh, God, I forgot to tell her about the parade!'

Bill put down the paper. 'Anne, she's a grown woman. She'll find out about the parade. It's out there.'

'But she was going to bring a pie. All those people!'

'You treat her like an infant. You do.'

'Well, she didn't put an extra lock on her door. And she forgets things.'

'She's made it fine for six months. Give her credit.'

'Do you like her, Bill?'

'Yeah, sure. Of course I like her.'

'We should have her over more often. I've neglected her.'

Bill got up, came into the kitchen and put his arms around Anne. 'Honey, your mother's tough.'

Anne pulled back. 'What do you mean by that?'

'I mean she doesn't need you to hold her hand. She has a boyfriend, doesn't she?'

'That's another thing. I think she does. And he's married.'

'Well, so's she.'

'That's not funny, Bill.'

She turned around and picked up the paring knife. 'How could anyone change so much? She always did what Dad wanted her to. And she was so – so – well, controlled.'

'I think she's terrific. You've got to let go, Anne.'

'I don't want her to get hurt.'

'I told you, she's tough. You'll see.'

At that moment Bonnie was spreading her feet, balancing in place as her purse arm curved around a slippery pole, the other holding a plastic-wrapped pumpkin pie. With Olympic precision she maintained her balance as the subway car bounced and jarred, started and stopped. The car was packed. She had fought her way in, vying for standing room. The door closed swiftly and silently, sending some people jumping back on the platform. She held her ground by the vertical pole. There was no way she could reach the high bar and balance the pumpkin pie.

Persons seated along the side stared vacantly ahead, solemnly ignoring the closeness of the swaying crowd. A well-dressed elderly man held his head erect before the red graffiti scrawled across the new paint, his dignity belying the ugly word on the wall. The lady next to him obviously belonged with him, although they did not speak to each other. She wore the same kind of 1950s elegant air, clothing conservative and new. And the hat ... stirring memories of the days when every woman on the street in Manhattan wore a hat. The young girl on his other side sat just as close, but her darkly outlined sad eyes and frosted pink lips placed her in a different milieu.

The car was so crowded. Pressure from behind grew more persistent. As she edged forward, the pressure followed. With growing horror, Bonnie identified the object pressing against her. The woman in the hat watched, jaw dropping.

Bonnie pivoted her head towards a dirt-streaked red nylon jacket. She forced her eyes up to the young face bearing a humourless smile and eyes without human softness. His cold steel eyes bore into hers, undressing and raping. His head slowly sank as his knees bent and his pelvis rotated against her hip.

Lights exploded and streaked, muscles jerked and rolled, and with the other passengers Bonnie watched her Thanksgiving dessert ooze and slide down stubbled cheeks. The crust in its foil pan covered his face briefly, then slid between them before careening to the floor as they wrenched apart. The plastic had protected his nose, forcing the spice-brown pumpkin out the sides into his hair, and off the edges of his chin onto the red jacket.

A murmur spread through the crowd like rising wind, expanding to laughter and cries of approval from persons close by, while others farther away craned their necks and asked each other what was happening. Bonnie felt the tone of the crowd sweep towards approval and she was suddenly onstage, in the spotlight, adored by the audience. Without a hearing, the man had been condemned. Bonnie did not dare look at him. She feared him, as she feared snakes and rodents. She feared the loathing that had moved her to violence.

Passengers held on as the car lurched to a stop. The block letters on the walls of the station said Times Square. Bonnie pushed her way to the door and escaped to the platform just before the door slammed shut. She looked back to see the train start up with the pie-faced man still aboard. Relief made her knees give way and she leaned against a post.

'Are you all right?' The kind voice came from the well-dressed man she had stood by on the train. He and the young girl with the sad eyes looked on with concern.

Bonnie nodded. 'I guess so.' She tried to relax her chattering teeth.

'I saw him,' the girl hissed. 'The son of a bitch had it coming.'

Bonnie nodded again. Nausea and dizziness were receding. Strength returned to her noodle knees.

Smiles slowly emerged from the man and girl. 'I shoulda had a camera,' the man said. 'You shoulda seen his face!'

The three of them roared together, suddenly close.

'Sure you're all right?' the man asked again.

'Yes, I'm sure,' Bonnie answered, looking out at the name on the approaching train. 'What a mob today.'

'It's the parade.'

'I know.'

They turned away from each other and she stood alone again in the crowd, wondering where she could find a bakery doing business on Thanksgiving.

Twenty-nine

'Which do you think is the cutest, the elephant or the giraffe?' Martha gravitated between the two giant stuffed animals, towering over their smaller animal friends on the wide table at Bloomingdale's.

'I don't know. They're both darling,' Bonnie answered, lifting her voice over the toyland commotion.

'Maybe I should take one, and you the other.'

'I don't think I could get it on the plane,' Bonnie hesitated.

'Worse than Amtrak to Buffalo? I could ship it ahead, but Angela would peek. I know she would.'

'Does it matter?'

'It should be a surprise. The baby isn't old enough yet, but Angela'll love it.'

'Is it for the baby, or for yourself and Angela?'

'He'll grow into it,' Martha answered complacently. 'I've a right to enjoy buying it.'

A small boy streaked past, a frantic woman in hot pursuit.

Bonnie looked around for the little cars. There were those tiny ones, made in England. Luke's eyes would light up when he opened it, giving him a few happy moments before the little truck disappeared into the fleet under his bed. Linda would be at his elbow cooing, 'Look at that, it's from Grandma,' and Luke would know Grandma hadn't forgotten him. Perhaps Luke had forgotten Grandma. Six months is a long time when you've just turned three. Maybe a bigger truck. Bonnie tried to visualize Linda's scarf drawer. A new scarf was always nice, but what would match Linda's wardrobe that she didn't already have?

'All I Want for Christmas Is My Two Front Teeth,' sang the store loudspeakers. If only it were that simple.

Bonnie had made plane reservations for December 23 months ago, assured by Martha that the Earth Savers office would be closed for two weeks after Christmas. A school semester would be ended. Both Linda and Karen had offered their spare bedrooms, but no real plans had been made. How would Frank be? Surely they could all be civilized together.

She returned to the apartment with one package, a handmade tote bag for Karen. She took her mail from the box, leafing quickly through the ones with stencilled addresses. John didn't write, preferring the telephone, but she always thought he might. She spotted a long envelope, hand-addressed. It was from Frank.

'Dear Bonnie,' she was reading a few moments later, in the easy chair, her coat thrown over the back.

Dear Bonnie,

I have to be in Washington for a conference December 10, so think I will come on to NYC to look in on Anne and you. There are some things we probably should talk about.

I will stay at the Hilton and will call you sometime on December 12.

Yours,
Frank.

Bonnie slowly lowered the letter to her lap, after reading it several times. The familiar handwriting reached out to pull her back through the open door. She breathed deeply and looked about the room. Were the loose tie-dyed pillows on the sofa silly and uncomfortable? She regarded the nude couple in the small print over the record player. She walked over and picked up the down pillows, fluffing them one at a time, carefully arranging them the way she wanted them, knowing they would not be moved.

Thirty

Hannah Rosenberg balanced her grocery sack on one raised knee as she struggled with the outside apartment door handle. Her oversized mittens were a handicap. She almost lost her balance when the door opened by itself. She drew back into the winter dusk as she juggled the sack to a secure armhold. The figure on the other side of the door focussed into a tall man. His expensive topcoat and curly, white hair reassured her and she stepped inside the foyer. She put the sack on the floor, pulled off the red and yellow mitten, and unlocked her mailbox. She felt the man watching her.

'Pardon me,' he finally said. 'My party doesn't answer the buzzer. Are you her neighbour?' Hannah turned to look at him. 'Mrs Forbes. She's in number 4.'

Hannah broke into a smile. So, this was Bonnie's wonder man. She slammed shut the mailbox for number 5. 'I sure am,' she said. 'I'll let you in.'

She used her key on the inside door. He picked up her groceries and reached his other hand for the door, but Hannah had already opened it.

'Does Bonnie know you're coming?' she asked, on the stairs.

'Yes. I guess I'm a little early.' His eyes were moving around the hall. Hannah hadn't noticed before that the paint was peeling on the baseboard. No doubt the paint didn't peel in Boston.

He waited while she unlocked her apartment door. 'Would you like to wait inside?' she asked.

245

He paused. His timidity irritated Hannah. 'All right. Thank you,' he said, following her in.

'She should be home soon,' Hannah said.

Coatless, each holding a cup of tea, they looked at each other across Hannah's coffee table. Hannah had pushed aside the magazines and the last three days' newspapers to make room for the teapot. She could tell by the way he held his cup that this man was a coffee drinker. His sober expression approached dislike as he sipped at the tea.

He's so old. Bonnie said he didn't look fifty-five. Something else was out of place.

'Did you forget your key?' she asked. She knew the question was presumptuous, but still was surprised at the response from the heretofore placid countenance. The man's face grew crimson, as his eyes opened wide. *Lord, Bonnie thinks he's so sophisticated.*

'Unfortunately, my wife hasn't furnished me with a key.'

The mischief in Hannah's eyes died slowly. She swallowed. 'Oh,' she said.

'We haven't introduced ourselves.' His composure recovered ahead of hers. 'I'm Frank Forbes.'

'Hannah Rosenberg,' she answered meekly. She stood up and began to fuss with the teapot, bracelets jangling. 'I haven't seen Bonnie for a few weeks. She didn't tell me you were coming.' *No, Hannah, that's not it.*

'She is expecting me. Do you know Bonnie well?'

'No,' Hannah said quickly, 'not really. We're just neighbours. Down the hall.' She smiled weakly.

Frank was relaxing. He wasn't so bad, now that he didn't have to be John. He looked tired.

'You don't really want that tea, do you?'

He laughed. 'Well, it's hot.'

'I'll get you some instant coffee.'

He didn't protest. They telephoned the apartment next door without success, and settled down to visit. Hannah crossed her legs so that her skirt fell open above the knee. Frank kept his eyes on her face. Hannah automatically locked onto the look, drawing it out, not dropping her eyes.

'You're a vice-president or something of a hardware factory,' she said, proving that she had heard of him.

'Yes.'

'I'm a singer.'

'Oh.' He didn't break the look. 'Where do you sing?'

'In a supper club, right now. It's called the Henry the Eighth. Ballads and blues.' Countdown until his eyes would hit the knee. 'I'm studying voice.' Bingo. Quickly down and away to the floor. He was a shy, sweet man.

He looked back again. 'I like a good song. You're so pretty, that must help.'

Time to drop her eyes, and lift them again. 'Thank you. It does.'

He looked pensive. He put down his cup and carefully stood up. 'I'll try again.' He walked to the phone. He picked up the receiver and stopped, before hanging up and reaching into his pocket for the number. This time there was an answer and he talked briefly.

His coat over his arm, Frank walked slowly to the door. Hannah laid her hand on his arm. 'Good to have met you, Frank,' she said. 'Have a good time in New York.'

He watched her with puzzled eyes, awkwardly put his hand over hers, said 'Good-bye,' and left.

Thirty-one

ANNIVERSARY

One tapestry.
You the warp, I the woof.
The shuttle has shot out a thousand times
Lashing us together in a taut tangle
*   of things.*

But the weave does not keep us touching.
We are apart

as the strings of a fish net.
Whales
dropping through the spaces.

Bonnie Forbes
English 231

Early on the grey morning of the twelfth, Bonnie had huddled in her easy chair and watched the breaking of the frigid dawn – the usual cup of black coffee in one hand and a rare cigarette in the other. She hadn't slept well, finally getting out of bed in the filtered darkness to rummage in the drawer for a cigarette pack buried there several months ago.

Only one window in the building across the street showed a light when she got up. Now there were four, less distinct in the growing daylight. Some must be wives, switching on the kitchen light and filling the coffeepot, eyes swollen from unfinished sleep after being up with the baby. But ultimately they would sit across from their husbands in their Madison Avenue suits and share a moment together. This was often the best time. Maybe a Manhattan apartment was different from a big house in the suburbs. Not so much space to escape. Hello there, in the downstairs den. Didn't we used to know each other?

She set the cold coffee on the table and walked over to switch on the radio. She learned that it was 7.02 AM and twenty-six degrees Fahrenheit in Greater New York. The easy listenin' station laid a cover of unobtrusive melody over the room, familiar old tunes not asking to be identified. She switched on the lamp and looked at the rumpled sofa bed. She could not picture Frank in this bed. She didn't want to sleep with Frank again. She tightened the sheets and tucked the edges in. Frank's letter had arrived two weeks ago. He had been sending the cheques to her lawyer, reducing their connection to a business transaction since her insistence upon a legal separation. They hadn't shared anything personal since she had left him last spring, back in Middle America.

She straightened and scratched her chin. She yanked the sheets off and took bright new ones from the drawer.

He called before noon. She knew it was Frank by the way he breathed before he said, 'Bonnie?'

'Yes.'

'This is Frank.'

'Yes, Frank.'

'I'm in town. I'd like to talk to you.'

'I have a class. I'll be home by six.'

'All right if I come over?'

'Yes.'

'Maybe we can go out to eat. Unless you'd like me to pick up some steaks.'

'Going out is fine.' Instant picture of Frank scrambling eggs alone in their daisy kitchen for the last six months. If she had a roast . . .

'I guess you'll know a good place,' he said.

'Yes, I do.' The hell with the roast.

'Six then.'

At ten after six Bonnie flew through the door, hanging up her coat before she hurried into the bathroom to renew her makeup. Odd to be putting on lipstick for Frank. She was combing her hair when the phone rang. He was next door, at Hannah's. Bonnie's young neighbour had offered him a place to wait.

Frank, walking into her efficiency living room after their first hellos, was a misplaced image. His curly, thick, white hair was carefully combed. He had a new suit, but it was just like all the other dark suits she used to take to the cleaners, and the maroon and navy striped tie could have been the same one he had worn when he was a young executive and she was his secretary, in another life.

She took his topcoat and offered him a chair. He sat in the tall rattan chair as though he could be out of it in an instant if there were a fire. He looked around the room. She sat across from him.

The high back and wings of the red chintz chair framed Frank's dark head. His fresh haircut minimized the black curls Bonnie had loved when she married him. There was triumph in his eyes as Matt gunned down the bad guy, and joined Chester in Kitty's saloon.

'I wish he would kiss her, just once,' Bonnie had commented. Frank shook his head. 'A true cowboy only loves his horse.'

'I was early,' he said.

'I was late.'

'You look settled in.'

'I feel settled.'

They avoided looking at each other except in quick glances.

'Have you seen Anne?'

'Yes, I was at her place this afternoon. She can't go with us.'

'Oh, that's too bad.' Bonnie hadn't thought of their daughter's joining them. 'How are things at work?' she asked.

'All right, fine,' he said. 'Good conference. Our lobbyists are getting results.'

'Do you see Linda and Karen?'

'Not much. They tried to look after Dad at first, but I soon set them straight.'

The radio played Bacharach; she couldn't remember the title.

'How are the kids?'

'Growing like weeds,' he answered. 'Baby's walking.'

'Come to Daddy. You can make it.' Eyes wide, lips parted, two wobbly steps to please him, to fall into the security of his open, strong arms. Linda adored her daddy.

'And you, Frank. How are you doing?'

'I'm all right,' his mouth in a thin, tight line.

He told her things she already knew from Linda's and Karen's letters. She saw him eyeing the cluttered makeshift desk.

'I'm writing a book,' she told him.

'Really?'

'I used to write before we were married.'

'I didn't know that.'

'I've always wanted to be a writer. I'll show you some of my stories. You can tell me if you think they're any good.'

It was over a late hamburger at the White Castle. The steamy, confined fragrance of the White Castle, forever tied to the taste of their juicy nickel hamburgers on a hot toasted bun.

The man on the end stool kept playing 'Straighten Up and Fly Right' on the jukebox. She thought he was drunk.

'I'm afraid I wouldn't be any judge,' Frank replied. 'I'm not very literary.'

'What's your book about?'

'It's a novel. About the war.'

250

'A war novel?'

'Love story. I guess I feel safer writing about kids the way they were when I was young.'

Frank studied the wall. 'That boy's living with her, isn't he?'

'What?' Bonnie asked, still thinking about Julie and Joe.

'She kept the bedroom doors closed, but there was Brut in the bathroom, and he brought milk and toilet paper when he came.'

'Oh.' Bonnie looked at the spot on the wall. 'Yes, he is living with her.'

'Well,' Frank said with a sigh, 'I'm glad they're in New York.

'Are you going to stay here, Bonnie?' he asked suddenly. 'Will you be back?' He didn't move, but his tone had toughened. They were on shakier ground now.

'I was planning to come back for Christmas. Just for a visit, I thought I'd pack some more things. Sort them out if you'd like me to.' She was trying to be gentle.

'Good idea. I'm going to put the house on the market.'

Bonnie caught her breath.

'Silly for me to go on living there by myself. We can split the profit ... over the balance of the mortgage.'

'Building costs are so high now. Maybe next year.'

'Please, Frank, it's my life. Her house is everything to a woman.'

She squeezed the arms of her chair. 'Where will you go?'

'A condominium maybe.' For the first time he looked hard at Bonnie. His lower lip twitched, he had raised the shield over his clear blue eyes. 'I might as well tell you. I've been seeing Dorothy. Dorothy Vance.'

'You have?' She groped for words. 'That's good, Frank. I'm glad.' She wasn't.

'Why don't you ask Dorothy Vance to go to the party?'

'Why would I want to do that?'

'It would be a nice thing to do for her; she's been out of things since Fred died. And you wouldn't have to go alone while I'm at the convention.'

'Bonnie, I don't need anyone to hold my hand.'

'She's had a lonely life. She and Fred didn't have children, and her family's all dead. She's glad to have someone needing her again.'

She hurried to say, 'And you have a lot in common.'

'Yes. I think we'll get married.' The creases in his forehead and around his mouth were deep and shadowed.

'Oh.' The design on the sofa looked unfamiliar. The chair was new and temporary. 'That's what you wanted to see me about.'

'Will you marry me, Bonnie? I've never been in love before, and never will be again. I knew the first time I saw you it had to be that way.'

'Yes. I think we should file.'

'All right.'

'Silent night, holy night ... ' sang the radio.

'Do you want to do it here?'

'I'll call my lawyer.' She spoke carefully, stepping over shattered glass. 'Of course, Dorothy wouldn't want the house. Or my things.'

'We haven't discussed it. I'm sure though, that a new place ... ' His voice grew weaker.

'You mean you haven't asked her yet?'

'I'm not free.'

Bonnie looked at her hands. The bare fingers.

He spoke slowly, 'I guess you haven't been lonely.'

'No. I have friends. And I see Anne and Bill.'

'That's not what I meant.'

Her face grew warm.

'You do have an extra key?'

He was bluffing. How could he know? She stood up and walked to the window. It was dark outside, and she meant to close the drapery, but felt suddenly self-conscious, and left it open. When she forced herself to look at Frank again he looked smug.

Their eyes could engage now, now that there were secrets.

'I don't know what you mean,' she answered.

He gave her a long sober look, neither of them breaking the stare. He said at last, 'Where shall we eat?'

They discussed New York restaurants, as though they hadn't just changed their lives.

'Hey,' Frank said, 'why don't we have supper at your friend's place?'

'Who?'

'Next door. Hannah. At the club where she sings. Henry the Eighth?'

Bonnie laughed, and Frank looked puzzled.

'I'll bet she's good,' Frank said.

'I haven't seen her perform. But you're right. Hannah has presence.' Bonnie smiled privately, and she could sense Frank's irritation. She had had years of practice anticipating Frank's irritation. She was tempted; it would serve him right.

'It's too early. She's on from nine to one.'

'It's seven-thirty.'

'Frank, she does it topless.'

She watched his face. Frank's mouth grew smaller. His neck reddened first and the glow spread across his face and onto his ears.

Bonnie said, 'Hannah's a good singer, she says it isn't vulgar ... it's expensive. But all the women ... '

'Forget it!' Frank said. 'The Italian place ... do we need reservations?'

They were back before ten. Bonnie went ahead to turn on the lamps, and looked back to find Frank standing by the door.

'I'd better get on,' he said.

She stopped by the second light. 'It's early.'

'I think there isn't any more to be said.'

'No, I guess not.'

They regarded each other from across the room. Bonnie sighed. 'Do you want to kiss me good-bye, Frank?'

She thought she had reached out for him, and he seemed to be moving towards her, and then she realized that they were both still standing in the same place.

He said, 'You aren't my wife anymore.'

'You don't have a kiss for the woman I am now?'

'I can't, Bonnie. I can't. Let him do it.'

'Forgive me?'

'I don't know if I ever will.'

She was grateful for the answer that made her glad to see him leave. Glad she didn't have to argue. Glad it was finished.

Thirty-two

His tongue was abnormally large in a padded mouth. His eyes locked onto the cold metal lamp and the plain door beyond it, his neck not wanting to wake up and go. For a bad moment, he floated in unidentified time and space before orienting himself to the New York Hilton. He moaned and raised a hand to his head. The blanket lumped and twisted about his body, rubbing against his legs. No pyjamas. He had apparently chosen to sleep in his underwear. He did not remember getting into bed last night. Only once before, when he was seventeen, had he awakened to blank memory. He had sworn it would never happen again. Frank Forbes never allowed himself to be out of control.

He moaned again, disgust mingling with pain. How many bourbons had he had last night? That little girl with her short gold velvet skirt and pleated stand-up collar and nothing in between, kept bringing him more bourbons.

How could she have gotten herself into this mess? The damned smog and the peeling paint on the baseboards in the hall. Those brave little yellow pillows. One room and all that confusion just outside the house ... foreigners and perverts around every corner.

His pulse speeded up at the thought of picking her up and reinstating her, kicking and screaming at the centre of his household. How would Cagney have handled it? It might even work if he, Frank, had the guts to carry it out. She might like it.

He sighed deeply. No, it was good he had come. It hurt like hell, but he faced the facts. *She's somebody else. Even if she wakes up someday and wants to come back, she can't. She will never again be my sweet Bonnie. Someone else has a key. There can be no return.*

A hint of movement, a faint rustle, drew his attention

254

sideways. The other twin bed ... Holy Jesus, there was someone in it! A mass of dark curls on the pillow culminated in the curves under the bedspread. Recognizing the curls instantly, Frank jerked the covers up to his neck and swallowed a new moan. How did Hannah Rosenberg get into his other twin bed?

He reached back desperately for a clue. He remembered leaving Bonnie's building, a burning sensation growing in his chest. He had stopped in the downstairs hall to pop two antacid tablets into his mouth. Outside, he walked towards the avenue to find a cab. There were many lights on the avenue, but it was dark and cold and empty inside of Frank. He didn't see the people he met. They were shadowed, in spite of city lights.

He flagged down a cab and slid inside. The empty hotel room and solitude for thinking was too much to face. 'Henry the Eighth,' he said, not believing he had said it. A quiet, dark corner with a drink and a chance to watch the lovely Hannah and listen to her sing. The indigestion let up a little and he was almost happy. No one would ever know. With some awe he realized that it didn't matter anymore. He was a man without fetters.

All the corners were dark in the Henry the Eighth. The decor was heavy, half-timbered, artificially Hampton Court. Flickering candles on the tables made all the ladies look lovely and mysterious, and the bared bosoms of the waitresses completed the intimacy. They were a harem of lovelies weaving in and out, sweet concubines, unattainable centrefolds. The prices were staggering, but he ordered with abandon when he realized that he would probably never reach the minimum anyway.

Now he saw his dark trousers neatly folded in the seat of the chair at the foot of the bed. The coat was draped around the chair back, a pale blue shirt showing underneath. He eased out of the bed and rescued the pants, hastily pulling them on. He did not feel up to facing Hannah in his boxer shorts. Bonnie always said he had nice legs, but he never wore the Bermuda shorts she bought him for lounging at home. Men's legs were meant to be covered.

He went into the bathroom and closed the door, still trying to remember. Clearly the image emerged, like a shimmering mirage, of Hannah on the stage at the piano. Her sweet, husky voice pleading 'Ne Me Quittes Pas' was directed only at Frank, although she could not have known he was there. The soft, pastel spotlight made her skin look like pale velvet. Her exquisite little pointed breasts – the thought now made him weak.

Seeing Bonnie again had stirred up emotion that frightened him. After seven celibate months he had just decided to yield gracefully to old age. The good-night kisses with Dorothy that brought a girlish flutter to her middle-aged composure had left him disturbingly calm and mildly concerned about their future nights. But yesterday he had realized that the rumours of his demise had been grossly exaggerated. Wrenched and drifting, he had turned to the artificial intimacy of the Henry the Eighth. There behind the protection of the table he knew for sure that he was not through being a man. *But what happened after?* That firm young body was at this moment in his bedroom.

The white hotel towel had black and pink smears on it, as did the little bar of soap. He picked up the soap gently, choosing to use it instead of a new one, sudsing away the makeup, watching the water clear. Headache forgotten, he opened the door.

Blue eyes looked out from the pillow. Hannah smiled and said, 'Hi.' He answered, 'Hi,' his heart jumping as she threw back the cover, and swung her legs to the floor. She had on a black lace slip and black panty hose. He watched her, appreciating the poetry of motion, the perfection of the design of her body. Even her scrubbed early morning face was beautiful. He had learned to see young girls as daughters. Now he was miraculously a participant again. The other time he had spoken to Hannah she had been a polite stranger. Now they had a secret. He put his hand to his head. God, if he only knew what it was.

'How do you feel?' she asked.

'I'm not sure,' he said. 'I think I drank too much.'

'I guess,' she agreed. 'You really tied one on.'

'You helped me get back here,' he said in a sudden flash of logic.

'Yes.' She grinned. 'You wanted to see a waitress home. You were going to buy her a brassiere.'

'I didn't!' Frank blanched.

'Yeah, you did.'

Frank shook his head and said in a low voice, 'What a fool.'

'No, you're not.' She leaned towards him. 'You were very sweet. Look, Frank, you needed somebody's shoulder to cry on last night. I lent you mine.'

He pulled the shirt from under the coat on the chair back and continued with his dressing, irritated at his inability to form the questions. He intently watched the buttons on his shirt, until they were all in place, and the shirt tucked in. He turned to look her full in the face and walked over and sat on the edge of the other bed. 'Now,' he said in his corporate voice, 'please tell me what took place here last night.'

A teasing smile played across Hannah's lips. 'Now, Frank, do I look like the kind who would take advantage?' He suddenly disliked her. The way she kept saying, 'Frank.'

She leaned across and put her hand over his. 'Look, Frank, you're a good, kind man. I like you a lot. Relax. It's okay to lose control sometimes.'

He allowed her eyes to take hold of his for the first time ... her lovely wide blue eyes. He said 'Hannah,' savouring the word. It seemed to help. He said 'Hannah,' again. He was beginning to feel good.

This time she looked away, removing her hand at the same time. She stood up and walked around the bed and took a full black skirt off a chair and pulled it over her head. She wasn't wearing a brassiere, and the glimpses of the swells of flesh through the low-cut slip were as tantalizing as her bare bosom had been from the stage last night. She put on the black linen shirt last, buttoning at the wrists, waiting to close the shirt front. Then it was done.

Daughter, mother, whore? The problem was a lovely one. She was as enigmatic as this town. He put on his coat and looked in the mirror. Distinguished. Even handsome.

'Shall we go down and get acquainted over breakfast?' he asked her.

'I have plenty of time,' she answered.

Thirty-three

It was the season of the child, of the family, of the happy ending, of togetherness; the triumph of candy over vegetables, red over dusky pink, major over minor, good over evil; snow was clean, not cold, tinsel was glittering, not gaudy; caring was cooking, loving was buying, and loneliness and anger and guilt waited in the wings.

The typewriter was situated to catch the last rays of daylight, but when December dark came early her spirit warmed with the act of lighting the lamp and closing the curtain. This room was a womb. She grew happily here.

O little town of Bethlehem, how still we see thee lie ...

Today's chapter was short, but right. It was the same chapter she wrote yesterday, but today it was right and that was happy growth. Linda's letter lay on the table by the big chair. It was an uneasy letter, full of unrest about change.

> *Please let me know soon when you are coming and where you will stay and if it is all right if Dad comes to Christmas dinner. You know how hard it is to get anything out of him.*
>
> *I don't know what to tell the kids except that Santa will arrive on Christmas morning. When will we open the family gifts? I haven't been able to sleep for thinking about this.*

Linda was caught up in the machinery of other people's lives. She could not light the lamp and close the curtain over her private world. She didn't live with the exciting possibility of a telephone call. Her mother's doing these things should not be an added burden for her. In a burst of movement, Bonnie returned to the typewriter and rolled in a sheet of paper.

I've decided to come the day after Christmas. Invite your dad for Christmas dinner, and ask him to bring Dorothy Vance. She'll love helping you with the dinner. I'll spend the day with friends here and see you after the holiday. We can visit then without the stress.

Bonnie contemplated the ultimate triumph, her first Christmas out of the kitchen. Still riding high, she hurried to take the letter to the box.

O come all ye faithful, joyful and triumphant . . .

Anne and Bill had planned the ski trip months in advance. Martha was going to Buffalo. But there was Jeanne. Bonnie called her.

'Of course you can spend Christmas with us,' Jeanne said emphatically. 'We'd love having you. Our plans aren't quite definite yet. I hate going to the house. Doug won't come to my apartment. Charlotte's boyfriend wants her to go to his folks', but she doesn't want to hurt her dad. Chuck would like us all to go to his grandpa's but they're mad at me. How considerate do you think I should be of Doug's new girl friend? She misses her kids.'

'I don't want to interfere,' Bonnie said lamely.

On December 20, Jeanne called to say that she and Chuck were going to Maryland, to Jeanne's Aunt Harriet's. 'Please come with us,' she urged. 'They'll have a houseful. You'd be very welcome.'

'Oh, no,' Bonnie stammered. 'I love your asking me. But no.'

While shepherds watched their flocks by night, all seated on the ground . . .

She knocked on Hannah's door. Hannah was Jewish – Hannah was buried in bright ribbon and shiny paper.

'Big plans?' Bonnie asked.

'I'll get over to The Bronx for Chanukah.'

'Christmas Eve?'

Hannah wrinkled her nose. 'Working. Lots of people go boozing on Christmas Eve.'

Bonnie lifted a bow and fingered it.

'It's hard on you, isn't it, going home?'

Bonnie shook her head. 'It's all right.' She wouldn't explain.

'What were Christmases like before?'

'Nice,' Bonnie answered. 'When the kids were small. Hectic but nice.'

'I'll bet Frank played Santa.'

'Oh, mercy, no. He didn't even help with the tree.'

'You didn't ask him,' Hannah said defensively.

'He was gone so much. Well, he did, I guess he did help the first few years. It's hard to remember.'

'I don't see how you could forget.'

'The company always came first.' She looked sharply at Hannah. 'Why? What makes you ask?'

Hannah shrugged. 'I don't know, he seems nice. I didn't think he would be. I feel kinda sorry for him, you know?'

'I never said he wasn't nice. Everyone feels sorry. Fact is, he's already found someone else.'

Hannah looked up. 'How do you know?'

'He told me. Someone we've known for a long time. Her husband was a company man, died a few years ago.'

Hannah turned away and worked with a bow. Then she said in a low tone, 'He's a gentleman. You don't meet many like that.'

'Yes,' Bonnie nodded, 'he's a gentleman all right. Let's don't talk about it, okay?'

'I'm sorry.'

God rest ye merry, gentlemen, let nothing you dismay.

On the yellow-flowered sofa Bonnie spread out the *Times* and nervously turned the latest *New Yorker* to 'Goings on About Town.' She would plan a never-to-be-forgotten night on the town for Christmas Eve, a night for a free soul, only in New York. Dinner at that forbidding restaurant on the avenue, without looking at the prices. Midnight mass at St Patrick's. Something special in between. She found it in a small item in the *Times*. An address in the village, a Christmas Eve programme of folk singing and poetry. She could splurge on a cab.

The ring of the telephone jerked her to attention. Standing up, on shaking knees, she went to answer.

'Hello,' she said in an unexpectedly tight voice.

'Bonnie?' the voice sounded concerned.

She sank into the desk chair and started crying, not softly but in a great flood.

'Bonnie?' The voice was really concerned now. 'Is that you?'

She nodded and managed to say, 'Yes, it's me. Oh, John,' she gasped, 'I hate Christmas.' Louder, and with less crying, 'I hate Christmas!'

'Well, good for you, darling. So do I.'

'I've hated it for years,' she was almost laughing. 'I hate having to buy presents that nobody wants. I hate cooking all day. I hate singing about peace on earth when there isn't. What do I write to the Osbornes? We haven't seen them in twenty years but we keep sending those dumb pictures.'

'Who cares? They don't. Just think how far you've come, to be able to say it.'

She was laughing now, between the sobs. 'Yes, I have.' She blew her nose and slowly regained control. 'You know, I think I already hate it less.'

'That's my girl.'

'I never knew what to do with those pictures, "Merry Christmas from all the Joneses," the kids and the dog in front of the tree, so I stored them away in boxes. It seemed unfriendly to throw them away.'

'Throw them away. They've served their purpose.'

'That's what I have to do next week. Throw them away.'

The phone was silent while she wiped her eyes.

'Poor baby,' John said at last. 'It's tough. I know it's tough.'

'Frank was here last week,' she said suddenly, remembering he didn't know. 'We're going to file.'

'How do you feel about that?'

'Relieved. Yes, I really am relieved.'

'He must be in a hurry.'

'Well, he was in Washington. Come to think of it, it looks like he wanted me to know before I came home that he has someone else.'

'Do you mind?'

'I don't know.' She hesitated. 'Well, of course, I'm glad. It takes away some of the guilt.'

'It gives him an armour. Sets the tone for your visit.'

'Cutting off retreat.' She straightened the envelopes on the desk.

'Is this bad?'

'Oh, no,' her words fell over his. 'I'm very, very sure, John. I've never wanted to go back.'

'You seem satisfied.' He sounded unsure. 'I thought this trip would settle your mind finally.'

'My mind has been settled. Since the day I left.'

He sighed. 'I wish I could see you.'

'Oh, so do I.'

'It's impossible until after the holidays. Right after you get back, I'll be there.'

'I'm not going until after Christmas.'

'What! Why?'

'To uncomplicate things for the children. It seemed a good idea.'

'That's crazy, Bonnie. Why shouldn't you be with your grandchildren?'

'They don't need me in all that hubbub. We'll have our own special Christmas when I get there.'

'You'll be alone on Christmas Eve? You know what you're doing? You're sacrifi – '

'No, I'm not,' she said fiercely. 'I'm going to celebrate my independence.' She hurried to keep talking. 'What will *you* do?'

She bit her lip. They didn't talk about John's other life.

'Christmas Eve is dinner at home – with Mother that is. I haven't missed many.'

So – Bonnie wouldn't want to be with John on Christmas Eve after all. Not with mother.

'How is your mother?'

'In excellent health. She never misses a board meeting.'

'Bill and Anne are going skiing.' They began to talk of less personal things. They talked for an hour and a half altogether. They rang off reluctantly, needing to touch, happy knowing they would touch again.

Thirty-four

The flowers in the Aubusson carpet at the Chateau d'Or were worn, the crystal chandeliers a little dusty, but the maitre d' was dressed in formal attire, and his smile was frigid. Bonnie felt conspicuous in her new red dress under the mink jacket, and wished she were dressed in black. He smiled the frigid smile at her, but approached the fat couple with three children first, and directed them to a table. The young couple who came after her were also seated before he spoke to Bonnie.

'Would madam like to be seated while you're waiting?'

She checked the impulse to look behind her. 'Oh,' she understood, 'I'm alone. I'm not waiting.'

He looked at his shoes, the frigid smile growing larger. He looked back at her and said in a confidential low tone, 'I'm so sorry, madam, there must have been a misunderstanding over the reservation. Ladies must be escorted in the dining room after six o'clock. I'm so sorry you weren't told.' He was trying hard to be sorry. Bonnie was telling herself it wasn't the red dress that did it. She turned without a word and walked with as much dignity as she could manage to the door, a long way.

'Ma'am,' she heard on the edge of consciousness. 'Ma'am,' repeated again a little louder. The girl in the cloak room was looking at her. Bonnie took a few steps to hear her better. The girl's eyes were warm and soft. 'There's a nice little tea room on the next block. Olga's.'

Bonnie nodded. 'I know.' She completed her exodus.

She hadn't walked far until feelings of rejection spilled over into anger. She would allow herself to steam on the walk over to Olga's. Once there, Olga's special borscht would taste very good, and save a lot of money. She didn't like the Chateau d'Or anyway, once she had seen the inside. Stuffy. Incredibly stuffy.

A man was standing on the sidewalk in front of Olga's,

looking at the door. As she walked towards him she noticed his straight back inside the worn overcoat. The back collar of the coat was turned up, and the man wore a hat, brim turned down over one eye, in a manner of another era. She was almost to the door when she noticed with a jar that Olga's neon sign was turned off. There was a neat printed sign on the door. This was what the man had been looking at. As she approached, he looked her full in the eye, seemed about to speak, but turned the other way instead and walked away. His face was kind and sad, one she would remember. She would like this man, if she knew him. She read the sign, already dreading what it would say.

WE WILL BE CLOSED FROM 6 PM DECEMBER 24 UNTIL 9 AM DECEMBER 26 TO ALLOW OUR EMPLOYEES A HOLIDAY WITH THEIR FAMILIES. MERRY CHRISTMAS!

There were no other restaurants in the neighbourhood. If she continued to walk, perhaps she would run into another. Perhaps she would not. Perhaps they were all giving their employees a holiday with their families.

Directionless, she walked on. Ahead of her, walking at about the same pace, was the man with the hat. He was an actor, probably Shakespearean, unemployed. He had been on the stage for many years, never quite making it to the top. His voice would be deep and resonant. If he had only said 'Isn't this bad luck? What are we supposed to do?' she could have said 'This is insane, but would you like to join me at the Chateau d'Or?'

He was a musician – violin, no, viola, never reaching first chair. He wasn't really poor, but dressed shabbily because he was too involved with his music to care about new clothes. They would visit over dinner about Schönberg while the maitre d' tried to figure out how the lady in the red dress had found an escort so quickly. She smiled secretly at the thought of his chagrin. He was a narrow little individual who wouldn't approve.

The man was a compulsive gambler. He had known wealth and poverty, but this last dry spell had been a long one. His wife and children had left him, and he was all alone at Christmas. Actually, the maitre d' wouldn't be interested enough to disapprove. Maybe he would be a little irritated over the red dress in his dining room.

Bonnie felt chills down her spine as for one brief moment she considered approaching the man. And then he was gone. He had quickly turned towards the subway entrance, and vanished down the steps. Gone forever. Bonnie put her hands to her face to quiet the grief she felt. She had lost him.

A cold wetness touched her cheek, and then another. In the light of the street lamp, small white flakes drifted down. The sidewalk was dry, but already the white flakes blew gently along next to the buldings. She turned into her street.

When she climbed the stairs she felt pain in a stiff knee she hadn't noticed before. She must force herself to go to the village. It would be so much easier to stay here and watch television. Bing Crosby or something. She heard a distant ringing.

She climbed faster. It was her phone. It would be the last thing to bear if she missed it. Trying to decide if the call was from John or her kids in Lancaster, she fought with the locks on the door and raced inside, stretching her arm ahead to grab the receiver.

'Hello.'

It was John. 'Is this by any chance Mrs Bonnie Forbes from Lancaster?' It wasn't John. He wouldn't say that.

'Yes. Yes it is.'

'Bonnie, how about that?' His voice was laughing. 'What in the world are you doing in New York?'

'Well, who is this?' she demanded.

'Oh, I'm sorry. It's Rick. Rick Baker.'

Who's Rick Baker? She struggled with the pictures the voice brought back – the McGovern campaign. 'Rick! Rick, of course. How in the world ...?'

'Somebody had told me Anne lived here now, and I looked her up in the phone book. And there you were! I thought I'd take a chance. What luck!'

'Anne's out of town. You couldn't get her.'

'I didn't even try. How about this? What in the world are you doing in New York?'

'It's a long story. I'm working, and going to school, and writing a book.'

'I want to hear the long story. Oh, but you're busy. I'm forgetting it's Christmas Eve. You've got company.'

'No, I haven't. I'm all alone, Rick.'

'No kidding. So am I.' It was one of her fantasies. She shook her head. There was a significant pause.

'Come over,' she said. 'Can you come over?'

'I thought you'd never ask. Where are you?'

She told him and hung up the phone. It was a new world. She straightened the pillows and carried the cup off the table over to the kitchen counter. She took off her fur jacket and hung it up and hurried to check on herself in the mirror. What if she had been given a lonely table at the Chateau d'Or? What if she had gone off with the man? He was probably a rapist, sought by police in six states.

The lady in the mirror had a certain sparkle. Her red dress rippled about her knees when she swung her hips so. The tight long sleeves and V-neck relied only upon gay colour for adornment. She didn't look like somebody's mother.

She had flown about the apartment, setting out candles and glasses for the Dubonnet fortunately chilling in the refrigerator. She lit the candles, even the little moulded bells Mrs Jacobshagen had given her at work. With the light of one table lamp, the room glowed and purred. Bonnie sat down and looked at it. She liked Christmas again. She leaned over and tuned the radio to soft rock. She jumped when the buzzer sounded, answered the intercom and heard, 'It's Rick.' After firmly pressing the button that would unlock the downstairs door, she waited for him in the open doorway.

They were both smiling, and their hands clasped. Two lone hands finding a connection, completing a circuit. Trusted friends miraculously drifted together over a sea of strangers.

She hadn't seen Rick since the day she moved out of McGovern headquarters. He had gone on to other towns by election night. Three long years ago.

She saw approval and admiration in his eyes as he looked about the apartment, and at her. He had a little red beard now, showing a touch of grey. How could that be? He was so young.

She filled him in briefly on the last eventful seven months, then waited to hear about him. He had been travelling for an organization lobbying against the development of nuclear power. Now he was looking to the campaign of 1976.

'I'm on my way to Georgia tomorrow. I think their governor's a viable contender for the Democratic nomination. Name's Jimmy Carter.'

'Never heard of him.'

'You will. At least I'm going to have a try on his team.'

She told him about her unsuccessful attempts at dining, and about the programme she had intended to see.

'Let's go,' he said. 'Sounds good to me, and we'll find us something to eat.'

They pulled back the curtain and looked out. Sidewalks were white now. In front of the house a man brushed the snow from his car windows while the wipers tracked semicircles on the windshield. Flakes had become large, soundlessly landing on the window ledge and multiplying as they watched. Bonnie changed her sandals for shiny black boots, and put on a dress-length black cape with a white fleece-lined hood. They blew out the candles and joyfully went out.

The city had been magically tidied up for Christmas. Squeaky clean sidewalks and streets stretched out in virginal purity. The violations of muddy footprints were quickly covered with fresh, feathery flakes. Traffic had slowed, and grown quieter behind the sheer white veil. The flakes fastened to their eyelashes as they walked, and a few floated under the hood, putting sparkles in her hair. Rick, hatless, accumulated frost across his sandy head. A cab appeared when they needed it, and they were soon on their way.

The address proved to be a deserted old store building. Their driver squinted at the numbers, as the snow stung his face through the rolled-down window glass. 'Yep, that's it. Sure you have the right address?'

'Look, over there.' Bonnie pointed to a group of strangely dressed people going through a side door.

'Yeah,' Rick said, 'it's upstairs.'

The driver rolled up the glass, only commenting through his stiff back.

'What do you think?' Bonnie asked Rick.

'Well, we've come this far. Might as well check it out.'

He gave the driver a large tip, asking him to wait a few minutes, and they got out.

The stairs were steep, the outside brightness yielded to gloom – dirty water puddled on the steps, and globs of dirt and red paint streaked across the walls. A small bare bulb at the top landing provided the only light. With some relief they found on the other side of the door a warm room, oppressively warm, with worn oriental-style rugs on the floor, and large pillows scattered around. There were a few chairs. Two couples in evening attire occupied some of these. Two men in leather jackets and caps conversed with a black man in an African caftan and beads. Young girls in tight jeans, long dark hair spread on their shoulders, were hard to classify in the dim light.

'Stay?' Rick asked.

'Let's,' she answered.

Rick paid a tired-looking white-haired woman sitting at a card table, making change from a muffin tin. He saw Bonnie seated on a low stool before going for coffee at another card table at the end of the room. She folded her cape on the floor beside her, reluctant to leave it out of her sight. The coffee was hot and delicious, unexpectedly rich. Rick sat on the floor nearby. Strings of brightly coloured Christmas tree bulbs wound around the window. Some were blinking, others were not. Bonnie tried to figure which bulbs were strung together, if the blue went with the green or if there was no plan. Soon the programme began.

A man whose very young face was surrounded by dark bushy hair and beard played the guitar and sang old country songs. His worn denim jeans and dirty cowboy shirt suggested origins that Bonnie doubted. He sang 'Big Rock Candy Mountain' which she remembered from hillbilly radio shows when she was a child. He was into a Dylan lyric when his glassy blue eyes centred on Bonnie. He would pull away, but quickly return his lazy gaze to her. Without changing expression, he looked over the red dress, the shiny boots, and knees elevated by the low stool. Regularly he would catch her eye, and slip away again. She felt young and sexy and beautiful. She took the moment to heart, took nourishment from it for all it could give to her, here and now.

The grimy young cowboy melted away into the background after his place in front of the room was taken by a couple giving a dramatic reading. Their voices were trained and as they traded the narrative back and forth, alto to baritone, Bonnie slipped into a hypnotic peace. She didn't understand the words, but the sounds were like a lullaby – caring and comforting. She was happy for the moment as she lived it, without connection to yesterday or tomorrow.

Blue, green, red, white, green, blue. 'Christmas is the agony of birth and lost angel songs.' Amber beads glowing against a black, strong neck. Rick's tow-coloured head, turning to smile, indicating a connection.

When the man with the curly, grey moustache and Indian shirt announced there would be more entertainment soon, Rick pulled Bonnie to her feet. 'Shall we look for food?' he asked. Reluctantly, she agreed.

Snow was accumulating on the sidewalk, and piling high in doorstep corners when they walked once again. A few short blocks and they were out on Washington Square, bright with coloured lights and full of people. They saw a seafood sign and went into a busy place with dancing in the back of the long room and the pounding beat of disco music and changing colours sifting through to the front. No Christmas bulbs these, but light itself, changing complexions from red to green to purple.

They were hungry, and ate fresh scallops and oysters without trying to converse over the music. When they were finished, Rick pulled her to her feet and as though it were the only thing to do she followed him to the dance floor. Fortunately the red dress knew how to disco, and she abandoned herself to the wriggling, swishing skirt.

They found a cab in time to head for St Patrick's at midnight, although they feared they had not allowed enough time for the crowd.

When Bonnie slid across the taxi seat and accidentally touched the door handle, sparks jumped out into the dim light. When Rick pulled the door closed, they both knew something had been added to the air. They were not the two people they had been at McGovern headquarters three years ago. Neither spoke, but there was no uncertainty when they met, a few blocks later in the middle of the seat, in a long, slow embrace, each kiss growing in intensity, urgency, necessity. His hand moved inside her cape, circling a breast through the red crepe dress, and slipping downward over the material bunched into her lap. 'Do you really want to go to mass?' he said, and she said, 'No.' Thus the driver changed his course, and it was Christmas Eve in New York as the bells chimed through the drifting snow.

Thirty-five

The eight-foot tree glittered, its shredded tinsel icicles incongruous against the dark Queen Anne furniture and the faded oriental rug. Marc Blake paused on the step leading through the archway into the oversized room. Behind him, Blanche's soft voice said, 'It's a beautiful tree. You did a good job, Marc.'

'I could do it in my sleep,' Marc answered. 'I haven't missed a tree in forty-five years.' *The same star on the top. The same goddamned star.* His earliest recollections of Christmas involved being lifted by his father to put on the star. He remembered sitting on the carpeted step, waiting, while John was allowed to climb the ladder and to decide where things would be placed. In recent years, after Brad died, John had been excused and the whole responsibility, now a large chore, had fallen on Marc. Mother and Blanche helping, of course.

He stepped down into the room and walked to the mahogany cabinet to fix a drink. He was adding the soda when it occurred to him that he didn't want a drink. He looked at the partially filled glass, set it down on the cabinet, and walked away.

Blanche had quietly disappeared. She would be checking on the progress of the traditional Christmas Eve dinner in the kitchen, and hurrying upstairs to report to mother and help her zip up her dress. Mother's arthritis was a source of embarrassment to her, and they all tried to help while

270

pretending not to. Blanche received a salary for acting the part of the old maid daughter Margaret Blake needed. *All she has is an old maid son.*

Marc reminded himself that it had been twenty years since he moved to his first bachelor apartment. That move had been made quickly when he had first perceived himself moving into the role of old maid son. Done with a callous disregard for his newly widowed mother's controlled disapproval. A private address gave a certain measure of freedom. The nights that June stayed over. At least mother pretended she didn't know. He wondered if his mother really hoped he was still a virgin.

He took the Kolstelanetz Christmas records from the cabinet and stacked them on the stereo turntable. The dulcet notes of 'Winter Wonderland' were already ringing though his head before they started. The needle engaged, he adjusted the volume and turned to the task of building a fire in the fireplace. He removed his coat, and pushed up the sleeves of the new cashmere turtleneck sweater. The sweater was as casual as you could get at mother's parties, even a very intimate family one. He guessed John would wear a tie.

The wood was starting to pop when Marc heard the mellow front door chime, overlapped by the sounds of an opening door and voices. He pulled down the sleeves and was putting on his coat when his sister-in-law appeared in the doorway.

Sara Anderson Blake paused on the step, balancing her weight carefully, head poised at a haughty angle. She was twenty pounds heavier than the lean, willowy girl who had posed for *Glamour* magazine, but she still retained an imposing grace.

'Hello, Marc.'

'Evening, Sara.'

She lifted her long black skirt enough to extend a sandalled toe down the step, and carefully walked to the bar. She was already scooping ice into the glass when John looked in. He smiled and nodded at Marc, eyes sweeping over the tree. He was wearing the red pure silk tie Blanche had given him last Christmas. Marc had a blue one at home. John had a small briefcase tucked under his arm.

'Mother's not down yet?'

'No.'

'We came a little early. I need to find something upstairs.'
Marc nodded as John disappeared down the hall.

Sara didn't look up. She finished making the drink with a quick squirt from the soda bottle, and walked over to sit on the sofa. She sat unsmiling, not looking at Marc or the tree. Marc remembered uneasily the first time he had seen her this way at Christmas. It was only four years ago, but seemed longer, that Brad was not with them for the first time in his twenty years. John and Sara's only child had been the focus of the family Christmases since his birth. He had called from Canada, while they were opening gifts, and Sara had collapsed. The memory of her agonized face, her large body without its usual balanced control, was one Marc wished he could erase. The Blakes never lost control. More typical was the strength that they all displayed the next Christmas when Brad was dead. He had come back from Canada and died appropriately for his country.

'Did you get the television?'

Marc stared at her, then found his tongue. 'Yes. Yes, I got the television.' It was a small colour set for his mother's bedroom. To replace the little black-and-white set she had used for years. She always insisted she didn't like television, but they all knew she often ran it into the early morning hours.

'I bought her a pink Dior blouse. John forgot to tell me he had bought a brooch in New York.' Her tone was accusing, missing its target.

'John's been working in New York?'

'Quite a lot lately.'

Marc wondered who the woman was. He went back to poke the fire.

'We got a Christmas card from June.'

Marc carefully turned the glowing log with the poker. His heart didn't jump any more at her name.

'Did you know she's pregnant?' Sara asked.

He finished the log and put the poker back in the rack.

'Yes. I got a card, too.'

'Must have been an accident. That's a terrible thing to happen at her age.'

'Maybe not. Maybe she wants a child.'

June – trim, efficient, fulfilled. He couldn't remember ever asking her if she missed children. They had both been smug about not wanting marriage. For ten years they had filled out each other's lives. 'I'm in love, Marc.' Now his heart did twist again. He could see her sitting on his leather sofa, where she belonged, saying 'I'm in love,' about another man.

'It could be retarded. She's over forty now, isn't she?'

'Somewhere around that.' He knew exactly how old June was. It was none of Sara's business.

'I think she should have an abortion.'

'For God's sake, Sara –' Marc was startled by the loudness of his voice. He sat down and stiffened his shaking hand.

'I'm sorry.' Sara's eyes focused on his for the first time. 'Sometimes I can really be obtuse. I don't mean to.'

He waved his hand at her, and shook his head. 'It's these damned family celebrations. They bring back the ghosts.'

'Why, Marc, I thought you liked tradition.'

'Why do you say that?'

'I don't know. You're the rock in the family. The only one who doesn't have problems.'

'Jesus, Sara! What a thing to say!'

'Why don't you find yourself another girl? Do you know how many women I know who'd give their teeth to go out with you?'

'I should know. You've exposed me to enough of them.'

'And you always find something wrong. Picky, picky!'

'Sara, let Marc be.'

They both looked towards the firm voice. Margaret Blake in a silk suit blooming with tastefully muted mauve and grey magnolias, stepped down with care and walked briskly to her chair. Blanche followed softly. The floor-length skirt made Margaret look taller than five feet two. Her white hair was carefully curled, her violet-shaded eyes bright. She eased into the chair, deliberately wiping away the fleeting expression of pain. 'That log is going to fall, Marc. Where's John?'

Marc looked at the fire and checked his impulse to go back to it. 'He went upstairs after something.'

'Whatever would he want upstairs?' Margaret looked at Sara.

Sara shrugged. 'Don't ask me.'

'Merry Christmas, Mother!' John came from the hall – straight to his mother's chair to kiss her on the cheek. His eyes were warm as he drew back to look at her. 'You're like a spring bouquet.'

'It's the perfume you gave me. Merry Christmas, darling.' She held to his hand until he moved out of reach. 'Marc, would you get us some sherry?'

'I'll get it,' John volunteered, changing direction.

The same pattern every year. Slight changes in the cast. John missing during the war years. Dad dying, and Brad. June, one of the few outsiders joining them for many years. Marc had never missed. Even when he was in the service, home for Christmas. And college. Should have taken the ski trip that time. That girl – Carol something – could have made the trip interesting. She was really stacked. Brad was still a toddler that year, a round-eyed cherub. Toy shopping made it Christmas. June.

Marc claimed his stale drink, and Sara was ready for another scotch and soda. Did John hesitate? Marc wondered about that. No one ever mentioned Sara was drinking too much, but Marc wondered.

John's stomach was flat, his shoulders erect. How does he do it? He's ten years older. Look how thick his hair is! In ten years I'll be – Marc turned his head to catch a look in the distant mirror. He straightened his shoulders, and decided to skip dessert.

'Marc!' He realized they were all looking at him. Mother had been speaking. The unabsorbed words must have been for him.

'John brought the papers – the Martin contract. He can get it recorded the day after Christmas. Don't forget to sign.'

'Yes, Mother. I know. We talked about it yesterday.'

The chairman of the board speaking to the president of the company. In a flash he felt his puppet strings chafe. Mother had been the backbone of the family company since Dad died. She didn't let go when her son succeeded her as president five years ago. Her physical presence was removed from the office, but she was up there watching – like God.

The four-course dinner was consumed, gifts torn into, and the three women had retired upstairs to try the new pink blouse with Mother's skirts when the two men went into the downstairs library. John removed the contract from the small case and laid it before Marc.

274

'It's ready?' Marc asked. 'You changed the restrictions we talked about?'

'Right.'

Marc looked at the new paragraph on the last page, and turned back to the beginning, rereading that also.

John turned away from the desk and slowly paced around the worn sofa that faced the bookshelves. He walked back and forth, a slight frown wrinkling his forehead, eyes sombre.

In the midst of his reading, Marc looked up abruptly and asked, 'Where's the list mentioned here?' He picked up John's case and poured out the meagre contents.

John stopped pacing, and sucked in his breath.

On the desk, topping the sheets of lengthy typing, was a photograph. The hand-painted photo of a pink-cheeked, red-lipped, young face looked at them, with a sweet, guileless smile. How fitting in this night of ghosts! Marc tenderly raised the ivoried photo and regarded it silently. As an adolescent boy he had often stared at this photo when it was framed on the piano, among many others. With the passion of puberty, he had adored the young woman pictured there. His brother's wife.

He looked up into John's blank face. John walked back and sat down.

'Where . . .?'

Marc sensed confusion behind John's controlled actions. Not ordinary for John. 'Bonnie,' Marc said, suppressing a smile, looking back at the picture. He laid it down quickly. 'Is this what you were after upstairs?'

John considered his answer, nodded.

'Well,' Marc said, 'I guess I'm not the only one remembering things tonight.'

John stood up and paced again. He glanced at the heavy door, walked back and said, 'She's in New York. I've seen her.'

'The hell you say!' The smile broke through now.

John's eyes dropped, and he slowly paced again, in front of the desk.

'Well, tell me, man,' Marc said, 'what's she like? What's happened to her?'

'Oh, she's been married, separated, grandchildren, going to school . . .'

'To make a long story short.'

John sighed and sat in the chair again. 'She's beautiful as ever. I love her. I still do.'

Marc sobered. 'I see. Your business trips to New York.' He picked up the old photo again. 'What's she like? I never thought of her middle-aged.'

John stared at the floor. 'She's like I knew she'd be.'

'How'd you find her?'

'She was at the Earth Savers convention last spring. I spoke at their banquet.'

'Did you say she's divorced?'

'Pending.'

'Pending before or after you saw her?'

'After.' The two men's eyes held together, neither giving way. 'Are you judging me? Don't do that.'

'Have I ever judged you?'

John turned away. 'No.'

'You don't ask for advice, and I don't offer it.'

John turned back. 'It's all right, Marc. We're handling it.'

'I hope so.'

John put the picture and other papers back in the case, handing one sheet to Marc. 'This is the list.'

Marc picked up the contract and looked at it. 'I think I'll go see her.'

'Why would you do that?'

'Why not? For myself. Nothing to do with you.'

John frownded. 'That's not a good idea.'

Marc slammed his fist on the desk, regarding the resulting pain with surprise. Slowly he looked back at the contract and continued to read without comprehension. Signed it. He had read it before.

Thirty-six

SKIN

I'm all covered up
with my skin
and you're over there
all wrapped up in yours.
The me and you locked inside
the flesh and hair and fingernails
forever must be two.

But
in my bed
skin to skin
limbs and bodies braided,
warmed by your heartbeat
wet from my joy,
we destroyed the space between us.

Your skin
slipped into my skin
and
for a flash in eternity
we were not alone.

Bonnie Forbes
English 231

Lean, hard shoulders and biceps above the sheet, a mussed, sandy head resting on the other pillow, greeted Bonnie's sleepy eyes on Christmas morning. She didn't move, but examined with fascination the density of Rick's little beard, and the variations in colour of the hair on his head, chin, and chest.

They had talked long into the morning hours. In the dark he

was a voice; warm, moist flesh; enfolding arms; a spirit revealing itself as it would never do in the daylight. He had admitted to his fear of lightning and had poured out the whole story of the girl he had made pregnant in high school. There was less time for Bonnie's confessing, but she did tell him there was a married man who had changed her life. From whom she would accept gratefully whatever he had to offer. Somewhere in the early hours Rick had said, 'I want a son, and a little girl. I love this gypsy life, but I don't want to miss the family thing either. Sometimes I panic. When will it be too late?' Bonnie couldn't tell him. She still didn't know how you make everything fit, even when there's time.

She started the coffee perking, and hurried into the bathroom where she removed yesterday's makeup and reapplied a minimal amount.

The table was set and bacon sizzling in the pan when Rick sat up and stretched. He asked, 'Why didn't you wake me?' swung his legs out to the floor and stood up to dress. Bonnie watched. It had been a long time since she had seen a male body this young, and it might well never happen again. There was a difference. But then she hadn't seen very many naked male bodies. Perhaps they were all different.

She ascertained his preference in eggs and provided them as ordered, along with bacon and toast, juice and coffee. He ate ravenously, which bothered Bonnie, she not being hungry at all.

'What time does your plane leave?'

'Two-thirty,' he confirmed what she remembered, looking at his watch. 'I'll have to be getting along soon . . . by the time I go back to the hotel and get to the airport . . . I'm sure stand-bys are waiting for my seat.'

'Why leave on Christmas?'

'I didn't expect anything to keep me here. I'll be ready to get down to work tomorrow. There's this guy I met in Washington in '74.' He launched into a long, enthusiastic account of the events leading to his involvement with Jimmy Carter. Bonnie's mind kept wandering and she would pull it back to hear him mentioning names she had missed. She decided it was something like corporation politics after all. Sometimes Rick had to be nice to people he didn't like.

During the night she had asked him if he would like to see her poems. She took them from a drawer after breakfast, holding them tentatively as Rick finished his anecdote. Before she could mention them, he said, 'Could I use your shower?'

'Of course,' she answered, still standing with the papers. 'These are my poems,' she said as she laid them on the desk. 'If you have time.'

'What? Oh, the poems,' he said, moving towards the bathroom. 'Yeah, great, I'll get back to them.'

She hurried to find him a large towel. Afterwards, he forgot, and she didn't mention it again.

When he was ready to leave they stood in front of the door, somewhat self-conscious. They had bumped into each other and she had said 'Sorry,' and felt silly for that. He took her two hands in his and squeezed them, and they traded smiles spiced with knowledge. Suddenly he threw his arms about her in a tight hug saying, swaying slightly, 'Good-bye, my love. Stay happy.'

She wriggled her arms around his broad back and spoke softly up towards his ear, 'Thank you for Christmas.'

He stood back and took his gloves from his overcoat pockets and pulled them on. 'I hope we're not snowed in.'

'Do you think . . .?'

'No, I don't think so,' he said with conviction. 'If we are, I'll come back.'

He didn't.

Thirty-seven

Dorothy Vance and Jenny Ames sat at a table overlooking the snow-covered golf course at the Lancaster Country Club. They both ordered the chef's salad, and quickly got down to business in their discussion of the playhouse committees. Dorothy was board chairman this year, with Jenny in an apprentice post as her assistant. Dorothy had been deeply grateful when Jenny suggested this arrangement. Dorothy needed the responsibility that went with the post, and it kept her in contact with the executive wives at Scott Manufacturing. They were a new, younger group now, but Dorothy was still maintaining her senior position, a notch above.

For instance, she was the one who could caution Jenny, 'Remember not to put Alice Long and Brenda Cullen on the same committee. They aren't speaking this month.'

'They aren't? Why?'

'I don't remember. Some dumb thing.'

'Alice is a problem anyway,' Jenny said. 'She can't be depended upon, ever.'

'But her husband is an assistant sales manager. You can't drop her.'

Jenny ordered another martini.

The big wooden bowls had been removed when Jenny sat back and said, 'I hear you're seeing Frank Forbes.'

Dorothy lowered her eyes to hide the pleasure and modestly answered, 'Well, yes. Poor Frank.'

Her eyes on her drink, Jenny ventured, 'I didn't get to know Bonnie very well, but I liked her.'

Dorothy nodded.

'She seemed very kind. It just shows that you can't tell what's really inside people. So sad. She seemed to have what we're all looking for.'

'She's in town now.' Dorothy felt it was time to get this straight.

Jenny's eyes widened. 'She is? Oh, I'm sorry, I didn't know. I probably shouldn't have brought it up.'

Dorothy shook her head. 'No problem. She's at her daughter's for Christmas. She called at the last minute and said she was coming the day after Christmas. Poor Linda's been so upset. Asked me to come for Christmas dinner. I was glad to help her out. It's so hard on the children, even when they're grown.'

'Do you think Bonnie's mentally ill? When I think about it, she sounded a little strange the night of the party. You expect men to do these things, but why would a woman? And at her age. What'll become of her?'

Dorothy shook her head. She couldn't say *I really don't care, as long as she doesn't come back*. Dorothy was frightened by the intensity of her feelings. She glimpsed a second chance for herself, to regain what she had lost. More, actually. Frank would make a better husband than Fred had been. Dorothy had done her share of silent suffering over Fred's philandering. She was sure Frank had never strayed. Indeed, Bonnie must have mental problems. Frank was well rid of her. 'They've filed for divorce,' Dorothy told Jenny. 'Bonnie's here to take what she wants from the house before Frank puts it on the market.' Her knowledge of Frank's personal life could imply things she couldn't tactfully say.

'Oh, will there be a sale?' Jenny perked up. 'They have some lovely pieces.'

'I don't know.' *I certainly don't want them.*

'I don't suppose George would want me to buy anything,' Jenny added, expressing the confusion she still felt about protocol. The hand that set the glass on the table trembled slightly.

Thirty-eight

Lancaster in December. The angels still blew their silent trumpets on Main Street looking down from the lamp posts on the swapping shoppers walking across the lull between Christmas shopping and the January clearance sales. How small downtown was – how calm and clean. You could stand in front of the old City Hall and look down the wide, well-lighted street, past Murray and Penn, and J. C. Penney, past most of the good stores. Barriers were up in some of the side streets. Lancaster was rejuvenating the downtown district, the city council putting up a good fight against the suburban shopping centre threat. Christmas snow had halted street work for the present.

Spencer's Drug Store, where Bonnie once sat on a stool and drank chocolate shakes, and later bought Kaopectate and birthday candles for the children, had given way to H. & R. Block's desks. They would be gone, too, when she came back again after tax time. Nobody drank milk shakes from a drug store stool anymore. Not even in Lancaster.

She turned down First Street towards the Wheatland Hotel. The marquee said HAPPY NEW YEAR but something was different. As she came closer, the large windows of the corner first floor loomed black and empty. The Comanche Room had closed long ago, followed by the Leopard Lounge (after liquor by the drink was legalized) and then by Hopkins Real Estate and Insurance. But now it was empty. She stood across the street and looked at the blank windows. Then she saw the boards across the main lobby entrance. And the coffee shop was gone. Bonnie swallowed hard.

A young meter maid finished writing a ticket and slipped it under an unlucky motorist's windshield wiper. Bonnie walked over to her and asked, 'What's happened to the Wheatland?'

'Gonna tear it down,' the girl answered cheerfully.

'Oh,' Bonnie said. 'Oh, how awful.'

The girl squinted up at the tall building. 'Yeah, I guess the new Hilton put them out of business.'

'I remember so many things about the hotel ...'

'Yeah,' the girl said, 'it's awfully old. But' – she looked back cheerfully – 'you can't stop progress.'

Bonnie used the key Frank had left with Linda. The living room looked as though she had just walked out and come back again. Nothing was changed.

Wait a minute, the bare spot on the table by the window. My begonia. I turned it every day, and watered it twice a week. Well, I'm sure Mrs Myers did her best.

Bonnie walked on numb legs into the panelled family room. Different here. Frank's chair had been moved closer to the television. Looked terrible here. The pretties she had kept on the shelf were gone. Everything was crooked.

She thought of the china and crystal in the dining room. The oil paintings throughout the house. How could she choose? She turned and walked back through the living room. On the antique table in the corner she saw a little music box that she had bought at a rummage sale twelve years ago for fifty cents. She had loved it then, and so had the girls. It had hand-painted violets on the lid and played 'Dream of Love', the melody from Schubert's Unfinished Symphony. She flipped open the lid and the litle waltz tune magically floated out. She couldn't know when the key on the bottom had been wound to make it ready. She stood still as the music grew slower and finally stopped – midphrase. Bonnie dropped the box into her purse and left the house. She put on the lock, by habit, and pulled the door shut.

'When your dad gets ready to move,' she told both daughters that evening, 'go in and pick out what you want, and then we'll have a big sale.'

'You didn't take *anything*?' Karen gasped.

'It would have cost a mint to ship. Besides, I don't have room.'

They were sitting on the floor, shoes kicked off. Bonnie leaned against the printed sofa and wiggled her toes into the shag carpet. 'There are keepsakes from when you were little in labelled boxes in the basement. You'll probably want to transfer those to your basement, Linda.' Her serene face looked into Linda's frowning one. 'There are things there from my childhood, too. You can pass them on to Luke and Bobby.'

The girls censured her with their silence.

'It's easier this way. Come on, let me do it easy.'

'It doesn't seem right. Not when you're still alive.'

'Well, pretend I died then,' Bonnie said. Her jovial tone was met with stony stares.

'Please,' she said quietly and soberly. 'This is the way I want it.'

They all looked at the floor. Bonnie reran in her mind the things she had just said – strange but necessary.

She stretched out her legs in front of her. 'I haven't told you about Christmas Eve. You can't guess what happened.'

Reluctantly, their eyes came back to hers. 'What?' Karen finally asked.

'Remember Rick Baker? Rick Baker – the McGovern campaign organizer.'

'Vaguely,' Karen murmured.

'He called me. On Christmas Eve. Can you imagine? Just when I was alone, and needed someone.'

'You said you had friends!' Linda accused loudly.

'They all had someplace else to go,' Bonnie explained hurriedly. 'I didn't know that when I decided to stay.'

'How terrible,' Linda said. 'How terrible. Mom, why did you do that?'

'Anyway, it worked out fine. Rick was alone, too, and he just happened to find out I was there, and we went out to this crazy place in the Village ...'

'I remember him,' Linda said. 'He was cute. You'd think he could have found a date.'

Bonnie slowly rolled against the sofa and stood up. 'Forgive me, kids. It has been a long day.' She turned around at the door to look at their worried faces, forced a smile and said, 'Forgive me', again. 'Good night.'

She closed the guest room door and sat down on the edge of the bed. Suddenly she was on her feet and hurrying to the bathroom. She dropped on her knees by the toilet, urgently fumbling with the lid and seat, to push them out of the way before she began retching. Her whole body jerked and heaved, expelling Linda's good dinner.

She rinsed her mouth and gargled with warm water and, trembling, returned to the bedroom, feeling a little better.

There were more good moments than bad in the visit. Most of the time they talked about inconsequential things, and enjoyed being in sight again. There were a few moments when they broke the barriers. One of these was when she and Linda were preparing dinner and Bonnie attempted to convey her feelings on the first day of poetry class. She described Debby, and her shopping bag full of radical poems. She stopped talking when she saw the twisted smile on Linda's face. 'You don't think this is funny,' Bonnie said abruptly.

'Well, it is,' Linda defended herself. 'Or it would be from someone else.'

Bonnie gripped the knife she was using to chop the cabbage, her eyes on the chopping board. 'Linda, why can't you see the woman I am? Give her a chance.'

When she looked at Linda she saw distress. Linda's words

284

emerged with difficulty. 'I don't want to lose a mother to gain a new friend.'

'But that wasn't me.' Bonnie's body turned to glass. 'I was born when I left Lancaster last May. Do I have to stay frozen forever in one place so you won't have to give up your mother? I gave up my cute little girls. They don't exist anymore. They're gone.'

Linda's face was ravaged. The softness Bonnie was begging for wasn't there.

Bonnie tried again. 'I was born ... there's so little time ... I already gave ...' Her voice broke.

Linda looked afraid. The bridge didn't grow.

Bonnie bent her head and put her hand to her forehead. She felt a touch, then arms slipping around her, and she turned quickly to a tight embrace.

The broken antique teacup lay in tiny pieces on the kitchen floor. The three-year-old braced herself in stiff-legged rebellion, her screams swelling her mother's shouts. The mother heard the violence, the futility of it, and stopped mid-scream. She threw her arms around the rigid body, feeling the surprised little girl let go and dissolve into her mother's tears.

They sniffed, and were smiling when they drew back to look at each other.

'I could never stop loving you and Karen and Anne. After all we've been through.'

'But you stopped loving Daddy.'

They backed apart and Bonnie looked away. 'I didn't stop loving him,' she said slowly. 'I just can't share this life with him. I either have to do it his way, or do it alone.'

'Isn't it terrible to be alone?'

'No, it isn't,' Bonnie said. 'I like living by myself. I was lonely with Frank.'

Linda stared out the window. 'Do I have to wait until I'm fifty?'

'No, don't wait, Linda.' Bonnie shook her head. 'But don't ask me how to do it.' Then she said sharply, with sudden insight, 'And don't always look at me and see yourself. It isn't inevitable that you turn into me. Your sisters don't look at me that way, but I think you always have.'

Luke burst into the kitchen, wailing as he held up a broken

285

plastic bulldozer, and Linda hurried to comfort him, holding him to her with extra passion.

Thirty-nine

Bonnie resigned her job that January and enrolled as a full-time college student. In a way, the decision was forced upon her by Martha. When Martha returned from Christmas in Buffalo, she carried her ample weight with new lightness. Her eyes glowed, and her cheeks were pink. She smiled often, said 'Please' and 'Thank you' and sometimes forgot what she was doing.

Bonnie had only been with her an hour when, finding the joy contagious, she asked with a smile, 'Martha, did you meet a man?'

Martha blushed and stammered, 'How did you know?'

'You've lighted up like a Christmas tree. I don't know what else could make you look like this.'

Martha sighed. 'He's in my son-in-law's office. His wife just died three months ago, and the poor dear is so helpless. Didn't want me to leave.'

'Well, that is news.' Bonnie hesitated. 'I'm glad, Martha. It has to be a good thing to make you look like this.'

'He's coming down this weekend. I'll introduce you.'

Harold Shields was portly, with a shock of greying red hair. He coughed a lot, always carried a cigarette. He teased waitresses and told ethnic jokes. He sprang to open doors and to carry small packages, gestures destined to end at the altar. He referred to Bonnie and Martha as 'handsome women'. After one evening of Harold, Bonnie was sick at the thought of Martha's surrender, but she didn't say this to Martha. She wanted to protest, but couldn't get it out.

286

The following Monday, Martha announced she was moving to Buffalo and offered Bonnie her job. 'You're the logical person. I know the board will want you.'

The job could mean many things. Contacts on a higher level with interesting and diverse persons. A salary. Not large, but more real than the mite she had been receiving. To be paid for one's contributions! 'Bonnie has a job,' her old friends back in Lancaster would say. 'She's running a national organization.' And the other old friend would be impressed, and maybe a little disappointed.

The bed wasn't made yet that Tuesday morning, and Bonnie hadn't dressed. She had been wakeful since dawn, sleeping and worrying in spurts. If she got up and dressed, she would have to sit at the desk and write. The writing had been neglected for Christmas, and then for the trip, and now her mind was on the new job. She looked at the stacks of paper. She had picked the manuscript up and spent a long time rereading – crossing out a word, changing a paragraph here and there. But she seemed paralyzed at just the thought of composing new pages.

When the phone rang, she scrambled across the sofa bed, happy for the diversion. Matt Fineberg's staccato voice cut into her disorganized morning. 'We got the counter offer on our settlement. Are you sitting down? $75,000 in bonds, plus half the profit from the house and its contents. That's it.'

'But he has that much in insurance. Nothing else? How about my tuition?'

'That's it. Nothing else.' He waited for the point to be made, then continued. 'Don't worry, this is standard. Now they have a low base to dicker from.'

Bonnie mumbled. 'I didn't think he'd do that. Is that all I've been worth?'

'He'll have to furnish a financial settlement. You're entitled to at least a third. I just wanted you to know what they offered.'

'I thought he'd be fair. He always said I helped.'

'Don't worry. We're just getting started.'

At fifty dollars an hour, Bonnie thought. He'll pay for that. He'll get the bill. She hung up and sat and thought, the son of a bitch. The lousy son of a bitch. Still words to be savoured unspoken. Frank? Was he this profane thing?

The phone, still resting beside her on the bed at the end of its long cord rang again. This time a strange male voice, deep and soft, said, 'Is this Bonnie Forbes?'

'Yes.'

'Well,' he said irrationally, 'I didn't think you'd be there in the morning.'

'Well,' she said after a pause, 'I am.'

The man laughed, and Bonnie felt a quick cutting memory. 'Who is this?' she asked sharply.

'This is Marc,' the voice said in a warmer tone. 'Marc Blake.'

'Really?' A thin thread of excitement quickened her breathing. Then apprehension. 'There's not anything wrong, is there?'

'No,' he answered lightly, then understanding, 'oh, no. I'm not calling for anyone else. I wanted to talk to you.'

Bonnie smiled into the phone. 'How nice, Marc. You're all grown up.'

They both laughed.

'I'll be in the city this week,' Marc said. 'Could I take you to dinner? Friday?'

'Lovely.'

'Maybe we could see the ballet. I have a friend who can get tickets.'

Bonnie hesitated. 'How did you know I was here?'

'John told me.' The name was mentioned. 'I told him I was going to call you.'

'Well, then, sure. Okay.'

A man who was interested in the ballet. This pleased her. It wasn't a surprise. The awkward, sensitive boy she had met in 1944 must still survive in some way inside the forty-five-year-old man she was going to meet.

She scrambled off the rumpled sofa bed and quickly straightened the covers and folded the bed into a sofa. Then she put on the teakettle, opened the refrigerator, and discovered she was out of homemade yogurt. In a burst of new energy, she put her long coat on over her breakfast robe, tied a scarf over her head, knotted it under her chin against the January wind, and trotted down the stairs to the health food store for strawberry yogurt.

It was a small store, Mum-and-Dad atmosphere, although Mum and Dad themselves were conspicuously absent. The waif at the cash register popped her gum and reluctantly laid down her paperback novel as Bonnie set down the yogurt and fresh apples and snapped open her coin purse.

'A dollar ten,' the girl said sleepily, then looked back at Bonnie. 'Senior?'

'I beg your pardon?'

'Senior-citizen discount?' The girl's eyes came alive as she looked into Bonnie's wide eyes and she stammered, 'We're supposed to ask.'

'No,' Bonnie gasped. 'Oh, no.'

The girl dropped her eyes and quickly sacked the groceries. 'I'm sorry,' she said, 'we're supposed to ask.'

Bonnie grabbed the sack and hurried out the door. She thought, *Poor thing. She was so embarrassed.* Inside Bonnie was dying. That is, she knew she was dying. She knew she was terminal.

Forty

Marc Blake dipped the half-inch brush into the mound of cobalt blue on the plywood board he used as a palette and slashed it boldly across the canvas, adding a softer afterthought in the corner and burying the paint left on the brush in the malleable softer blues at the top. The buildings in the cityscape were receding into masses of sharp, almost violent colour – at once disintegrating as precise architecture and reemerging as emotional blurs, less identifiable but infinitely more exciting.

His studio was the attic of the building he lived in. The partially finished interior was impervious to splattered paint, and the skylight and one dirty window on the street side of the building gave him good daylight to work by. All the landlord asked was that Marc keep his paints stored in a fireproof metal cabinet. The cobwebs on the exposed rafters and the dead crickets were not objectionable to him here. The unfinished, uncleaned atmosphere freed his inhibitions in painting, though it was a direct contradiction to the rest of his life.

He had efficiently set a trap for the little mouse who had shown up when he first moved into the attic, feeling bad later about this reaction to his only visitor. Marc seemed to be spending more time here lately, in spite of the frequent trips to New York. Or was it because of them?

His brush stood still as his mind went to Bonnie, as it so often did these days. Her voice on the phone that first morning had been pitched lower, quieter, but familiar. It stirred, excited, intimidated him. He remembered turning to a mirror to reaffirm the balding, middle-aged man he was, while feeling strangely adolescent.

They had seen each other several times since then. Easy, relaxed encounters, happy, comfortable. More low-key than the multiple moments like this one, when the memory of being near her was more upsetting than the real thing. Was this because of years of idolizing a memory? She had been the first woman to arouse him – how acute the pain of a fourteen-year-old's desire for his brother's lonely wife. A grown-up goddess, near enough to evoke real physical distress, but completely unattainable.

After the first ten minutes together, Bonnie became the woman he remembered. She was more self-assured now, *finished* somehow. But then, so was he. He needed to remind himself that society at this point would see the advantage on his side. Actually they were even. They were warm friends, and the inappropriate physical yearnings of the fourteen-year-old were a curse he still had to bear. Big brother again stood between them.

Marc recalled once more the feel of her lips brushing his cheek as she said goodnight after their first date. He had helped her that night. She had talked brightly of the classes she was taking, and the novel that was taking on impressive thickness on her desk. They had returned to her apartment after the performance before she mentioned the new job assuming he would be impressed by this.

'It's a real job. Contributing to society, nine to five. Paying taxes and all that.'

'Is this important to you?'

'I think so,' she answered, without conviction. 'I think it is something I need to do. It'll validate my worth somehow, when people ask me, "What do you do?" They expect me to do something. If I'm not a housewife anymore, what am I?'

'It seems to me you're much more than a job.'

She stared at him. 'How would you answer them if you weren't a president?'

'It's different for a man.'

'Why?'

Marc said, 'God knows I'm tied to the concept of my job. There's no real self-worth in it for me. I don't like my job.' He was astounded at what he was saying. He had never said that to anyone.

'I thought maybe a year or two. Then I could resign.'

He had nodded, not pushing the matter. It wasn't his business. Maybe she needed the money. He wondered if John ever gave her money, but pushed the thought away. They never talked about John. Marc hadn't seen John alone since Christmas Eve. Legal advice at the office was another matter, but Marc had learned long ago to listen quietly to Mother's and John's advice about his personal life, and then do as he pleased. But John was there when Bonnie kissed Marc's cheek, blocking the actions or words that filled Marc's fantasies but defied realization.

He jabbed the brush into the cadmium orange and destroyed another building.

Forty-one

Hannah sat back in the cab, her overnight bag on the seat beside her, the train station receding. The name of the hotel she had given the driver seemed familiar to him, though it was not to her. Frank had made the reservation and she was on her way there to meet him.

The letter in her box with a Lancaster return address had been a pleasant surprise. The envelope contained a round-trip train ticket to Washington, D.C., and a brief handwritten letter.

Business takes me to Washington, D.C., March 16 for four or five days. You said you have Monday nights off, and can get extra time occasionally. If you would care to see me again, I would find it very pleasant to spend some time together in the evenings. If the idea appeals to you, let me know and I will see to reservations. I will be staying at the L'Enfant Plaza where our conferences are scheduled, but a friend has advised me of a pleasant little place close by where we could have some quiet time. If you can't manage it at this time, I will of course understand.

Sincerely,
Frank Forbes

P.S. I'm sure you will be discrete about this around my wife. We have finally reached an agreement and have a court date a the end of the month, so our long commitment is coming to an end.

She remembered a reserved but pleasant older man. She counted on her fingers to see if he was old enough to be her grandfather. If two men sired babies at nineteen – well, not likely. She had never known anyone like him. Her own father was jolly and undependable. Older men came into the club, polished shiny on the outside, but often crude under the veneer. She thought of Edward and shivered. Frank was different. So what if his sense of humour was not up to par? He was a gentleman. And rich. Probably not rich rich, but the figures Bonnie was talking about in the settlement sounded rich to Hannah. She hoped Bonnie wouldn't bankrupt him. Going to school every day and typing far into the night, she was still living on Frank's money. Bonnie had turned down the new job, and left Earth Savers behind.

Hannah blocked out the cherry blossoms they were passing as she speculated about Frank's plans for the next two nights. How proper was he? Also, he might be impotent, have to consider that. An affair without sex. He hadn't tried anything at the hotel that day. Far too drunk the night before. Well, it was a new adventure. Frank was the kind of man you would vote for. A man who would take care of you, and be aware of old-fashioned things like honour and dependability.

It was deceiving Bonnie that bothered Hannah most. Even though Bonnie didn't want him anymore, Hannah hated lying to her, and she had been forced to lie – at least by omission when Bonnie saw her packing her bag. When Bonnie asked 'Who's the lucky man?' Hannah didn't say, 'It's your husband.' That was lying by omission when she replied, 'Someone new. From out of town.'

She arrived at the little hotel. The lobby was small, the contemporary furniture clean and unobtrusive. Discreet, as their affair must be. The desk clerk said everything was arranged and she returned his smile, accepting his admiration as a fact of life, as it was indeed of hers.

Frank Forbes scowled at his reflection in the hotel mirror. The turtleneck sweater was plain and grey and expensive, but his chin settling into it looked different. He was used to this chin above a neatly knotted necktie, usually striped maroon, or in more casual moments an open, soft-collared shirt. The turtleneck was a costume, casting his familiar chin into an unfamiliar role. Appropriate, he thought. A disguise.

Frank put his hand to his forehead and squinted. At this moment in a small hotel nearby, a young woman waited for him. A girl born the same year as his youngest daughter. A girl who did things Anne would never do. Obviously, Hannah had chosen the way long ago, and Frank felt no responsibility for her choice. In fact, it was the other way around. He hesitated and considered taking off the sweater and returning to the tie. A quiet dinner in the Plaza dining room alone and early to bed. Message in Miss Rosenberg's box – 'Unavoidable conflict, will not be able to see you.' Before the note was finished in his head, he was turning off the lights and recalling for the hundredth time the unblemished satin smoothness of Hannah's skin. Her face on the pillow, uncomplicated, naturally pink and innocent. The rest of her in the topless bar, accessible but just out of reach.

Frank had never bothered with women he didn't respect. Not since Louise Culbertson in high school, a necessary step in a young man's maturing. He had never understood why some of his friends cheated on their wives with little tramps at the office. Fred Vance, for instance, with a good little wife like Dorothy. Frank wouldn't do that if he married Dorothy – wouldn't put her through that again. But now. He wasn't responsible to anyone.

He knew exactly what it was he wanted from Hannah. Her baring of her breasts nightly in public, and her choice of disrobing and climbing into the other twin bed in his room had established her availability. Things were progressing smoothly and he found himself humming as he took a last look at the room. No matter the mess, they wouldn't come back here. He pulled the door shut and ended the humming abruptly as he confronted a couple in the hall.

When Hannah stepped off the tiny elevator, the lobby was almost empty. A lone man stood in front of the closed cigar counter, turned towards the street. The way he wore the expensive clothes, his quiet confident air as he turned, excited her. She extended her hands before she reached him, and he accepted them. They looked each other over, refreshing their memories, liking what they saw. In his eyes she saw pleasure and appreciation.

'I asked the cab to wait,' he told her and they hurried out, she remembering to step back so he could open the outside door and help her into the cab.

They dined in a small restaurant, simple but expensive. He insisted she order the highest-priced dinner, and the rarest wine. She had let her shawl drop back in the cab, and felt the long slow look he gave to the low-sweeping curved neckline of her gathered voile blouse. She could not explain the shyness she felt, the suppressed desire to pull the shawl back up. In the restaurant his eyes were guarded again, and remained on her face. His ease with the maître d' and the waiter pleased her. She was sure there could be no social situation beyond his control.

After they had ordered, he said, 'I can't tell you how glad I am that you're here. Any trouble at work?'

'No,' she said. 'I have to be back Wednesday night.'

He nodded. She realized with some distress that she had almost asked, 'Is that all right?'

'I'm sorry I can't see you during the day ...' he said.

'That's okay. I'll check out the Capitol tomorrow.'

He leaned back and fixed his eyes on her, saying shyly, 'I almost didn't write. I mean, I wasn't sure.'

'Why not? You could have survived a no.'

'Oh, no,' he answered quickly. 'I don't think I could.'

She laughed uneasily. 'Don't be silly. Of course, you could.'

'No,' he said. 'No, I couldn't.'

The matter was closed.

'You look beautiful,' he told her.

She smiled quietly, knowing this was true.

The ritual of dinner took a long time. The dim lights and distant music relaxed them as the wine warmed. She asked what brought him to Washington and he replied at some length. She didn't know what he was talking about, but she liked the ease with which he dropped the names of congressmen and bureaucrats. He showed no shortage of confidence in his ability to manipulate the wheels of government for the good of the corporation which, of course, was for the good of his community and state. She recognized power which could be equated to wisdom, and she was complimented by the laying out of details he presumed she would understand. She even wished she could.

He didn't mention what was scheduled for them after dinner and she was surprised when he gave the driver the name of her hotel.

'It's still early,' she suggested, after some consideration.

'We'll go up to your room,' he said. 'And talk.'

She thought there might be some fumbling in the cab, but Frank remained on his side of the seat. He pointed out the Library of Congress and the Supreme Court.

'I've talked too much,' he said suddenly. 'Tomorrow night we will talk only about you.'

'I haven't done anything important. Not yet, anyway.'

'You'll be famous someday.'

'Maybe I will. If I get the breaks.'

'It's all ahead. I envy you. It's the fight that counts.'

The desk clerk looked up when they came in, and returned to

the book he was reading. They rode up silently in the elevator, and she started to put the key in the lock, saw Frank's extended hand and gave it to him instead. He unlocked the door, pushed it open and stepped back.

Inside she flipped the switch that lit the large lamp on the dresser. Frank walked over and laid down the key. He turned without overture, reached out and pulled her towards him. He kissed her, then turned to switch off the lamp at its base. Total darkness covered them.

She felt hands, competent and sure, open up the shawl, disappear with it and come back to spread across her back and pull her very close for a longer, more open kiss.

She felt like a virgin. She hadn't been ready to lose the lights. They usually wanted to look. He tugged at the back of her blouse, pulling it out of the wide gathered skirt and sliding his hands under it. This threw them off balance and they swayed, still glued together. Then she realized that his hands were searching for something that wasn't there. A funny little sound came from her lips. He stopped, still holding her against him.

'I don't wear one,' she whispered.

He stood quite still, then said, 'Oh, hell!'

The outline of the window was beginning to clear around the blind. Simultaneously they laughed. He let go and they stepped apart. Hannah crossed her arms and grasped the bottom of the blouse, pulling it over her head and tossing it towards the dresser. She could see him dimly now and she reached over and took both his hands and placed them low under her breasts, pushing up. She could hear a long, hard intake of breath. His hands slowly, gently, cupped and kneaded. His head bent down. He tasted. He was so careful she felt precious, fourteen-karat.

When he touched her skirt, she helped him push everything down together. The bunching of lined gathered voile forced the yielding of elastic, and cobweb nylon, leaving pale, smooth flesh taut and high and round.

Frank let go of her to get out of his coat. When he raised his arms to pull off the sweater, she unfastened his belt and released his swollen sex. After dropping to the edge of the bed to get rid of his trousers, they locked together again and fell back across the bedspread. Through one long, desperate kiss, he crushed her hair and stroked her back. As he rolled to loom over her, a violence in him erupted in accelerating motion. He thrust hard, powerful, and fast. They were drenched with his sweat and he was breathing audibly when his cry turned to whimpers and the violence slowly drained out of him. She felt his weight coming down, and the gentleness returning until he was holding on instead of holding down. In time he let go and rolled over on his back, quiet. The window was a clear rectangle now, the dresser and lamp and chair all recognizable. She could see him, lying undressed beside her. He stood up and went into the bathroom.

When he came back she was still lying on top of the bed, liking what she had done for him, but disturbed and empty.

He lifted the outside of the spread and whispered, 'Get under.' She turned to her stomach and climbed under the covers as he turned them back, placing the pillow under her head. He slid in beside her and pulled her to him.

His two hands contacted her body, skimming the full length, up and down, arriving at the vital terminals, finding the connections, lighting the fire, starting the mounting cries of pleasure. He was taking care of her.

Much later when she was relaxed and warm, and looked after, he said, 'I'm sorry I came so fast. It has been so long.' He turned his head on the pillow and she knew he was looking at her in the dark. She couldn't form an answer. This was not a fuck they wrote books about. More versatile lovers she had sent packing. So what was happening to her?

She turned over and moved across. He put his arm under her shoulders and cradled her against him. They touched with their whole bodies, pushing back the lonely dark.

Frank left at 3.00 a.m., not wanting to return to his hotel later when there was a remote possibility of seeing someone he knew. Hannah said he had slept, but it didn't seem so. His body ached, his eyes were full of gravel, he found it hard to think straight through the process of returning to the Plaza. It wasn't far, but it wasn't smart to walk the deserted streets alone at this hour.

Back in his own bed, ready for sleep, his brain suddenly cleared and he was wide awake. The evening replayed in his head, and he relished every moment. He could not believe this had happened. It made it easier to understand adultery. Not that he would ever condone that, or do it, but how could he have failed to see what it could mean to have a beautiful young girl adoring you? Hannah was undoubtedly impressed, she thought he was wonderful. She got off work, travelled this distance, waited all day for him to come to her. She wanted only to please him. She trusted him, and was grateful. But she was different from a wife. He didn't owe her anything. He had cleared this up during some of their late night talking.

'I've never had affairs,' he told her. 'Until now, everything has always been for real.' He thought that was putting it clearly. She wasn't dumb, she understood that there was no permanence in what they were doing. If she didn't hear from him again, it wouldn't ruin her life. On the other hand, he was sure she would be receptive to another visit. How convenient that his job now involved occasional regular visits to Washington.

He slowly watched in his mind's eye the shadowy figure pulling the filmy blouse over her head and tossing it away. Taking his hands and placing them. Reliving this moment was almost as good as the real thing. He was grateful for the stirrings in his groin right now. To think he had almost missed this.

Tomorrow's meeting with Congressman Schmidt suddenly projected itself. He had left a call for 6.30 a.m. Plenty of time to dress and breakfast before a long, busy day. It wouldn't be easy, as tired as he was at this moment, but he would handle it. He could have made the call for 7.00 or even 7.30, but he wasn't accustomed to pampering himself. He'd always been able to handle long workdays, and loss of sleep if necessary.

He turned over. They'd better look up a movie tonight. He could rest at a movie. Hannah was of a different generation. She had probably tried new things. She might be bored. Maybe he should read one of those books. The idea of learning from Hannah did not please him. He might have to tell her that sometime. On the other hand ...

He sighed and turned again. The room was filled with light – must be a sign nearby, or a streetlight. Hannah's room was much darker. He preferred the dark. God, the feel of her. He thought ahead to when he would come east again. Maybe he could arrange to move the date up.

He looked over at the rococo chair and long French dresser, and there sat Dorothy. She wasn't welcome tonight. God-damn, the perfect wife. She adored the corporate life, and she wanted a Winnebago Coach, too. She would follow him anywhere, but she was so unexciting. What country is it where it is acceptable to have a wife and a mistress – or several wives? How convenient to have both the homemaker and the whore. Why couldn't life be set up that way?

He sat up and switched on the bedside lamp. Inside the dresser was a well-stocked liquor cabinet. This was a good hotel. He poured a stiff drink and went to the window to see where the light was coming from while he drank it. It didn't take long. He didn't believe in pills, but sometimes a drink could help sleep.

Forty-two

By the time she registered for the fall semester, Bonnie's life had fallen into a predictable pattern. She was rooted into Manhattan like a native flower. Her income was larger after the divorce settlement than it had been when she lived on her small job and Frank's generosity. She had attended classes through another summer – soaking up knowledge like a sponge. Her thirst to question, to discuss, to look for understanding, was unquenchable. In her former college days she had studied for grades, memorizing facts, missing the most exciting revelation of education – the fact that not all questions are answerable. She debated with her new friends in class. She enjoyed their enjoyment of her – the one who was different.

She got up early enough every morning to work an hour on her novel before the day began. Sharing this, too, with writing classmates was a help and a joy. Sometime during the summer she started over, using only a few choice phrases from the original manuscript and a little dialogue here and there that she could not bear to discard.

Three afternoons a week she stopped at the YWCA for an exercise class and a quick swim. She was exhausted at night, and – like a native – she no longer saw as many shows and museums as she had the first few months in town.

These were things now left to be enjoyed with her 'public Mr Blake.' Marc came often. Her young classmates thought this was cute. They knew nothing about the other Mr Blake who came and went quietly and was the 'maybe' and 'will be again' that kept her young and alive.

She loved Marc. He was bread-and-butter, and didn't mind if her hair needed washing. But she was 'in love' with John. That silly thing that girls look for that is supposed to dissipate with marriage. Bonnie didn't know, because she had never been 'in love' with Frank. Hannah had once remarked that being 'in love' only indicated an accelerated degree of lust. Hannah had softened lately. She wouldn't talk about the trips to Washington, but they seemed to be making a change in her. Bonnie suspected this had something to do with love and lust.

Marc's deep interest in art had opened another door for Bonnie. As they sat now over drinks in the darkened Flamingo Room, he was explaining the photorealism that they had seen in the opening of a gallery show earlier in the evening.

'I can't get into it,' he said, 'but I can appreciate what these artists are trying to do.'

'Well, I guess most people know what they like,' Bonnie said.

'The truth is,' Marc replied rapidly, tapping his fingers on the table, 'that most people like what they know. They limit their world with that silly statement.'

'You could say that about lots of things,' Bonnie answered, looking at the crowded floor and wishing Marc would dance.

'We'll have to take disco lessons one of these days,' he said. She looked back, feeling closer to him because he had read her mind.

He stopped tapping and leaned back. 'Did you see me talking with Mr Gibson tonight?'

She shook her head slowly.

'He owns the gallery. Little fellow with a beard. Picked me out – asked about my paintings. I may do a show.' Marc was beaming and Bonnie took his hand with both of hers and squeezed it as she expressed her delight.

'I've been working on this quietly, or friends of mine have, for a long time. I've had some shows in Boston, but no galleries this important.' His other hand slipped over hers.

'You've been painting forever?'

'Almost. I squeezed in all the art I could in college. It's not something a red-blooded American boy does for a living.'

'I wish I could see your paintings.'

'You will if we do the show. Not something easily brought along on the train.'

Bonnie looked at the stem of her glass as she turned it slowly. 'I don't suppose your mother knows about me.'

'No,' he said hesitantly. 'She knows something is going on. Can't fool her about business trips since she's still so involved. Our lawyer usually handles our New York trips.' He stopped talking, as though he had lost his train of thought. 'Anyway,' he started again, 'I just told her there was a lady. She has this sad way of looking at me like a naughty little boy caught with jam on his face.' His jaw set firmly. 'I did lie. I don't like it, I don't do it well, but there was no choice. I told her your name was Betty.'

'Do I have a last name?'

'No. She didn't ask. Any suggestions?'

'No, you decide.'

'Would it matter if she knew?' he asked presently.

It hadn't occurred to Bonnie that it might not matter. *Both your sons, Margaret. And you thought you had disposed of me.* Bonnie shook her head firmly. 'I think it would be better if she didn't.' Margaret was too close to Sara. Suddenly Bonnie felt the thinness of the ice.

The dancers had left the floor, and a man was talking. He had made the announcement while Bonnie was speaking, and she didn't understand. Marc looked distracted and didn't reply to her last comment. The spotlight shone on the stage and a beautiful girl appeared in it. She had shining, thick red hair and clear brown eyes. Her voice was strong, with a touch of huskiness that made it more private. Bonnie felt an unexplainable antagonism towards the girl. And a familiarity. Who was this? She pulled at the back of her mind for a connection. She leaned towards Marc and asked, 'Who is she?'

Marc looked ahead and didn't answer. Then, without turning he said, 'It's Barbara Aiken.'

Bonnie hoped Marc didn't hear her sudden intake of breath. She had seen Barbara's picture in *People* magazine. She had heard her voice once – on the telephone. How had they missed seeing her name outside?

She was good. The room quieted. As Bonnie looked around she saw people sitting attentively, all heads turned to the stage. As Barbara neared the song's close, her voice grew huskier and softer, projecting an intimacy that drew in every listener. Tenderly she touched the tips of her long fingers to her shining lips, and extended them towards a table next to the stage where a dark-haired man waited, his back to the room. Words in a hoarse whisper ended the song, the audience holding the silence, vainly waiting for more. At last they broke away and applauded. They loved her.

Bonnie's mouth turned to cotton. She felt awkward and ugly and a hundred years old, filled with dread at what she would see when the lights went up, but they didn't. Barbara began another song. Bonnie could not bring herself to look at Marc. She forced another glance at the stage-side table. She was sure. Very sure.

The songs went on and on. Applause and encores. Two more times Barbara looked or gestured towards the silent man. During the final applause, Bonnie suddenly remembered she didn't have to stay here, and she stood up and said, 'Shall we go?'

Marc offered no objection, and they quickly wound their way out of the ballroom.

They were settled in a cab when Marc said, 'I'm sorry. I didn't check on the floor show. I didn't know she was there.'

Bonnie looked straight at him for the first time. 'It was John, wasn't it?'

Marc said soberly, 'We can't be sure.'

'But you thought so.'

'Yes. I did.' He took her hand. 'But we could be projecting.'

Bonnie gave a short, dry laugh. 'Poor Marc. Standing in the wings. Does Sara cry on your shoulder?'

He shook his head. 'No. She doesn't.'

'Does she know?'

'Of course she does.'

'Whom does she cry to?'

'No one I guess. She's a private person. Private as a man.' They were on untrodden ground. 'Of course, she has her analyst.'

Bonnie tried to swallow from her cotton mouth. 'Do I have a right to cry, Marc?'

'If you feel like crying, you have the right.' He held her hand tighter. 'And the shoulder is here. Any time.' His mouth was a straight line, and she realized that he was as tight as she was loose at this moment. Alive as she was dead. She longed to slip into his arms and get lost in his sweet goodness. John was lost in a shadow world, and she wondered if she hated him.

Marc slid across the seat and put his arms tightly around her. His shoulder felt substantial under her head. She could feel the movement of his chest, and hear his laboured breathing. Slowly she realized that a slight turn of her head would bring the kind of kissing they had been avoiding. This was not her gentle friend. She twisted her neck and his mouth came down hard over hers. She parted her lips and tried to respond, but there was no feeling. His hand clutching her breast helped a little. She was anxious. This was not the man she knew.

'I don't want ...' she said, pulling back, but he resisted. His mouth covered hers again while his hands explored her body, not yielding to her squirming. 'Hold still,' was a quiet command.

'Maaaaaarc ...' she protested as his hand slid from her knee up the panty hose under her full skirt. 'Marc, for heaven's sakes, people can see.' She hissed in a whisper, aware of the stiff-necked cab driver on the other side of the glass.

'Let them enjoy it,' came back into her ear, as the passing lights flashed on and off into the back of the cab. His warm, agile fingers through taut, sheer nylon, were stirring her chilled blood. The other hand cuddled and caressed arm, neck, cleavage. Soon she was kissing back without trying. She barely arched her back and raised her hips, moaning softly into his ear. The movement of the cab played counterpoint to the movement within it.

They were just scaling the mountaintops when the cab

swerved to the kerb and stopped. Without turning around, the driver reached back and opened up the partition, saying, 'This is 140.'

She pulled herself together and giddily got out on the sidewalk. She was still breathing thin air when the cab finally pulled away and Marc joined her, taking her arm without pause and pulling her towards the house.

'Marc,' she gasped, trotting beside him, 'wait, let's think about this.' He didn't answer, looking grimly ahead as he unlocked the entry door with her keys. She felt an impulse to giggle that had no connection with anything. 'Marc,' she said again, trying to think as they hurried up the stairs. 'Marc. Now wait. I know how you feel, but ...'

They met her neighbour, Mr Shapiro, in the hall. She nodded. 'Marc,' she hissed again in a lowered tone, coming up closer behind him. 'We need to talk. I've thought about this. You know how much I care for you ...' He threw open the door and stepped back. She stood uncertainly in the hall, looking anxiously into his unsmiling face. He waited quietly as she slowly walked through. The door closed behind him, shutting out the light, and ending the one-sided conversation.

Forty-three

Marc sent flowers, but she didn't hear from him or John the following week, or the week after. She had thought Marc would call, maybe every day, but he didn't. Sometimes after the phone rang and it was a *TV Guide* salesperson, or the wrong number, she would feel alone. Coming home tonight, noticing that the days were getting shorter, the vision of finding someone waiting at home, or waiting for someone to come home, flashed across her mind. At these moments she always remembered the married years when these same longings would come over her. The long evenings when she couldn't settle down to anything because Frank hadn't gotten home for dinner yet. And after he was there, behind his paper or in front of the television, they would sit for long periods without speaking.

We could laugh at the same thing. He could put down the paper for no reason and touch me. He never did. And too often, she would feel in her bones, *What I want is to be hugged while I cry. I don't know why. He would expect me to know why.* That was loneliness. Why must everyone want connection so much, and never be able to find it? Except as it is savoured in fleeting moments. Moments that cannot be held, except in memory. Two can never be one. When she got home she turned on all the lamps, dialled the jazz station, had a second helping of ice cream for dessert, and assured herself she was whole.

When the dishes were washed and draining, Bonnie put her keys in her jeans pocket and went down the hall to Hannah's. She wanted company tonight, and Hannah was the most accessible friend, although she hadn't been coming around much lately.

Bonnie received a warm greeting, and kicked off her shoes to tuck her feet under in the massive armchair.

A pamphlet with a cover picture of the Eiffel Tower topped the mess on the chairside table.

'Reading about Paris?' Bonnie asked.

'Yes,' Hannah answered. She took the chair across from Bonnie. 'I'm going next month.'

Bonnie shrieked, 'Oh, Hannah, you are? To Paris? It's the dream I've had as long as I can remember.'

'Me, too.'

'You can tell me about it. I've never even known anyone who's been there. Well, yes, I have. People who said France is a rip-off. They don't count.'

'You think I'm a romantic like you?'

'Ah, yes, you are, Hannah. You can't fool me.'

Hannah looked at the floor. She asked, 'How are things going for you? How's school? And life?'

'School's fine. Life's a little mixed up.'

Hannah waited.

'You knew I've been seeing Marc Blake. It's been nice. The

first regular escort I've had since I've been here. Nice.' Why did she keep using that word about Marc?

'And ...?'

'We've kept our distance. He's John's brother, it was understood. But a couple of weeks ago we – we got carried away.'

'So? Did you like it?'

'I'm afraid I did. But he's not John. And he is John's brother.' Bonnie knew that the loneliness that plagued her tonight was not for Marc.

'What does Marc want?'

'I don't know, I haven't heard from him. Well, yes, he sent flowers, but I haven't heard from him.'

'Figures. Sometimes intimacy scares the shit out of men.'

'That's crazy –'

'It's true. Get too close and watch them run. Fortunately, they're not all like that.'

Bonnie straightened her stiffening legs. 'Are you going to Paris with a man?' she asked.

Hannah nodded soberly.

'The one you've been meeting in Washington?'

'Yes.' Hannah leaned forward. 'Bonnie,' she said, 'it's Frank.'

Bonnie blinked.

'Frank Forbes. Your husband. That's who I've been meeting in Washington.'

Bonnie gasped. 'My Frank? You and my Frank? You don't even know him. He's in Lancaster.'

'I met him when he came to see you. He waited in my apartment, remember?'

Bonnie tried to assimilate these facts. 'But I can't think of two people less likely –' she said. 'What in God's name could you ever see in Frank?'

Hannah bristled. 'He's a fine man. What did you see in him?'

'He's a stuffed shirt,' Bonnie stammered over the inadequate words, ' a bigot, a chauvinist – You? Frank and you?' She was laughing, and stopped as with some alarm she heard the hollowness of the laugh. Hannah looked hurt. Bonnie wondered if it was supposed to be the other way around. 'Wait a minute,' she said in a strange voice. 'Did you say Frank is taking you to Paris?'

'Yes.'

Bonnie's voice was stranger still, and cold. 'Thirty years I waited for him to take me to Paris. Thirty years – thirty years.'

Hannah looked near tears. 'I'm sorry, Bonnie. That's not my fault, is it?'

Bonnie stood up and looked for her shoes. 'No, of course not. That's not your fault.' She leaned down and fastened a strap.

'Bonnie, please don't be mad. He didn't want me to tell you. I promised I wouldn't, but I just can't lie to you any longer.'

'It's all right.' She didn't mean for her voice to be so cold. 'We'll talk about it later. I don't feel good.'

Hannah took her arm, but she walked away. She returned to solitude where she could shut and bar the door. Now she could scream, and smash a cup against the wall. But she stood still and couldn't scream, and couldn't break the dishes.

From behind the kitchen wastebasket, a small brown spot moved out and crossed the floor. Bonnie pounced upon the cockroach, crushing it under her shoe and grinding it into greasy pulp, feeling nausea close in, making it impossible to wipe up the mess. Violence and destruction were so abhorrent that even this consuming anger could not release her. *My fault I haven't been to Paris, with or without Frank. If I hadn't been with Marc HE wouldn't have seen Barbara again.* Her rage turned in upon herself.

She recalled skin-to-skin with Rick and Marc – isolated moments of connection without meaning and value. She was deprived of righteous rage without rationalization. True evil had never existed for her, and so true anger never could. But there was nothing rational in her fear of Barbara Aiken. Not hatred or anger but cold, paralyzing fear. Even the little brown cockroach was an innocent victim. She shrank from the mess on the bottom of her shoe. *John – just love me. I can't hate you anymore. Just come and love me again.*

Forty-four

The following Wednesday, John called. He arrived that evening bearing cartons of Chinese food. He often called after he had arrived in town, expecting her to be available. She always was, even if it meant cancelling other plans.

The sight of him stirred up the same excitement she had felt the first time she saw him. She knew now that this excitement was not something felt by her alone. Some men awaken women by just walking into the room. Like rarefied air they invisibly quicken the pulse and narrow the vision of women everywhere. Was it a privilege or a curse to be a woman favoured by such a man?

Over dinner they talked about the coming election, neither of them very excited about Carter or Ford. She thought about things she couldn't bring herself to ask. John seemed somewhat preoccupied, too, and she wondered if he was picking up her unrest.

He folded the dishtowel while she wiped out the sink, and kissed her before they sat down – a ritual they had fallen into. John looked a little out of place in the kitchen, but he always insisted they do the dishes. It was something to do, since they never went out.

Bonnie was wearing a soft ivory-coloured gauze shirt, the high plain neckline unbuttoned several notches, and a long Indian cotton skirt. Her curly hair was tousled these days, no longer needing protection from the rain or wind. John had taken off his coat and turned back his sleeves, but hadn't loosened his tie.

She felt his eyes following her as she turned on the lamps. He was still standing when she finished. She returned his stare, smiled and extended her hand. 'Sit,' she suggested. They both sat on the sofa, not touching.

'How are you and Marc doing?' John said.

Bonnie looked up quickly. 'I saw him a couple of weeks ago. He was in town for an art exhibit.'

'You're why he's in town.' He looked at her and she looked away. 'He used to come here once or twice a year. No more than that.'

'It's been nice, he takes me out. Does it bother you?'

'Hell, yes, it bothers me. I figured you were seeing other men – I hadn't the right – didn't want to know – but my brother –'

'I'm sorry.' She pulled her thoughts together and said positively, 'Of course, it's true, you don't have the right –'

He reached out for her, his voice changing, 'Except that I love you so much.'

'She whispered into his ear, 'What about Barbara?'

He jerked back, frowning. 'What about her?'

'You *have* seen her.'

'Where'd you hear this?'

'I saw you.'

'What?'

'Yes. I was at the Flamingo Room with Marc.'

He looked at the rug and said carefully, 'I had to come down on the Fletcher case and stopped by the plant to pick up some things. Marc had left two numbers with his secretary. One of them was yours. I didn't call you. Decided to take in Barbara's show.'

Bonnie winced at hearing him say 'Barbara'. 'If you had called ahead,' she said. 'I don't like this, John. Maybe we can't talk about it.'

'I think we should talk about it.' He took her by both shoulders. 'Bonnie, I didn't take her home, we just talked there in the Flamingo Room. We're old friends.'

'You don't have to explain.'

'I want to explain,' his voice was growing louder. 'Goddamnit, there isn't anybody else. Hasn't been for a year.'

She shouted back, 'How can you say there isn't anybody else? How can you say that, John Blake? You have a wife in Boston!'

John looked slapped. She waited to hear him say, *It's not a real marriage*. His stoic face didn't change. She sighed, 'It's been working, we haven't tried to tie each other down, it can't be any other way. I'm sorry.'

'Maybe it's over.' He stood up and started slowly pacing. 'Maybe we'll have to figure out a way to get married.'

Bonnie's reactions were a step behind what he was saying – dismay followed by disbelief. In a flash she heard a young lieutenant say, '*How long does it take to get married here?*' 'You mean us?' she stammered. 'You and me?'

He stopped walking. 'She'd want the house, and plenty besides. I don't think she'd make a scandal but I'm not sure – can't tell about Sara.'

He walked again. 'Some of my clients are pretty conservative, could be messy. If she really wanted to dig . . . Oh, Lord!' He stopped. 'When she finds out it's you. She's never suspected . . .'

'Wait a minute, John.'

'She's always hated you. If she finds out about the past year . . .'

'John, wait a minute. Will you listen to me?'

'What?'

'I don't want to marry you, darling.'

'What?' he said again.

'I said I don't want to marry you, love. I like the way we are.' She hurried on, 'I don't want to run your big house – seat the dinner guests and redo the slip covers and be nice to people I don't like. I'm free. I don't have to worry about responsibility or building a nest for the future, or what the neighbours will say.'

Deep creases settled between John's eyes. Slowly and deliberately she finished, 'But most of all, I don't want to sit at home alone and wonder who you're with tonight.'

The creases remained while his eyes tried to catch up. She felt that ripple of submerged laughter deep inside her again. She went to him and hugged his taut shoulders. 'It's all right, darling,' she said. 'Soon you'll wake up and see what a narrow escape you've had.'

Slowly he put his arms around her and they stood quietly embracing, both overwhelmed by the things that had been said.

Forty-five

Margaret Blake set her jaw, spasms of the little muscles below her ear giving her away. as she stared without any other betrayal of emotion at the gift her youngest son had just presented to her.

Marc, through a finely tuned sense of what pleases or displeases Mother, knew she didn't like it. He didn't care.

The painting, still a little sticky in the impasto, leaned against the rosewood table in the living room. Its multi-directional stabs of riotous colour tore into the peace and stability of the quiet room.

He knew she was choosing her words carefully. He anticipated with some excitement the challenge.

She leaned back and looked him full in the eye. 'All right, Marc,' she said. 'Why did you do this?'

Marc was her innocent child. 'What do you mean? It's your birthday present.'

'It would fit in this house like a hungry elephant.'

'You're rejecting my gift?' His lips curved down, even as his eyes gleamed.

'The days of my hanging your inadequate scribblings ended when you reached your majority.'

'Inadequate scribblings!'

'Marc, don't play games with me. You know I don't accept abstract art, if that's what this is. The lovely landscape you did for my bedroom suits me very well. This could only go into the vault.'

'Not the furnace room?'

'It's a nice hobby for you, dear. But you and I know each other too well for this to be a mistake. I think you are trying to tell me something.'

Marc shook his head and sighed. She was right of course.

Mother met everything head-on. Well, he hadn't been very subtle. He walked slowly the length of the room and back again to stand beside her chair. 'Mother, I don't paint landscapes anymore. I haven't painted landscapes for years. This is the way I paint now.'

'And that's quite all right, I have no objection. You probably hang them all the time in that apartment, I wouldn't know. But you know how I feel about modern art. I consider it a cop-out for people who can't paint real things. I'm sorry, but I just want you to understand why it won't be hung.' She glared at him, then added, 'Why are you inviting rejection, dear?'

The mellow notes of the door chime interrupted, followed by the sound of someone letting himself in the front door. They both turned to watch. John stopped in the doorway to look into their silent faces.

'Am I interrupting something?'

Marc said 'Yes' at the same time Margaret said 'No.'

John walked in. 'What's this?' He looked at the painting. 'Yours?' he asked Marc, examining it.

'Yes.'

'Dynamite. You always surprise me. They're so belligerent.'

'It's a birthday present, but she doesn't like it.'

John turned to him. 'Well, of course it's not Mother's style. You should have known that. Trying to upset her?'

'That's what *she* said.'

John laughed. 'This your day for taking on windmills?'

Words fell over each other in his brain, but he didn't know how put them together. He wanted to pick up the painting and stalk out of the room, but somehow stayed quietly where he was.

'Oh, I'm so glad the two of you stopped by. My boys. Sit down and talk to me.'

They sat. 'I can't stay long, we're going to something tonight. I forget what.' John fished in his pocket and brought out a small package which he gave to her. 'It's a scarf,' he said, as she tore at the shiny paper. She wore scarves often, covering the veins under her chin.

She cooed over it, squeezed his hand, went to the mirror to hold it close to her face. 'Yes, it's perfect,' she said. 'Thank you, dear.'

'I'll take it back,' Marc said. 'I should have saved it for the New York show anyway.'

'You both are making so many trips these days.'

The two men looked at the floor.

'John, have you met Marc's lady?'

John gave Marc a fleeting glance. 'Uh, yes,' he answered.

'You have?' Margaret responded with interest. 'Well, I'm glad someone has. What's she like?'

'She's lovely. I really have to get along, Mother. It's marvellous to have you so beautiful on your seventy-seventh birthday.'

'Oh, I'm not done in yet.'

With the painting squeezed into the backseat, Marc guided his little sports car through the intricacies of freeway traffic. He wouldn't buy her another present. She had declined this one, she would just have to do without. She had pointed out the childishness of his making the inappropriate gift. If she had responded as a mother should, pretending to like it, that wouldn't have made him feel any better. He had set himself up, any way it turned out. He hated her. It wasn't the first time he had admitted hating his mother; the thought didn't upset him anymore. He assumed the love was still there, underneath, but he wanted to be free. He wanted to be respected for what he was. He wanted to be first with someone. Mother would always respect John more. So would Bonnie.

He had seen her once since that special night. It had been an evening full of activity, ending with the night train – a schedule arranged to preclude lovemaking. He was punishing them both, he wasn't sure why. He hadn't touched her, not even to say good-bye. She had looked confused. He had enjoyed hurting her. Why must it always be Marc who was hurt?

He clamped his jaw so that the muscles stood out. The landscape in mother's bedroom, painted twenty years ago. She thought it was a better painting than the one still drying on the canvas. She didn't think he had gone anyplace. She didn't want him to go anyplace.

He remembered gratefully the show coming up in New York in December. Those people would only know the artist – the artist he was today. They didn't care that he was sandwiched

313

between the chairman of the board and her ultimatums and the vice-presidents who carried them out. They saw only a creator walking alone. He checked the mirror and swerved into the exit lane. Fuck the office; there was still an hour of daylight.

Forty-six

Bonnie heard the phone ringing in her dream. Pulling herself painfully back she gradually knew that she was in bed and it was the middle of the night and she was frightened. She reached for the phone without getting up, sitting straight and saying 'Hello?' in a small voice.

'Mom? It's Linda,' she heard. Long distance.

'What is it?'

'Did I wake you? I'm sorry,' Linda said. 'I thought maybe you'd still be up.'

Bonnie felt foolish, looking at the clock and seeing it was only 11.15. 'I went to bed early,' she said, trying to collect her thoughts. 'I was so sound asleep. You scared me.'

'I do have some bad news, but it's not us. We're all okay.'

'What?' Bonnie asked, the dread returning.

'I decided I should call you, before you hear about it. It was just on our evening news.'

'What?'

'It's George and Jenny Ames. They were killed this afternoon. The company plane crashed.'

Relief made her weak, then she remembered it was Jenny. 'That's awful. How sad. I'm sorry.'

'Dad called this afternoon. Mom, he was supposed to be on that flight. Some union trouble came up and he had to stay behind. Jenny went at the last minute because they had an empty seat.'

Bonnie was seeing Jenny that night in the red dress – so

314

worried about her future. She thought about Frank. 'Your dad, Linda. What will this mean?'

'I don't know. For the moment, he's in charge. I guess it isn't automatic, like president of the United States.'

'They expected George to be around for a long time. So Frank outlives him.'

They talked briefly about the children, and Linda hung up.

Bonnie eased herself back under the covers and pulled her knees up to her stomach. Wide-awake now, she allowed herself to deal with mortality, feeling the dread that violence opens us to, pointing out life's tentativeness.

What now, Paris – and Hannah! The necessity of breaking the news to Hannah loomed at her. They had been uneasy with each other lately, not spending any time together. But of course, Frank would have to handle it. Frank had always left such delicate matters to Bonnie. But this time he would have to handle it. Bonnie rolled to her back and looked at the black ceiling. Poor Hannah. Frank's mistress, the company, would surely score again.

Forty-seven

She was sitting in Miss Nolan's office in a royal-blue silk suit, with a filmy white thing at the neck. Frank had been the first one out of the board room, striding down the hall and into the elevator. The men with him dropped back, as Frank was the only one going up.

His head was whirling – the immediate tasks before him being numbered off while in the back of his mind major personal decisions awaited attention. Dorothy stood up, almost passed by, as Frank crossed the small anteroom that was his secretary's office. He braked and turned around when the impression of royal-blue silk and filmy white registered in his mind.

'Dorothy,' he said.

'I know you're busy.' Her face was flushed. 'I was in the building and decided to stop by.'

'Come in.'

Miss Nolan silently held up a stack of notes.

'In a moment,' he told her.

He smiled and stepped back from the opened door.

Dorothy walked through. The suit was a perfect fit, and a perfect match for her slender-heeled plain pumps. The waistline was only suggested, but he could tell that her waistline was thick. There were no deep curves there to swirl into breast or behind. Everything would just sort of lump together.

'Sit down,' he said warmly, walking to his tall leather chair behind the desk. 'I'm sorry we haven't gotten together lately, so much has happened. I saw you at the funeral, but you were gone before I could speak.'

'I didn't go to the cemetery. I just couldn't face it.'

'You should have gone with us. Linda chewed me out for not asking you.'

Her eyes were looking watery. Oh, God, was she going to cry?

'You have been different lately. Even before the accident. What is it, Frank? What did I do?'

'You didn't do anything, Dorothy, don't be silly.' He squirmed in the chair. 'I've been so tied up at work – spending a lot of time in Washington.'

'I never thought I'd come begging like this. I didn't mean to.'

'As a matter of fact, you've been on my mind lately. I have to sort things out.'

She blew her nose, and sat straighter. 'You don't owe me anything. I just want you to know that I appreciate what we had, or what I thought we had.' She sighed and changed the subject. 'Will this change your plans for Europe?'

She had named one of the big problems. 'Probably. I may be able to settle our French contracts without the trip.' He had found a few errands to run in Paris, so he could charge it off as a combination business and pleasure trip. 'I have to think about the offer the board made this morning.'

She looked up. 'An offer? Surely they'll ask you to take the job. There isn't anyone else.'

'Unfortunately there are strings attached. I have to decide whether to do it their way, or to just continue as acting president until we can hire someone else.'

'What kind of strings? I think that's pretty shitty of them.'

'You know about company politics, Dorothy.'

She did. She would understand that part of the problem.

'Would you like to talk about it? I could fix some chicken the way you like it. Tonight at my house?'

It sounded like a good idea. He needed to talk about it to someone not involved with the company. Dorothy had a good mind, but she wasn't exactly uninvolved. 'I'd like that,' he answered, and then remembered it was Monday. 'I can't make it by six. Would eight be too late?'

'Of course not.' She was smiling now. She stood up. Dorothy moved with aristocratic dignity, like a queen. This was appropriate. He was trying on his king's robe these days.

He walked around the desk and slipped an arm around her shoulders. She leaned against him. She was soft and smelled of violet-scented powder. The gold in her carefully swirled hair picked up the light. Strange, he had always assumed her hair was grey. He bent and kissed her on the lips, then moved back, holding her hand. 'Be patient with me, dear,' he said.

'Of course,' she answered, eyes shining. 'You can count on me, Frank.'

Frank set his bourbon glass down on the table by his big chair and stared at the telephone. He had walked away from the mess on his desk early enough to stop at home before going to Dorothy's. He wasn't comfortable using the phone at work, even in the privacy of his office.

Monday night was Hannah's night; he always called. Only last Monday they had talked through a golden glow for an hour and a half. Anticipation of the trip coming at the end of this month had them both a little cockeyed. He had told her he was flying to Kansas City the next day with George Ames. Frank could have been dead now. He might have been in the graveyard instead of Jenny. But he wasn't dead. He was facing an impossible phone call.

For the tenth time he sighed, reached for the phone and pulled away. He grabbed the receiver and dialled, without knowing what he was going to say.

317

'Hello, darling,' she answered.

'What if it isn't darling?' he asked.

'Maybe you're not the only darling I know. How are you, darling?'

'Not so good, I'm afraid, baby. The roof's fallen in since I talked to you last.'

Her tone changed. 'What do you mean?'

'Well, to start at the beginning, I didn't fly to Kansas City last week. George's wife went instead. The company plane crashed in a wheat field. All killed.'

After the shocked silence Hannah said, 'They were good friends of yours.'

'Well, I guess you could say that. He was also president of the company.'

'And what does that mean?'

'It means I'm acting president now. It means I can't get away to go to Europe.'

He heard no response.

'Hannah, are you still there?'

'Yes,' she said in a small voice. 'Well, you're still alive. That's good, isn't it?'

'Yes, I'd say it is.'

Hannah sighed. 'Well, I always thought it was too good to be true.'

'It's tough about the trip. You know I'm disappointed, too.'

'Will we do it later?'

'I don't know.'

'Why don't you know?'

It was a stupid question. His voice grew louder. 'The shit's in the fan here, and it's up to me to clean it up. It's no time for a vacation.'

'I see.' Now she was going to pout. She didn't understand about priorities.

'I have to make some decisions.'

'About me?'

'About my job.' About her, too, but this wasn't the way to approach it. She was probably crying; he couldn't tell. It was so impractical for them to cry. His stomach burned. 'I don't know when I'll see you again.' You'd think she would be interested in his future with the company. She hadn't even asked, only thinking of herself.

318

'Well,' Hannah said in a flat voice. 'It's been nice.'

'Don't talk that way, we'll be together again.' But he wasn't sure.

'When did you say George Ames was – killed?'

'Last Tuesday.'

'Almost a week! And you let me go on getting ready.'

'I didn't know what the future was going to be. I still don't.'

'But we could have talked about it.'

'You're probably right. I'm sorry.'

'You're sorry! You forgot all about me.' She was being so female. What the hell was he supposed to say now? He was exhausted.

'Hannah, the trip is off for now. My future is uncertain. The time I have spent with you has been wonderful – wonderful. I'll never forget. Sorry I didn't call sooner. So damned tired.'

She *was* crying now. 'I wish I could help you.'

'You can. Just wait. I'll get back to you. Okay?'

'Yes. Don't forget Paris. We can still do it.'

'I hope so. Good night, baby.'

He hung up the phone, feeling confused and fragmented. This bit of spring didn't fit now with his autumn plans.

He found he was looking forward to Dorothy's chicken, served effortlessly with Wedgwood and sterling, and her intelligent understanding eyes as she asked, 'Now, Frank, what are the strings? What is that bastard board of directors trying to hang on you now?'

He told her. It was good to lay it all out before someone. 'They offered me the presidency, but want me to sign an agreement to resign in four years. Part of my job would be to groom a successor.'

'Would that be so bad?'

'Maybe not. It's just that they're assuming that in four years I'll be finished, incapable. If I can do it now, why can't I do it then?'

'I know what you mean.' He felt she did. 'It's tough to be discarded. Very tough. You *could* just tell them to go to hell.'

Frank reached back to recent moments when he knew he wasn't finished. Like a skyrocket the Washington trips lit up the sky – Hannah. The rocket blazed and died as his mind clicked on to the well-meshed gears of industry rolling without slip or slowdown after his takeover last week. And now, he looked at Dorothy. She understood his dilemma – shared it. He was not onstage here. He was home.

'You know what I think?' she asked, looking him straight in the eye.

'Tell me.'

'I think there's no conflict at all. I can't by any stretch of the imagination see you refusing the chance to run this company on any terms. No cost would be too great.'

She was half smiling, sure of herself, and by God she was right. There wasn't any conflict. He took a deep breath and felt the tension flowing out. 'Give me some more chicken,' he said, suddenly hungry, returning her smile.

Later, as they sat having wine in front of the fire, she said, 'Think how well you can plan your life now. You'll have four years to live out your goal. Then there'll still be time to buy the Winnebago.' She smiled and he knew they were both remembering previous conversations. Conversations when he had already been planning to ask Dorothy to share his life, though he hadn't said it out loud. Her face looked smooth and glowing in the firelight, the wrinkles at the eyes and arcs around the mouth adding strength, matching his own.

'I like being the boss,' he confessed with conviction. 'Goddamn, I like it when they scurry around.' He still didn't want to think about letting go, but she was right. He wanted all he could get.

New York and Washington and Paris were fading fast.

Forty-eight

Her first Christmas card was in the box when she checked her mail – a bright red envelope from Christy, of Christy's Fashion Corner. Bonnie had bought a designer dress there once. There was also a letter from Boston. The Blake on the return address was Marc. The first feeling of disappointment was quickly followed by anticipation.

The outside door opened and Hannah came in. Bonnie, still holding her mail out in front of her and balancing an armload of books, smiled and greeted her. Hannah returned the greeting, unsmiling. Her eyes were veiled. Bonnie switched the books to accommodate the mail and went on up the stairs while Hannah checked her box. They hadn't talked for months, only passing now and then in the hall. But even in this brief contact, Bonnie saw that the joyful aura that had surrounded Hannah lately had disappeared.

Bonnie climbed slowly, wanting to go back, but unsure of what to say. Then she remembered Marc's letter and hurried on to her own door.

The letter was in Marc's barely legible handwriting. He gave some details about his New York show, coming up in two weeks. The letter ended with what she decided was his reason for writing it.

I'm sorry, Bonnie, that it won't work out for me to take you to the opening. Sara has made an issue (she thinks in my behalf) of the family's attending the opening, so it looks like they will all be there. I'm sure you don't want to walk into this. I will come back later in the week and will perhaps see you then. If you want to drop in during the week you know where the gallery is.

She indulged in a fleeting fantasy of appearing on Marc's arm to greet John and Sara, and the formidable Margaret. That would get things off to a roaring start!

She missed Marc. He was a rare man friend; his regular visits, no longer regular, had been an important part of her new life. She had lost him when she allowed him to take her to bed.

She slowly lay back on the sofa and recalled step by step their passionate interlude after the Flamingo Room. He had called her beautiful, and sweet, and had left her feeling loved, although he hadn't used the word.

The dark-haired man waiting for Barbara was the key. Bonnie suddenly saw this. For one night they had felt justified in removing John from the picture. But John came back and now they both were embarrassed.

Marc, undressing her; Marc kissing her navel and knees. It was wicked of her to remember, between visits from John, but sometimes she did. Marc had been distant on the two times she had seen him since. They had moved on a tight schedule, with no private time. They pretended it hadn't happened.

Hannah called it fear of intimacy. Which called up an uneasy image of Hannah being intimate with Frank. Bonnie never allowed her imagination to dwell on this. She remembered Hannah's eyes. Hannah had looked old and tired this afternoon. Bonnie reached for her keys and went down the hall.

Hannah came to the door in an old corduroy wraparound robe. She looked surprised, invited Bonnie in. Bonnie sat in the only chair that didn't have clothing piled on it, and Hannah curled her legs beneath her on the Indian cotton sofa, one brown knee poking through.

'How've you been?' Bonnie asked, and Hannah answered 'Fine.'

'It's almost Christmas again. I don't know where the time goes.'

'It's been a short year.'

'You could stop by sometime.'

'Actually, Bonnie, I didn't think I would be welcome.'

'I wasn't mad. I thought you were uncomfortable with me.'

'Why don't you ask why I'm still here? You just want to know why I didn't go, don't you?'

'I think I know why.'

'You probably know more than I do.'

'I wouldn't say that. Tell me, what happened to Paris?'

'Nothing happened to Paris. Something happened to Hannah.'

'I know from my daughters about Frank's promotion. I think he couldn't have avoided cancelling the trip.'

Hannah's set lips gave a different message than her eyes.

'Hannah, I'm not jealous. You're more important to me than Frank now. Don't you know that?'

'What promotion?'

'He didn't tell you?'

'I know that his company's president got killed.'

'Didn't he explain?'

'He said he was acting president and couldn't get away. I haven't heard from him for two weeks.'

Linda had written that Dorothy was joining them for Christmas. The bastard. 'Frank has real problems with communication.' The understatement of the year.

Hannah stood up and swooped her coat and scarf off a chair, opening the closet door for a hanger.

'I'm all right, Bonnie,' she said in a new, firmer voice. 'I knew it wasn't forever. I counted too much on the trip. It was an adventure, *c'est fini.*'

Bonnie still had trouble associating this kind of high emotion with Frank. 'He may call again.'

'True. He told me to wait.'

'And will you be here, on hold?'

'No. *C'est fini!*'

'You really care for him, don't you?'

'He cared for me. More than he intended to.'

'I don't think Frank would ever let emotion get the upper hand over good judgment.'

'And good judgment wouldn't include me?'

'Don't put words in my mouth.'

'You're glad I didn't fare any better than you did.'

'That's cruel, Hannah. I don't want you hurt.'

'But you're glad. You were only upset with me when I was making it to Paris with Frank.'

Bonnie stopped to wonder if this was true. Hannah shut the closet door and came back and stood over Bonnie. 'I made him happy. I gave him a lot.'

'I expect you did.' Bonnie felt criticized. She spoke her mind. 'He's used to women giving.'

Hannah paced away once and turned around. 'Do you think I could be his wife?'

'What happened to "*c'est fini*"?'

'Just as a rhetorical question. Why couldn't I?'

Bonnie shook her head, weary. 'You're at the beginning of the road, Hannah. I'm at the end. You don't want to hear my opinion. Ask *him*.'

When she left, she had the uneasy feeling that Hannah was going to do just that.

Forty-nine

LONG AGO

long ago
I suppose
we could have
hewn reasons for
our flesh.
talked of great
black books
and pearl crosses.
smiled and sipped
the finest wine
at quiet tables.
walked in the
brightest streets
with carefully
locked fingers.
long ago
the precipice
was a gentle slope
of daisies.
too late,
naked darling,
too far
for retreat
and fear of our
joining.

Bonnie Forbes
English 331

When the door closed, Hannah walked about the room, not
looking at the phone. Mother always said, 'Girls don't call

boys,' but Hannah never bought that. When she was eleven she hid under her father's desk in the den every day and called Bobby Brandt while her mother was taking her bath. Bobby tried to sound bored, but she knew he liked it. Yet Mother's admonition still lurked in the back of her mind and now when it really counted she waited for him to call.

She hurried over to sit in the chair by the phone. She called area information for the number, then dialled. He wouldn't be home – but he was. His militant 'Hello' came through the line immediately. She pulled her robe tighter, feeling cold.

'Frank, it's Hannah.'

His tone changed. 'Hannah, baby, what a surprise.' Warmer – anxious? 'I came home early today. You just caught me.'

'You didn't call Monday – or the one before.'

After a short silence, he said, 'I'm sorry. I've been working late.'

'You could call late.'

'Well, how are you? Did you have your auditions?'

'Not yet. I'm working hard, too.' She wished she had turned up the heat. 'What's happening?'

'That's why I didn't call,' he said quickly. 'I've been making decisions, it's a trying time. I didn't know what to tell you.'

'Couldn't you have talked it over with me?' The suggestion didn't even sound logical to her.

'I'm sorry, dear, I don't think I could have. I had to decide for myself. I've signed a contract with the company to be president for four more years, when I'll automatically retire. I'll be sixty-eight years old in four more years. That must sound incredible to you.'

'I know your age. I can add. But this is good, isn't it? Why does it change things for us?'

'It means that I won't be making regular trips to the capital. Someone else will take over that job.'

'I see.' She swallowed, and asked in an artificially strong voice. 'Are you trying to tell me we're finished?'

'Oh, of course not – no one knows for sure what the future will be.' His cheerful voice infuriated her. 'We'll just have to wait and see what happens. I don't have any hold on you. You probably have lots of men friends ...'

'I see. I guess you've answered my question.'

'You know I'll always be grateful. Our time together was so good . . .' Frank heard the click and knew he had been hung up on. He slowly put down the phone. He had done the right thing, made a decision after considering all the angles, and he would stick by it. But the days were getting very short; it was dark around his chair. And his stomach hurt like hell.

Fifty

Marc scooted off the stool and carried his glass to a table when he saw his brother come through the lobby door into the hotel bar, forty-five minutes before closing time. Marc wondered if he would sleep at all tonight; the opening had left him on a splendid high. Sara and Margaret had chosen to go to their rooms after the party, but John had agreed to meet him for a nightcap.

John pulled out a chair. 'I don't need another drink, think I'll have tomato juice.'

Marc looked at the floating olive and wished he had done the same. 'I don't feel like going to bed.'

'It's been a big night.'

'Several things are already spoken for. Would you believe I hate to turn some of them loose?'

'Must be like children. You created them.'

'Can you see that?'

John nodded. 'Halliday was smiling. Is that a good sign?'

'Can't tell about critics, it was a coup to get him there. Now I can start worrying about what he'll write – or if he'll mention me at all.'

John nodded again. 'I'm bushed; I wound up the Spencer deal before we left.'

'You mean we're ready to sign?'

'We did sign. I signed for you.'

'You what?'

'I signed for you. We needed to close while they were in the mood to sell.'

'But I don't even know what the final agreement was. I haven't been *that* inaccessible.'

'You did tell Ben to go ahead and negotiate. We got a good deal, we didn't think you'd have any objections.'

Marc's heartbeat accelerated. 'That's a million dollar deal. You didn't think I needed to be consulted at all?'

'Ben called Mother yesterday and said they were ready to sign. You were out of town. She told him to go ahead, and they called me to draw up the papers. *Did* you have any objections?'

'No,' Marc answered in a strained cold voice. 'No, of course not.'

John looked around for a waitress.

Marc's voice sank to a low monotone. 'What am I doing in that office? I'll tell you, I'm there because the four of us own seventy-nine percent of the company. Otherwise I'd be out on my ear so fast.'

John looked down at the table. He shifted in his chair, but wasn't coming up with an answer, because there wasn't any.

'If I never went back there they wouldn't miss a beat. Maybe one or two little beats, that's all. Isn't that right?' He glared at John.

John looked back soberly. 'You know the answer to that better than I do.'

Marc slammed his fist on the table. 'What if I didn't go back?' They were only words, but slowly they began to take on meaning. 'By God, what if I didn't?'

'I don't think this is the time to make a decision like that. You'll sleep it off.'

'No, I won't.' He was feeling stronger. 'No, by God, I mean it. What am I going back for?'

John shook his head, but his eyes were not hostile. 'Is this really the first time you've thought of this?'

It was. It had never occurred to Marc that he could walk out. His head was light.

John seemed to be considering his lines. He finally said slowly, 'Don't think I would stop you. If I'd been in your shoes I would have taken off twenty years ago.'

And Marc had never guessed – the way his brother saw him. 'Where'd I go?'

'I don't know, this is your fantasy.'

Marc leaned forward. 'I'll bet you'd like to do it, too.'

A curtain closed over John's face and he shook his head again.

'Know what I'm going to do? I'm gonna go out right now and get a taxi and go to Bonnie's and ask her to marry me and go to Europe to live.' He was feeling so powerful that it seemed like she would.

John paled. Marc felt that his brother had come closer for a moment and that he had pushed him away. He regretted this. He stood.

'Don't you think you'd better wait till morning?'

Marc shook his head. 'No, I've waited too long already.' He walked out without looking back. He had reached the front door before he remembered it was December and his coat was upstairs. Swearing to himself he hurried to the elevator.

The insistent buzzer woke Bonnie and she sat up, listening for it to come again, before stumbling to the door to switch on the intercom. The raspy speaker responded to her weak 'Yes?' with 'It's Marc Blake, I need to talk to you.'

'What time is it?'

'I don't know, let me in.'

She pushed the button that unlocked the downstairs hall door. Turning on the lamp, she caught a look at her reflection. She hurried to the closet for her robe and managed to run a comb through her hair before the doorbell sounded, and she admitted her caller.

'Marc, what in the world?'

He was the familiar friend, dark suit and topcoat, thinning hair not covered with a hat. He looked excited, younger.

'Oh,' she said, 'your opening was a success!'

'I almost forgot; it's not why I came.'

'What?'

'I'm going to Europe to be a gypsy. Will you come with me?'

She laughed and shook her head.

'I mean it,' he said sobering. 'I am going. Come be my love.'

She sobered, too. She reached for his coat and laid it on a chair. He went to sit across from her.

'I just proposed,' he said.

'I'm mixed up. What was that again about a gypsy?'

'Bonnie, I'm going to quit, just like you did.'

'When did you decide?'

'About an hour ago.'

'Things will look different tomorrow.'

'That's why I came right over. I'll sign you up to come with me and then I can't back out.'

'Fill me in. Is this a marriage proposal?'

'That's up to you, any way you want it. I've loved you since I was fourteen. I could make you happy. You'd be important.'

She said slowly, 'Thank you, Marc.'

'Thank you? I don't like the sound of that.'

'Will you really move to Europe? I couldn't live in Boston.' What was she saying? She would be John's sister-in-law.

'I know that. We wouldn't live there.'

She started to speak and he leaned over and laid a finger over her lips. 'Think about it, please. You'd be first with me – and only. You deserve that.' His finger touching her lips hovered and she thought his hand would spread out to her cheek; but he withdrew it.

'We couldn't go first class, but I have enough to retire on if we travel coach – the little pensiones.' He was assuming full responsibility for them, pretending she would be dependent.

'All right, I'll think about it.' Softly. She wanted to say, *I love you, Marc,* because she did, but it would confuse the issue.

Bonnie didn't sleep that night. She stayed in bed with the lights out, her mind churning. While the clock crept through the early morning hours, she saw herself walking with Marc through the ruins in Rome, riding a gondola in Venice, strolling among flowers in the streets of Paris. All movie sets, with Charles Boyer and Rossano Brazzi waiting in the little cafés. She was shopping for fresh vegetables and fish in little markets, and cooking with garlic when she needed a break from writing. And the nights were as romantic as their one night had been – her dependable friend turning into forbidden lover in the dark. You'd be first with me – and only.

First and only. Was Marc after all another Frank for her, safe and loving and nice and dependable and permanent? She didn't know him either. She would never have dreamed he would do this. He would change now. You couldn't rely on anybody but yourself.

Things were racing to an end for her. Finals to close the semester, by spring she would have the degree. Then the novel would be finished, ending the resurrection of the 1940s, freeing her to live in the present. She couldn't stop now. It would soon be two years since she had turned her life around. She had to finish what she started. Everything neat and tidy and in its proper place – finished with distinction. She hadn't after all escaped the lifelong habits.

By 2.00 AM she knew the answer. Marc's moment of change was his alone, she would not share it.

Fifty-one

In January, Frank and Dorothy were married. Bonnie and Hannah, feeling in different ways the stress of that wedding day, joined in planning a reception. They bought a cake (un-iced angel food from the grocery store), pistachio ice cream, and Cold Duck with which they toasted the bride and groom and, repeatedly, their own liberation.

Hannah was rehearsing a Broadway musical. She was on-stage a lot, singing in the chorus with a six-bar solo in spotlight to set her up for discovery. She would leave the Henry the Eighth when the play opened, unmindful of the cut in pay.

They lounged in Bonnie's living room, a little tipsy, and told wedding night jokes, although they could only remember two.

They understood each other better than either had ever understood Frank. They had both put in a lot of time trying to guess what this man was feeling. 'Rots of ruck, Dorothy,'

Hannah solemnly toasted, glass held high. 'Heartfelt sympathy,' Bonnie mumbled, joining in the toast. 'She can have him, I don't want him, he's too fat for me,' Bonnie sang. Hannah stood up, steadying herself, and in full voice delivered her six-bar solo. They laughed hysterically, and had another glass of champagne.

In February, Karen, and Bob got their divorce. Bonnie remembered the ecstatic seventeen-year-old bride, fragile, vulnerable, unformed, and wondered how she, Bonnie, might have raised her daughter to avoid this mistake. Remembered that mistakes are a part of living. At least Karen didn't have to wait so long.

In early March, a letter arrived from Rick Baker, written in a large scrawl on White House stationery.

Dear Bonnie,

I thought of you on Christmas Eve – we did have a jolly time last year.

Things are moving along for me. My man won this time, and I have become part of the White House staff. Looks like I will stay put at last, for a while at least. One never knows in politics.

I am engaged to be married. My girl and I are planning a May wedding. She's a journalist, a sweet, attractive and very bright young woman. Her name is Mary Cassidy.

I wonder sometimes about what has happened to you. Are you still with Earth Savers? You are a woman of many talents, and I am sure you are doing something worthwhile. You kept your light under a bushel for too many years.

Is That Man still in your life?

If you are ever going to be in Washington, let me know and I will give you a grand tour.

Affectionately,
Rick

She read the letter through a number of times. Pleased to be remembered, happy over Rick's good fortune, a little jealous of the sweet, attractive, very bright young woman.

Only two weeks later, she heard from Rick again. This one secretary-typed.

Dear Bonnie:

Enjoyed your long letter.

How would you like to represent the U.S.A. in Paris next fall at a conference on pollution and the world's water supply? Our only female delegate will be unable to attend (as a matter of fact, she died) and we need a replacement. I'm in a position to recommend someone and it occurs to me that your years as an Earth Saver (both volunteer and professional) would make you eligible.

I should warn you that there will be some time-consuming preparation involved, but the pay is good and you would have an expense-paid trip with first-class accommodations, plus a chance to make an input with a bunch of interesting, dedicated people.

Frankly, I am pessimistic about any long-reaching benefits coming out of this conference, but the U.S. government is at least giving it token support.

If you are interested, call me collect and I will give you more details. Action must be taken very soon.

Best personal regards,
Rick Baker

Fifty-two

It was raining in Cleveland. On the window of the Airport Motel the drops gathered, joined, meandered uncertainly downward to join again. The window looked down over the parking lot which Bonnie watched now, while she waited for That Man. A woman got out of a station wagon while two

332

children scrambled out of the backseat and stepped into the puddles. She grabbed one with each arm and dragged them to the shelter of the overhang next to the building. Her man ignored the family as he opened the trunk and struggled with luggage. They looked at the numbers, found the right one, and stiffly sought shelter from the cold rain.

Bonnie's room was warm and dry – and quiet, childless. She burrowed into the quiet, waited for the man bringing only himself, his beautiful, bright self, and his Morocco leather carry-on bag. He had called to ask her to fly to Cleveland for their first time together away from the apartment – a time at last to walk before other people with John on her arm. Strangers thinking what a handsome couple – what a lucky woman.

When she saw him park the Hertz coupe she flew for a last look in the mirror, feeling the same tremors she had felt before a special date at eighteen. The face that looked back from the mirror was a living face, opened, unafraid. She didn't need the comb.

She heard a gentle tap on the door, such a small sound for such an important entry. She let him in and he pushed the door shut. They kissed and kissed again. His all-weather coat bunched up in the way and he slid out of one arm, still holding her with the other. She pulled at the sleeve next to her. They stepped apart, and he looked at her with eyes as enveloping as his arms had been.

'Hello,' she said. They smiled a greeting. His legal work was completed, and they had twenty-four hours before taking the separate Sunday afternoon flights to Boston and New York. Twenty-four hours removed from the gravity of planet Earth to an outer space station called Cleveland.

'Hello, Bonnie,' he said in that voice.

'What shall we do tonight?' she asked.

'First things first,' he answered, looking for the cord to close the curtains. She undid her blouse down the front and at the cuffs, and sat down to unbuckle the straps of her sandals. Freed of blouse and shoes, she unzipped her skirt and stepped carefully out. He was ready before her, and came to help free her breasts and toss away the last veil. They embraced again, sparking at contact where their bodies reached out, longing made flesh, desire answered. This would never be again, and they must savour, savour before it slipped away.

Their lovemaking progressed slowly, moving to the bed, inside stiff white motel sheets, sometimes slowing for words, building happily to the bursting of the rainbow, turning point, splintering hues raining over the descending action, where love became the epilogue to passion.

'I saw a poster in the lobby,' he told her when they were resting, her head on his arm. 'The Starlight Ballroom, in a place called Morganville, wherever that is.'

'Starlight Ballroom?'

'Dress-up. No jeans. Somebody's swing band. Remember swing?'

'I remember swing.'

'Coloured spotlights on a revolving sequin ball on the ceiling. I'd bet on it.'

'Shall we go see?'

'Why not.'

It was dark when they came outside after dinner. The parking lot was shining, and the slow mist stung their cheeks. 'It's freezing,' Bonnie exclaimed. The windows of the rented car were glazed over. When they got inside and closed the doors, they were enclosed in an opaque box. John started the engine and defrosters and got out to chisel with a scraper found in the glove compartment, creating jagged holes in the middle of each side window and in the back. Ice crystals rested in his hair and eyebrows when he slid back into the driver's seat.

'This is a hell of a note,' he said. 'I thought it was spring.' He started the wipers and they watched the chunks break away.

'Do you think we should go?' Bonnie asked.

'Oh, sure, it's only twenty miles.'

He drove carefully. All traffic was slowed.

'Do you know,' she reminded him, feeling their isolation, 'that this is the first time we've ever ridden in a car together?'

'Hmmmmm, I guess that's right.'

'What kind of a car do you drive?'

'I drive a Mustang to work. We have a Continental.'

'You never drive to New York.'

'Not by myself, car's a nuisance in Manhattan. We drove the Lincoln down for Marc's opening.'

They both considered whether to follow up on this.

'What do you hear from Marc?' she asked.

'Very little. A postcard from Paris. Don't you hear?'

'No.'

'No?'

'He asked me not to write.'

John eased into the turn that would take them onto the highway. 'What do you think about little brother's abdication?'

'It seems like it could be a good thing. I'm not sure.'

'I think it's good. High time he got away.'

'I wonder how it will change him.' She had speculated about this a good deal. 'How's your mother taking it?' Speaking of getting away.

'Very badly. She leaned on him a lot. Everybody sees Mother as strong and Marc as weak, but she leans on him. It took courage.'

'Big question, isn't it? How much we owe the leaners.'

He laid his hand over hers in the seat without taking his eyes from the road. 'It sure is.'

They fell into silence, remembering Bonnie's withdrawal and John's uninterrupted commitment. Where were Frank and Sara tonight because John and Bonnie had celebrated their love this afternoon? Responsibility? To others? To themselves? Happiness in ideals? In action? This moment, alone together, to hold forever – for the diminishing forever that remained for them. A treasure – life is short on treasures.

That other icy night she gave him her treasure – her virginity – served up in a prescribed way – withheld until the words were spoken, documents signed. The future was short then, too, uncertain, but she knew the answers – you followed the rules. Today there were no rules, you made your own. She had learned this from him. He had freed her from the security of rules. Now she did it like a man.

'What if?' she broke the silence. 'What if we had stayed in the apartment? What if we had slept together that night, without the wedding? We were safe. I had the diaphragm.'

She was mildly surprised that he had to collect his thoughts, that he had been going along another path. 'You keep coming back to what if? Why does it matter?'

'Don't you find it exciting to think that a small change in the

335

path taken at one point could make a large change at the destination reached at another?'

'I suppose it is. Exciting. I've never been inhibited about taking what I wanted at the moment. And I've never tried to push anyone else to do it my way. At least, I don't think I have.'

'Women are encouraged to manipulate – perfume, chocolate cake, padded bras.'

'Maybe it's a side effect of the economic thing. Because women and their children have been dependent for food and shelter.'

'Make them feel obligated so they'll take care of you. Then they call us petty, unpredictable.'

'I didn't call you that. I called you sweet, worth fighting for.'

'Meaning my worth is less when I can do my own fighting?'

'No, no, not that at all. But it is different. You can see why men and women are getting fouled up by the changing roles. It changes lots of things. Not that change is bad.'

'I love change,' she proclaimed. 'But most people don't. You have to cram it down their throats.'

'But it happens anyway. Yesterday's radical idea is tomorrow's safe harbour.'

They could feel the back of the car pull slightly to one side and he released the accelerator until they were straight.

Morganville was off the highway. Morganville was very dead this Saturday night. Cars and pickups clustered around a small frame building at the end of Main Street with an electric Milwaukee beer sign in the window. For a bad moment, they wondered if this might be the Starlight Ballroom but driving a little farther, out of greater Morganville, they were relieved to see a large structure fronted by the curved lines of an aluminium Quonset hut. A red and blue neon sign on a post in front identified the Starlight Ballroom, complete with three white stars flashing on and off with twinkling regularity.

Despite the inclement weather, the parking lot already contained rows of automobiles. The place obviously had an appeal that was not limited to local inhabitants.

John eased the car into a space at the end of a row. In low gear, the momentum gradually lost was still felt briefly after they stopped.

'Careful,' he cautioned as she unlatched her door while he

336

was climbing out. He came around to offer a welcome arm, and they leaned together as they walked. Halfway across, Bonnie stopped, looking towards a grove of trees behind the building.

'I thought I saw him,' she said. 'Up in a tree. An old man in a pointed cap and cowboy boots.'

'By God, you're right, he's been waiting for us all this time. Thought you'd never make it, he says.'

'With Grandmother in her shawl on your arm.'

'And what a granny she is!' Granny laughed, feeling glamorous.

They walked faster, with confidence, until she slipped and clutched his arm again. 'Wanta slide?' she asked recklessly.

'Not on your life,' he answered. 'These old bones won't bounce like they used to.'

The sweet clear wail of a trumpet undercut by the gentle persistent slapping of a bass fiddle wafted through the double doors to grip and pull them into a dimly lit, whitewashed time machine. Beyond the check room, a little man in a tweed suit stamped the backs of their hands with marks that showed purple under the ultraviolet lamp for identification if you wanted to sneak out to the parking lot for a snort or a smooch.

The dance floor was huge, gleaming, made slick by powdered wax (could it be cornmeal?) sprinkled on from time to time to be polished by the frantic gyrations of dancers' feet. Tables around the edge were there for intermission only. These people came to dance.

There it was, splendid in the centre ceiling, the big ball covered with a thousand mirrors, shooting back the coloured lights like illuminated confetti across the dancers in the dark.

They danced close, her head on his chest on the slow ones, or his hand guiding her twisting waist while their feet tapped out the slow, slow, quick quick steps of the Lindy Hop on the fast ones. 'One O'Clock Jump,' 'Five O'Clock Whistle,' and 'Chattanooga Choo-Choo' set them jivin' and truckin' on down. They shook their hips and shoulders for Miranda and Cugat on 'Green Eyes' and 'Frenesi,' and stole kisses during the yearning notes of 'Deep Purple' and the immortal 'Stardust.' When 'In the Mood' began they thought their hearts would burst with the glory of it, the power of their music, their youth, their lost innocence and dreams.

In a slow descent by parachute, they returned to the table where their glasses of bourbon and Coke sat – warmed up, watered down, and fizzless. Accustomed now to the dim lights, they looked away from each other to the folks around them. Everyone else was older than they were. Veterans of the big one, double-u double-u two, and the belles of the U.S.O – fatter, greyer, far-sighted. They had danced to this music when Dorsey and Goodman introduced it. On the dance floor they left behind the gas shortage, the children's (grandchildren's?) grass and speed, the rising price of a loaf of bread, and they danced. They were graceful and light on their feet. In my day we knew how to dance! In my day we respected our parents. In my day we were proud to be American. In my day you wanted to do it, you got married!

'Whatever happened to chlorophyll?'

'To what?'

'Chlorophyll. It kept things from smelling bad.'

'I remember. Turned them green.'

'And bowl covers. Little plastic ones in assorted sizes with elastic around.'

'Don't remember. How about men's garters?'

'How about women's garters? And silk chiffon hose. And anklets.'

'Three-D movies.'

'Jeanette MacDonald and Nelson Eddy.'

'Bank night.'

'Washing your hair in Dreft. And pin curls. Remember fenders?'

'Hell, I remember running boards.'

'And inner tubes.'

'Packards and Studebakers.'

'Window iceboxes.'

'Cream-top milk?'

'Milk bottles!'

'Milkmen.'

'That's history, damnit,' she cried. 'We're historical, the good old days,' and tears streaked her cheeks.

He came around to her side and consoled her. They sang softly with the band, remembering all the words, and where they had first heard the song – Maine summer camp, triple trio at Joy Night. 'Little Marjorie Geisler,' John said when the band played 'Cheek to Cheek.' 'That was our song!'

Fifty-three

Going back, they drove thirty miles an hour on the ice. Her feet and thighs ached dully, but she couldn't relax.

'Too bad they didn't remember "American Patrol," ' he said.

'You didn't remember either.'

'Sure I did, after you reminded me. I remembered "Speak Low." I remember it was so appropriate at the time.'

'Most lyrics would have been appropriate at the time. We were typical, you know.'

'Yes, we were typical,' he agreed. 'Now we're not typical.' He sang in a wavering, but not unmelodious baritone, 'Speak low, when you speak love. The curtain descends, everything ends, too soon, too soon . . .'

'Don't say that. I'll be glad when we get there, I hate this drive.'

He leaned forward, intent on the job at hand.

They did make it, easing around the incline into the lot in low gear and finally rolling to a safe stop. They walked stiffly past the ice-coated shrubbery, and laughed in relief as they came into the lobby.

She felt married as they shared the small bedroom and bath that night. On the rare occasions she and Frank had stayed at motels, she had always felt a little wicked – it was as wicked as she could get in those days. Tonight was what she once thought marriage was supposed to be – two separate persons in one space. Not needing room of their own.

She assumed John liked her imperfect body – probably because she liked it now. As she stood looking into her suitcase, considering whether to use the new long white nightgown, she remembered how she had always covered up when she was young. Even when she was alone, she had pulled a robe around her as quickly as possible after bathing, embarrassed over what was too wide or too flat or just not supposed to be seen. In the past two years she had become so comfortable with Bonnie Forbes that the feeling extended to her body. This is me, the whole package, even though things are slipping a little, as on a snowmaiden in early sunshine. Don't think about the thaw to come.

The gown was lovely, and she put it on.

'You had a blue one,' he said as she smoothed the cloth down over her hips. She turned around.

It was as though they hadn't spent the night before. There was something about a motel room.

They talked most of the night. They usually slept well in her apartment, except for brief moments when they came close and woke to discover each other. But tonight sleep seemed a waste of time. They kept saying 'Good night,' only to begin talking again.

'I can finish the book now. I know how it will end. Let me tell you.'

'I won't let myself be dragged into the company. Did you know about our last merger?'

They drove to the airport Sunday, midafternoon. Her plane was scheduled to leave an hour and a half before his. He stood with her in line for seat assignment.

The young clerk, in her red and blue vest, frowned as Bonnie said, 'I really would like a window seat.'

'I'm afraid they're all gone in nonsmoking. I can give you an aisle seat up front.'

John stepped closer and the girl raised round eyes, suddenly alive. He said, 'My friend would like to sleep. Sure you can't find one more?' His smile, his eyes.

The girl reached a nervous hand to push back her long hair. 'Well, just a minute.' She walked over to speak to the man serving the other line, and returned with quicker steps and a grin. 'We can move back one more row, if you don't mind being in the last.'

'All right,' Bonnie said.

The girl said to John, 'Those little pillows do work better against the wall,' and John answered, 'Yes, they do. The airline needs more people like you.'

As they walked away from the counter, Bonnie said, 'It wasn't that important. You didn't have to give her your bedroom smile.'

'What!' he responded in good spirits. 'That was my courtroom smile. "Your honour, you are dealing with a man of integrity." '

'Sure it was. That smile would get you thirty days, easy.'

She laughed then, and touched his arm.

They said good-bye in a crowd, kissing as the rest did, as though it were of no consequence. She heard distant gunfire, and kept reassuring herself that the void that threatened her was not real, that there was no war, and she was not empty. She fell into step between a pair of teen-agers carrying backpacks, and a frowning stocky man with a portfolio under his arm. She was by choice a free and independent woman.

John Blake watched her sky-blue coat vanish into the tunnel. A fat man followed and hid her from view. John's eyes moved to the observation window. Sun glared off the runways. No trace of last night's ice. Everything changes. Life goes on.

His legs were stiff. What a workout, the Starlight Ballroom. But he was restless, not sleepy. He turned back towards the lobby, to find a newspaper. Falling into long strides down the corridor, he recognized a red and blue vest coming towards him, covering a nicely curved chest. Out from behind the counter, the rest of her was revealed as slim, purring hips and a good pair of legs.

'Hey there,' she called to him. 'Your friend get off okay?' They stopped in the middle of the hall.

'She did.'

'I'm off for a coffee break. Care to join me?'

'Well, I do have some time to kill. Taking the Boston flight at five.'

He thought she looked a little disappointed. 'It's this way.' She led the way to the coffee shop.

'I thought maybe you lived her,' she said when they were seated. 'But I should have recognized the Boston accent.'

'I come here from time to time on business,' he told her.

'What's your business?'

'Law. I'm an attorney.' He felt himself smiling – bedroom or courtroom? He'd never thought of classifying it. It worked both places. It was working now.

She leaned closer. 'You're a very attractive man.' She dropped her eyes and fumbled with the silverware. 'I don't usually act like this.'

'There's no reason a lady shouldn't ask a man for coffee if she feels like it.'

'No, I mean I don't usually get shy.' She was blushing.

John reached for words to put her at ease, and wondered why the hell he was doing this. He'd rather be reading the paper. 'That was quite a storm last night.'

'Yes, I'm glad I wasn't on duty; we shut down for a while.'

'Must be a trick to stop a jet on ice. I'm still a propeller man myself.'

'You fly?'

'Learned during the war.'

Viet Nam?'

'No. World War Two.'

He saw her jaw drop. 'No. Come on, you're kiddin' me.'

He sighed. He really didn't care. 'Yeah, I'm kiddin' you. It was Korea.'

'I thought so. I like older men. They're intelligent. All the young guys want to do is fu . . .' she stopped and laughed. 'Well, you know. I think there's more than that to life.'

'How old are you?'

He had stopped smiling, and she looked uncomfortable.

'I'm no kid. I'm twenty-one.'

That's what *she* had been. Twenty-one. How sad to be twenty-one. 'You're a beautiful woman. Take your time. You don't have to do it all at once.'

'You're in love with her, aren't you?' she asked suddenly.

He nodded, feeling choked up.

'I noticed, you're wearing a ring. She wasn't. She's not your wife, is she?'

'No.'

'Want to talk about it?'

He felt like laughing. Talk about it? To this child? To this child who was a stranger? 'No,' he answered.

342

She sighed. 'Men can't talk about it. You'd probably feel better.'

'I'm a lawyer,' he said with irritation. 'I know how to talk. I'm a trial lawyer.'

'But that's other people's problems. I'll bet you never talk about your own.'

'I don't have any problems.'

'The wedding ring, silly. Anybody's got a wife and loves somebody else has got a problem.'

'What's your name?'

'Gail. What's yours?'

'John. I have a headache, Gail. Don't make me think, okay?'

'Okay. Sorry I got nosy.'

'That's all right. You meant well.'

So, another path not taken. John bought a paper and sat in a deserted corner of the main waiting room. He read the lead article on the front page over three times before he folded the paper and walked back to the observation window. He watched the silver 747 taxi around into the wind, stop, then streak down the runway, its wheels finally letting go of the earth to rise magnificently into the wild blue yonder.

Her plane was almost home by now. Soon she would take off again for the Champs-Elysees, Maxim's, and the Louvre. Next, a best-seller. It was his critical judgment that she was creating one.

He breathed a slow lingering intake of air and turned back towards the gift shop. Creams for Margaret, and for Sara, caramel with nuts, preferably pecans.

His feet dragged; they had become heavy. What was freedom? Where was guilt? The house, the Continental, the growing estimated worth. For what? Brad was dead. No one waited in the wings. The clock was still running. The curtain descends, everything ends.

How many find their true mate? Despite all the women he had known, only one continued to matter. They hadn't ridden in a car together. A diet of high drama. Afraid to face urbanity, monotony, mediocrity – dependency, boredom. Afraid. He wanted to be with her when he lost the case, when the water pipes broke, when she had a bad cold, when it wasn't a good day. Through paralysis and hospital vigils, as well as for dancing.

He could go to Paris and be the delegate's husband, and bring her home to be the attorney's wife. He had given her wings, he liked her flying. She was the yin for his yang. Yet words were not right, the lines were jammed. Blood could not flow from his heart to her heart.

He turned back to squint into the sky, at the expanding white trail of the jet stream. He wanted the risk of coupling. They had grown towards the same sun. He was going to try. If she could hear. Over the music.

STAR BOOKS BESTSELLERS

FICTION

WAR BRIDES	*Lois Battle*	£2.50 ☐
AGAINST ALL GODS	*Ashley Carter*	£1.95 ☐
THE STUD	*Jackie Collins*	£1.75 ☐
SLINKY JANE	*Catherine Cookson*	£1.35 ☐
THE OFFICERS' WIVES	*Thomas Fleming*	£2.75 ☐
THE CARDINAL SINS	*Andrew M. Greeley*	£1.95 ☐
WHISPERS	*Dean R. Koontz*	£1.95 ☐
LOVE BITES	*Molly Parkin*	£1.60 ☐
GHOSTS OF AFRICA	*William Stevenson*	£1.95 ☐

NON-FICTION

BLIND AMBITION	*John Dean*	£1.50 ☐
DEATH TRIALS	*Elwyn Jones*	£1.25 ☐
A WOMAN SPEAKS	*Anais Nin*	£1.60 ☐
I CAN HELP YOUR GAME	*Lee Trevino*	£1.60 ☐
TODAY'S THE DAY	*Jeremy Beadle*	£2.95 ☐

BIOGRAPHY

IT'S A FUNNY GAME	*Brian Johnston*	£1.95 ☐
WOODY ALLEN	*Gerald McKnight*	£1.75 ☐
PRINCESS GRACE	*Gwen Robyns*	£1.75 ☐
STEVE OVETT	*Simon Turnbull*	£1.80 ☐
EDDIE: MY LIFE, MY LOVES	*Eddie Fisher*	£2.50 ☐

STAR Books are obtainable from many booksellers and newsagents. If you have any difficulty tick the titles you want and fill in the form below.

Name_____

Address_____

_____

Send to: Star Books Cash Sales, P.O. Box 11, Falmouth, Cornwall. TR10 9EN.

Please send a cheque or postal order to the value of the cover price plus: UK: 45p for the first book, 20p for the second book and 14p for each additional book ordered to the maximum charge of £1.63.

BFPO and EIRE: 45p for the first book, 20p for the second book, 14p per copy for the next 7 books, thereafter 8p per book.

OVERSEAS: 75p for the first book and 21p per copy for each additional book.

While every effort is made to keep prices low, it is sometimes necessary to increase prices at short notice. Star Books reserve the right to show new retail prices on covers which may differ from those advertised in the text or elsewhere.

STAR BOOKS BESTSELLERS

THRILLERS

OUTRAGE	*Henry Denker*	£1.95 ☐
FLIGHT 902 IS DOWN	*H Fisherman &*	£1.95 ☐
	B. Schiff	
TRAITOR'S EXIT	*John Gardner*	£1.60 ☐
ATOM BOMB ANGEL	*Peter James*	£1.95 ☐
HAMMERED GOLD	*W.O. Johnson*	£1.95 ☐
DEBT OF HONOUR	*Adam Kennedy*	£1.95 ☐
THE FIRST DEADLY SIN	*Laurence Sanders*	£2.60 ☐
KING OF MONEY	*Jeremy Scott*	£1.95 ☐
DOG SOLDIERS	*Robert Stone*	£1.95 ☐

CHILLERS

SLUGS	*Shaun Hutson*	£1.60 ☐
THE SENTINEL	*Jeffrey Konvitz*	£1.65 ☐
OUIJA	*Andrew Laurance*	£1.50 ☐
HALLOWEEN III	*Jack Martin*	£1.80 ☐
PLAGUE	*Graham Masterton*	£1.80 ☐
MANITOU	*Graham Masterton*	£1.50 ☐
SATAN'S LOVE CHILD	*Brian McNaughton*	£1.35 ☐
DEAD AND BURIED	*Chelsea Quinn Yarbo*	£1.75 ☐

STAR Books are obtainable from many booksellers and newsagents. If you have any difficulty tick the titles you want and fill in the form below.

Name_____

Address_____

Send to: Star Books Cash Sales, P.O. Box 11, Falmouth, Cornwall. TR10 9EN.

Please send a cheque or postal order to the value of the cover price plus:
UK: 45p for the first book, 20p for the second book and 14p for each additional book ordered to the maximum charge of £1.63.

BFPO and EIRE: 45p for the first book, 20p for the second book, 14p per copy for the next 7 books, thereafter 8p per book.

OVERSEAS: 75p for the first book and 21p per copy for each additional book.

While every effort is made to keep prices low, it is sometimes necessary to increase prices at short notice. Star Books reserve the right to show new retail prices on covers which may differ from those advertised in the text or elsewhere.